Hornblower
and the 'Hotspur'

C. S. FORESTER

Introduction by Bernard Cornwell

PENGUIN BOOKS

PENGUIN BOOKS

UK | USA | Canada | Ireland | Australia
India | New Zealand | South Africa

Penguin Books is part of the Penguin Random House group of companies
whose addresses can be found at global.penguinrandomhouse.com.

First published by Michael Joseph 1962
Published in Penguin Books 1980
Reissued in this edition 2017

001

Typeset in 11/13 pt Monotype Dante
by Palimpsest Book Production Limited, Falkirk, Stirlingshire
Printed in Great Britain by Clays Ltd, St Ives plc

A CIP catalogue record for this book is available from the British Library

ISBN: 978-1-405-92831-1

www.greenpenguin.co.uk

MIX
Paper from
responsible sources
FSC® C018179

Penguin Random House is committed to a
sustainable future for our business, our readers
and our planet. This book is made from Forest
Stewardship Council® certified paper.

Introduction

Hornblower and the 'Hotspur' was the last complete novel Forester wrote about Horatio Hornblower. It is the third novel in chronological order but was the tenth to be written and was first published in 1962. During the 1950s Forester wrote just two Hornblower novels, so the patience of his many fans was severely tested. And not just his fans. There is a story that whenever his American publishers found their profits threatened they despatched an envoy to California with orders to stay with Forester until he finally agreed, however reluctantly, to write another Hornblower. We should be grateful to them.

Writing was Forester's life and he was extremely successful at it, but he never talks about writing without using words like 'hard', 'exacting' and 'exhausting'. 'I would rather be in the dentist's chair,' he claimed in *The Hornblower Companion*. After completing his daily quota of words he felt 'sick, weary, flat'. 'There is no pleasure left in life,' he wrote. 'I am drained and empty.' *Hornblower and the 'Hotspur'* was written under even more pressure. By the 1960s Forester was ill, he lost his secretary while the book was being written and the Internal Revenue Service, America's implacable equivalent of the Inland Revenue, audited his accounts – a truly dreadful experience (though in Forester's case it ended happily with the taxman owing *him* money). And to cap it all, the house across the street was being built so his day's work was interrupted by 'every pneumatic drill, every concrete mixer, bulldozer, and air-compressor in California'.

The book reflects none of this. From the wonderful opening chapter it sweeps the reader along and contains one of literature's great sea-chases, the beat to windward as the *Hotspur* pursues the *Loire*. It is a tale of blockade, and blockade duty was the primary purpose of the Royal Navy throughout the long Napoleonic wars. The French navy was mostly in port and their harbours had to be stopped up, and so through good weather and bad, through summer days and winter gales, the wooden ships of Britain patrolled off the French coast. It was hard, boring duty, and dangerous too, especially for the small ships which beat to and fro just off the rocky approaches to Brest, which were badly charted. The only respite for the crews came if a gale blew up from the west, in which case, to prevent being driven on to the rocks, the blockading fleet would run for Torbay in Devon. It was safe to do that, for the westerly gales that threatened the British ships also kept the French ships safely in harbour, but as soon as the gales abated the British would hurry back to resume the blockade.

Hornblower had been cast on to the beach at the end of *Lieutenant Hornblower*, put there by the Treaty of Amiens that was supposed to bring peace to France and Britain, but the peace has broken down and Hornblower, who had been earning a living as a professional gambler, receives command of His Majesty's sloop *Hotspur*. It comes as a huge relief, not just because a naval officer ashore is an unhappy fellow, but also because Hornblower is escaping his new wife, Maria. The marriage ceremony begins the book, and it is excruciating. Maria calls him

'Horry'. Horry! His new mother-in-law, deputized to provide his cabin stores, buys him rotten eggs. In all, Hornblower has just two days of married life before he goes to sea, and two days are sufficient. Not that he can totally escape Maria, for her letters follow him. She is anxious that 'her Hero was not running into danger, and how necessary it was to change his socks if they should get wet'. Poor Maria. She is a harmless, loving creature, and Forester invented her solely to embarrass Hornblower. In many ways Maria is very like Kitty, the first Duke of Wellington's wife. Kitty was much better born, but equally ill-suited for marriage to a warrior. 'She has grown ugly,' Wellington complained to his clergyman brother as Kitty came to the altar, while Maria is charitably described as 'plain'. 'I married her because they asked me to,' Wellington was to write. 'In short, I was a fool.' Hornblower married Maria because he did not know how to escape her cloying affections, and while he commands the *Hotspur* he learns he is to become a father and 'for the life of him he could not tell if he were pleased or not'. This ill-made marriage is a superb portrait, Forester at his glowing best.

Cecil Scott Forester was born in Egypt to British parents in 1899. His real name was Cecil Lewis Troughton Smith and he was raised in Britain, where, as a child, he was an avid reader, usually the first step in the making of a writer. In 1917, before his eighteenth birthday, he volunteered for the British army, fully expecting to fight on the Western Front, but he was rejected as medically unfit. He was a skinny, short-sighted six-footer who enjoyed sports, but the army's physical examination revealed a dangerously weak heart. So instead of serving as a soldier, Forester entered Guy's Hospital as a medical student – an experience as unhappy as it was unsuccessful. There is something feckless about these early years, but Forester's ambitions were fixed on writing. His first efforts failed, but he persevered and in 1924, with *Payment Deferred*, enjoyed his first success. The filming of that novel introduced Forester to Hollywood and, more crucially, California. During the Second World War he moved to the United States at the request of the British government, who wanted him to produce articles and stories that would encourage American support for the British war effort. It was sophisticated propaganda, and Forester was good at it. He also liked living in the States and most of the Hornblower books were written in California, where, with his second wife, he remained until his death in 1966. By then he had become one of the world's most popular authors with almost sixty novels to his name and, even if he had never dreamed up Hornblower, he would be famous as the author of *The African Queen*, *The Gun*, *Brown on Resolution* and *Hunting the Bismarck*.

Hornblower and the 'Hotspur' is full of good things. Who can forget Doughty, the perfect cabin steward, or the moment when Poole saves the *Hotspur* from Hornblower's inattention? Forester, in writing this book, was at the height of his powers, and we can only be grateful that neither the IRS nor every pneumatic drill, concrete mixer, bulldozer and air-compressor in California could keep him from his desk.

'Repeat after me,' said the parson. '"I, Horatio, take thee, Maria Ellen –"'

The thought came up in Hornblower's mind that these were the last few seconds in which he could withdraw from doing something which he knew to be ill-considered. Maria was not the right woman to be his wife, even admitting that he was suitable material for marriage in any case. If he had a grain of sense, he would break off this ceremony even at this last moment, he would announce that he had changed his mind, and he would turn away from the altar and from the parson and from Maria, and he would leave the church a free man.

'To have and to hold –' he was still, like an automaton, repeating the parson's words. And there was Maria beside him, in the white that so little became her. She was melting with happiness. She was consumed with love for him, however misplaced it might be. He could not, he simply could not, deal her a blow so cruel. He was conscious of the trembling of her body beside him. That was not fear, for she had utter and complete trust in him. He could no more bring himself to shatter that trust than he could have refused to command the *Hotspur*.

'And thereto I plight thee my troth,' repeated Hornblower. That settled it, he thought. Those must be the final deciding words that made the ceremony legally binding. He had made a promise and now there was no going back on it. There was a comfort in the odd thought that he had really been committed from a week back, when Maria had come into his arms sobbing out her love for him, and he had been too soft-hearted to laugh at her and too – too weak? too honest? – to take advantage of her with the intention of betraying her. From the moment that he had listened to her, from the moment that he had returned her kisses, gently, all these later results, the bridal dress, this ceremony in the church of St Thomas à Becket – and the vague future of cloying affection – had been inevitable.

Bush was ready with the ring, and Hornblower slipped it over Maria's finger, and the final words were said.

'I now pronounce that they are man and wife,' said the parson, and he went on with the blessing, and then a blank five seconds followed, until Maria broke the silence.

'Oh, Horry,' she said, and she laid her hand on his arm.

Hornblower forced himself to smile down at her, concealing the newly discovered fact that he disliked being called 'Horry' even more than he disliked being called Horatio.

'The happiest day of my life,' he said; if a thing had to be done it might as well be done thoroughly, so that in the same spirit he continued. 'In my life so far.'

It was actually painful to note the unbounded happiness of the smile that answered this gallant speech. Maria put her other hand up to him, and he realized she expected to be kissed, then and there, in front of the altar. It hardly seemed a proper thing to do, in a sacred edifice – in his ignorance he feared lest he should affront the devout – but once more there was no drawing back, and he stooped and kissed the soft lips that she proffered.

'Your signatures are required in the register,' prompted the parson, and led the way to the vestry.

They wrote their names.

'Now I can kiss my son-in-law,' announced Mrs Mason loudly, and Hornblower found himself clasped by two powerful arms and soundly kissed on the cheek. He supposed it was inevitable that a man should feel a distaste for his mother-in-law.

But here was Bush to disengage him, with outstretched hand and unusual smile, offering felicitations and best wishes.

'Many thanks,' said Hornblower, and added, 'Many thanks for many services.'

Bush was positively embarrassed, and tried to brush away Hornblower's gratitude with the same gestures as he would have used to brush away flies. He had been a tower of strength in this wedding, just as he had been in the preparation of the *Hotspur* for sea.

'I'll see you again at the breakfast, sir,' he said, and with that he withdrew from the vestry, leaving behind him an awkward gap.

'I was counting on Mr Bush's arm for support down the aisle,' said Mrs Mason, sharply.

It certainly was not like Bush to leave everyone in the lurch like this; it was in marked contrast with his behaviour during the last few whirlwind days.

'We can bear each other company, Mrs Mason,' said the parson's wife. 'Mr Clive can follow us.'

'You are very kind, Mrs Clive,' said Mrs Mason, although there was nothing in her tone to indicate that she meant what she said. 'Then the happy pair can start now. Maria, take the captain's arm.'

Mrs Mason marshalled the tiny procession in businesslike fashion. Hornblower felt Maria's hand slipped under his arm, felt the light pressure she could not help giving to it, and – he could not be cruel enough to ignore it – he pressed her hand in return, between his ribs and his elbow, to be rewarded by another smile. A small shove from behind by Mrs Mason started him back in the church, to be greeted by a roar from the organ. Half a crown for the organist and a shilling for the blower was what that music had cost Mrs Mason; there might be better uses for the money. The thought occupied Hornblower's mind for several seconds, and was naturally succeeded by the inevitable wonderment as to how anyone could possibly find enjoyment in these distasteful noises. He and Maria were well down the aisle before he came back to reality.

'The sailors are all gone,' said Maria with a break in her voice. 'There's almost no one in the church.'

Truth to tell, there were only two or three people in the pews, and these obviously the most casual idlers. All the few guests had trooped into the vestry for the signing, and the fifty seamen whom Bush had brought from *Hotspur* – all those who could be trusted not to desert – had vanished already. Hornblower felt a vague disappointment that Bush had failed again to rise to the situation.

'Why should we care?' he asked, groping wildly for words of comfort for Maria. 'Why should any shadow fall on our wedding day?'

It was strangely painful to see and to feel Maria's instant response, and her faltering step changed to a brave stride as they marched down the empty church. There was bright sunshine awaiting them at the west door, he could see; and he thought of something else a tender bridegroom might say.

'Happy is the bride the sun shines on.'

They came out of the dim light into the bright sun, and the transition was moral as well as physical, for Bush had not disappointed them; he had not been found wanting after all. Hornblower heard a sharp word and a ragged clash of steel, and there were the fifty seamen in a double rank stretching away from the door, making an arch of their drawn cutlasses for the couple to walk beneath.

'Oh, how nice!' said Maria, in childish delight; furthermore the array of seamen at the church door had attracted a crowd of spectators, all craning forward to see the captain and his bride. Hornblower darted a professional glance first down one line of seamen and then down the other. They were all dressed in the new blue and white checked shirts with which he had stocked the slop chest of the *Hotspur*; their white duck trousers were mostly well worn but well washed, and long enough and baggy enough to conceal the probable deficiencies of their shoes. It was a good turnout.

Beyond the avenue of cutlasses stood a horseless post-chaise, with Bush standing behind it. Wondering a little, Hornblower led Maria towards it; Bush gallantly handed

Maria up into the front seat and Hornblower climbed up beside her, finding time now to take his cocked hat from under his arm and clap it on his head. He had heard the cutlasses rasp back into their sheaths; now the guard of honour came pattering forward in a disciplined rush. There were pipe-clayed drag ropes where the traces should have been, and the fifty men seized their coils, twenty-five to a coil, and ran them out. Bush craned up towards Hornblower.

'Let the brake off, if you please, sir. That handle there, sir.'

Hornblower obeyed, and Bush turned away and let loose a subdued bellow. The seamen took the strain in half a dozen quickening steps and then broke into a trot, the post-chaise rattling over the cobbles, while the crowd waved their hats and cheered.

'I never thought I could be so happy – Horry – darling,' said Maria.

The men at the drag ropes, with the usual exuberance of the seaman on land, swung round the corner into the High Street and headed at the double towards the George, and with the turn Maria was flung against him and clasped him in delicious fear. As they drew up it was obvious that there was a danger of the chaise rolling forward into the seamen, and Hornblower had to think fast and reach for the brake lever, hurriedly casting himself free from Maria's arm. Then he sat for a moment, wondering what to do next. On this occasion there should be a group to welcome them, the host of the inn and his wife, the boots, the ostler, the drawer, and the maids, but as it was there was no one. He had to leap down from the chaise unassisted and single-handed help Maria down.

'Thank you, men,' he said to the parting seamen, who acknowledged his thanks with a knuckling of foreheads and halting words.

Bush was in sight now round the corner, hurrying towards them; Hornblower could safely leave Bush in charge while he led Maria into the inn with a sad lack of ceremony.

But here was the host at last, bustling up with a napkin over his arm and his wife at his heels.

'Welcome, sir, welcome, madam. This way, sir, madam.' He flung open the door into the coffee-room to reveal the wedding breakfast laid on a snowy cloth. 'The Admiral arrived only five minutes ago, sir, so you must excuse us, sir.'

'Which Admiral?'

'The Honourable Admiral Sir William Cornwallis, sir, commanding the Channel Fleet. 'Is coachman says war's certain, sir.'

Hornblower had been convinced of this ever since, nine days ago, he had read the King's message to Parliament, and witnessed the activities of the press gangs, and had been notified of his appointment to the command of the *Hotspur* – and (he remembered) had found himself betrothed to Maria. Bonaparte's unscrupulous behaviour on the Continent meant –

'A glass of wine, madam? A glass of wine, sir?'

Hornblower was conscious of Maria's enquiring glance when the innkeeper asked this question. She would not venture to answer until she had ascertained what her new husband thought.

'We'll wait for the rest of the company,' said Hornblower. 'Ah –'

A heavy step on the threshold announced Bush's arrival.

'They'll all be here in two minutes,' said Bush.

'Very good of you to arrange about the carriage and the seamen, Mr Bush,' said Hornblower, and he thought that moment of something else that a kind and thoughtful husband would say. He slipped his hand under Maria's arm and added – 'Mrs Hornblower says you made her very happy.'

A delighted giggle from Maria told him that he had given pleasure by this unexpected use of her new name, as he expected.

'Mrs Hornblower, I give you joy,' said Bush, solemnly, and then to Hornblower, 'By your leave, sir, I'll return to the ship.'

'Now, Mr Bush?' asked Maria.

'I fear I must, ma'am,' replied Bush, turning back at once to Hornblower. 'I'll take the hands back with me, sir. There's always the chance that the lighters with the stores may come off.'

'I'm afraid you're right, Mr Bush,' said Hornblower. 'Keep me informed, if you please.'

'Aye aye, sir,' said Bush, and with that he was gone.

Here came the others, pouring in, and any trace of awkwardness about the party disappeared as Mrs Mason marshalled the guests and set the wedding breakfast into its stride. Corks popped and preliminary toasts were drunk. There was the cake to be cut, and Mrs Mason insisted that Maria should make the first cut with Hornblower's sword; Mrs Mason was sure that in this Maria would be following the example of naval brides in good society in London. Hornblower was not so sure;

he had lived for ten years under a strict convention that cold steel should never be drawn under a roof or a deck. But his timid objections were swept away, and Maria, the sword in both hands, cut the cake amid general applause. Hornblower could hardly restrain his impatience to take the thing back from her, and he quickly wiped the sugar icing from the blade, wondering grimly what the assembled company would think if they knew he had once wiped human blood from it. He was still engaged on this work when he became aware of the innkeeper whispering hoarsely at his side.

'Begging your pardon, sir. Begging your pardon.'

'Well?'

'The Admiral's compliments, sir, and he would be glad to see you when you find it convenient.'

Hornblower stood sword in hand, staring at him in momentary uncomprehension.

'The Admiral, sir. 'E's in the first floor front, what we always calls the Admiral's Room.'

'You mean Sir William, of course?'

'Yes, sir.'

'Very well. My respects to the Admiral and – No, I'll go up at once. Thank you.'

'Thank'ee, sir. Begging your pardon again.'

Hornblower shot his sword back into its sheath and looked round at the company. They were watching the maid bustling round handing slices of wedding cake and had no eyes for him at present. He settled his sword at his side, twitched at his neck-cloth, and unobtrusively left the room, picking up his hat as he did so.

When he knocked at the door of the first floor front a deep voice that he well remembered said, 'Come in.'

It was so large a room that the four-poster bed at the far end was inconspicuous; so was the secretary seated at the desk by the window. Cornwallis was standing in the middle, apparently engaged in dictation until this interruption.

'Ah, it's Hornblower. Good morning.'

'Good morning, sir.'

'The last time we met was over that unfortunate business with the Irish rebel. We had to hang him, I remember.'

'Yes, sir.'

Cornwallis, 'Billy Blue', had not changed perceptibly during those four years. He was still the bulky man with the composed manner, obviously ready to deal with any emergency.

'Please sit down. A glass of wine?'

'No, thank you, sir.'

'I expected that, seeing the ceremony you've just come from. My apologies for interrupting your wedding, but you must blame Boney, not me.'

'Of course, sir.' Hornblower felt that a more eloquent speech would have been in place here, but he could not think of one.

'I'll detain you for as short a time as possible. You know I've been appointed to the command of the Channel Fleet?'

'Yes, sir.'

'You know that *Hotspur* is under my command?'

'I expected that, but I didn't know, sir.'

'The Admiralty letter to that effect came down in my coach. You'll find it awaiting you on board.'

'Yes, sir.'

'Is *Hotspur* ready to sail?'

'No, sir.' The truth and no excuses. Nothing else would do.

'How long?'

'Two days, sir. More if there's delay with the ordnance stores.'

Cornwallis was looking at him very sharply indeed, but Hornblower returned glance for glance. He had nothing with which to reproach himself; nine days ago *Hotspur* was still laid up in ordinary.

'She's been docked and breamed?'

'Yes, sir.'

'She's manned?'

'Yes, sir. A good crew – the cream of the press.'

'Rigging set up?'

'Yes, sir.'

'Yards crossed?'

'Yes, sir.'

'Officers appointed?'

'Yes, sir. A lieutenant and four master's mates.'

'You'll need three months' provisions and water.'

'I can stow a hundred and eleven days at full rations, sir. The cooperage is delivering the water-butts at noon. I'll have it all stowed by nightfall, sir.'

'Have you warped her out?'

'Yes, sir. She's at anchor now in Spithead.'

'You've done well,' said Cornwallis.

Hornblower tried not to betray his relief at that speech; from Cornwallis that was more than approval – it was hearty praise.

'Thank you, sir.'

'So what do you need now?'

'Bos'n's stores, sir. Cordage, canvas, spare spars.'

'Not easy to get the dockyard to part with those at this moment. I'll have a word with them. And then the ordnance stores, you say?'

'Yes, sir. Ordnance are waiting for a shipment of nine-pounder shot. None to be had here at the moment.'

Ten minutes ago Hornblower had been thinking of words to please Maria. Now he was selecting words for an honest report to Cornwallis.

'I'll deal with that, too,' said Cornwallis. 'You can be certain of sailing the day after tomorrow if the wind serves.'

'Yes, sir.'

'Now for your orders. You'll get them in writing in the course of the day, but I'd better tell you now, while you can ask questions. War's coming. It hasn't been declared yet, but Boney may anticipate us.'

'Yes, sir.'

'I'm going to blockade Brest as soon as I can get the fleet to sea, and you're to go ahead of us.'

'Yes, sir.'

'You're not to do anything to precipitate war. You're not to provide Boney with an excuse.'

'No, sir.'

'When war's declared you can of course take the appropriate action. Until then you have merely to observe. Keep your eye on Brest. Look in as far as you can without provoking fire. Count the ships of war – the number and rate of ships with their yards crossed, ships still in ordinary, ships in the roads, ships preparing for sea.'

'Yes, sir.'

'Boney sent the best of his ships and crews to the West Indies last year. He'll have more trouble manning his fleet even than we have. I'll want your report as soon as I arrive on the station. What's the *Hotspur*'s draught?'

'She'll draw thirteen feet aft when she's complete with stores, sir.'

'You'll be able to use the Goulet pretty freely, then. I don't have to tell you not to run her aground.'

'No, sir.'

'But remember this. You'll find it hard to perform your duty unless you risk your ship. There's folly and there's foolhardiness on one side, and there's daring and calculation on the other. Make the right choice and I'll see you through any trouble that may ensue.'

Cornwallis' wide blue eyes looked straight into Hornblower's brown ones. Hornblower was deeply interested in what Cornwallis had just said, and equally interested in what he had left unsaid. Cornwallis had made a promise of sympathetic support, but he had refrained from uttering the threat which was the obvious corollary. This was no rhetorical device, no facile trick of leadership – it was a simple expression of Cornwallis' natural state of mind. He was a man who preferred to lead rather than to drive; most interesting.

Hornblower realized with a start that for several seconds he had been staring his commander-in-chief out of countenance while following up this train of thought; it was not the most tactful behaviour, perhaps.

'I understand, sir,' he said, and Cornwallis rose from his chair.

'We'll meet again at sea. Remember to do nothing to provoke war before war is declared,' he said, with a smile

– and the smile revealed the man of action. Hornblower could read him as someone to whom the prospect of action was stimulating and desirable, and who would never seek reasons or excuses for postponing decisions.

Cornwallis suddenly withheld his proffered hand.

'By Jove!' he exclaimed. 'I was forgetting. This is your wedding day.'

'Yes, sir.'

'You were only married this morning?'

'An hour ago, sir.'

'And I've taken you away from your wedding breakfast.'

'Yes, sir.' It would be cheap rhetoric to add anything trite like 'For King and Country', or even 'Duty comes first.'

'Your good lady will hardly be pleased.'

Nor would his mother-in-law, more especially, thought Hornblower, but again it would not be tactful to say so.

'I'll try to make amends, sir,' he contented himself with saying.

'It's I who should make amends,' replied Cornwallis. 'Perhaps I could join the festivities and drink the bride's health?'

'That would be most kind of you, sir,' said Hornblower.

If anything could reconcile Mrs Mason to his breach of manners, it would be the presence of Admiral the Hon. Sir William Cornwallis, KB, at the breakfast table.

'I'll come, then, if you're certain I shan't be unwelcome. Hachett, find my sword. Where's my hat?'

So that when Hornblower appeared again through

the door of the coffee-room Mrs Mason's instant and bitter reproaches died away on her lips, the moment she saw that Hornblower was ushering in an important guest. She saw the glittering epaulettes, and the red ribbon and the star which Cornwallis had most tactfully put on in honour of the occasion. Hornblower made the introductions.

'Long life and much happiness,' said Cornwallis, bowing over Maria's hand, 'to the wife of one of the most promising officers in the King's service.'

Maria could only bob, overwhelmed with embarrassment in this glittering presence.

'Enchanted to make your acquaintance, Sir William,' said Mrs Mason.

And the parson and his wife, and the few neighbours of Mrs Mason's who were the only other guests, were enormously gratified at being in the same room as – let alone being personally addressed by – the son of an Earl, a Knight of the Bath, and a Commander-in-Chief combined in one person.

'A glass of wine, sir?' asked Hornblower.

'With pleasure.'

Cornwallis took the glass in his hand and looked round. It was significant that it was Mrs Mason whom he addressed.

'Has the health of the happy couple been drunk yet?'

'No, sir,' answered Mrs Mason, in a perfect ecstasy.

'Then may I do so? Ladies, gentlemen. I ask you all to stand and join me on this happy occasion. May they never know sorrow. May they always enjoy health and prosperity. May the wife always find comfort in the knowledge that the husband is doing his duty for King and Country, and may the husband be supported in his duty by the loyalty of the wife. And let us hope that in time to come there will be a whole string of young gentlemen who will wear the King's uniform after their father's example, and a whole string of young ladies to be mothers of further young gentlemen. I give you the health of the bride and groom.'

The health was drunk amid acclamation, with all eyes turned on the blushing Maria, and then from her all eyes turned on Hornblower. He rose; he had realized, before Cornwallis had reached the midpoint of his speech, that the Admiral was using words he had used scores of times before, at scores of weddings of his officers. Hornblower, keyed up on the occasion, met Cornwallis' eyes and grinned. He would give as good as he got; he would reply with a speech exactly similar to the scores that Cornwallis had listened to.

'Sir William, ladies and gentlemen, I can only thank you in the name of' – Hornblower reached down and took Maria's hand – 'my wife and myself.'

As the laughter died away – Hornblower had well known that the company would laugh at his mention of Maria as his wife, although he himself did not think it a subject for laughter – Cornwallis looked at his watch, and Hornblower hastened to thank him for his presence and to escort him to the door. Beyond the threshold Cornwallis turned and thumped him on the chest with his large hand.

'I'll add another line to my orders for you,' he said; Hornblower was acutely aware that Cornwallis' friendly smile was accompanied by a searching glance.

'Yes, sir?'

'I'll add my written permission for you to sleep out of your ship for tonight and tomorrow night.'

Hornblower opened his mouth to reply, but no words came; for once in his life his readiness of wit had deserted him. His mind was so busy reassessing the situation that it had nothing to spare for his organ of speech.

'I *thought* you might have forgotten,' said Cornwallis, grinning. '*Hotspur*'s part of the Channel Fleet now. Her captain is forbidden by law to sleep anywhere except on board without the permission of the Commander-in-Chief. Well, you have it.'

'Thank you, sir,' said Hornblower, at last able to articulate.

'Maybe you won't sleep ashore again for a couple of years. Maybe more than that, if Boney fights it out.'

'I certainly think he'll fight, sir.'

'In that case you and I will meet again off Ushant in three weeks' time. So now goodbye, once more.'

For some time after Cornwallis had left Hornblower stood by the half-closed door of the coffee-room in deep thought, shifting his weight from one foot to the other, which was the nearest he could get to pacing up and down. War was coming; he had always been certain of that, because Bonaparte would never retreat from the position he had taken up. But until this moment Hornblower had thought recklessly that he would not be ordered to sea until war was declared, in two or three weeks' time, after the final negotiations had broken down. He had been utterly wrong in this surmise, and he was angry with himself on that account. The facts that he had a good crew – the first harvest of the press – that his ship could be quickly made ready for sea, that she was small and of no account in the balance of power, even that she was of light draught and therefore well adapted to the mission Cornwallis had allotted her, should have warned him that he would be packed off to sea at the earliest possible moment. He should have foreseen all this and he had not.

That was the first point, the first pill to swallow. Next he had to find out why his judgement had been so faulty. He knew the answer instantly, but – and he despised himself for this even more – he flinched from expressing it. But here it was. He had allowed his judgement to be clouded on account of Maria. He had shrunk from hurting her, and in consequence he had refused to allow his mind to make calculations about the future. He had gone recklessly forward in the wild hope that some stroke of good fortune would save him from having to deal her this blow.

He pulled himself up abruptly at this point. Good fortune? Nonsense. He was in command of his own ship, and was being set in the forefront of the battle. This was his golden chance to distinguish himself. That was his good fortune – it would have been maddening bad luck to have been left in harbour. Hornblower could feel the well-remembered thrill of excitement at the thought of seeing action again, of risking reputation – and life – in doing his duty, in gaining glory, and in (what was really the point) justifying himself in his own eyes. Now he was sane again; he could see things in their proper proportion. He was a naval officer first, and a married man only second, and a bad second at that. But – but – that did not make things any easier. He would still have to tear himself free from Maria's arms.

Nor could he stay here outside the coffee-room any longer. He must go back, despite his mental turmoil. He turned and re-entered the room, closing the door behind him.

'It will look well in the *Naval Chronicle*,' said Mrs Mason, 'that the Commander-in-Chief proposed the health of the happy pair. Now, Horatio, some of your guests have empty plates.'

Hornblower was still trying to be a good host when he saw across the room the worried face of the innkeeper again; it called for a second glance to see what had caused him to come in. He was ushering in Hornblower's new coxswain, Hewitt, a very short man who escaped observation across the room. Hewitt made up in breadth a good deal of what he lacked in height, and he sported a magnificent pair of glossy black side-whiskers in the style which was newly fashionable on the lower-deck. He came rolling across the room, his straw hat in his hand, and, knuckling his forehead, gave Horatio a note. The address was in Bush's handwriting and in the correct phrasing, although now a little old-fashioned – Horatio Hornblower, Esq., Master and Commander. Silence fell on the assembled company – a little rudely, Hornblower thought – as he read the few lines.

HM Sloop Hotspur
April 2nd, 1803
Sir,

I hear from the dockyard that the first of the lighters is ready to come alongside. Extra pay is not yet authorized. for dockyard hands, so that work will cease at nightfall. I respectfully submit that I can supervise the embarkation of the stores if you should find it inconvenient to return on board.

> *Your obdt servant,*
> *Wm Bush.*

'Is the boat at the Hard?' demanded Hornblower.

'Yes, sir.'

'Very well. I'll be there in five minutes.'

'Aye aye, sir.'

'Oh, Horry,' said Maria, with a hint of reproach in her voice. No, it was disappointment, not reproach.

'My dear –' said Hornblower. It occurred to him that he might now quote 'I could not love thee, dear, so much –' but he instantly discarded the idea; it would not be at all suitable at this moment, with this wife.

'You're going to the ship again,' said Maria.

'Yes.'

He could not stay away from the ship while there was work to be done. Today, by driving the hands, they could get half the stores on board at least. Tomorrow they could finish, and if Ordnance responded to the prodding of the Admiral, they could get the powder and shot on board as well. Then they could sail at dawn the day after tomorrow.

'I'll be back again this evening,' he said. He forced himself to smile, to look concerned, to forget that he was on the threshold of adventure, that before him lay a career of possible distinction.

'Nothing shall keep me from you, dear,' he said.

He clapped his hands on her shoulders and gave her a smacking kiss that drew applause from the others;

that was the way to reintroduce a note of comedy into the proceedings, and, under cover of the laughter, he made his exit. As he hastened down to the Hard two subjects for thought intertwined in his mind, like the serpents of the medical caduceus – the tender love that Maria wished to lavish upon him, and the fact that the day after tomorrow he would be at sea, in command.

2

Someone must have been knocking at the bedroom door for some time; Hornblower had been conscious of it but was too stupid with sleep to think more about it. But now the door opened with a clank of the latch, and Maria, awakening with a start, clutched at him in sudden fright, and he was now fully awake. There was the faintest gleam of light through the thick bed curtains, a shuffling step on the oak floor of the bedroom, and a high-pitched female voice.

'Eight bells, sir. Eight bells.'

The curtains opened an inch to let in a ray of brighter light still, and Maria's grip tightened, but they came together again as Hornblower found his voice.

'Very well. I'm awake.'

'I'll light your candles for you,' piped the voice, and the shuffling step went round the room and the light through the curtains grew brighter.

'Where's the wind? What way's the wind?' asked Hornblower, now so far awake as to feel the quickening of his heartbeat and the tensing of his muscles as he realized what this morning meant to him.

'Now that I can't tell you, sir,' piped the voice. 'I'm not one who can box the compass, and there's no one else awake as yet.'

Hornblower snorted with annoyance at being kept in ignorance of this vital information, and without a thought reached to fling off the bedclothes so as to get up and find out for himself. But there was Maria clasping him, and he knew that he could not leap out of bed in such a cavalier fashion. He had to go through the proper ritual and put up with the delay. He turned and kissed her, and she returned his kisses, eagerly and yet differently from on other occasions. He felt something wet on his cheek; it was a tear, but there was only that one single tear as Maria forced herself to exert self-control. His rather perfunctory embrace changed in character.

'Darling, we're being parted,' whispered Maria. 'Darling, I know you must go. But – but – I can't think how I'm going to live without you. You're my whole life. You're . . .'

A great gust of tenderness welled up in Hornblower's breast, and there was compunction too, a pricking of conscience. Not the most perfect man on earth could merit this devotion. If Maria knew the truth about him she would turn away from him, her whole world shattered. The cruellest thing he could do would be to let her find out; he must never do that. Yet the thought of being loved so dearly set flowing deeper and deeper wells of tenderness in his breast and he kissed her cheeks and sought out the soft eager lips. Then the soft lips hardened, withdrew.

'No, angel, darling. No, I mustn't keep you. You would be angry with me – afterwards. Oh, my dear life, say goodbye to me now. Say that you love me – say that you'll always love me. Then say goodbye, and say that you'll think of me sometimes as I shall always think of you.'

Hornblower said the words, the right words, and in his tenderness he used the right tone. Maria kissed him once more, and then tore herself free and flung herself on to the far side of the bed face downward. Hornblower lay still, trying to harden his heart to rise, and Maria spoke again; her voice was half muffled by the pillow, but her forced change of mood was apparent even so.

'Your clean shirt's on the chair, dear, and your second-best shoes are beside the fireplace.'

Hornblower swung himself out of bed and out through the curtains. The air of the bedroom was certainly fresher than that inside. The door latch clanked again and he had just time to whip his bedgown in front of him as the old chambermaid put her head in. She let out a high cackle of mirth at Hornblower's modesty.

'The ostler says light airs from the s'uth'ard, sir.'

'Thank you.'

The door closed behind her.

'Is that what you want, darling?' asked Maria, still behind the curtains. 'Light airs from the s'uth'ard – that means south, does it not?'

'Yes, it may serve,' said Hornblower, hurrying over to the wash basin and adjusting the candles so as to illuminate his face.

Light airs from the south now, at the end of March, were hardly likely to endure. They might back or they might veer, but would certainly strengthen with the coming of day. If *Hotspur* handled as well as he believed she would he could weather the Foreland and be ready for the next development, with plenty of sea room. But of course – as always in the Navy – he could not afford to waste any time. The razor was rasping over his cheeks, and as he peered into the mirror he was vaguely conscious of Maria's reflection behind his own as she moved about the room dressing herself. He poured cold water into the basin with which to wash himself, and felt refreshed, turning away with his usual rapidity of movement to put on his shirt.

'Oh, you dress so fast,' said Maria in consternation.

Hornblower heard her shoes clacking on the oaken floor; she was hurriedly putting on a fresh mob cap over her hair, and clearly she was dressing as quickly as she could, even at the cost of some informality.

'I must run down to see that your breakfast is ready,' she said, and was gone before he could protest.

He folded his neckcloth carefully, but with practised fingers, and slipped on his coat, glanced at his watch, put it in his pocket and then put on his shoes. He rolled his toilet things into his housewife and tied the tapes. Yesterday's shirt and his nightshirt and bedgown he stuffed in the canvas bag that awaited them, and the housewife on top. A glance round the room told him that he had omitted nothing, although he had to look more carefully than usual because there were articles belonging to Maria scattered here and there. Bubbling with excitement, he opened the window curtains and glanced outside; no sign of dawn as yet. Bag in hand, he went downstairs and into the coffee-room. This smelt of stale living, and was dimly lit by an oil lamp dangling from the ceiling. Maria looked in at him from the farther door.

'Here's your place, dear,' she said. 'Only a moment before breakfast.'

She held the back of the chair for him to be seated.

'I'll sit down after you,' said Hornblower; it went against the grain to have Maria waiting on him.

'Oh, no,' said Maria. 'I have your breakfast to attend to – only the old woman is up as yet.'

She coaxed him into the chair. Hornblower felt her kiss the top of his head, felt a momentary touch of her cheek against his, but before he could seize her, reaching behind him, she was gone. She left behind her the memory of something between a sniff and a sob; the opening of the door into the kitchen admitted a smell of cooking, the sizzling of something in a pan, and a momentary burst of conversation between Maria and the old woman. Then in came Maria, her rapid steps indicating that the plate she held was too hot to be comfortable. She dropped it in front of him, a vast rump steak, still sizzling on the plate.

'There, dear,' she said, and busied herself with putting the rest of the meal within his reach, while Hornblower looked down at the steak with some dismay.

'I picked that out for you specially yesterday,' she announced proudly. 'I walked over to the butcher's while you were on the ship.'

Hornblower steeled himself not to wince at hearing a naval officer's wife speak about being 'on' a ship; he also had to steel himself to having steak for breakfast, when steak was by no means his favourite dish, and when he was so excited that he felt he could eat nothing. And dimly he could foresee a future – if ever he returned, if ever, inconceivably, he settled down in domestic life – when steak would be put before him on any special occasion. That thought was the last straw; he felt he could not eat a mouthful, and yet he could not hurt Maria's feelings.

'Where's yours?' he asked, temporising.

'Oh, I shan't be having any steak,' replied Maria. The tone of her voice proved that it was quite inconceivable to her that a wife should eat equally well as her husband. Hornblower raised his voice and turned his head.

'Hey, there!' he called. 'In the kitchen! Bring another plate – a hot one.'

'Oh, no, darling,' said Maria, all fluttered, but Hornblower was by now out of his chair and seating her at her own place.

'Now, sit there,' said Hornblower. 'No more words. I'll have no mutineers in my family. Ah!'

Here came the other plate. Hornblower cut the steak in two, and helped Maria to the larger half.

'But darling –'

'I said I'll have no truck with mutiny,' growled Hornblower parodying his own quarterdeck rasp.

'Oh, Horry, darling. You're good to me, far too good to me.' Momentarily Maria clapped hands and handkerchief to her face, and Hornblower feared she would break down finally, but then she put her hands in her lap and straightened her back, controlling her emotions in an act of the purest heroism. Hornblower felt his heart go out to her. He reached out and pressed the hand she gladly proffered him.

'Now let me see you eat a hearty breakfast,' he said; he was still using his mock-bullying tone, but the tenderness he felt was still evident. Maria took up her knife and fork and Hornblower did the same. He forced himself to eat a few mouthfuls, and so mangled the rest of his steak that it did not appear as if he had left too much. He took a pull at his pot of beer – he did not like drinking beer for breakfast, not even beer as small as this, but he realized that the old woman could not be expected to have access to the tea-caddy.

A rattling at the windows attracted their attention. The ostler was opening the shutters, and they could dimly see his face for a moment, but it was still quite dark outside. Hornblower looked at his watch; ten minutes to five, and he had ordered his boat to be at the Sally Port at five. Maria saw the gesture and looked over at him. There was a slight trembling of her lips, a slight moisture in her eyes, but she kept herself under control.

'I'll get my cloak,' she said quietly, and fled from the room. She was back in no time, her grey cloak round her, and her face shadowed in her hood; in her arms was Hornblower's heavy coat.

'You're leaving us now, sir?' piped the old woman coming into the coffee-room.

'Yes. Madam will settle the score when she returns,' said Hornblower; he fumbled out half a crown from his pocket and put it on the table.

'Thank you kindly, sir. And a good voyage, and prize money galore.' The sing-song tone reminded Hornblower that she must have seen naval officers by the hundreds leaving the George to go to sea – her memories must go back to Hawke and Boscawen.

He buttoned up his coat and took up his bag.

'I'll have the ostler come with us with a lantern to escort you back,' he said, consideringly.

'Oh, no please, darling. It's so short a way, and I know every step,' pleaded Maria, and there was enough truth in what she said for him not to insist.

They walked out into the keen cold air, having to adjust their eyes to the darkness even after the miserable light of the coffee-room. Hornblower realized that if he had been an Admiral, or even a distinguished Captain, he would never have been allowed to leave with so little ceremony; the innkeeper and his wife would certainly have risen and dressed to see him on his way. They turned the corner and started on the steep slope down to the Sally Port, and it was borne in anew on Hornblower that he was about to start out for the wars. His concern for Maria had actually distracted him from this thought, but now he found himself gulping with excitement.

'Dear,' said Maria. 'I have a little present for you.'

She was bringing something out from the pocket of her cloak and pressing it into his hand.

'It's only gloves, dear, but my love comes with them,' she went on. 'I could make nothing better for you in this little time. I would have liked to have embroidered something for you – I would have liked to give you something worthy of you. But I have been stitching at these every moment since – since –'

She could not go on, but once more she straightened her back and refused to break down.

'I'll be able to think of you every moment I wear them,' said Hornblower. He struggled into the gloves despite the handicap of the bag he was carrying; they were splendid thick woollen gloves, each with separate thumb and forefinger.

'They fit me to perfection. I thank you for the kind thought, dear.'

Now they were at the head of the steep slope down the Hard, and this horrible ordeal would soon be over.

'You have the seventeen pounds safely?' asked Hornblower – an unnecessary question.

'Yes, thank you, dearest. I fear it too much –'

'And you'll be able to draw my monthly half-pay,' went on Hornblower harshly, to keep the emotion from his voice, and then, realising how harshly, he continued. 'It is time to say goodbye now, darling.'

He had forced himself to use the unaccustomed last word. The water level was far up the Hard; that meant, as he had known when he had given the orders, that the tide was at the flood. He would be able to take advantage of the ebb.

'Darling!' said Maria, turning to him and lifting up her face to him in its hood.

He kissed her; down at the water's edge there was the familiar rattle of oars on thwarts, and the sound of male voices, as his boat's crew perceived the two shadowy figures on the Hard. Maria heard those sounds as clearly as Hornblower did, and she quickly snatched away from him the cold lips she had raised to his.

'Goodbye, my angel.'

There was nothing else to say now, nothing else to do; this was the end of this brief experience. He turned his back on Maria; he turned his back on peace and on civilian married life and walked down towards war.

3

'Slack water now, sir,' announced Bush. 'First of the ebb in ten minutes. And anchor's hove short, sir.'

'Thank you, Mr Bush.' There was enough grey light in the sky now to see Bush's face as something more definite than a blur. At Bush's shoulder stood Prowse, the acting-master, senior master's mate with an acting-warrant. He was competing unobtrusively with Bush for Hornblower's attention. Prowse was charged, by Admiralty instructions, with 'navigating and conducting the ship from port to port under the direction of the captain.' But there was no reason at all why Hornblower should not give his other officers every opportunity to exercise their skill; on the contrary. And it was possible, even likely, that Prowse, with thirty years of sea duty behind him, would endeavour to take the direction of the ship out of the hands of a young and inexperienced captain.

'Mr Bush!' said Hornblower. 'Get the ship under way, if you please. Set a course to weather the Foreland.'

'Aye aye, sir.'

Hornblower watched Bush keenly, while doing his best not to appear to be doing so. Bush took a final glance round him, gauging the gentle wind and the likely course of the ebb.

'Stand by there, at the capstan,' he ordered. 'Loose the heads'ls. Hands aloft to loose the tops'ls.'

Hornblower could see in a flash that he could place implicit reliance on Bush's seamanship. He knew he should never have doubted it, but his memories were two years old and might have been blurred by the passage of time. Bush gave his orders in a well-timed sequence. With the anchor broken out *Hotspur* gathered momentary sternway. With the wheel hard over and the forecastle hands drawing at the headsail sheets she brought her head round. Bush sheeted home and ordered hands to the braces. In the sweetest possible way *Hotspur* caught the gentle wind, lying over hardly more than a degree or two. In a moment she was under way, slipping forward through the water, rudder balanced against sail-pressure, a living, lovely thing.

There was no need to drop any word of commendation to Bush regarding such a simple operation as getting under way. Hornblower could savour the pleasure of being afloat, as the hands raced to set the topgallant sails and then the courses. Then suddenly he remembered.

'Let me have that glass, please, Mr Prowse.'

He put the massive telescope to his eye and trained it out over the port quarter. It was still not yet full daylight, and there was the usual hint of haze, and *Hotspur* had left her anchorage half a mile or more astern. Yet he could just see it; a solitary, lonely speck of grey, on the water's edge, over there on the Hard. Perhaps – just possibly – there was a flicker of white; Maria might be waving her handkerchief, but he could not be sure. In fact he thought not. There was just the solitary grey speck. Hornblower looked again, and then he made himself lower the telescope; it was heavy, and his hands were trembling a trifle so that the image was blurred. It was the first time in all his life that he had put to sea leaving behind him someone who was interested in his fate.

'Thank you, Mr Prowse,' he said, harshly, handing back the telescope.

He knew he had to think about something different, that he must quickly find something else to occupy his thoughts; fortunately as captain of a ship just setting sail there was no lack of subjects.

'Now, Mr Prowse,' he said, glancing at the wake and at the trim of the sails. 'The wind's holding steady at the moment. I want a course for Ushant.'

'Ushant, sir?' Prowse had a long lugubrious face like a mule's, and he stood there digesting this piece of information without any change of expression.

'You heard what I said,' snapped Hornblower, in sudden irritation.

'Yes, sir,' answered Prowse, hastily. 'Ushant, sir. Aye aye, sir.'

There was, of course, some excuse for his first reaction. Nobody in the ship save Hornblower knew the content of the orders which were taking *Hotspur* to sea; nobody knew to what point in the whole world she was destined to sail. The mention of Ushant narrowed down the field to some extent at least. The North Sea and the Baltic were ruled out. So were Ireland and the Irish Sea and the St Lawrence across the Atlantic. But it still might be the West Indies or the Cape of Good Hope or the Mediterranean; Ushant was a point of departure for all those.

'Mr Bush!' said Hornblower.

'Sir!'

'You may dismiss the watch below, and send the hands to breakfast when you think proper.'

'Aye aye, sir.'

'Who's the officer of the watch?'

'Cargill, sir.'

'He has charge of the deck, then.'

Hornblower looked about him. Everything was in order, and *Hotspur* was standing out for the Channel. But there was something odd, something different, something unusual. Then it dawned upon him. For the first time in his life he was going to sea in time of peace. He had served ten years as a naval officer without this experience. Always before, whenever his ship emerged from harbour, she was in instant danger additional to the hazards of the sea. In every previous voyage any moment might bring an enemy up over the horizon; at an hour's notice ship and ship's company might be fighting for their lives. And the most dangerous time of all was when first putting to sea with a raw crew, with drill and organization incomplete – it was a likely moment to meet an enemy, as well as the most inconvenient one.

Now here they were putting to sea without any of these worries. It was an extraordinary sensation, something new – something new, like leaving Maria behind. He tried to shake that thought from him; as a buoy slithered past the starboard quarter he tried to leave the thought with it. It was a relief to see Prowse approaching again, with a piece of paper in his hand as he glanced up to the commission pendant and then out to the horizon in an attempt to forecast the weather.

'Course is sou'west by west, half west, sir,' he said. 'When we tack we may just be able to make that good, close-hauled.'

'Thank you, Mr Prowse. You may mark it on the board.'

'Aye aye, sir,' Prowse was pleased at this mark of confidence. He naturally had no idea that Hornblower, revolving in his mind, yesterday afternoon, all the responsibilities he would be carrying on the morrow, had made the same calculation to reach the same result. The green hills of the Isle of Wight were momentarily touched by a watery and level sun.

'There's the buoy, sir,' said Prowse.

'Thank you. Mr Cargill! Tack the ship, if you please.'

'Aye aye, sir.'

Hornblower withdrew aft. He wanted not merely to observe how Cargill handled the ship, but also how *Hotspur* behaved. When war should come it was not a mere possibility, but a definite probability, that success or failure, freedom or captivity, might hinge on how *Hotspur* went about, how handy she was in stays.

Cargill was a man of thirty, red-faced and corpulent in advance of his years; he was obviously trying hard to forget that he was under the simultaneous scrutiny of the captain, the first lieutenant, and the sailing master, as he applied himself to the manoeuvre. He stood beside the wheel looking warily up at the sails and aft at the wake. Hornblower watched Cargill's right hand, down by his thigh, opening and shutting. That might be a symptom of nervousness or a mere habitual gesture of calculation. The watch on deck were all at their stations. So far the men were all unknown faces to Hornblower;

it would be profitable to devote some of his attention to the study of their reactions as well.

Cargill obviously braced himself for action and then gave his preliminary order to the wheel.

'Helm's a-lee!' he bellowed, but not a very effective bellow, for his voice cracked halfway.

'Headsail sheets!' That was hardly better. It would not have served in a gale of wind, althought it carried forward in present conditions. Jib and foretopsail began to shiver.

'Raise up tacks and sheets!'

Hotspur was coming round into the wind, rising to an even keel. She was coming round, coming round – now was she going to hang in stays?

'Haul, mains'l! Haul!'

This was the crucial moment. The hands knew their business; the port-side bowlines and braces were cast off smartly, and the hands tailed on to the starboard-side ones. Round came the yards, but the *Hotspur* refused to answer. She baulked. She hung right in the eye of the wind, and then fell off again two points to port, with every sail ashiver and every yard of way lost. She was in irons, helpless until further action should be taken.

'A fine thing if we were on a lee shore, sir,' growled Bush.

'Wait,' said Hornblower. Cargill was glancing round at him for orders, and that was disappointing. Hornblower would have preferred an officer who went stolidly on to retrieve the situation. 'Carry on, Mr Cargill.'

The hands were behaving well. There was no chatter, and they were standing by for further orders. Cargill was drumming on his right thigh with his fingers, but for his own sake he must find his way out of his troubles unaided. Hornblower saw the fingers clench, saw Cargill glance ahead and astern as he pulled himself together. *Hotspur* was slowly gathering stern-way as the wind pushed directly back on the sails. Cargill took the plunge, made the effort. A sharp order put the wheel hard-a-port, another order brought the yards ponderously round again. *Hotspur* hung reluctant for a moment, and then sulkily turned back on the starboard tack and gathered way as Cargill in the nick of time sent the wheel spinning back and took a pull on the braces. There was no lack of sea room, there was no dangerous lee shore to demand instant action, and Cargill could wait until every sail was drawing full again and *Hotspur* had plenty of way on her to enable the rudder to bite. Cargill even had the sense to allow her head to fall off another point so as to give plenty of momentum for his next attempt, although Hornblower noticed with a slight pang of regret that he hurried it a trifle more than he should have done. He should have waited perhaps two more minutes.

'Headsail sheets!' ordered Cargill again; his fingers started drumming on his thigh once more with the strain of waiting.

But Cargill's head was clear enough to give his orders in the correct sequence. Round came *Hotspur* into the wind again. Sheets and braces were handled smartly. There was a paralysing moment as she baulked again, hung as though she was determined once more to miss stays, but this time she had a trifle more momentum, and in the last possible second a fortunate combination of wind and wave pushed her bows round through the vital final degrees of swing. Round she came, at last.

'Full and bye!' said Cargill to the helmsman, the relief very evident in his voice. 'Fore tack, there! Sheets! Braces!'

With the operation completed he turned to face the criticism of his superiors; there was sweat trickling down his forehead. Hornblower could feel Bush beside him ready to rate him thoroughly; Bush believed sincerely that everyone was the better for a severe dressing-down in any circumstance, and he was usually right. But Hornblower had been watching *Hotspur*'s behaviour closely.

'Carry on, Mr Cargill,' he said, and Cargill, relieved, turned away again, and Bush met Hornblower's glance with some slight surprise.

'The ship's trimmed too much by the head,' said Hornblower. 'That makes her unhandy in stays.'

'It might do so,' agreed Bush, doubtfully.

If the bow gripped the water more firmly than the stern *Hotspur* would act like a weather-vane, persisting in keeping her bow to the wind.

'We'll have to try it,' said Hornblower. 'She'll never do as she is. We'll have to trim her so that she draws six inches more aft. At least that. Now, what is there we can shift aft?'

'Well –' began Bush.

In his mind's eye he called up a picture of the interior of the *Hotspur*, with every cubic foot crammed with stores. It had been a Herculean feat to prepare her for sea; to find room for everything necessary had called for the utmost ingenuity. It seemed as if no other arrangement could be possible. Yet maybe –

'Perhaps –' went on Bush, and they were instantly deep in a highly technical discussion.

Prowse came up and touched his hat, to report that *Hotspur* was just able to make good the course for Ushant. Bush could hardly help but prick up his ears at the mention of the name; Prowse could hardly help but be drawn into the discussion regarding the alteration in the trim of the ship. They had to move aside to make room for the hourly casting of the log; the breeze flapped their coats round them. Here they were at sea; the nightmare days and nights of fitting out were over, and so were the – what was the right word? Delirious, perhaps – the delirious days of marriage. This was a normal life. Creative life, making a living organism out of *Hotspur*, working out improvements in material and in personnel.

Bush and Prowse were still discussing possible alteration in the ship's trim as Hornblower came back into his present world.

'There's a vacant port right aft on each side,' said Hornblower; a simple solution had presented itself to his mind, as so often happened when his thoughts had strayed to other subjects. 'We can bring two of the forward guns aft.'

Prowse and Bush paused while they considered the matter; Hornblower's rapid mind was already dealing with the mathematics of it. The ship's nine-pounders weighed twenty-six hundredweight each. Along with the gun carriages and the ready use shot which would have to be brought aft too there would be a total transfer of four tons. Hornblower's eye measured the distances, forward and aft of the centre of flotation, from forty feet before to thirty feet abaft. No, the leverage would be a little excessive, even though *Hotspur*'s dead weight was over four hundred tons.

'Maybe she'd gripe a little, sir,' suggested Prowse, reaching the same conclusions two minutes later.

'Yes. We'll take the No. 3 guns. That should be exactly right.'

'And leave a gap, sir?' asked Bush in faint protest.

It certainly would, as conspicuous as a missing front tooth. It would break into the two ordered rows of cannon, conveying a makeshift appearance to the ship.

'I'd rather have an ugly ship afloat,' said Hornblower, 'than a good-looking one on the rocks of a lee shore.'

'Yes, sir,' said Bush, swallowing this near-heresy.

'As the stores are consumed we can put things to rights again,' added Hornblower soothingly. 'Perhaps you'll be good enough to attend to it now?'

'Aye aye, sir.' Bush turned his mind to the practical aspects of the problem of shifting cannon in a moving ship. 'I'll hoist 'em out of the carriages with the stay tackles and lower them on to a mat –'

'Quite right. I'm sure you can deal with it, Mr Bush.'

No one in his senses would try to move a gun in its carriage along a heeling deck – it would go surging about out of control in a moment. But out of its carriage, lying helpless on a mat, with its trunnions prohibiting any roll, it could be dragged about comparatively easily, and hoisted up into its carriage again after that had been moved into its new position. Bush had already passed the word for Mr Wise, the boatswain, to have the stay-tackles rigged.

'The quarter-bill will have to be changed,' said Hornblower incautiously as the thought struck him – the guns' crews would need to be reallotted.

'Aye aye, sir,' said Bush. His sense of discipline was

too acute to allow more than a hint of reproach to be apparent in his tone. As first lieutenant it was his business to remember these things without being reminded by his captain. Hornblower made amends as best he could.

'I'll leave it all in your charge, then, Mr Bush. Report to me when the guns are moved.'

'Aye aye, sir.'

Hornblower crossed the quarterdeck to go to his cabin, passing Cargill as he went; Cargill was keeping an eye on the hands rigging the stay-tackles.

'The ship will be more handy in stays when those guns are shifted, Mr Cargill,' said Hornblower. 'Then you'll have another opportunity to show how you can handle her.'

'Thank you, sir,' replied Cargill. He had clearly been brooding over his recent failure.

Hornblower walked along to his cabin; the moving cogs in the complex machine that was a ship always needed lubrication, and it was a captain's duty to see that it was provided. The sentry at his door came to attention as he passed in. He glanced round at the bare necessities there. His cot swung from the deck-beams; there was a single chair, a mirror on the bulkhead with a canvas basin on a frame below it. On the opposite bulkhead was clamped his desk, with his sea chest beneath it. A strip of canvas hanging from the deck-beams served as a wardrobe to screen the clothes hanging within. That was all; there was no room for anything else, but the fact that the cabin was so tiny was an advantage in one way. There were no guns mounted in it – it was right aft – and there would be no necessity when the ship cleared for action, to sweep all this away.

And this was luxury, this was affluence, this was the most superlative good fortune. Nine days ago – no, ten days, now – he had been a half-pay lieutenant, under stoppage of pay because the Peace of Amiens had resulted in his promotion not being confirmed. He had been doubtful where his next meal would be coming from. A single night had changed all this. He had won forty-five pounds at a sitting of whist from a group of senior officers, one of them a Lord of Admiralty. The King had sent a message to Parliament announcing the government's decision to set the Navy on a war footing again. And he had been appointed Commander and given the *Hotspur* to prepare for sea. He could be sure now of his next meal, even though it would be salt beef and biscuit. And – not so much as a coincidence, but rather as a sequel to all this – he had found himself betrothed to Maria and committed to an early marriage.

The fabric of the ship transmitted the sound of one of the nine-pounders being dragged aft; Bush was a fast worker. Bush had been a half-pay lieutenant too, ten days ago, and senior to Hornblower. It was with diffidence that Hornblower had asked him if he would care to serve as first lieutenant – as the only lieutenant allowed on the establishment of a sloop of war – of the *Hotspur*, under Hornblower's command. It had been astonishing, and extremely flattering, to see the delight in Bush's face at the invitation.

'I'd been hoping you'd ask me, sir,' said Bush. 'I couldn't really think you'd want me as a first lieutenant.'

'Nobody I'd like better,' Hornblower had replied.

At this moment he nearly lost his footing as *Hotspur* heaved up her bows, rolled, and then cocked up her stern in the typical motion of a ship close-hauled. She was out now from the lee of the Wight, meeting the full force of the Channel rollers. Fool that he was! He had almost forgotten about this; on the one or two occasions during the past ten days when the thought of seasickness had occurred to him he had blithely assumed that he had grown out of that weakness in eighteen months on land. He had not thought about it at all this morning, being too busy. Now with his first moment of idleness here it came. He had lost his sea legs – a new roll sent him reeling – and he was going to be sick. He could feel a cold sweat on his skin and the first wave of nausea rising to his throat. There was time for a bitter jest – he had just been congratulating himself on knowing where his next meal was coming from, but now he could be more certain still about where his last meal was going to. Then the sickness struck, horribly.

Now he lay face downward across his cot. He heard the rumble of wheels, and cleared his thoughts sufficiently to make the deduction that, with the guns brought aft, Bush was bringing the gun-carriages aft as well. But he hardly cared. His stomach heaved again and he cared even less. He could think about nothing but his own misery. Now what was that? Someone pounding vigorously on the door, and he realized that the pounding had grown-up from an earlier gentle tapping that he had ignored.

'What is it?' he called, croaking.

'Message from the master, sir,' said an unknown voice. 'From Mr Prowse.'

He had to hear what it was. He dragged himself from his cot, and staggered over and dumped himself into his chair, hunching his shoulders over his desk so that his face could not be seen.

'Come in!' he called.

The opening of the door admitted considerably more of the noise that had been more and more insistently making itself heard.

'What is it?' repeated Hornblower, hoping that his attitude indicated deep concentration upon the paper-work of the ship.

'Message from Mr Prowse, sir,' said a voice that Hornblower could hardly place. 'Wind's freshening an' hauling forward. Course will have to be altered, sir.'

'Very well. I'll come.'

'Aye aye, sir.'

He certainly would have to come. He stood up, holding on to the desk with one hand while he adjusted his clothes with the other. He braced himself, and then he plunged out on to the quarterdeck. He had forgotten all these things; he had forgotten how fresh the wind blew at sea, how the rigging shrieked in a gust, how the deck heaved under unwary feet. As the stern rose he was hurried forward, struggling vainly to retain his dignity, and just managed to fetch up without disaster against the hammock netting. Prowse came up at once.

'Course is sou'west by south, now, sir,' he said. 'I had to let her fall off a couple of points. Wind's still backing westerly.'

'So I see,' said Hornblower. He looked at sky and

sea, making himself think. 'How's the glass?'

'Hardly fallen at all, sir. But it's going to blow harder before nightfall, sir.'

'Perhaps you're right.'

Bush appeared at this moment, touching the hat that was now pulled down hard on to his head.

'The guns are shifted aft, sir. The lashings are bowsed up taut.'

'Thank you.'

Hornblower kept his hands on the hammock netting, and his gaze steadily forward, so that, by not turning either to Bush on one side or to Prowse on the other, the whiteness of his landlubber's face might not be noticed. He struggled to picture the chart of the Channel that he had studied so carefully yesterday. There was the twenty-league gap between the Casquets and the Start; an incorrect decision now might keep them windbound for days inside it.

'We might just weather the Start on this course, sir,' prompted Prowse.

Unexpected nausea suddenly welled up in Hornblower, and he moved restlessly as he fought with it. He did not want Prowse to prompt him, and as he swung about he caught sight of Cargill standing by the wheel. It was still Cargill's watch – that was one more factor to bring Hornblower to a decision, along with Bush's report and Prowse's prompting.

'No,' he said. 'We'll put the ship about.'

'Aye aye, sir,' said Prowse, in reluctant agreement.

Hornblower looked towards Cargill, summoning him with a glance; he did not wish to leave the comforting support of the hammock netting.

'Mr Cargill,' said Hornblower. 'Let's see you tack the ship again, now that we've altered her trim.'

'Aye aye, sir,' answered Cargill. That was the only thing the poor devil could say in any case, in reply to a direct order. But he was clearly nervous. He went back to the wheel and took the speaking trumpet from its beckets – the freshening wind made that necessary.

'Hands 'bout ship!' he called, and the order was instantly underlined by the calls of the bos'n's mates and the bellowings of Mr Wise. The hands ran to their stations. Cargill stared round at wind and sea; Hornblower saw him swallow as he nerved himself. Then he gave the order to the wheel; this time it was the fingers of his left hand that drummed upon his thigh, for his right was occupied by the speaking-trumpet. *Hotspur* rose to an even keel while sheets and braces were being handled. She was turning – she was turning.

'Let go and haul!' yelled Cargill into the speaking-trumpet. Hornblower felt he would have waited three or four more seconds before giving that order, but he knew that he might be wrong; not only was seasickness dulling his judgement but, standing as he did, looking aft, he did not have the 'feel' of the ship. Events proved that Cargill did, or else was lucky, for *Hotspur* came on round without hesitation.

'Hard-a-lee!' snapped Cargill to the helmsman, and the wheel spun round in a blur of spokes, catching *Hotspur* at the moment when she was beginning to fall off. A straining group of men hauled out the foretack; others tailed on to the bowlines. *Hotspur* was on the new tack, having handled as sweetly, apparently, as anyone could ask.

Hornblower walked up to the wheel.

'Does she gripe?' he asked the quartermaster.

The quartermaster eased off the wheel a couple of spokes, squinting up at the leech of the maintopsail, and then brought her up to the wind again.

'Can't say that she does, sir,' he decided. 'Mebbe she does, a trifle. No, sir, I can't say that she gripes. Just a touch of weather helm's all she needs now, sir.'

'That's as it should be,' said Hornblower. Bush and Prowse had not spoken a word, and there was no need even for a glance to underline the situation, but a word to Cargill would not be out of place. 'You can go off watch feeling better pleased with yourself now, Mr Cargill.'

'Yes, sir, thank you, sir,' said Cargill.

Cargill's round red face split into a grin. *Hotspur* rose to a wave, lay over, and Hornblower, taken by surprise, staggered down the deck on to Cargill's broad chest. Luckily Cargill was a heavyweight and fast of footing; he took the shock without staggering – otherwise he and his captain might have gone reeling across the deck into the scuppers. Hornblower felt a burst of shame. He had no more sea legs than the merest landlubber; his envy of Cargill and Bush and Prowse, standing firm and swaying easily with the send of the ship, amounted to positive dislike. And his stomach was about to betray him again. His dignity was in peril, and he summoned up all that was left of it, turning to Bush stiff-legged and stiff-necked.

'See that I am called when any alteration of course is necessary, if you please, Mr Bush,' he said.

'Aye aye, sir.'

The deck was heaving, but he knew it was not heaving as much as his distorted mind told him it was. He forced himself somehow to walk aft to his cabin; twice he had to stop and brace himself, and when *Hotspur* rose to a wave he was nearly made to run – certainly he had to walk faster than a captain should – past the sentry, and he fetched up against the door with some little violence. It was no comfort – in fact it added to his distress – to see that the sentry had a bucket on the deck beside him. He wrenched open the door, hung suspended for a moment as *Hotspur* completed her pitch, with her stern in the air, and then crashed down groaning on to his cot, his feet dragging on the deck as the cot swung.

4

Hornblower sat at his desk in his cabin holding a package in his hand. Five minutes earlier he had unlocked his chest and taken this out; in five minutes more he would be entitled to open it – at least, that was what his dead reckoning indicated. It was a remarkably heavy package; it might be weighted with shot or scrap metal, except that Admiral Cornwallis was hardly likely to send shot or scrap metal to one of his captains. It was heavily sealed, in four places, and the seals were unbroken. Inked upon the canvas wrapper was the superscription:

'Instructions for Horatio Hornblower, Esq., Master and Commander, HM Sloop *Hotspur*. To be opened on passing the Sixth Degree of Longitude West of Greenwich.'

Sealed orders. Hornblower had heard about such things all his professional life, but this was his first contact with them. They had been sent on board the *Hotspur* on the afternoon of his wedding day, and he had signed for them. Now the ship was about to cross the sixth meridian; she had come down-Channel with remarkable ease; there had been only one single watch when she had not been able to make good her direct course. Putting her about in order to restore Cargill's self-confidence had been extraordinarily fortunate. The wind had hardly backed westerly at all, and only momentarily even then. *Hotspur* had escaped being embayed in Lyme Bay; she had neatly weathered the Casquets, and it all stemmed from that fortunate order. Hornblower was aware that Prowse was feeling a new respect for him as a navigator and a weather prophet. That was all to the good, and Hornblower had no intention of allowing Prowse to guess that the excellent passage was the result of a fortunate fluke, of a coincidence of circumstances.

Hornblower looked at his watch and raised his voice in a shout to the sentry at the door.

'Pass the word for Mr Bush.'

Hornblower could hear the sentry shouting, and the word being passed on along the quarterdeck. *Hotspur* rose in a long, long pitch with hardly any roll about it. She was meeting the long Atlantic swell now, changing her motion considerably, and all for the better, in Hornblower's opinion – and his seasickness was rapidly coming under control. Bush was taking a long time to respond to the call – he obviously was not on the quarterdeck, and the chances were he was taking a nap or was engaged on some other private business. Well, it would do him no harm and cause him no surprise to be summoned from it, for that was the way of the Navy.

At last came the knock on the door, and Bush entered.

'Sir?'

'Ah, Mr Bush,' said Hornblower pedantically. Bush was the closest friend he had, but this was a formal matter, to be carried through normally. 'Can you tell me the ship's position at this moment?'

'No, sir, not exactly, sir,' replied the puzzled Bush. 'Ushant bears ten leagues to the east'ard, I believe, sir.'

'At this moment,' said Hornblower, 'we are in longi-

tude six degrees and some seconds west. Latitude 48°
40', but we do not have to devote any thought to our
latitude at present, oddly enough. It is our longitude
that matters. Would you be so kind as to examine this
packet?'

'Ah. I see, sir,' said Bush, having read the superscription.

'You observe that the seals are unbroken?'

'Yes, sir.'

'Then perhaps you will have the further kindness,
when you leave this cabin, to make sure of the ship's
longitude so that, should it become necessary, you can
bear witness that I have carried out my orders?'

'Yes, sir, I will,' said Bush, and then, after a pause
long enough for him to realize that Hornblower
intended the interview to be at an end, 'Aye aye, sir.'

The temptation to tease Bush was a very strong one,
Hornblower realized as Bush left the cabin. It was a
temptation he must resist. It might be indulged to the
extent of causing resentment; in any case, Bush was too
easy a target – he was a sitting bird.

And thinking along those lines had actually delayed
for several seconds the exciting moment of opening the
orders. Hornblower took out his penknife and cut the
stitching. Now the weight of the packet was explained.
There were three rolls of coins – golden coins.
Hornblower spilt them out on to his desk. There were
fifty small ones, about the size of sixpences; twenty
larger ones, and ten larger still. Examination revealed
that the medium-sized ones were French twenty-franc
pieces, exactly like one he had seen in Lord Parry's
possession a week or two ago, with 'Napoleon First

Consul' on one side and 'French Republic' on the other. The small ones were ten franc pieces, the larger ones forty francs. Altogether it made a considerable sum, over fifty pounds without allowing for the premium on gold in an England plagued by a depreciating paper currency.

And here were his supplementary instructions, explaining how he should employ the money. 'You are therefore required –' said the instructions after the preliminary sentences. Hornblower had to make contact with the fishermen of Brest; he had to ascertain if any of them would accept bribes; he had to glean from them all possible information regarding the French fleet in that port; finally he was informed that in case of war information of any kind, even newspapers, would be acceptable.

Hornblower read his instructions through twice; he referred again to the unsealed orders he had received at the same time; the ones that had sent him to sea. There was need for thought, and automatically he rose to his feet, only to sit down again, for there was no chance whatever of walking about in that cabin. He must postpone his walk for a moment. Maria had stitched neat linen bags in which to put his hair brushes – quite useless, of course, seeing that he always rolled his brushes in his housewife. He reached for one, and swept the money into it, put the bag and the orders back into his chest and was about to lock it when a further thought struck him, and he counted out ten ten-franc pieces and put them into his trouser pocket. Now, with his chest locked, he was free to go on deck.

Prowse and Bush were pacing the weather side of the quarterdeck in deep conversation; no doubt the news that their captain had opened his sealed orders would spread rapidly through the ship – and no one on board save Hornblower could be really sure that *Hotspur* was not about to set course for the Cape and India. It was a temptation to keep them all on tenterhooks, but Hornblower put the temptation aside. Besides, it would be to no purpose – after a day or two of hanging about outside Brest everyone would be able to guess *Hotspur*'s mission. Prowse and Bush were hurriedly moving over to the lee side, leaving the weather side for their captain, but Hornblower halted them.

'Mr Bush! Mr Prowse! We are going to look into Brest and see what our friend Boney is up to.'

Those few words told the whole story to men who had served in the last war and who had beaten about in the stormy waters off the Brittany coast.

'Yes, sir,' said Bush, simply.

Together they looked into the binnacle, out to the horizon, up to the commission pendant. Simple enough to set a course; Bush and Prowse could do that easily, but it was not so simple to deal with problems of inter-national relations, problems of neutrality, problems of espionage.

'Let's look at the chart, Mr Prowse. You can see that we'll have to keep well clear of Les Fillettes.'

The islands of the Little Girls, in the middle of the fairway into Brest; it was a queer name for rocks that would be sites for batteries of guns.

'Very well, Mr Prowse. You can square away and set course.'

There were light airs from the north-westward today, and it was the easiest matter in the world to stand down towards Brest; *Hotspur* was hardly rolling at all and was pitching only moderately. Hornblower was fast recovering his sea legs and could trust himself to walk the deck, and could almost trust his stomach to retain its contents. There was a certain feeling of well-being that came with a remission from seasickness. The April air was keen and fresh, but not paralysingly cold; Hornblower's gloves and heavy coat were barely necessary. In fact Hornblower found it hard to concentrate on his problems; he was willing to postpone their consideration, and he halted his step and looked across at Bush with a smile that brought the latter over with hurried steps.

'I suppose you have plans for exercising the crew, Mr Bush?'

'Yes, sir.' Bush did not say, 'Of course, sir,' for he was too good a subordinate. But his eyes lit up, for there was nothing Bush enjoyed more than reefing topsails and unreefing them, sending down top-gallant yards and sending them up again, rousting out cables and carrying them to a stern port in readiness to be used as a spring, and in fact rehearsing all the dozens – hundreds – of manoeuvres that weather or war might make necessary.

'Two hours of that will do for today, Mr Bush. I can only remember one short exercise at the guns?'

Tortured by seasickness while running down the Channel he could not be sure.

'Only one, sir.'

'Then after dinner we'll have an hour at the guns. One of these days we might use them.'

'We might, sir,' said Bush.

Bush could face with equanimity the prospects of a war that would engulf the whole world.

The pipes of the bos'n's mates called all hands, and very soon the exercises were well under way, the sweating sailors racing up and down the rigging tailing on to ropes under the urgings of the petty officers and amid a perfect cloud of profanity from Mr Wise. It was as well to drill the men, simply to keep them exercised, but there were no serious deficiencies to make up. *Hotspur* had benefited by being the very first ship to be manned after the press had been put into force. Of her hundred and fifty hands no fewer than a hundred were prime seamen, rated AB. She had twenty ordinary seamen and only ten landsmen all told, and no more than twenty boys. It was an extraordinary proportion, one that would never be seen again as the manning of the fleet continued. Not only that, but more than half the men had seen service in men o' war before the Peace of Amiens. They were not only seamen, but Royal Navy seamen, who had hardly had time to make more than a single voyage in the merchant navy during the peace before being pressed again. Consequently most of them had had experience with ship's guns; twenty or thirty of them had actually seen action. The result was that when the gun exercise was ordered they went to their stations in businesslike fashion. Bush turned to Hornblower and touched his hat awaiting the next order.

'Thank you, Mr Bush. Order "silence" if you please.'

The whistles pealed round the deck, and the ship fell deathly still.

'I shall now inspect, if you will be so kind as to accompany me, Mr Bush.'

'Aye aye, sir.'

Hornblower began by glowering down at the starboard-side quarterdeck carronade. Everything was in order there, and he walked down into the waist to inspect the starboard-side nine-pounders. At each he stopped to look over the equipment. Cartridge, crowbar, hand-spike. Sponge, quoin. He passed on from gun to gun.

'What's your station if the larboard guns are being worked?'

He had picked for questioning the youngest seaman visible, who moved uneasily from one foot to another finding himself addressed by the captain.

'Stand to attention, there!' bellowed Bush.

'What's your station?' repeated Hornblower, quietly.

'Oh–over there, sir. I handle the rammer, sir.'

'I'm glad you know. If you can remember your station when the captain and the first lieutenant are speaking to you I can trust you to remember it when round-shot are coming in through the side.'

Hornblower passed on; a captain could always be sure of raising a laugh if he made a joke. Then he halted again.

'What's this? Mr Cheeseman!'

'Sir.'

'You have an extra powder-horn here. There should be only one for every two guns.'

'Er – yessir. It's because –'

'I know the reason. A reason's no excuse, though, Mr Cheeseman. Mr Orrock! What powder-horns have you in your section? Yes, I see.'

Shifting No. 3 gun aft had deprived Orrock's section

of a powder-horn and given an additional one to Cheeseman's.

'It's the business of you young gentlemen to see that the guns in your section are properly equipped. You don't have to wait for orders.'

Cheeseman and Orrock were two of the four 'young gentlemen' sent on board from the Naval College to be trained as midshipmen. Hornblower liked nothing he had seen as yet of any of them. But they were what he had to use as petty officers, and for his own sake he must train them into becoming useful lieutenants – his needs corresponded with his duty. He must make them and not break them.

'I'm sure I won't have to speak to you young gentlemen again,' he said. He was sure he would, but a promise was better than a threat. He walked on, completing the inspection of the guns on the starboard side. He went up to the forecastle to look at the two carronades there, and then back down the maindeck guns of the port side. He stopped at the marine stationed at the forehatchway.

'What are your orders?'

The marine stood stiffly at attention, feet at an angle of forty-five degrees, musket close in at his side, forefinger of the left hand along the seam of his trousers, neck rigid in its stock, so that, as Hornblower was not directly in front of him, he stared over Hornblower's shoulder.

'To guard my post –' he began, and continued in a monotonous sing-song, repeating by rote the sentry's formula which he had probably uttered a thousand times before. The change in his tone was marked when he reached the final sentence added for this particular station – 'To allow no one to go below unless he is carrying an empty cartridge bucket.'

That was so that cowards could not take refuge below the waterline.

'What about men carrying wounded?'

The astonished marine found it hard to answer; he found it hard to think after years of drill.

'I have no orders about them, sir,' he said at last, actually allowing his eyes, though not his neck, to move.

Hornblower glanced at Bush.

'I'll speak to the sergeant of marines, sir,' said Bush.

'Who's on the quarter-bill to attend to the wounded?'

'Cooper and his mate, sir. Sailmaker and his mate. Four altogether, sir.'

Trust Bush to have all those details at his fingers' ends, even though Hornblower had found two small points to find fault with, for which Bush was ultimately responsible. No need to stress those matters with Bush – he was burning with silent shame.

Down the hatchway to the magazine. A candle glimmered faintly through the glass window of the light-room, throwing just enough light for powder boys to see what they were doing as they received loaded cartridges through the double serge curtains opening into the magazine; inside the magazine the gunner and his mate, wearing list slippers, were ready to pass out, and, if necessary, fill cartridges. Down the after hatchway to where the surgeon and his lob-lolly boy were ready to deal with the wounded. Hornblower knew that he himself might at some time be dragged in here with blood streaming from some shattered limb

– it was a relief to ascend to the maindeck again.

'Mr Foreman,' – Foreman was another of the 'young gentlemen' – 'what are your orders regarding lanterns during a night action?'

'I am to wait until Mr Bush expressly orders them, sir.'

'And who do you send if you receive those orders?'

'Firth, sir.'

Foreman indicated a likely-looking young seaman at his elbow. But was there perhaps the slightest moment of hesitation about that reply? Hornblower turned on Firth.

'Where do you go?'

Firth's eyes flickered towards Foreman for a moment. That might be with embarrassment; but Foreman swayed a little on his feet, as if he were pointing with his shoulder, and one hand made a small sweeping gesture in front of his middle, as if he might be indicating Mr Wise's abdominal rotundity.

'For'rard, sir,' said Firth. 'The bos'n issues them. At the break of the fo'c'sle.'

'Very well,' said Hornblower.

He had no doubt that Foreman had quite forgotten to pass on Bush's orders regarding battle lanterns. But Foreman had been quick-witted enough to remedy the situation, and Firth had not merely been quick-witted but also loyal enough to back up his petty officer. It would be well to keep an eye on both those two, for various reasons. The break of the forecastle had been an inspired guess, as being adjacent to the bos'n's locker.

Hornblower walked up on to the quarterdeck again, Bush following him, and he cast a considering eye about him, taking in the last uninspected gun – the port-side quarterdeck carronade. He selected a position where the largest possible number of ears could catch his words.

'Mr Bush,' he said, 'we have a fine ship. If we work hard we'll have a fine crew too. If Boney needs a lesson we'll give it to him. You may continue with the exercises.'

'Aye aye, sir.'

The six marines on the quarterdeck, the helmsman, the carronades' crews, Mr Prowse and the rest of the afterguard had all heard him. He had felt it was not the time for a formal speech, but he could be sure his words would be relayed round the ship during the next dog watch. And he had chosen them carefully. That 'we' was meant as a rallying call. Meanwhile Bush was continuing with the exercise. 'Cast loose your guns. Level your guns. Take out your tompions,' and all the rest of it.

'We'll have them in shape soon enough, sir,' said Bush. 'Then we'll only have to get alongside the enemy.'

'Not necessarily alongside, Mr Bush. When we come to burn powder at the next exercise I want the men schooled in firing at long range.'

'Yes, sir. Of course,' agreed Bush.

But that was lip-service only on Bush's part. He had not really thought about the handling of *Hotspur* in battle – close action, where the guns could not miss, and only needed to be loaded and fired as rapidly as possible, was Bush's ideal. Very well for a ship of the line in a fleet action, but perhaps not so suitable for *Hotspur*. She was only a sloop of war, her timbers and her scantlings more fragile even than those of a frigate.

Her twenty nine-pounders that gave her 'rate' – the four carronades not being counted – were 'long guns', better adapted for work at a couple of cables' lengths than for close action when the enemy's guns stood no more chance of missing than hers did. She was the smallest thing with three masts and quarterdeck and forecastle in the Navy List. The odds were heavy that any enemy she might meet would be her superior in size, in weight of metal, in number of men – probably immeasurably her superior. Dash and courage might snatch a victory for her, but skill and forethought and good handling might be more certain. Hornblower felt the tremor of action course through him, accentuated by the vibrating rumble of the guns being run out.

'Land ho! Land ho!' yelled the look-out of the fore-topmast head. 'Land one point on the lee bow!'

That would be France, Ushant, the scene of their future exploits, perhaps where they would meet with disaster or death. Naturally there was a wave of excitement through the ship. Heads were raised and faces turned.

'Sponge your guns!' bellowed Bush through his speaking-trumpet. Bush could be relied on to maintain discipline and good order through any distraction. 'Load!'

It was hard for the men to go through the play-acting of gun drill in these circumstances; discipline on the one side, resentment, disillusionment on the other.

'Point your guns! Mr Cheeseman! The hand-spike man on No. 7 gun isn't attending to his duty. I want his name.'

Prowse was training a telescope forward; as the

officer responsible for navigation that was his duty, but it was also his privilege.

'Run your guns in!'

Hornblower itched to follow Prowse's example, but he restrained himself; Prowse would keep him informed of anything vital. He allowed the drill to go on through one more mock broadside before he spoke.

'Mr Bush, you may secure the guns now, thank you.'

'Aye aye, sir.'

Prowse was offering his telescope.

'That's the light-tower on Ushant, sir,' he said.

Hornblower caught a wavering glimpse of the thing, a gaunt framework topped by a cresset, where the French government in time of peace maintained a light for the benefit of the ships – half the world's trade made a landfall off Ushant – that needed it.

'Thank you, Mr Prowse.' Hornblower visualized the chart again; recalled the plans he had made in the intervals of commissioning his ship, in the intervals of his honeymoon, in the intervals of seasickness, during the past crowded days. 'Wind's drawing westerly. But it'll be dark before we can make Cape Matthew. We'll stand to the s'uth'ard under easy sail until midnight. I want to be a league off the Black Stones an hour before dawn.'

'Aye aye, sir.'

Bush joined them from the business of securing the guns.

'Look at that, sir! There's a fortune passing us by.'

A large ship was hull-up to windward, her canvas reflecting the westering sun.

'French Indiaman,' commented Hornblower, turning his glass on her.

'A quarter of a million pounds, all told!' raved Bush. 'Maybe a hundred thousand for you, sir, if only war were declared. Doesn't that tease you, sir? She'll carry this wind all the way to Havre and she'll be safe.'

'There'll be others,' replied Hornblower soothingly.

'Not so many, sir. Trust Boney. He'll send warnings out the moment he's resolved on war, and every French flag'll take refuge in neutral ports. Madeira and the Azores, Cadiz and Ferrol, while we could make our fortunes!'

The possibilities of prize money bulked large in the thoughts of every naval officer.

'Maybe we will,' said Hornblower. He thought of Maria and his allotment of pay; even a few hundreds of pounds would make a huge difference.

'Maybe, sir,' said Bush, clearly discounting the possibility.

'And there's another side to the picture,' added Hornblower, pointing round the horizon.

There were half a dozen other sails all visible at this time, all British. They marked the enormous extent of British maritime commerce. They bore the wealth that could support navies, sustain allies, maintain manufactories of arms – to say nothing of the fact that they provided the basic training for seamen who later would man the ships of war which kept the seas open for them and closed them to England's enemies.

'They're only British, sir,' said Prowse, wonderingly. He had not the vision to see what Hornblower saw. Bush had to look hard at his captain before it dawned upon him.

The heaving of the log, with the changing of the

watch, relieved Hornblower of the temptation to preach a sermon.

'What's the speed, Mr Young?'

'Three knots and a half, sir.'

'Thank you.' Hornblower turned back to Prowse. 'Keep her on her present course.'

'Aye aye, sir.'

Hornblower was training his telescope out over the port bow. There was a black dot rising and falling out there towards Molene Island. He kept it under observation.

'I think, Mr Prowse,' he said, his glass still at his eye, 'we might edge in a little more inshore. Say two points. I'd like to pass that fishing-boat close.'

'Aye aye, sir.'

She was one of the small craft employed in the pilchard fishery, very similar to those seen off the Cornish coast. She was engaged at the moment in hauling in her seine; as *Hotspur* approached more closely the telescope made plain the rhythmical movements of the four men.

'Up with the helm a little more, Mr Prowse, if you please. I'd like to pass her closer still.'

Now Hornblower could make out a little area of water beside the fishing-boat that was of a totally different colour. It had a metallic sheen quite unlike the rest of the grey sea; the fishing-boat had found a shoal of pilchards and her seine was now closing in on it.

'Mr Bush. Please try to read her name.'

They were fast closing on her; within a few moments Bush could make out the bold white letters on her stern.

'From Brest, sir. *Duke's Freers.*'

With that prompting Hornblower could read the name for himself, the *Deux Frères*, Brest.

'Back the maintops'l, Mr Young!' bellowed Hornblower to the officer of the watch, and then, turning back to Bush and Prowse, 'I want fish for my supper tonight.'

They looked at him in ill-concealed surprise.

'Pilchards, sir?'

'That's right.'

The seine was close in alongside the *Deux Frères*, and masses of silver fish were being heaved up into her. So intent were the fishermen on securing their catch that they had no knowledge of the silent approach of the *Hotspur*, and looked up in ludicrous astonishment at the lovely vessel towering over them in the sunset. They even displayed momentary panic, until they obviously realized that in time of peace a British ship of war would do them less harm than a French one might, a French one enforcing the *Inscription Maritime*.

Hornblower took the speaking-trumpet from its beckets. He was pulsing with excitement now, and he had to be firm with himself to keep calm. This might be the first step in the making of the history of the future; besides, he had not spoken French for a considerable time and he had to concentrate on what he was going to say.

'Good day, captain!' he yelled, and the fishermen, reassured, waved back to him in friendly fashion. 'Will you sell me some fish?'

Hurriedly they conferred, and then one of them replied.

'How much?'

'Oh, twenty pounds.'

Again they conferred.

'Very well.'

'Captain,' went on Hornblower, searching in his mind not only for the necessary French words but also for an approach to bring about the situation he desired. 'Finish your work. Then come aboard. We can drink a glass of rum to the friendship of nations.'

The beginning of that sentence was clumsy, he knew, but he could not translate 'Get in your catch'; but the prospect of British navy rum he knew would be alluring – and he was a little proud of *l'amitié des nations*. What was the French for 'dinghy'? *Chaloupe*, he fancied. He expanded on his invitation, and someone in the fishing-boat waved in assent before bending to the business of getting in the catch. With the last of it on board two of the four men scrambled into the dinghy that lay alongside the *Deux Frères;* it was nearly as big as the fishing-boat itself, as was to be expected when she had to lay out the seine. Two oars stoutly handled brought the dinghy rapidly towards *Hotspur*.

'I'll entertain the captain in my cabin,' said Hornblower. 'Mr Bush, see that the other man is taken forward and well looked after. See he has a drink.'

'Aye aye, sir.'

A line over the side brought up two big buckets of fish, and these were followed by two blue-jerseyed men who scrambled up easily enough despite their sea-boots.

'A great pleasure, captain,' said Hornblower in the waist to greet him. 'Please come with me.'

The captain looked curiously about him as he was led up to the quarterdeck and aft to the cabin. He sat down cautiously in the only chair while Hornblower perched on the cot. The blue jersey and trousers were spangled with fish scales – the cabin would smell of fish for a week. Hewitt brought rum and water, and Hornblower poured two generous glasses; the captain sipped appreciatively.

'Has your fishing been successful?' asked Hornblower, politely.

He listened while the captain told him, in his almost unintelligible Breton French, about the smallness of the profits to be earned in the pilchard fishery. The conversation drifted on. It was an easy transition from the pleasures of peace to the possibilities of war – two seamen could hardly meet without that prospect being discussed.

'I suppose they make great efforts to man the ships of war?'

The captain shrugged.

'Certainly.'

The shrug told much more than the word.

'It marches very slowly, I imagine,' said Hornblower, and the captain nodded.

'But of course the ships are ready to take the sea?'

Hornblower had no idea of how to say 'laid-up in ordinary' in French, and so he had to ask the question in the opposite sense.

'Oh, no,' said the captain. He went on to express his contempt for the French naval authorities. There was not a single ship of the line ready for service. Of course not.

'Let me refill your glass, captain,' said Hornblower. 'I suppose the frigates receive the first supplies of men?'

Such supplies as there were, perhaps. The Breton captain was not sure. Of course there was – Hornblower had more than a moment's difficulty at this point. Then he understood. The frigate *Loire* had been made ready for sea last week (it was the Breton pronunciation of that name which had most puzzled Hornblower) for service in Far Eastern waters, but with the usual idiocy of the naval command had now been stripped of most of her trained men to provide nuclei for the other ships. The Breton captain, whose capacity for rum was quite startling, did nothing to conceal either the smouldering Breton resentment against the atheist regime now ruling France or the contempt of a professional user of the sea for the blundering policies of the Republican Navy. Hornblower had only to nurse his glass and listen, his faculties at full stretch to catch all the implications of a conversation in a foreign language. When at last the captain rose to say goodbye there was a good deal of truth in what Hornblower said, haltingly, about his regrets at the termination of the visit.

'Yet perhaps even if war should come, captain, we may still meet again. As I expect you know, the Royal Navy of Great Britain does not make war on fishing vessels. I shall always be glad to buy some of your catch.'

The Frenchman was looking at him keenly now, perhaps because the subject of payment was arising. This was a most important moment, calling for accurate judgement. How much? What to say?

'Of course I must pay for today's supply,' said Hornblower, his hand in his pocket. He took out two ten-franc pieces and dropped them into the horny palm, and the captain could not restrain an expression of astonishment from appearing in his weatherbeaten face. Astonishment, followed instantly by avarice, and then by suspicion, calculation, and finally by decision as the hand clenched and hurried the money into a trouser-pocket. Those emotions had played over the captain's face like the colours of a dying dolphin. Twenty francs in gold, for a couple of buckets of pilchards; most likely the captain supported himself, his wife and children for a week on twenty francs. Ten francs would be a week's wage for his hands. This was important money; either the British captain did not know the value of gold or –. At least there was the indubitable fact that the French captain was twenty francs richer, and there was at least the possibility of more gold where this came from.

'I hope we shall meet again, captain,' said Hornblower. 'As of course you understand, out here at sea we are always glad to have news of what is happening on land.'

The two Bretons went over the side with their two empty buckets, leaving Bush ruefully contemplating the mess left on the deck.

'That can be swabbed up, Mr Bush,' said Hornblower. 'It will be a good ending to a good day.'

5

The cabin was quite dark when Hornblower awoke; there was not even the glimmering of light through the two stern windows. He lay curled on his side only half conscious, and then a single sharp note from the ship's bell recalled him to the world, and he turned over on his back and stretched himself, half fretfully and half luxuriously trying to put his thoughts into order. That must be one bell in the morning watch, because one bell in the middle watch had sounded as he was getting back into bed after being roused when the ship was put about at midnight. He had had six hours of sleep, even after making allowance for that break; there were great advantages about being in command of a ship; the watch which had retired to bed at that time had been up on deck again for half an hour already.

The cot on which he lay was swaying easily and slowly. *Hotspur* must be under very easy sail indeed, and, as far as he could judge, with a moderate wind on the starboard beam. That was as it should be. He would soon have to get up – he turned on to his other side and went to sleep again.

'Two bells, sir,' said Grimes, entering the cabin with a lighted lamp. 'Two bells, sir. Bit of haze, and Mr Prowse says he'd like to go about on the other tack.' Grimes was a weedy young seaman who affirmed that he had acted as captain's steward in a West India packet.

'Get me my coat,' said Hornblower.

It was cold in the misty dawn, with only a greatcoat on over his nightshirt. Hornblower found Maria's gloves in a pocket and pulled them on gratefully.

'Twelve fathoms, sir,' reported Prowse as the ship steadied on her new course with the lead going in the forechains.

'Very well.'

There was time to dress, there was time to have breakfast. There was time for – Hornblower felt a wave of temptation breaking round him. He wanted a cup of coffee. He wanted two or three cups of coffee, strong and scalding hot. Yet he had on board no more than two pounds of coffee. At seventeen shillings a pound that was all he had been able to afford to buy. The miraculous forty-five pounds had melted away which he had won at whist the night before the appearance of the King's message regarding the fleet. There had been his sea-going clothing and his sword to get out of pawn, his cabin furniture to buy, and he had had to leave seventeen pounds with Maria for her support until she could draw his allotment of pay. So there had been little enough left over for 'captain's stores'. He had not bought a sheep or a pig; not a single chicken. Mrs Mason had bought six dozen eggs for him – they were packed in shavings in a tub lashed to the deck in the chart room – and six pounds of heavily salted butter. There was a loaf of sugar and some pots of jam, and then the money had run out. He had no bacon, no potted meat. He had dined yesterday on pilchards – the fact that they had been bought with secret service money was some kind of sauce for them, but pilchards were unattractive fish. And of course there was the absurd prejudice of seamen regarding fish, creatures from their own element. They hated having their eternal round of salt beef and pork interrupted by a meal of fish – allowance must be made, of course, for the fact that the cooking of fish left behind a lingering scent, hard to eradicate from utensils sketchily washed in seawater. At this very moment, in the growing dawn, one of the lambs netted down in the boat chocked in the waist emitted a lingering baa-aaa as it woke. The wardroom officers had invested in four of the creatures while the *Hotspur* was commissioning, and any day now they would be dining on roast lamb – Hornblower determined to get himself invited to dinner in the wardroom that day. The thought reminded him that he was hungry; but that was quite minor compared with his yearning for coffee.

'Where's my servant?' he suddenly roared. 'Grimes! Grimes!'

'Sir?'

Grimes put his head round the chart room door.

'I'm going to dress, and I'll want my breakfast. I'll have coffee.'

'Coffee, sir?'

'Yes.' Hornblower bit off the 'damn you' he nearly added. To swear at a man who could not swear back and whose only offence lay in being unoffending was not to his taste, just as some men could not shoot foxes. 'You don't know anything about coffee?'

'No, sir.'

'Get the oak box and bring it in to me.'

Hornblower explained about coffee to Grimes while working up a lather with a quarter of a pint of fresh water.

'Count out twenty of those beans. Put them in an open jar – get that from the cook. Then you toast 'em over the galley fire. And be careful with 'em. Keep shaking 'em. They've got to be brown, not black. Toasted, not burnt. Understand?'

'Well, yes, sir.'

'Then you take 'em to the surgeon, with my compliments.'

'The surgeon? Yes, sir.' Grimes, seeing Hornblower's brows come together like thunderclouds, had the sense to suppress in the nick of time his astonishment at the entry of the surgeon's name into this conversation.

'He has a pestle and mortar to pound his jalap with. You pound those beans in that mortar. You break 'em up small. Small, mark you, but you don't make dust of 'em. Like large grain gunpowder, not mealed gunpowder. Understand?'

'Yes, sir. I suppose so, sir.'

'Next you – oh go and get that done and then report to me again.'

Grimes was clearly not a man to do things quickly. Hornblower had shaved and dressed and was pacing the quarterdeck, raging for his breakfast, before Grimes appeared again with a panful of dubious powder. Hornblower gave him brief instructions on how to make coffee with it, and Grimes listened doubtfully.

'Go and get it done. Oh, and Grimes!'

'Sir?'

'I'll have two eggs. Fried. Can you fry eggs?'

'Er – yes, sir.'

'Fry 'em so the yolk's nearly hard but not quite. And get out a crock of butter and a crock of jam.'

Hornblower was throwing discretion to the winds; he was determined on a good breakfast. And those winds to which he had thrown discretion suddenly asserted themselves. With hardly a warning puff there was a sudden gust which almost took *Hotspur* aback, and with it, while *Hotspur* paid off and recovered herself, there came driving rain, an April shower, icy cold. Hornblower shook off Grimes the first time he appeared to report that breakfast was ready, and only went off with him on his second appearance, after *Hotspur* was steady on her course again. With the weather clearing and daylight growing there was little time he could spare.

'I'll be on deck again in ten minutes, Mr Young,' he said.

The chart room was a minute compartment beside his cabin – cabin, chart room, and the captain's pantry and head occupied the whole space of the *Hotspur*'s tiny poop. Hornblower squeezed himself into the chair at the little table.

'Sir,' said Grimes. 'You didn't come when breakfast was ready.'

Here were the eggs. The rim of the whites was black; the yolks were obviously hard.

'Very well,' growled Hornblower. He could not blame Grimes for that.

'Coffee, sir?' said Grimes. With the chart room door shut he was wedged against it hardly able to move. He poured from a jug into a cup, and Hornblower sipped. It was only just hot enough to drink, which meant that it was not hot enough, and it was muddy.

'See that it's hotter than this another time,' said

Hornblower. 'And you'll have to strain it better than this.'

'Yes, sir.' Grimes voice seemed to come from a great distance. The man could hardly whisper. 'Sir –'

Hornblower looked up at him; Grimes was cold with fright.

'What is it?'

'I kept these to show you, sir.' Grimes produced a pan containing a bloody and stinking mess. 'The first two eggs was bad, sir. I didn't want you to think –'

'Very well.' Grimes was afraid in case he should be accused of stealing them. 'Take the damned things away.'

Now was it not exactly like Mrs Mason to buy eggs for him of which half were bad? Hornblower ate his unpleasant eggs – even these two, although not exactly bad, were flavoured – while reconciling himself with the prospect of making up for it all with the jam. He spread a biscuit with the precious butter, and here was the jam. Blackcurrant! Of all the misguided purchases! Grimes, squeezing back into the chart room, positively jumped as Hornblower let out the oath that had been seeking an outlet for several minutes.

'Sir?'

'I'm not speaking to you, damn you,' said Hornblower, his restraint at an end.

Hornblower was fond of jam, but of all the possible varieties he liked blackcurrant least. It was a poor last best. Well, it would have to do; he bit at the iron-hard biscuit.

'Don't knock at the door when you're serving a meal,' he said to Grimes.

'No, sir. I won't, sir. Not any more, sir.'

Grimes' hand holding the coffeepot was shaking, and when Hornblower looked up he could see that his lips were trembling too. He was about to ask sharply what was the matter, but he suppressed the question as the answer became apparent to him. It was physical fear that was affecting Grimes. A word from Hornblower could have Grimes bound to a grating at the gangway, there to have the flesh flogged from the bones of his writhing body. There were captains in the navy who would give just that order when served with such a breakfast. There would never be a time when more things went wrong than this.

There was a knocking at the door.

'Come in!'

Grimes shrank against the bulkhead to avoid falling out through the door as it opened.

'Message from Mr Young, sir,' said Orrock. 'Wind's veering again.'

'I'll come,' said Hornblower.

Grimes cowered against the bulkhead as he pushed his way out; Hornblower emerged on to the quarter-deck. Six dozen eggs, and half of them bad. Two pounds of coffee – far less than a month's supply if he drank coffee every day. Blackcurrant jam, and not much even of that. Those were the thoughts coursing through his mind as he walked past the sentry, and then they were expunged by the blessed air from the sea, and the instant approach of professional problems.

Prowse was peering out to port through his telescope; it was almost full daylight, and the haze had dissipated with the rain.

'Black Stones broad on the port-beam, sir,' reported Prowse. 'You can see the breakers sometimes.'

'Excellent,' said Hornblower. At least his breakfast troubles had kept him from fretting during these final minutes before entering on to a decisive day. In fact he had actually to pause for several seconds to collect his thoughts before issuing the orders that would develop the plans already matured in his fevered mind.

'Do you have good eyesight, Mr Orrock?'

'Well, sir –'

'Have you or haven't you?'

'Well, yes, sir.'

'Then take a glass and get aloft. See what you can see of the shipping as we pass the entrance to the road-stead. Consult with the lookout.'

'Aye aye, sir.'

'Good morning, Mr Bush. Call the hands.'

'Aye aye, sir.'

Not for the first time Hornblower was reminded of the centurion in the New Testament who illustrated his authority by saying: 'I say to one, come, and he cometh, and to another, go, and he goeth.' The Royal Navy and the Roman Army were identical in discipline.

'Now, Mr Prowse. How far is the horizon now?'

'Two miles, sir. Perhaps three miles,' answered Prowse, looking round and collecting his thoughts after being taken by surprise by the question.

'Four miles, I should think,' said Hornblower.

'Maybe, sir,' admitted Prowse.

'Sun's rising. Air's clearing. It'll be ten miles soon. Wind's north of west. We'll go down to the Parquette.'

'Aye aye, sir.'

'Mr Bush, get the topgallants in, if you please. And the courses. Tops'ls and jib's all we need.'

'Aye aye, sir.'

That way they would attract less notice; also they would, by moving more slowly, have longer for observation as they crossed the passage that led into Brest.

'Sunset on a clear day,' said Hornblower to Prowse. 'Would be a better moment. Then we could look in with the sun behind us.'

'Yes, sir. You're right, sir,' answered Prowse. There was a gleam of appreciation in his melancholy face as he said this; he knew, of course, that the Goulet lay almost east and west, but he had not made any deductions or plans on that basis.

'But we're here. We have this chance. Wind and weather serve us now. It may be days before we have another opportunity.'

'Yes, sir,' said Prowse.

'Course east by south, Mr Prowse.'

'Aye aye, sir.'

Hotspur crept along. The day was cloudy but clear, and the horizon was extending every minute. There was the mainland of France, Pointe St Mathieu – Point Matthew – in plain view. From there the land trended away out of sight again.

'Land on the lee bow!' yelled Orrock from the foretopmasthead.

'That'll be the other headland, sir,' said Prowse.

'Toulinguet,' agreed Hornblower and then he corrected his pronunciation of 'Toolingwette.' For months or years to come he might be beating about this coast,

78

and he wanted no chance of misunderstanding with any of his officers when he gave orders.

Between those two headlands the Atlantic broke in through the wild Breton coast and reached deep inland to form the roadstead of Brest.

'Can you make out the channel yet, Mr Orrock?' yelled Hornblower.

'Not yet, sir. At least, not very well.'

A ship of war – a King's ship – approaching a foreign coast was under a handicap on this sort of mission in peacetime. She could not enter into foreign territorial waters (except under stress of weather) without permission previously asked and obtained; she certainly could not trespass within the limits of a foreign naval base without occasioning a series of angry notes between the respective governments.

'We must keep out of long cannon shot of the shore,' said Hornblower.

'Yes, sir. Oh yes, of course, sir,' agreed Prowse.

The second more hearty agreement was called forth when Prowse realized the implications of what Hornblower was saying. Nations asserted sovereignty over all the waters that could be dominated by their artillery, even if there was no cannon mounted at any particular point. In fact international law was hardening into a convention fixing an arbitrary limit of three miles.

'Deck!' yelled Orrock. 'I can see masts now. Can just see 'em.'

'Count all you can see, very carefully, Mr Orrock.'

Orrock went on with his report. He had an experienced sailor beside him at the masthead, but Hornblower, listening, had no intention of trusting

79

entirely to their observation, and Bush was fuming with impatience.

'Mr Bush,' said Hornblower. 'I'll be wearing ship in fifteen minutes. Would you be so kind as to take a glass to the mizzen topmasthead? You'll have a good chance of seeing all that Orrock's seeing. Please take notes.'

'Aye aye, sir,' said Bush.

He was at the mizzen shrouds in a moment. Soon he was running up the ratlines at a speed that would have been a credit to any young seaman.

'That makes twelve of the line, sir,' yelled Orrock. 'No topmasts hoisted. No yards crossed.'

The seaman beside him interrupted his report.

'Breakers on the lee bow!'

'That's the Parquette,' said Hornblower.

The Black Stones on the one side, the Parquette on the other, and, farther up, the Little Girls in the middle, marked off the passage into Brest. On a clear day like this, with a gentle wind, they were no menace, but lives by the hundred had been lost on them during storms. Prowse was pacing restlessly back and forward to the binnacle taking bearings. Hornblower was carefully gauging the direction of the wind. If the French squadron had no ship of the line ready for sea there was no need to take risks. A shift in the wind might soon find *Hotspur* embayed on a lee shore. He swept his glass round the wild coast that had grown up round his horizon.

'Very well, Mr Prowse. We'll wear ship now, while we can still weather the Parquette.'

'Aye aye, sir.'

Prowse's relief was obvious. His business was to keep

the ship out of danger, and he clearly preferred a wide margin of safety. Hornblower looked round at the officer of the watch.

'Mr Poole! Wear the ship, if you please.'

The pipes shrilled and the orders were passed. Hands went to the braces as the helm was put up while Hornblower scanned the shore warily.

'Steady as you go!'

Hotspur settled sweetly on her new course. Hornblower was growing intimate with her ways, like a bridegroom learning about his bride. No, that was an unlucky simile, to be discarded instantly. He hoped that he and *Hotspur* were better suited to each other than he and Maria. And he must think about something else.

'Mr Bush! Mr Orrock! You will please come down when you are sure you will see nothing more useful.'

The ship was alive with a new atmosphere; Hornblower was sensitively aware of it as the hands went about their duties. Everyone on board was conscious that they were bearding Boney in his den, that they were boldly looking into the principal naval base of France, proclaiming the fact that England was ready to meet any challenge at sea. High adventure was looming up in the near future. Hornblower had the gratifying feeling that during these past days he had tempered a weapon ready for his hand, ship and ship's company ready for any exploit, like a swordsman knowing well the weight and balance of his sword before entering upon a duel.

Orrock appeared, touching his hat, and Hornblower listened to his report. It was fortunate that Bush in the mizzentop still had a view up the Goulet and had not descended; reports should be made independently, each officer out of the hearing of the other, but it would have been tactless to ask Bush to stand aside. Bush did not descend for several more minutes; he had methodically taken notes with paper and pencil, but Orrock could hardly be blamed for not having done so. The thirteen or fourteen ships of the line at anchor in the Roads were none of them ready for sea and three of them were missing at least one mast each. There were six frigates, three with their topmast sent up and one with her yards crossed and sails furled.

'That will be the *Loire*,' commented Hornblower to Bush.

'You know about her, sir?' asked Bush.

'I know she's there,' answered Hornblower. He would gladly have explained further, but Bush was going on with his report, and Hornblower was content to have something more added to his reputation for omniscience.

On the other hand, there was considerable activity in the roadstead. Bush had seen lighters and tenders moving about, and believed he had identified a sheer hulk, a vessel rigged solely for the purpose of putting new masts into large ships.

'Thank you, Mr Bush,' said Hornblower. 'That is excellent. We must look in like this every day if possible.'

'Yes, sir.'

Constant observation would increase their information in geometrical progression – ships changing anchorage, ships sending up topmasts, ships setting up their rigging. The changes would be more significant than anything that could be deduced from a single inspection.

'Now let's find some more fishing boats,' went on Hornblower.

'Yes, sir.'

Bush trained his glass out towards the Parquette, whose sullen black rocks, crowned by a navigation beacon, seemed to rise and fall as the Atlantic swell surged round them.

'There's one in the lee of the reef there, sir,' said Bush.

'What's he doing there?'

'Lobster pots, sir,' reported Bush. 'Getting in his catch, I should say, sir.'

'Indeed?'

Twice in his life Hornblower had eaten lobster, both occasions being during those bleak bitter days when under the compulsion of hunger and cold he had acted as a professional gambler in the Long Rooms. Wealthy men there had called for supper, and had tossed him an invitation. It was a shock to realize that it was only a fortnight ago that that horrible period in his life had ended.

'I think,' said Hornblower, slowly, 'I should like lobster for my supper tonight. Mr Poole! Let her edge down a little towards the reef. Mr Bush, I would be obliged if you would clear away the quarterboat ready for launching.'

The contrast between these days and those was quite fantastic. These were golden April days; a strange limbo between peace and war. They were busy days, during which Hornblower had friendly chats with fishing boats' captains and dispensed gold pieces in exchange for a small portion of their catch. He could drill his crew and he could take advantage of those exercises to learn all he could about the behaviour of the *Hotspur*. He could peep up the Goulet and measure the preparation of the French fleet for sea. He could study this Gulf of Iroise – the approaches to Brest, in other words – with its tides and its currents. By observing the traffic there he could obtain an insight into the difficulties of the French naval authorities in Brest.

Brittany was a poor province, neither productive nor well populated, at the extremity of France, and by land the communications between Brest and the rest of the country were more inferior. There were no navigable rivers, no canals. The enormously ponderous materials to equip a fleet could never be brought to Brest by road. The artillery for a first-rate weighed two hundred tons; guns and anchors and shot could only be brought by sea from the foundries in Belgium round to the ships in Brest. The mainmast of a first-rate was a hundred feet long and three feet thick; only ships could transport those, in fact only ships specially equipped.

To man the fleet that lay idle in Brest would call for twenty thousand men. The seamen – what seamen there were – would have to march hundreds of miles from the merchant ports of Le Havre and Marseille if they were not sent round by sea. Twenty thousand men needed food and clothing, and highly specialized food and clothing moreover. The flour to make biscuit, the cattle and pigs and the salt to salt them down, and the barrel-staves in which to store them – where were they to come from? And provisioning was no day-to-day, hand-to-mouth operation, either. Before going to sea the ships would need rations for a hundred days – two million rations to be accumulated over and above daily consumption. Coasting vessels by the hundred were needed – Hornblower observed a constant trickle of them heading into Brest, rounding Ushant from the north and the Pointe du Raz from the south. If war should come – when war should come – it would be the business of the Royal Navy to cut off this traffic. More particularly it would be the business of the light craft to do this – it would be *Hotspur*'s business. The more he knew about all these conditions the better.

These were the thoughts that occupied Hornblower's mind as *Hotspur* stood in once more past the Parquette for a fresh look into Brest. The wind was south-easterly this afternoon, and *Hotspur* was running free – creeping along under topsails – with her lookouts posted at her mastheads in the fresh morning sunshine. From foremast and mizzenmast came two successive hails.

'Deck! There's a ship coming down the channel!'

'She's a frigate, sir!' That was Bush supplementing Cheeseman's report.

'Very well,' hailed Hornblower in return. Maybe the appearance of the frigate had nothing to do with his own evolutions in the Iroise, but the contrary was much more likely. He glanced round the ship; the hands were engaged in the routine of holystoning the decks, but he could effect a transformation in five minutes. He could clear for action or he could set all sail at a moment's notice.

'Steady as you go,' he growled at the quartermaster. 'Mr Cargill, we'll hoist our colours, if you please.'

'There she is, sir,' said Prowse. The glass showed a frigate's topgallant sails; she was reaching down the

Goulet with a fair wind, on a course that would inter-
sect *Hotspur*'s some miles ahead.

'Mr Bush! I'd like you on deck, if you please, as soon
as you have completed your observations.'

'Aye aye, sir.'

Hotspur stole quietly along; there was no purpose in
hurriedly setting additional sail and pretending to be
innocent – the French fleet must have heard from a
dozen sources about her continued presence in the
approaches.

'You're not going to trust 'em, sir?' This was from
Bush, back on the quarterdeck and in a state of some
anxiety; the anxiety was not displayed by any change in
Bush's imperturbable manner, but by the very fact that
he volunteered advice in this positive form.

Hornblower did not want to run away. He had the
weather gauge, and in a moment he could set all sail
and come to the wind and stand out to sea, but he did
not want to. He could be quite sure that if he were to
do so the frigate would follow his example and chase
him, ignominiously, out into the Atlantic with his tail
between his legs. A bold move would stimulate his crew,
would impress the French and – this was the point –
would subdue his own doubts about himself. This was
a test. His instinct was to be cautious; but he told himself
that his caution was probably an excuse for cowardice.
His judgment told him that there was no need for
caution; his fears told him that the French frigate was
planning to lure him within range of her guns and then
overwhelm him. He must act according to his judgement and he must abhor the counsel of his fears, but
he wished his heart would not beat so feverishly, he

wished his palms would not sweat nor his legs experience these pins-and-needles feelings. He wished Bush were not crowding him at the hammock netting, so that he might take a few paces up and down the quarterdeck, and then he told himself that he could not possibly at this moment pace up and down and reveal to the world that he was in a state of indecision.

Today coasters had been swarming out of Brest, taking advantage of the fair wind; if war had been declared they would have been doing nothing of the sort. He had spoken to three different fishing boats, and from none of them had he received a hint of war – they might all have been taking part in a conspiracy to lull him into a sense of security, but that was most unlikely. If news of war had reached Brest only an hour ago the frigate could never have prepared herself for sea and come down the Goulet in this time. And to support his judgement from the other direction was the thought that the French naval authorities, even if war was not declared, would act in just this way. Hearing of the audacious British sloop cruising outside they would find men enough for the frigate by stripping other ships of their skeleton crews and would send her out to scare the British ship away. He must not be scared away; this wind could easily persist for days, and if he once ran down to leeward it would be a long time before he could beat back and resume his observation of Brest.

The frigate was hull-up now; through his glass he could see her down to the waterline. She was big; there were her painted ports, twenty of them a side besides the guns on quarterdeck and forecastle. Eighteen-pounders, probably; she had not merely twice as many guns as *Hotspur* but would discharge a weight of broadside four times as great. But her guns were not run out, and then Hornblower raised his glass to study her yards. He strained his eyes; this time he must not only trust his judgement but his eyesight. He was sure of what he saw. Foreyard and foretopsailyard, mainyard and maintopsailyard; they were not supported by chain slings. If the frigate were ready for action they would never have omitted that precaution. She could not be planning to fight; this could not be an ambush.

'Any orders, sir?' asked Bush.

Bush would have liked to clear for action, to open the ports and run out the guns. If anything could precipitate hostilities it would be that, and Hornblower remembered how his orders from Cornwallis, both written and oral, had stressed the necessity to do nothing that would bring on England the odium of starting a war.

'Yes,' said Hornblower in reply to Bush's question, but the relief that showed instantly in Bush's expression changed back into concern as he noted the gleam in Hornblower's eyes.

'We must render passing honours, Mr Bush,' said Hornblower. There was something madly stimulating in forcing himself to be coldly formal when internally he was boiling with excitement. That must be what went on inside one of Mr Watt's steam engines when the safety valve did not function.

'Aye aye, sir,' said Bush; the disciplined answer, the only answer when a superior officer spoke.

'Do you remember the procedure, Mr Bush?'

Never in his life had Hornblower rendered honours

to a French ship of war; through his whole professional career until now sighting had meant fighting.

'Yes, sir.'

'Then be so good as to give the orders.'

'Aye aye, sir. All hands! All hands! Man the side! Mr Wise! See that the men keep order. Sergeant of marines! Parade your men on the quarterdeck! Smartly now. Drummer on the right. Bos'n's mates! Stand by to pipe on the beat of the drum.' Bush turned to Hornblower. 'We've no music, sir, except the drum and the pipes.'

'They won't expect more,' said Hornblower, his eye still at his glass. One sergeant, one corporal, twelve privates and a drummer were all the marines allotted to a sloop of war, but Hornblower was not devoting any further thought to the marines. His whole attention was concentrated on the French frigate. No doubt on the Frenchman's deck a dozen glasses were being trained on the *Hotspur*. As the bustle began on the *Hotspur*'s deck he could see a corresponding bustle on the Frenchman's. They were manning the side, an enormous crowd of them. Carried by the water came the noise as four hundred excited Frenchmen took up their stations.

'Silence!' ordered Bush at that very moment. There was a certain strangeness about his voice as he continued, because he did not want his words to be overheard in the Frenchman, and so he was endeavouring to bellow *sotto voce*. 'Show the Frogs how a British crew behaves. Heads up, there, and keep still.'

Blue coats and white breeches; these were French soldiers forming up on the frigate's quarterdeck; Hornblower's glass detected the flash of steel as bayonets were fixed, and the gleam of brass from the musical instruments. The ships were closing steadily on their converging courses, with the frigate under her greater canvas drawing ahead of the sloop. Nearer and nearer. *Hotspur* was the visiting ship. Hornblower put away his telescope.

'Now,' he said.

'Drum!' ordered Bush.

The drummer beat a long roll.

'Present-arr-ums!' ordered the sergeant of marines, and in a much lower voice, 'One. Two. Three!'

The muskets of the marines and the half-pike of the sergeant came to the present in the beautiful movements of the prescribed drill. The pipes of the bos'n's mates twittered, long and agonisingly. Hornblower took off his hat and held it before his chest; the off-hand salute with hand to the brim was not for this occasion. He could see the French captain on his quarterdeck now, a bulky man, holding his hat over his head in the French fashion. On his breast gleamed a star, which must be this newfangled Legion of Honour which Boney had instituted. Hornblower came back to reality; he had been the first to render the honours, and he must be the first to terminate them. He growled a word to Bush.

'Drum!' ordered Bush, and the long roll ended. With that the twittering of the pipes died away, a little more raggedly than Hornblower liked. On the French quarterdeck someone – the drum major, perhaps – raised a long staff hung with brass bells into the air and brought it down again with a thump. Instantly the drums rolled, half a dozen of them, a martial, thrilling sound, and then over the water came the sound of music, that incomprehensible blend of noises which Hornblower could never appreciate; the drum major's staff rose and fell rhythmically. At last the music stopped, with a final roll of the drums. Hornblower put on his hat, and the French captain did the same.

'Sl-o-o-ope arrums,' yelled the sergeant of marines.

'All hands! Dismiss!' yelled Bush, and then, reverting to his softer tone, 'Quietly, there! Silence!'

The hands were excited and prone to chatter with the order to dismiss – never in any of their lives, either, had they passed a French ship of war so close without guns firing. But Bush was determined to make the Frenchman believe that *Hotspur* was manned entirely by stoics. Wise with his rattan enforced the order, and the crew dispersed in an orderly mob, the good order only disturbed by a single quickly suppressed yelp as the rattan struck home on some rash posterior.

'She's the *Loire*, surely enough, sir,' said Bush. They could see the name entwined in gilded letters amid the scrollwork of the frigate's stern; Hornblower remembered that Bush still was in ignorance of his source of information. It was amusing to be thought omniscient, even without justification.

'And you were right, sir, not to run away from them,' went on Bush. Why was it so intolerable in this case to note the gleam of admiration in Bush's eyes? Bush did not know of the quickening heartbeats and the sweaty palms.

'It's given our fellows a close look at a Frenchman,' said Hornblower, uneasily.

'It certainly did that, sir,' agreed Bush. 'I never expected in all my life to hear that tune from a French frigate!'

'What tune?' asked Hornblower unguardedly, and was instantly furious with himself for this revelation of his weakness.

'God Save The King, sir,' answered Bush, simply. Luckily it never occurred to him that anyone could possibly fail to recognize the national anthem. 'If we'd had any music on board we'd have had to play their Marseillaise.'

'So we would,' said Hornblower; it was desperately necessary to change the subject. 'Look! He's getting in his topgallants. Quick! Time him! We'll see what sort of seamen they are.'

6

Now it was blowing a gale, a two-reef gale from the westward. The unbelievably fine weather of the past week had come to an end, and now the Atlantic was asserting itself in its usual fashion. Under her close-reefed topsails *Hotspur* was battling against it, close-hauled on the port tack. She was presenting her port bow to the huge rollers that were advancing upon her, unimpeded in their passage over three thousand miles of water, from Canada to France. She would roll, lift, pitch, and then roll again. The tremendous pressure of the wind on her topsails steadied her to the extent that she hardly leaned over at all to windward; she would heel over to starboard, hang for a moment, and then come back to the vertical. But even with her roll restricted in this fashion, she was pitching extravagantly, and she was rising and falling bodily as each wave passed under her bottom, so that a man standing on her deck would feel the pressure of his feet on her planking increasing and diminishing as she ascended and dropped away again. The wind was shrieking in the rigging, and her fabric groaned as the varying strains worked on her, bending her lengthwise, upward in the centre first and then upward at the ends next. But that groaning was a reassuring sound; there were no sharp cracks or disorderly noises, and what could be heard was merely an indication that *Hotspur* was being flexible and sensible instead of being rigid and brittle.

Hornblower came out on to the quarterdeck. He was pallid with seasickness because the change of motion had found him out, but the attack had not been as severe as he had experienced during the run down-channel. He was muffled in his coat, and he had to support himself against the roll, for his sea legs had not yet learned this advanced lesson. Bush appeared from the waist, followed by the boatswain; he touched his hat and then turned, with Wise beside him, to survey the ship in searching fashion.

'It's not until the first gale that you know what can carry away, sir,' said Bush.

Gear that seemed perfectly well secured would begin to show alarming tendencies to come adrift when submitted to the unpredictable strains of continued heavy weather, and Bush and Wise had just completed a long tour of inspection.

'Anything amiss?' asked Hornblower.

'Only trifles, sir, except for the stream anchor. That's secure again now.'

Bush had a grin on his face and his eyes were dancing; obviously he enjoyed this change of climate, this bustling of the wind, and the activity it called for. He rubbed his hands and breathed deep of the gale. Hornblower could console himself with the memory that there had been times when he had enjoyed dirty weather, and even the hope that there would be more, but as he felt at present, he bitterly told himself, it was a hollow memory and an empty hope.

Hornblower took his glass and looked about him. Momentarily the weather was fairly clear and the horizon at some distance. Far away on the starboard quarter the telescope picked up a flash of white; steadying himself as best he could he managed to catch it in the field again. That was the surf on Ar Men – curious Breton name, that – the most southerly and the most seaward of the rocks and reefs that littered the approaches to Brest. As he watched a fresh roller came in to catch the rock fully exposed. The surf burst upon it in a towering pillar of white water, reaching up as high as a first-rate's maintopsails, before the wind hurled it into nothingness again. Then a fresh squall hurtled down upon the ship bringing with it driving rain, so that the horizon closed in around them, and *Hotspur* became the centre of a tiny area of tossing grey sea, with the lowering clouds hardly clear of the mastheads.

She was as close in to that lee shore as Hornblower dared risk. A timid man would have gone out farther to sea at the first sign of bad weather, but then a timid man would be likely next to find himself with a shift of wind far away to leeward of the post he was supposed to be watching. Then whole days might pass before he could be back at his post – days when that wind would be fair for the French to do whatever they wanted, unobserved. It was as if there were a line drawn on the chart along with the parallels of longitude – rashness on the one side, boldness on the other, and Hornblower keeping to the very boundary of rashness. Now there was nothing further to do except – as always in the navy – to watch and wait. To battle with the gale with a wary eye noting every shift in the wind, to struggle northward on one tack and then to go about and struggle southward on the other, beating up and down outside Brest until he had a chance to risk a closer view again.

So he had done all day yesterday, and so he would do for countless days to come should the threatening war break out. He went back into his cabin to conceal another flurry of seasickness.

Some time after the misery had in part subsided he was summoned by a thundering at the door.

'What is it?'

'Lookout's hailing from the masthead, sir. Mr Bush is calling him down.'

'I'll come.'

Hornblower emerged just in time to see the lookout transfer himself to the backstay and come sliding all the way down the deck.

'Mr Cargill,' said Bush. 'Send another hand aloft to take his place.'

Bush turned to Hornblower.

'I couldn't hear what this man was saying, sir, thanks to the wind, so I called him down. Well, what d'you have to say?'

The lookout stood cap in hand, a little abashed at confronting the officers.

'Don't rightly know if it's important, sir, but during that last clear spell I caught a glimpse of the French frigate.'

'Where away?' demanded Hornblower; at the last moment before he spoke he had managed to modify his originally intended brusqueness. There was nothing to be gained and something to be lost by bullying this man.

'Two points on the lee bow, sir. She was hull-down but I could see her tops'ls, sir. I know 'em.'

Since the incident of the passing honours *Hotspur* had frequently sighted the *Loire* at various points in the Iroise channel – it had been a little like a game of hide-and-seek.

'What was her course?'

'She was close-hauled, sir, under double-reefed tops'ls, on the starboard tack, sir.'

'You were quite right to report her. Get back to your post now. Keep that other man aloft with you.'

'Aye aye, sir.'

The man turned away and Hornblower gazed out to sea. Thick weather had closed round them again, and the horizon was close in. Was there anything odd about the *Loire*'s coming out and braving the gale? She might well wish to drill her men in heavy weather. No; he had to be honest in his thinking, and that was a rather unFrench notion. There was a very marked tendency in the French navy to conserve material in a miserly fashion.

Hornblower became aware that Bush was standing beside him waiting for him to speak.

'What do you think, Mr Bush?'

'I expect she anchored last night in Berthon Bay, sir.'

Bush was referring to Bertheaume Bay, just on the seaward side of the Goulet, where it was just possible to ride to a long cable with the wind anywhere to the north of west. And if she lay there she would be in touch with the shore. She could receive news and orders sent overland from Brest, ten miles away. She might have heard of a declaration of war. She might be hoping to take *Hotspur* by surprise, and he must act on that assumption. In that case the safest thing to do would be to put the ship about. Heading south on the starboard tack he would have plenty of sea room, would be in no danger

97

from a lee shore, and would be so far ahead of the *Loire* as to be able to laugh at pursuit. But – this was like Hamlet's soliloquy, at the point where Hamlet says 'There's the rub' – he would be far from his post when Cornwallis should arrive, absent perhaps for days. No, this was a case where he must risk his ship. *Hotspur* was only a trifle in the clash of two enormous navies. She was important to him personally, but the information she had gleaned was a hundred times more important than her fabric to Cornwallis.

'We'll hold our course, Mr Bush,' said Hornblower.

'She was two points on our lee bow, sir,' said Bush. 'We ought to be well to windward of her when we meet.'

Hornblower had already made that calculation; if the result had been different he would have put *Hotspur* about five minutes ago and would have been racing for safety.

'Clearing again a little, sir,' commented Bush, looking about him, and at that very moment the masthead yelled again.

'There she is, sir! One point before the starboard beam!'

'Very well!'

With the moderation of the squall it was just possible to carry on a conversation with the masthead from the deck.

'She's there all right, sir,' said Bush, training his glass.

As *Hotspur* lifted to a wave Hornblower saw her topsails, not very plainly. They were braced sharp round, presenting only their edge to his telescope. *Hotspur* was at least four miles to windward of her.

'Look! She's going about, sir!'

The topsails were broadening into oblongs; they wavered for a moment, and then settled down; they were braced round now parallel to the *Hotspur*'s topsails; the two ships were now on the same tack.

'She went about the moment she was sure who we were, sir. She's still playing hide-and-seek with us.'

'Hide-and-seek? Mr Bush, I believe we are at war.'

It was hard to make that momentous statement in the quiet conversational tone that a man of iron nerve would employ; Hornblower did his best. Bush had no such inhibitions. He stared at Hornblower and whistled. But he could follow now the same lines of thought as Hornblower had already traced.

'I think you're right, sir.'

'Thank you, Mr Bush.' Hornblower said that spitefully, to his instant regret. It was not fair to make Bush pay for the tensions his captain had been experiencing; nor was it in accord with Hornblower's ideal of imperturbability to reveal that such tensions had existed. It was well that the next order to be given would most certainly distract Bush from any hurt he might feel.

'I think you had better send the hands to quarters, Mr Bush. Clear for action, but don't run out the guns.'

'Aye aye, sir!'

Bush's grin revealed his instant excitement. Now he was bellowing his orders. The pipes were twittering through the ship. The marine drummer came scrambling up from below. He was a child of no more than twelve, and his equipment was all higgledy-piggledy. He made not only a slapdash gesture of coming to attention on the quarterdeck, he quite omitted the formal drill of raising the drumsticks high before he began to beat the long roll, so anxious was he to begin.

Prowse approached; as acting-master his station in battle was on the quarterdeck beside his captain.

'She's broad on the starboard beam now, sir,' he said, looking over at the *Loire*. 'She took a long time to go about. That's what you'd expect.'

One of the factors that had entered into Hornblower's calculations was the fact that *Hotspur* would be quicker in stays than the *Loire*. Bush came up, touching his hat.

'Ship cleared for action, sir.'

'Thank you, Mr Bush.'

Now here was navy life epitomized in these few minutes. A moment of decision, of bustle, and excitement, and then – settle down to a long wait again. The two ships were thrashing along close-hauled, four miles apart. *Hotspur* almost dead to windward of the *Loire*. Those four miles, that direction of the wind, conferred immunity upon *Hotspur*. As long as she could preserve that distance she was safe. If she could not – if some accident occurred – then the *Loire*'s forty eighteen-pounders would make short work of her. She could fight for honour, but with no hope of victory. Clearing for action was hardly more than a gesture; men would die, men would be horribly mutilated, but the result would be the same as if *Hotspur* had tamely surrendered.

'Who's at the wheel?' asked Prowse of nobody in particular, and he walked over to supervise the steering – perhaps his thoughts were running along those same lines.

The boatswain came rolling aft; as the warrant officer charged with the general supervision of sails and rigging he had no particular station in action, and was justified in moving about. But he was being very formal at the moment. He took off his hat to Bush, instead of merely touching it, and stood holding it, his pigtail thumping his shoulders in the gale. He must be asking permission to speak.

'Sir,' said Bush. 'Mr Wise is asking on behalf of the hands, sir. Are we at war?'

Yes? Or no?

'The Frogs know, and we don't – yet, Mr Wise.' There was no harm in a captain admitting ignorance when the reason for it should be perfectly clear as soon as the hands had time to consider the matter, as they would have. This might be the time to make a resplendent speech, but second thoughts assured Hornblower it was not. Yet Hornblower's instinct told him that the situation demanded something more than his last bald sentence.

'Any man in this ship who thinks there's a different way of doing his duty in peacetime is likely to have his back scratched, Mr Wise. Say that to the hands.'

That was sufficient for the occasion; Prowse was back again, squinting up at the rigging and gauging the behaviour of the ship.

'Do you think she could carry the maintopmast stays'l, sir?'

That was a question with many implications, but there was only one answer.

'No,' said Hornblower.

That staysail might probably give *Hotspur* a little more speed through the water. But it would lay her over very considerably, which along the additional area exposed to the wind would increase her leeway by an appreciable proportion. Hornblower had seen *Hotspur* in dry dock, knew the lines of the turn of her bilge, and could estimate the maximum angle at which she could retain her grip on the water. Those two factors would balance out, and there was a third one to turn the scale – any increase in the amount of canvas exposed would increase the chances of something carrying away. A disaster, petty or great, from the parting of a line to the loss of a topmast, would thrust *Hotspur* helplessly within range of the enemy's guns.

'If the wind moderates that's the first extra canvas I'll set,' went on Hornblower to modify the brusqueness of his refusal, and he added, 'Take note of how that ship bears from us.'

'I've done that, sir,' answered Prowse; a good mark to Prowse.

'Mr Bush! You may dismiss the watch below.'

'Aye aye, sir.'

This chase – this race – might continue for hours, even for days, and there was no purpose in fatiguing all hands prematurely. The gale developed a new gust within itself, hurling rain and spray across the deck; the *Loire* faded from sight again as he looked at her, while the *Hotspur* plunged and tossed like a toy boat as she battled against wind and wave.

'I wonder how many hands are seasick over there?' said Hornblower. He uttered that distasteful word in the same way that a man might tease a sore tooth.

'A good few, I dare say, sir,' answered Bush in a completely neutral tone.

'Call me when she's in sight again,' said Hornblower. 'Call me in any case of need, of course.'

He said these words with enormous dignity. Then it was an exhausting physical exercise to struggle aft again back into his cabin; his dizziness exaggerated the leaping of the deck under his feet, and the swing of his cot as he sank groaning across it. It was Bush himself who roused him later on.

'Weather's clearing, sir,' came Bush's voice through the cabin door, over the clamour of the storm.

'Very well. I'll come.'

A shadowy shape was already visible to starboard when he came out, and soon the *Loire* was revealed sharply as the air cleared. There she was, lying steeply over, yards braced up, her gun ports plain enough to be counted when she rose level again, spray bursting in clouds over her weather bow, and then, as she lay over again, a momentary glimpse, pinky-brown, of her copper bottom. Hornblower's eye told him something that Prowse and Bush put simultaneously into words.

'She's head-reaching on us!' said Bush.

'She's a full point for'ard of the beam now,' said Prowse.

The *Loire* was going faster through the water than *Hotspur*, gaining in the race to that extent. Everyone knew that French ship desingners were cleverer than English ones; French ships were usually faster. But in this particular case it might mean tragedy. But there was worse news than this.

'I think, sir,' said Bush, slowly, as if each word caused him pain, 'she's weathering on us, too.'

Bush meant that the *Loire* was not yielding to the same extent as the *Hotspur* to the thrust of the wind down to leeward; relatively *Hotspur* was drifting down upon the *Loire*, closer to her guns. Hornblower, with a twinge of apprehension, knew that he was right. It would only be a question of time, if the present weather conditions persisted, before the *Loire* could open her ports and commence fire. So the simplest way of keeping out of trouble was denied him. If *Hotspur* had been the faster and the more weatherly of the two he could have maintained any distance he chose. His first line of defence was broken through.

'It's not to be wondered at,' he said. He tried to speak coldly, or nonchalantly, determined to maintain his dignity as captain. 'She's twice our size.'

Size was important when clawing to windward. The same waves battered against small ships as against big ones, but they would push the small ships farther to leeward; moreover the keels of big ships reached down farther below the surface, farther below the turbulence, and maintained a better hold in the more tranquil water.

The three telescopes, as of one mind, trained out towards the *Loire*.

'She's luffing up a little,' said Bush.

Hornblower could see the *Loire*'s topsails shiver momentarily. She was sacrificing some of her headway to gain a few yards to windward; having superior speed through the water she could afford to do so.

'Yes. We've drawn level with her again,' said Prowse.

That French captain knew his business. Mathematically, the best course to take when trying to close on a ship to windward was to keep the ship being chased right in the wind's eye, and that was where the *Hotspur* now found herself again, relative to the *Loire*, while the latter, resuming her former course, close-hauled, was twenty or thirty yards nearer to her in the direction of the wind. A gain of twenty or thirty yards, repeated often enough, and added to the steady gain resulting from being the more weatherly ship, would eventually close the gap.

The three telescopes came down from the three eyes, and Hornblower met the gaze of his two subordinates. They were looking to him to make the next move in this crisis.

'Call all hands, if you please, Mr Bush. I shall put the ship about.'

'Aye aye, sir.'

Here was a moment of danger. If *Hotspur* were mishandled she was lost. If she missed stays – as she once had done with Cargill handling her – she would lie dead in the water for minutes, sagging down to leeward with the *Loire* coming up fast upon her, while in this gale the sails might thrash themselves to ribbons leaving her more helpless still, even if nothing more vital carried away. The operation must be carried out to perfection. Cargill by coincidence was officer of the watch. He could be given the task. So might Bush, or Prowse. But Hornblower knew perfectly well that he could not tolerate the thought of anyone other than himself bearing the responsibility, whether in his own eyes or in those of the ship's company.

'I'm going to put the ship about, Mr Cargill,' he said, and that fixed the responsibility irrevocably.

He walked over the wheel, and stared round him. He felt the tension, he felt the beating of his heart, and noticed with momentary astonishment that this was pleasurable, that he was enjoying this moment of danger. Then he forced himself to forget everything except the handling of the ship. The hands were at their stations; every eye was on him. The gale shrieked past his ears as he planted his feet firmly and watched the approaching seas. This was the moment.

'Handsomely, now,' he growled to the hands at the wheel. 'Put your wheel down.'

There was a brief interval before *Hotspur* answered. Now her bow was turning.

'Helm's a-lee!' shouted Hornblower.

Headsail sheets and bowlines were handled, with Hornblower watching the behaviour of the ship like a tiger stalking its prey.

'Tacks and sheets!' and then turning back to the wheel. 'Now! Hard over!'

She was coming rapidly into the wind.

'Mains'l haul!' The hands were keyed up with the excitement of the moment. Bowlines and braces were cast off and the yards came ponderously round at the exact moment that *Hotspur* was pointing directly into the wind.

'Now! Meet her! Hard over!' snapped Hornblower to the wheel. *Hotspur* was turning fast, and still carrying so much way that the rudder could bite effectively, checking the swing before she could turn too far.

'Haul off all!'

The thing was done; *Hotspur* had gone from one tack to the other without the unnecessary loss of a second or a yard, thrashing along now with her starboard bow butting into the waves. But there was no time to feel relief or pleasure; Hornblower hurried to the port quarter to train his glass on the *Loire*. She was tacking naturally; the mathematics of the theory of the pursuit to windward demanded that the pursuer should tack at the same moment as the pursued. But she was bound to be a little late; her first inkling that *Hotspur* was about to tack would be when she saw her foretopsail shiver, and even if *Loire* had all hands at their stations for going about the *Hotspur* would have two minutes' grace. And she was far slower in stays. Even now, when *Hotspur* was settled on the new tack with every inch of sail drawing, the *Loire*'s foretopsail was still shivering, her bows were still turning. The longer she took to go about the more distance she would lose in the race to windward.

'We've weathered on her, sir,' said Prowse, watching through his glass. 'Now we're head-reaching on her.'

Hotspur had won back some of her precious lead, and Hornblower's second line of defence was proving at least stronger than his first.

'Take the bearing again,' ordered Hornblower.

Once settled on the new tack the *Loire*'s natural advantages asserted themselves once more. She showed her extra speed and extra weatherliness; she drew up again from *Hotspur*'s quarter to her beam; then she could luff up briefly and gain a little more to windward on the *Hotspur*. The minutes passed like seconds, an hour like a minute, as the *Hotspur* plunged along, with every man braced on the heeling deck and the wind shrieking.

'Time to go about again, sir?' asked Bush, tentatively and greatly daring, but the theoretically correct moment was passing.

'We'll wait a little longer,' said Hornblower. 'We'll wait for that squall.'

It was hurtling down wind upon them, and as it reached them the world was blotted out with driving rain. Hornblower turned from the hammock netting over which he was peering and climbed up the steep deck to the wheel. He took the speaking-trumpet.

'Stand by to go about.'

In the gusts that were blowing the crew could hardly hear what he said, but every eye was on him, everyone was alert, and, drilled as they were, they could not mistake his orders. It was a tricky business to tack while the squall prevailed, because the gusts were liable to veer a point or two, unpredictably. But the *Hotspur* was so handy – as long as the manoeuvre was well timed – that she had a good deal to spare for emergencies. The slight change in the wind's direction which threatened to take her aback was defeated because she still had sufficient steerage way and command to keep her swinging. The gust died away and the blinding chilly rain ceased while the hands were trimming all sharp, and the last of the squall drove off to leeward, still hiding the *Loire* from view.

'That's done him!' said Bush with satisfaction. He was revelling in the mental picture of the *Loire* still thrashing along on the one tack while the *Hotspur* was comfortably on the other and the gap between the two ships widening rapidly.

They watched the squall travelling over the foam-flecked grey water, shrieking towards France. Then in the thickness they saw a more solid nucleus take shape; they saw it grow sharper in outline.

'God –' exclaimed Bush; he was too disconcerted, too dumbfounded, to finish the oath. For there was *Loire* emerging from the squall, comfortably on the same tack as *Hotspur*, plunging along in her relentless pursuit with the distance in no way diminished.

'That's a trick we won't try a second time,' said Hornblower. He was forcing a smile, tight-lipped.

The French captain was no fool, evidently. He had observed the *Hotspur* delaying past the best moment for tacking, he had seen the squall engulfing her, and had anticipated her action. He must have tacked at the very same moment. In consequence he had lost little while tacking, and that little had been regained by the time the two ships were in sight of each other once more. Certainly he was a dangerous enemy. He must be one of the more able captains that the French navy possessed. There were several who had distinguished themselves in the last war; true, in consequence of the overpowering British naval strength, most of them had ended the war as prisoners, but the Peace of Amiens had set them free.

Hornblower turned away from Bush and Prowse and tried to pace the heeling deck, to think out all the implications. This was a dangerous situation, as dangerous as the worst he had envisaged. Inexorably wind and wave were forcing *Hotspur* closer to the *Loire*. Even as he tried to pace the deck he felt her shudder and lurch, out of the rhythm of her usual pitch and roll. That was the 'rogue wave', generated by some unusual combination of wind and water, thumping against *Hotspur*'s weather side like a battering ram. Every few seconds rogue waves made themselves felt, checking *Hotspur*'s way and pushing her bodily to leeward; *Loire* was encountering exactly similar rogue waves, but with her greater size she was not so susceptible to their influence. They played their part along with the other forces of nature in closing the gap between the two ships.

Supposing he were compelled to fight a close action? No, he had gone through that before. He had a good ship and well-trained crew, but on this tossing sea that advantage would be largely discounted by the fact that the *Loire* provided a steadier gun platform. Odds of four to one in weight of metal were greater than it was advisable to risk. Momentarily Hornblower saw himself appearing in the written history of the future. He might have the distinction of being the first British captain in the present war to fall a victim to the French navy. What a distinction! Then even in the cold gale blowing round him he could feel the blood hot under his skin as he pictured the action. Horrors presented themselves in endless succession to the crack of doom like the kings in *Macbeth*. He thought of death. He thought of mutilation, of agony under the surgeon's knife, and of being wheeled about legless through a blank future. He thought of being a prisoner of war; he had experienced that already in Spain and only by a miracle he had achieved release. The last war had gone on for ten years; this one might do the same. Ten years in prison! Ten years during which his brother officers would be gaining fame, distinguishing themselves, making fortunes in prize money while he would fret himself to pieces in prison, emerging at the end a cranky eccentric, forgotten by all his world – forgotten even by Maria, he fancied. He would rather die, just as he would rather die than be mutilated; or so he thought (he told himself brutally) until the choice should be more imminently presented to him. Then he might well flinch, for he did not want to die. He tried to tell himself that he was not afraid of death, that he merely regretted the prospect of missing all the interesting and amusing things that life held in store for him, and then he found himself sneering at himself for not facing the horrid truth that he was afraid.

Then he shook himself out of this black mood. He was in danger, and this was no time for morbid introspection. It was resolution and ingenuity that he demanded of himself. He tried to make his face a mask to hide his recent feelings as he met the gaze of Bush and Prowse.

'Mr Prowse,' he said. 'Bring your journal. Let's look at the chart.'

The rough log recorded every change of course, every hourly measurement of speed, and by its aid they could calculate – or guess at – the present position of the ship starting from her last point of departure at Ar Men.

'We're making fully two points of leeway,' said Prowse despondently. His long face seemed to grow longer and longer as he looked down at Hornblower seated at the chart-table. Hornblower shook his head.

'Not more than a point and a half. And the tide's been making in our favour for the last two hours.'

'I hope you're right, sir,' said Prowse.

'If I'm not,' said Hornblower, working the parallel rulers, 'we'll have to make fresh plans.'

Despondency for the sake of despondency irritated Hornblower when displayed by other people; he knew too much about it.

'In another two hours,' said Prowse, 'The Frenchman'll have us under his guns.'

Hornblower looked fixedly at Prowse, and under that unwavering gaze Prowse was at length reminded of his omission, which he hastily remedied by belatedly adding the word 'sir'. Hornblower was not going to allow any deviation from discipline, not in any crisis whatever – he knew well enough how these things might develop in the future. Even if there might be no future. Having made his point there was no need to labour it.

'You can see we'll weather Ushant,' he said, looking down at the line he had pencilled on the chart.

'Maybe, sir,' said Prowse.

'Comfortably,' went on Hornblower.

'I wouldn't say exactly comfortably, sir,' demurred Prowse.

'The closer the better,' said Hornblower. 'But we can't dictate that. We daren't make an inch more of leeway.'

He had thought more than once about that possibility, of weathering Ushant so close that *Loire* would not be able to hold her course. Then *Hotspur* would free herself from pursuit like a whale scraping off a barnacle against a rock; an amusing and ingenious idea, but not practicable as long as the wind stayed steady.

'But even if we weather Ushant, sir,' persisted Prowse, 'I don't see how it will help us. We'll be within range by then, sir.'

Hornblower put down his pencil. He had been about to say 'Perhaps you'd advise saving trouble by hauling down our colours this minute, Mr Prowse,' but he remembered in time that such a mention of the possibility of surrender, even with a sarcastic intention, was contrary to the Articles of War. Instead he would penalize Prowse by revealing nothing of the plan he had in mind; and that would be just as well, in case the plan should fail and he should have to fall back on yet another line of defence.

'We'll see when the time comes,' he said, curtly, and rose from his chair. 'We're wanted on deck. By now it'll be time to go about again.'

On deck there was the wind blowing as hard as ever; there was the spray flying; there was the *Loire*, dead to leeward and luffing up to narrow the gap by a further important trifle. The hands were at work on the pumps; in these weather conditions the pumps had to be employed for half an hour every two hours to free the ship from the seawater which made its way on board through the straining seams.

'We'll tack the ship, Mr Poole, as soon as the pumps suck.'

'Aye aye, sir.'

Some way ahead lay Ushant and his plan to shake off the *Loire*, but before that he had to tack twice more at least, each time with its possibilities of making a mistake, of handing *Hotspur* and himself over to the enemy. He must not stumble over an obstacle at his feet through keeping his eyes on the horizon. He made himself perform the manoeuvre as neatly as ever, and made himself ignore any feeling of relief when it was completed.

'We gained a full cable's length on him that time, sir,' said Bush, after watching *Loire* steady herself on the starboard tack on *Hotspur*'s beam.

'We may not always be so lucky,' said Hornblower. 'But we'll make this leg a short one and see.'

On the starboard tack he was heading away from his

objective; when they went about on the port tack again he must hold on for a considerably longer time, but he must make it appear as though by inadvertence. If he could deceive Bush it would be an indication that he was deceiving the French captain.

The hands seemed to be actually enjoying this sailing contest. They were light-hearted, revelling in the business of cheating the wind and getting every inch of way out of the *Hotspur*. It must be quite obvious to them that *Loire* was gaining in the race, but they did not care; they were laughing and joking as they looked across at her. They had no conception of the danger of the situation, or, rather, they made light of it. The luck of the British navy would save them, or the unhandiness of the French. Or the skill of their captain – without faith in him they would be far more frightened.

Time to go about again and beat towards Ushant. He resumed charge of the ship and turned her about. It was only after the turn was completed that he noted, with satisfaction, that he had forgotten his nervousness in the interest he was taking in the situation.

'We're closing fast, sir,' said Prowse, gloomy as ever. He had his sextant in his hand and had just finished measuring the angle subtended between the *Loire*'s masthead and her waterline.

'I can see that for myself, thank you, Mr Prowse,' snapped Hornblower. For that matter the eye was as trustworthy as any instrumental observation on that heaving sea.

'My duty, sir,' said Prowse.

'I'm glad to see you executing your duty, Mr Prowse,' said Hornblower. The tone he used was the equivalent of saying, 'Damn your duty,' which would have also been contrary to the Articles of War.

Northward the *Hotspur* held her steady course. A squall engulfed her, blinding her, while the quarter-masters juggled desperately at the wheel, allowing her, perforce, to pay off in the worst of the gusts, and putting down the wheel to keep her to the wind when the wind backed a point. The final gust went by, flapping Hornblower's coat-tails. It whipped the trouser-legs of the quartermasters at the wheel so that a momentary glance would make a stranger believe that, with their swaying arms and wavering legs, they were dancing some strange ritual dance. As ever, when the squall passed on, all eyes not dedicated to present duty turned to leeward to look for the *Loire*.

'Look at that!' yelled Bush. 'Look at that, sir! We've fooled him properly!'

Loire had gone about. There she was, just settling down on the starboard tack. The French captain had been too clever. He had decided that Hotspur would go about when concealed by the squall, and had moved to anticipate her. Hornblower watched the *Loire*. That French captain must be boiling with rage at having his too-great-cleverness revealed to his ship's company in this fashion. That might cloud his judgement later. It might make him overanxious. Even so, he showed little sign of it from here. He had been about to haul his bowlines, but he reached a rapid and sensible decision. To tack again would necessitate standing on for some-time on his present course while his ship regained speed and manoeuvrability, so that instead he made use of the turning momentum she still possessed, put up his helm

115

and completed the circle, wearing his ship round so that she momentarily presented her stern to the wind before arriving at last on her original tack again. It was a cool-headed piece of work, making the best of a bad job, but the *Loire* had lost a good deal of ground.

'Two full points abaft the beam,' said Prowse.

'And he's farther down to loo'ard, too,' supplemented Bush.

The greatest gain, Hornblower decided, watching her, was that it made possible, and plausible, the long leg to the northward that his plan demanded. He could make a long beat on the port tack without the French captain seeing anything unusual in that.

'Keep her going, there!' he shouted to the wheel. 'Let her fall off a little! Steady as you go!'

The race was resumed, both ships plunging along, battling with the unremitting gale. Hornblower could see the wide angle from the vertical described by the *Loire*'s masts as she rolled; he could see her yards dipped towards the sea, and he could be sure that *Hotspur* was acting in the same way, rolling even a trifle more deeply, perhaps. So this very deck on which he stood was over at that fantastic angle too; he was proud of the fact that he was regaining his sea legs so rapidly. He could stand balanced, one knee straight and rigid, the other considerably bent, while he leaned over against the heel, and then he could straighten with the roll almost as steadily as Bush could. And his seasickness was better as well – no; a pity he had let that subject return to his mind, for he had to struggle with a qualm the moment it did so.

'Making a long leg like this gives him a chance, sir,'

grumbled Prowse, juggling with telescope and sextant. 'He's drawing up on us fast.'

'We're doing our best,' answered Hornblower.

His glass could reveal many details of the *Loire* now, as he concentrated upon her to distract himself from his seasickness. Then, as he was about to lower the glass to ease his eye he saw something new. The gun ports along her weather side seemed to change their shape, and as he continued to look he saw, first from one gun port and then from another and finally from the whole line, the muzzles of her guns come nosing their way out, as the invisible crews strained at the tackles to drag the ponderous weights up against the slope of the deck.

'She's running out her guns, sir,' said Bush, a little unnecessarily.

'Yes.'

There was no purpose in imitating her example yet. It would be the lee side guns that *Hotspur* would have to run out. They would increase her heel and render her by that much less weatherly. Lying over as she was she would probably take in water over the port sills at the low point of her roll. Lastly, even at extreme elevation, they would nearly all the time be depressed by the heel below the horizontal, and would be useless, even with good timing on the part of the gun captains, against a target at any distance.

The lookouts at the foretopmasthead were yelling something, and then one of them launched himself into the rigging and came running aft to the quarterdeck.

'Why don't you use the backstay like a seaman?' demanded Bush, but Hornblower checked him.

'What is it?'

'Land, sir,' spluttered the seaman. He was wet to the skin with water streaming from every angle, whisked away by the wind as it dripped.

'Where away?'

'On the lee bow, sir.'

'How many points?'

He thought for a moment.

'A good four, sir.'

Hornblower looked across at Prowse.

'That'll be Ushant, sir. We ought to weather it with plenty to spare.'

'I want to be sure of that. You'd better go aloft, Mr Prowse. Make the best estimate you can.'

'Aye aye, sir.'

It would not do Prowse any harm to make the tiring and exacting journey to the masthead.

'He'll be opening fire soon, sir,' said Bush, referring to the Frenchman and not to Prowse's departing figure. 'Not much chance of replying as yet. On the other tack, maybe, sir.'

Bush was ready for a fight against any odds, and he was unaware that Hornblower had no intention of tacking again.

'We'll see when the time comes,' said Hornblower.

'He's opening fire now, sir.'

Hornblower whipped round, just in time to see a puff of smoke vanishing in the gale, and then others, all down the *Loire*'s side, enduring hardly for a second before the wind overcame the force of the powder that impelled them. That was all. No sound of the broadside reached them against the wind, and there was not a sight of the fall of shot.

'Long range, sir,' said Bush.

'A chance for him to exercise his guns' crews,' said Hornblower.

His glass showed him the *Loire*'s gun-muzzles disappearing back into the ship as the guns were run in again for reloading. There was a strange unreality about all this, about the silence of that broadside, about the fact that *Hotspur* was under fire, about the fact that he himself might be dead at any moment now as the result of a lucky hit.

'He's hoping for a lucky hit, I suppose, sir,' said Bush, echoing the very words of Hornblower's thoughts in a manner that made the situation all the more uncanny and unreal.

'Naturally.' Hornblower forced himself to say that word, and in this strange mood his voice, pitched against the gale, seemed to come from very far away.

If the Frenchman had no objection to a prodigious waste of powder and shot he might as well open fire at this range, at extreme cannon shot, in the hope of inflicting enough damage on *Hotspur*'s rigging to slow her down. Hornblower could think clearly enough, but it was as if he was looking on at someone else's adventure.

Now Prowse was returning to the quarterdeck.

'We'll weather the land by a good four miles, sir,' he said; the spray tossed up by the weather-bow had wetted him just as thoroughly as the seamen. He looked over at the *Loire*. 'Not a chance of our paying off, I suppose, sir.'

'Of course not,' said Hornblower. Long before such a plan could bear fruit he would be engaged in close action were he to drop down to leeward, in the hope of forcing the *Loire* to go about to avoid running ashore. 'How long before we're up to the land?'

'Less than an hour, sir. Maybe half. It ought to be in sight from the deck any minute.'

'Yes!' said Bush. 'There it is, sir!'

Over the lee bow Hornblower could see the black bold shoreline of Ushant. Now the three points of the triangle, Ushant, *Hotspur* and *Loire*, were all plain to him, and he could time his next move. He would have to hold on to his present course for some considerable time; he would have to brave further broadsides, whether he liked it or not – insane words those last, for no one could like being under fire. He trained his glass on the land, watching his ship's movement relative to it, and then as he looked away he saw something momentarily out of the corner of his eye. It took him a couple of seconds to deduce what it was he had seen; two splashes, separated by a hundred feet in space and by a tenth of a second in time. A cannon ball had skipped from the top of one wave crest and plunged into the next.

'They're firing very deliberately, sir,' said Bush.

Hornblower's attention was directed to the *Loire* in time to see the next brief puff of smoke from her side; they saw nothing of the ball. Then came the next puff.

'I expect they have some marksman on board moving along from gun to gun,' said Hornblower.

If that were the case the marksman must wait each time for the right conditions of roll – a slow rate of firing, but, allowing for the length of time to reload and run up, not impossibly slower than firing broadsides.

'You can hear the guns now, sir. The sound's carried by the water.'

It was an ugly, flat, brief clap, following just after each puff of smoke.

'Mr Bush,' said Hornblower speaking slowly as he felt the excitement of the approaching crisis boiling up within him. 'You know your watch – and quarter-bills off by heart, I'm sure.'

'Yes, sir,' replied Bush, simply.

'I want –' Hornblower checked the position of *Loire* again. 'I want sufficient hands at the braces and bowlines to handle the ship properly. But I want crews sufficient for the guns of one side too.'

'Not very easy, sir.'

'Impossible?'

'Nearly, sir. I can do it, though.'

'Then I want you to arrange it. Station crews at the port-side guns, if you please.'

'Aye aye, sir. Port side.'

The repetition was in the usual navy style to ensure against misunderstanding; there was only the faintest questioning note in Bush's voice, for the port side was that turned away from the enemy.

'I want –' went on Hornblower, still slowly. 'I want the port-side guns run out when we go about, Mr Bush. I'll give the order. Then I want them run in again like lightning and the ports closed. I'll give the order for that, too.'

'Aye aye, sir. Run 'em in again.'

'Then they're to cross to the starboard side and run those guns out ready to open fire. You understand, Mr Bush?'

'Y-yes, sir.'

Hornblower looked round at the *Loire* and at Ushant again.

'Very well, Mr Bush. Mr Cargill will need four hands for a special duty, but you can start stationing the rest.'

Now he was committed. If his calculations were incorrect he would appear a fool in the eyes of the whole ship's company. He would also be dead or a prisoner. But now he was keyed up, the fighting spirit boiling within him as it had done once when he boarded *Renown* to effect her recapture. There was a sudden shriek overhead, so startling that even Bush stopped short as he was moving forward. A line mysteriously parted in mid-air, the upper end blowing out horizontal in the wind, the lower end flying out to trail overside. A luckier shot than any so far had passed over the *Hotspur* twenty feet above her deck.

'Mr Wise!' yelled Hornblower into the speaking-trumpet. 'Get that halliard re-rove.'

'Aye aye, sir.'

The spirit of mischief asserted itself in Hornblower's mind along with his excitement, and he raised the trumpet again.

'And Mr Wise! If you think proper you can tell the hands we're at war!'

That raised the laugh that Hornblower anticipated, all over the ship, but there was no more time for frivolity.

'Pass the word for Mr Cargill.'

Cargill presented himself with a faint look of anxiety on his round face.

'You're not in trouble, Mr Cargill. I've selected you for a responsible duty.'

'Yes, sir?'

'Arrange with Mr Bush to give you four steady hands and take your station on the fo'c'sle at the jib halliard and jib sheet. I shall be going about very shortly, and then I shall change my mind and come back on my original tack. So now you can see what you have to do. The moment you get my signal run the jib up the stay and then flat it out to port. I want to be quite sure you understand?'

Several seconds went by while Cargill digested the plan before he answered 'Yes, sir.'

'I'm relying on you to keep us from being laid flat a-back, Mr Cargill. You'll have to use your own judgment after that. The moment the ship's turning and under command again run the jib down. You can do that?'

'Yes, sir.'

'Very well, carry on.'

Prowse was standing close by, straining to hear all this. His long face was longer than ever, it seemed.

'Is it the gale that's making your ears flap, Mr Prowse?' snapped Hornblower, in no mood to spare anyone; he regretted the words as soon as they were said, but now there was no time to compensate for them.

Loire was dead to leeward, and beyond her was Ushant. They had opened up the Bay of Lampoul on Ushant's seaward side, and now were beginning to close it again. The moment had come; no, better to wait another minute. The scream of a cannon ball and a simultaneous crash. There was a gaping hole in the weather-side bulwark; the shot had crossed the heeling deck and smashed its way through from within outwards. A seaman at the gun there was looking stupidly at his left arm where the blood was beginning to flow from a splinter wound.

'Stand by to go about!' yelled Hornblower.

Now for it. He had to fool the French captain, who had already proved he was no fool.

'Keep your glass on the Frenchman, Mr Prowse. Tell me just what he's doing. Quartermaster, a little lee helm. Just a little. Handsomely. Helm's a-lee!'

The foretopsail shivered. Now every moment was precious, and yet he must delay so as to induce the Frenchman to commit himself.

'His helm's a-lee, sir! He's coming round.'

This would be the moment – actually it was just past the moment – when the Frenchman would expect him to tack to avoid the gunfire, and the Frenchman would try to tack as nearly simultaneously as possible.

'Now, quartermaster. Hard down. Tacks and sheets!'

Hotspur was coming to the wind. Despite the brief delay she was still well under command.

'Mr Bush!'

On the weather side they opened the gun ports, and the straining gun crews dragged the guns up the slope. A rogue wave slapping against the side came in through the ports and flooded the deck knee deep in water; but the Frenchman must see those gun muzzles run out on the port side.

'He's coming about, sir!' reported Prowse. 'He's casting off the braces!'

He must make quite sure.

'Mainsail haul!'

This was the danger point.

'He's past the wind's eye, sir. His foretops'ls coming round.'

'Ava-a-ast!'

The surprised crew stopped dead as Hornblower screamed into the speaking-trumpet.

'Brace all back again! Jump to it! Quartermaster! Hard-a-port! Mr Cargill!'

Hornblower waved his hand, and the jib rushed up the stay. With its tremendous leverage on the bowsprit the jib, given a chance, would turn the ship back irresistibly. Cargill and his men were hauling it out to port by main force. There was just enough of an angle for the wind to act upon it in the right direction. Was there? Yes! *Hotspur* was swinging back again, gallantly ignoring her apparent mistreatment and the wave that she met bows-on which burst over her forecastle. She was swinging, more and more rapidly, Cargill and his men hauling down the jib that had played so great a part in the operation.

'Braces, there! She's coming before the wind. Stand by! Quartermaster, meet her as she swings. Mr Bush!'

The guns' crews flung themselves on the tackles and ran the guns in again. It was a pleasure to see Bush restraining their excitement and making certain that they were secure. The ports slammed shut and the crews raced over to the starboard side. He could see the *Loire* now that *Hotspur* had completed her turn, but Prowse was still reporting, as his order dictated.

'She's in irons, sir. She's all a-back.'

That was the very thing Hornblower had hoped for. He had believed it likely that he would be able to effect his escape to leeward, perhaps after an exchange of broadsides; this present situation had appeared possible but too good to materialize. The *Loire* was hanging helpless in the wind. Her captain had noted *Hotspur*'s manoeuvre just too late. Instead of going round on the other tack, getting his ship under command, and then tacking once more in pursuit, he had tried to follow *Hotspur*'s example and revert to his previous course. But with an unskilled crew and without a carefully prepared plan the improvisation had failed disastrously. While Hornblower watched he saw *Loire* yaw off the wind and then swing back again, refusing obstinately, like a frightened horse, to do the sensible thing. And *Hotspur*, dead before the wind, was rushing down upon her. Hornblower measured the dwindling gap with a calculating eye all the keener for his excited condition.

'We'll render passing honours, Mr Bush!' he yelled – no trumpet needed with the wind behind him. 'You gunners! Hold your fire until her mainmast comes into your sights. Quartermaster! Starboard a little. We'll pass her close.'

'Pistol shot' was the ideal range for firing a broadside according to old tradition, or even 'half pistol shot,' twenty yards or ten yards. *Hotspur* was passing *Loire* starboard side to starboard side but on the starboard side *Hotspur* had her guns run out, manned, and ready, while *Loire* presented to his gaze a line of blank ports – no wonder, with the ship in her present state of confusion.

They were level with her. No. 1 gun went off with a crash; Bush was standing beside it and gave the word, and apparently he intended to walk along the battery firing each gun in turn, but *Hotspur* with the wind behind her was going far too fast for him. The other guns went off in a straggling roll. Hornblower saw the splinters fly from the Frenchman's side, saw the holes battered in it. With the wind behind her *Hotspur* was hardly rolling at all; she was pitching, but any cool-headed gun captain could make sure of hitting his mark at fifteen yards.

Hornblower saw a single gun port open in *Loire*'s side – they were trying to man the guns, minutes too late. Then he was level with the *Loire*'s quarterdeck. He could see the bustling crowd there; for a moment he thought he distinguished the figure of the French captain, but at that moment the carronade beside him went off with a crash that took him by surprise so that he almost leaped from the deck.

'Canister on top of the round-shot, sir,' said the gun captain turning to him with a grin. 'That'll learn 'em.'

A hundred and fifty musket bullets in a round of canister would sweep the *Loire*'s quarterdeck like a broom. The marines posted on the deck were all biting fresh cartridges and plying their ramrods – they must have been firing too, without Hornblower perceiving it. Bush was back beside him.

'Every shot told!' he spluttered. 'Every single shot, sir!'

It was amazing and interesting to see Bush so excited, but there was still no time for trifles. Hornblower looked back at the *Loire*, she was still in irons – that broadside must have thrown her crew into complete disorder again. And over there was Ushant, grim and black.

'Port two points,' he said to the men at the wheel. A sensible man would conserve all the sea room available.

'Shall we come to the wind and finish her off, sir?' asked Bush.

'No.'

That was the sensible decision, reached in spite of his fighting madness. Despite the advantage gained by firing an unanswered broadside *Hotspur* was far too weak to enter voluntarily into a duel with *Loire*. If *Loire* had lost a mast, if she had been disabled, he would have tried it. The ships were already a mile apart; in the time necessary to beat back to his enemy she would recover and be ready to receive him. There she was; now she had swung, she had come under control again. It simply would not do.

The crew were chattering like monkeys, and like monkeys they were dancing about the deck in their excitement. Hornblower took the speaking-trumpet to magnify his order.

'Silence!'

At his bellow the ship instantly fell silent, with every eye turned towards him. He was impervious to that, strangely. He paced across the quarterdeck and back again, judging the distance of Ushant, now receding over the starboard quarter, and of the *Loire*, now before the wind. He waited, almost reached his decision, and then waited again, before he gave his orders.

'Helm a-weather! Mr Prowse, back the maintops'l, if you please.'

They were in the very mouth of the English Channel now, with *Loire* to windward and with an infinite avenue of escape available to leeward. If *Loire* came down upon him he would lure her up-channel. In a stern chase and with night coming on he would be in little enough danger, and the *Loire* would be cutting herself off from safety with every prospect of encountering powerful units of the British Navy. So he waited, hove-to, on the faint chance that the Frenchman might not resist temptation. Then he saw her yards swing, saw her come about, on to the starboard tack. She was heading for home, heading to keep Brest under her lee. She was acting conservatively and sensibly. But to the world, to everyone in *Hotspur* – and to everyone in the *Loire*, for that matter – *Hotspur* was challenging her to action and she was running for safety with her tail between her legs. At the sight of her in flight the *Hotspur*'s crew raised an undisciplined cheer; Hornblower took the speaking-trumpet again.

'Silence!'

The rasp in his voice came from fatigue and strain, for reaction was closing in upon him in the moment of victory. He had to stop and think, he had to prod his mind into activity before he could give his next orders. He hung the speaking-trumpet on its becket and turned to Bush; the two unplanned gestures took on a highly dramatic quality in the eyes of the ship's company, who were standing watching him and expecting some further speech.

'Mr Bush! You can dismiss the watch below, if you would be so kind.' Those last words were the result of a considerable effort.

'Aye aye, sir.'

'Secure the guns, and dismiss the men from quarters.'

'Aye aye, sir.'

'Mr Prowse!' Hornblower gauged by a glance at Ushant the precious distance they had lost to leeward. 'Put the ship on the port tack close-hauled, if you please.'

'Close-hauled on the port tack. Aye aye, sir.'

Strictly speaking, that was the last order he need give at this moment. He could abandon himself to his fatigue now, this very second. But a few words of explanation were at least desirable, if not quite necessary.

'We shall have to beat back. Call me when the watch

is changed.' As he said those words he could form a mental picture of what they implied. He would be able to fall across his cot, take the weight off his weary legs, let the tensions drain out of him, abandon himself to his fatigue, close his aching eyes, revel in the thought that no further decisions would be demanded of him for an hour or two. Then he recalled himself in momentary surprise. Despite those visions he was still on the quarterdeck with all eyes on him. He knew what he had to say; he knew what was necessary – he had to make an exit, like some wretched actor leaving the stage as the curtain fell. On these simple seamen it would have an effect that would compensate them for their fatigue, that would be remembered and quoted months later, and would – this was the only reason for saying it – help to reconcile them to the endless discomforts of the blockade of Brest. He set his tired legs in motion towards his cabin, and paused at the spot where the greatest number of people could hear his words to repeat them later.

'We are going back to watch Brest again.' The melodramatic pause. '*Loire* or no *Loire*.'

7

Hornblower was seated in the cramped chart room eating his dinner. This salt beef must have come from the new cask, for there was an entirely different tang about it, not unpleasant. Presumably it had been pickled at some other victualling yard, with a different quality of salt. He dipped the tip of his knife into the mustard pot; that mustard was borrowed – begged – from the wardroom, and he felt guilty about it. The wardroom stores must be running short by now – but on the other hand he himself had sailed with no mustard at all, thanks to the distractions of getting married while commissioning his ship.

'Come in!' he growled in response to a knock.

It was Cummings, one of the 'young gentlemen', First Class Volunteers, King's Letter Boys, with whom the ship was plagued in place of experienced midshipmen, thanks again to the haste with which she had been commissioned.

'Mr Poole sent me, sir. There's a new ship joining the Inshore Squadron.'

'Very well. I'll come.'

It was a lovely summer day. A few cumulus clouds supplied relief to the blue sky. *Hotspur* was hardly rocking at all as she lay hove-to, her mizzen-topsail to the mast, for she was so far up in the approaches to Brest that the moderate easterly wind had little opportunity, since leaving the land, to raise a lop on the water. Hornblower swept his eye round as he emerged on the quarterdeck, landward at first, naturally. They lay right in the mouth of the Goulet, with a view straight up into the Outer Roads. On one side was the Capuchins, on the other the Petit Minou, with *Hotspur* carefully stationed – as in the days of peace but for a more forceful reason – so that she was just out of cannon shot of the batteries on those two points. Up the Goulet lay the reefs of the Little Girls, with their outlier, Pollux Reef, and beyond the Little Girls, in the outer roadstead, lay the French navy at anchor, forced to tolerate this constant invigilation because of the superior might of the Channel Fleet waiting outside, just over the horizon.

Hornblower naturally turned his gaze in that direction next. The main body was out of sight, so as to conceal its strength; even Hornblower did not know its present numbers correctly – some twelve ships of the line or so. But well in sight, only three miles out to sea, lay the Inshore Squadron, burly two-deckers lying placidly hove-to, ready at any minute to support *Hotspur* and the two frigates, *Doris* and *Naiad*, should the French decide to come out and drive off these insolent sentries. There had been three of these ships of the line; now, as Hornblower looked, a fourth was creeping in close-hauled to join them. Automatically Hornblower looked over again at the Petit Minou. As he expected, the semaphore arms of the telegraph on the cliffs at the point there were swinging jerkily, from vertical to horizontal and back again. The watchers there were signalling to the French fleet the news of the arrival of this fourth ship to join the inshore squadron; even the smallest activity was noted and reported, so that in clear weather the French admiral was informed within minutes. It was an intolerable nuisance – it helped to smooth the path of the coasters perennially trying to sneak into Brest through the passage of the Raz. Some action should be taken about that semaphore station.

Bush was rating Foreman, whom he was patiently – impatiently – training to be the signal officer of the *Hotspur*.

'Can't you get that number yet?' he demanded.

Foreman was training his telescope; he had not acquired the trick of keeping the other eye open, yet idle. In any case it was not easy to read the flags, with the wind blowing almost directly from one ship to the other.

'Seventy-nine, sir,' said Foreman at length.

'You've read it right for once,' marvelled Bush. 'Now let's see what you do next.'

Foreman snapped his fingers as he recalled his duties, and hastened to the signal book on the binnacle. The telescope slipped with a crash to the deck from under his arm as he tried to turn the pages, but he picked it up and managed to find the reference. He turned back to Bush, but a jerk of Bush's thumb diverted him to Hornblower.

'*Tonnant*, sir,' he said.

'Now, Mr Foreman, you know better than that. Make your report in proper form and as fully as you can.'

'*Tonnant*, sir. Eighty-four guns. Captain Pellew.' Hornblower's stony face and steady silence spurred Foreman into remembering the rest of what he should say. 'Joining the Inshore Squadron.'

'Thank you, Mr Foreman,' said Hornblower with the utmost formality, but Bush was already addressing Foreman again, his voice pitched as loudly as if Foreman were on the forecastle instead of three yards away.

'Mr Foreman! The *Tonnant*'s signalling! Hurry up, now.'

Foreman scuttled back and raised his telescope.

'That's our number!' he said.

'So I saw five minutes ago. Read the signal.'

Foreman peered through the telescope, referring to the book, and checked his reference before looking up at the raging Bush.

'"Send boat," it says, sir.'

'Of course it does. You ought to know all routine signals by heart, Mr Foreman. You've had long enough. Sir, *Tonnant* signals us to send a boat.'

'Thank you, Mr Bush. Acknowledge, and clear away the quarter boat.'

'Aye aye, sir. Acknowledge!' A second later Bush was blaring again. 'Not that halliard, you careless – you careless young gentleman. *Tonnant* can't see the signal through the mizzen-tops'l. Send it up to the maintops'l yardarm.'

Bush looked over at Hornblower and spread his hands in resignation. Partly he was indicating that he was resigned to this duty of training ignorant young subordinates, but partly the dumb show conveyed some of the feelings aroused by having, in view of Hornblower's known preferences, to call Foreman a 'young gentleman' instead of using some much more forcible expression. Then he turned away to supervise Cummings as he hoisted out the quarterboat. There was everything to be said in favour of these young men being harassed and bullied as they went about their duties, although Hornblower did not subscribe to the popular notion that young men were actually the better for harassment and bullying. They would learn their duties all the quicker; and one of these days Foreman might easily find himself having to read and transmit signals amid the smoke and confusion and slaughter of a fleet action, while Cummings might be launching and manning a boat in desperate haste for a cutting out expedition.

Hornblower remembered his unfinished dinner.

'Call me when the boat returns, if you please, Mr Bush.'

This was the last of the blackcurrant jam; Hornblower, ruefully contemplating the sinking level in the final pot, admitted to himself that compulsorily he had actually acquired a taste for blackcurrant. The butter was all gone, the eggs used up, after forty days at sea. For the next seventy-one days, until the ship's provisions were all consumed, he was likely to be living on seamen's fare, unrelieved salt beef and pork, dried peas, biscuit. Cheese twice a week and suet pudding on Sundays.

At any rate there was time for a nap before the boat returned. He could go to sleep peacefully – a precaution in case the exigencies of the service disturbed his night – thanks to the naval might of Britain, although five miles away there were twenty thousand enemies any one of whom would kill him on sight.

'Boat coming alongside, sir.'

'Very well,' answered Hornblower sleepily.

The boat was deeply laden, right down to her gunwales. The hands must have had a long stiff pull back to the *Hotspur*; it was the purest bad luck on them that they could run under sail to the *Tonnant* when lightly laden and then have to row all the way back deeply laden in the teeth of the gentle wind. From the boat as she approached there came a strange roaring noise, a kind of bellow.

'What the devil's that?' asked Bush of himself as he stood beside Hornblower on the gangway.

The boat was heaped high with sacks.

'There's fresh food, anyway,' said Hornblower.

'Reeve a whip at the main-yardarm!' bellowed Bush – odd how his bellow was echoed from the boat.

Foreman came up the side to report.

'Cabbages, potatoes, cheese, sir. And a bullock.'

'Fresh meat, by God!' said Bush.

With half a dozen hands tailing on to the whip at the yardarm the sacks came rapidly up to the deck; as the boat was cleared there lay revealed in the bottom a formless mass of rope netting; still bellowing. Slings were passed beneath it and soon it lay on deck; a miserable undersized bullock, lowing faintly. A terrified eye rolled at them through the netting that swathed it. Bush turned to Hornblower as Foreman completed his report.

'*Tonnant* brought twenty-four cattle out for the fleet from Plymouth, sir. This one's our share. If we butcher it tomorrow, sir, and let it hang for a day, you can have steak on Sunday, sir.'

'Yes,' said Hornblower.

'We can swab the blood off the deck while it's still fresh, sir. No need to worry about that. An' there'll be tripe, sir! Ox tongue!'

He could still see that terrified eye. He could wish that Bush was not so enthusiastic, because he felt quite the reverse. As his vivid imagination pictured the butchering he felt no desire at all for meat provided by such a process. He had to change the subject.

'Mr Foreman! Were there no messages from the fleet?'

Foreman started guiltily and plunged his hand into his side pocket to produce a bulky packet. He blanched as he saw the fury on Hornblower's face.

'Don't you ever do that again, Mr Foreman! Despatches before everything! You need a lesson and this is the time for it.'

'Shall I pass the word for Mr Wise, sir?' asked Bush.

The boatswain's rattan could make vigorous play over Foreman's recumbent form bent over the breech of a gun. Hornblower saw the sick fright in Foreman's face. The boy was as terrified as the bullock; he must have the horror of corporal punishment that occasionally was evident in the navy. It was a horror that Hornblower himself shared. He looked into the pleading desperate eyes for five long seconds to let the lesson sink in.

'No,' he said, at length. 'Mr Foreman would only remember that for a day. I'll see he gets reminded every day for a week. No spirits for Mr Foreman for seven days. And anyone in the midshipman's berth who tries to help him out will lose his ration for fourteen days. See to that, if you please, Mr Bush.'

'Aye aye, sir.'

Hornblower snatched the packet from Foreman's lifeless hand, and turned away with contempt in the gesture. No child of fifteen would be any the worse for being deprived of ardent spirits.

In the cabin he had to use his penknife to open the tarred canvas packet. The first thing to tumble out was a grape-shot; the navy had developed through the centuries a routine in these matters – the tarred canvas preserved the contents from salt water if it had to be transported by boat in stormy weather, and the grape-shot would sink it if there were danger of its falling into the hands of the enemy. There were three official letters and a mass of private ones; Hornblower opened the official ones in haste. The first was signed 'Wm Cornwallis, Vice Ad.' It was in the usual form, beginning with the statement of the new situation. Captain Sir Edward Pellew, KB, in the *Tonnant*, had, as senior officer, received the command of the Inshore Squadron. 'You are therefore requested and required' to obey the orders of the said Captain Sir Edward Pellew, and to pay him the strictest attention, as issued with the authority of the Commander in Chief. The next was signed 'Ed. Pellew, Capt', and was drily official in three lines, confirming the fact that Pellew now considered Hornblower and *Hotspur* as under his command. The third abandoned the formal 'Sir' which began the others.

My dear Hornblower,
    It is with the greatest of pleasure that I hear that you
are serving under me, and what I have been told of your
actions already in the present war confirms the opinion I
formed when you were my best midshipman in the old
Indefatigable. *Please consider yourself at liberty to make*

any suggestions that may occur to you for the confounding
of the French and the confusion of Bonaparte.
    Your sincere friend,
    Edward Pellew.

Now that was a really flattering letter, warming and comforting. Warming, indeed; as Hornblower sat with the letter in his hand he could feel the blood running faster through his veins. For that matter he could almost feel a stirring within his skull as the ideas began to form, as he thought about the signal station on Petit Minou, as the germs of plans began to sprout. They were taking shape; they were growing fast in the hothouse atmosphere of his mind. Quite unconsciously he began to rise from his chair; only by pacing briskly up and down the quarterdeck could he bring those plans to fruition and create an outlet for the pressure building up inside him. But he remembered the other letters in the packet; he must not fall into the same fault as Foreman. There were letters for him – one, two, six letters all in the same handwriting. It dawned upon him that they must be from Maria – odd that he did not recognize his own wife's handwriting. He was about to open them when he checked himself again. Not one of the other letters was addressed to him, but people in the ship were probably anxiously waiting for them.

'Pass the word for Mr Bush,' he bellowed; Bush, when he arrived, was handed the other letters without a word, nor did he stay for one, seeing that his captain was so deeply engaged in reading that he did not even look up.

Hornblower read, several times, that he was Maria's Dearest Husband. The first two letters told him how much she missed her Angel, how happy she had been during their two days of marriage, and how anxious she was that her Hero was not running into danger, and how necessary it was to change his socks if they should get wet. The third letter was dated from Plymouth. Maria had ascertained that the Channel Fleet was based there, and she had decided to move so as to be on the spot should the necessities of the Service send *Hotspur* back into port; also, as she admitted sentimentally, she would be nearer her Beloved. She had made the journey in the coasting hoy, committing herself (with many thoughts of her Precious) to the Briny Deep for the first time, and as she gazed at the distant land she had reached a better understanding of the feelings of her Valiant Sailor Husband. Now she was comfortably established in lodgings kept by a most respectable woman, widow of a boatswain.

The fourth letter began precipitately with the most delightful, the most momentous news for her Darling. Maria hardly knew how to express this to her most Loved, her most Adored Idol. Their marriage, already so Blissful, was now to be further Blessed, or at least she fancied so. Hornblower opened the fifth letter in haste, passing over the hurried postscript which said that Maria had just learned the news of her Intrepid Warrior adding to his Laurels by engaging with the *Loire*, and that she hoped he had not exposed himself more than was necessary to his Glory. He found the news confirmed. Maria was more sure than ever that she was destined to be so vastly fortunate in the future as to be the Mother of the Child of her Ideal. And the sixth letter repeated the confirmation. There might be a Christmas

Baby, or a New Year's Child; Hornblower noted wryly that much more space in these later letters was devoted to the Blessed Increase than to her Longed-for but Distant Jewel. In any case Maria was consumed with hope that the Little Cherub, if a Boy, would be the Image of his Famous Father, or, if a Girl, that she should display his Sweetness of Disposition.

So that was the news. Hornblower sat with the six letters littered before him, his mind in just as much disorder. Perhaps to postpone realization he dwelt at first on the thought of the two letters he had written – addressed to Southsea they would be a long time before they caught up with Maria – and their comparatively formal and perhaps chilling content. He would have to remedy that. He would have to write a letter full of affection and full of delight at the news, whether he were delighted or not – and at that point he could reach no decision. Plunged as he was into professional problems the episode of his marriage was suffused in his memory with unreal quality. The affair was so brief, and even at the time it had been so overlain by the business of getting to sea, that it had seemed strange to him that it should involve the lasting effects of marriage; and this news was an indication of more lasting and permanent effects still. He was going to be a father. For the life of him he could not tell if he were pleased or not. Certainly he was sorry for the child if he – or she – were destined to inherit his accursed unhappy temperament. The more the child should prove to be like him, whether in looks or in morals, the sorrier he would be. Yet was that quite true? Was there not something flattering, something gratifying, in the thought that his own characteristics might be perpetuated? It was hard to be honest with himself.

He could remember, with his mind now diverted from his present life, more clearly the details of his honeymoon. He could conjure up more exactly his memories of Maria's doting affection, of the whole-hearted way in which she gave herself to believe, that she could not give so much love without its being as hotly reciprocated. He must never let her guess at the quality of his feelings for her, because that would be a cruelty that he could not contemplate. He reached for pen and paper, returning to the commonplace world with his routine annoyance at having a left-wing pen. Pens from the left wing of the goose were cheaper than right-wing ones, because when held in position for writing they pointed towards the writer's eye and not conveniently out over his elbow as right-wing ones did. But at least he had cut a good point and the ink had not yet grown muddy. Grimly he applied himself to his task. Partly it was a literary exercise, an Essay on Unbounded Affection, and yet – and yet – he found himself smiling as he wrote; he felt tenderness within him, welling out perhaps along his arm and down his pen. He was even on the verge of admitting to himself that he was not entirely the cold-hearted and unscrupulous individual he believed himself to be.

Towards the close of the letter, as he searched for synonyms for 'wife' and 'child', his glance strayed back to the letters from Pellew, and he actually caught his breath, his thoughts reverting to his duty, to his plans for slaughter, to the harsh realities of the world he was living in. *Hotspur* was riding easily over the placid sea, but the very fact that she was lying hove-to meant that there was a fair wind out of Brest and that at any moment a shout from the topmasthead would announce that the French Navy was on its way out to contest in thunder and smoke the mastery of the sea. And he had plans; even as he reread the latest lines of his letter to Maria his vision was blurred by the insistence on his attention of his visualization of the chart of the entrance to Brest. He had to take tight hold of himself to compel himself to finish the letter to Maria in the same strain as he had begun it. He made himself finish it, he made himself reread it, he made himself fold it; a shout to the sentry brought in Grimes with a lighted dip with which to seal it, and when he had completed the tiresome process it was with eager relief that he laid the letter aside and reached for a fresh sheet of paper.

HM *Sloop* Hotspur, *at sea, the Petit Minou bearing north one league.*
May 14th, 1803
Sir –

This was an end of mellifluous phrasing, of blundering attempts to deal with a totally unfamiliar situation; no longer was he addressing (as if in a dream) the Dear Companion of our Lives Together in Happy Years to Come. Now he was applying himself to a task that he felt competent and eager to do, and for phrasing he had only to draw upon the harsh and unrelieved wording of a myriad official letters before this one. He wrote rapidly and with little pause for consideration, because fantastically his plans had reached complete maturity during his preoccupation with Maria. The sheet was covered, turned and half covered again, and the plan was sketched out in full detail. He wrote the conclusion:

Respectfully submitted by
Your ob'd't servant
Horatio Hornblower.

He wrote the address:

Captain Sir E. Pellew, KB
HMS Tonnant.

When the second letter was sealed he held the two of them in his hand; new life in the one, and death and misery in the other. That was a fanciful thought – of far more importance was the question as to whether Pellew would approve of his suggestions.

8

Hornblower lay stretched out on his cot waiting for the time to pass. He would have preferred to be asleep, but during the afternoon sleep had refused to come to him. It was better to go on lying here in any case, for he would need all his strength during the night to come, and if he followed his inclinations and went on deck he would not only tire himself but he would reveal his anxieties and tensions to his subordinates. So he lay as relaxed as he could manage, flat on his back with his hands behind his head; the sounds that he heard on deck told him of the progress of the ship's routine. Just over his head the tell-tale compass which he had had fitted to the deckbeams was literally carrying out its functions and telling the tale of *Hotspur*'s small alterations of heading as she lay hove-to, and these could be correlated with the play of the beams of sunshine that came in through the stern windows. Those were now curtained, and the sunbeams came in around the curtains as they swayed gently with the ship's motion. Most captains curtained – and furnished – their cabins with gay chintz, or even, if wealthy, with damask, but these curtains were of canvas. They were of the finest, No. 8, sailcloth to be found in the ship and had only hung there for the last two days. Hornblower thought about this pleasantly, for they had been a present to him from the wardroom; Bush and Prowse, and the surgeon, Wallis, and the purser, Huffnell, had made the presentation after a mysterious request from Bush that they should be allowed to enter his cabin for a moment in his absence. Hornblower had returned to the cabin to find the deputation there and the cabin transformed. There were curtains and cushions – stuffed with oakum – and a coverlet, all gay with red and blue roses and green leaves painted on with ship's paint by some unknown artist in the ship's company. Hornblower had looked round in astonishment that made it impossible to conceal his pleasure. There was no time to glower or look stern, as nine captains out of ten would have done at such an unwarrantable liberty on the part of the wardroom. He could do no more than thank them in halting phrases; and the greatest pleasure only came after later consideration, when he faced the situation realistically. They had not done this as a joke, or in a silly attempt to win his favour. He had to believe the unbelievable, and accept the fact that they had done it because they liked him. That showed their poor judgement; gratification warred with guilt in his mind, yet the fact that they had dared to do such a thing was a strange but undeniable confirmation that the *Hotspur* was welding herself into a fighting entity.

Grimes knocked at the door and entered.

'They're calling the watch, sir,' he said.

'Thank you. I'll come.' The squeals of the pipes and the bellowings of the petty officers echoing through the ship made Grimes' words a little superfluous, but Hornblower had to act the part of a newly awakened man. He retied his neckcloth and pulled on his coat, slipped on his shoes and walked out on deck. Bush was there with paper and pencil in his hand.

'The semaphore's been signalling, sir,' he reported. 'Two long messages at fifteen minutes past four and four-thirty. Two short ones at – there they go again, sir.'

The long gaunt arms of the semaphore were jerkily swinging out and up and back again.

'Thank you, Mr Bush.' It was sufficient to know that the semaphore had been busy. Hornblower took the glass and trained it out to seaward. The Inshore Squadron was sharply silhouetted against the clear sky; the sun just down on the horizon, was still so bright that he could not look towards it at all, but the squadron was well to the northward of it.

'*Tonnant* signalling again, sir, but it's a ninety-one signal,' reported Foreman.

'Thank you.'

It had been agreed that all flag-signals from *Tonnant* preceded by the numerals ninety-one should be disregarded; *Tonnant* was only making them to deceive the French on Petit Minou into thinking some violent action was being planned by the inshore squadron.

'There goes *Naiad*, sir,' said Bush.

Under easy sail the frigate was creeping northward from her station to the south where she had been watching over Camaret Bay, heading to join the big ships and the *Doris*. The sun was now touching the sea; small variations in the water content of the nearly clear air were causing strange freaks of refraction, so that the reddening disc was slightly out of shape as it sank.

'They're heaving the long boat up out of its chocks, sir,' commented Bush.

'Yes.'

The sun was halfway down in the sea, the remaining

half pulled by refraction into twice its normal length. There was still plenty of light for an observer with a good glass on Petit Minou – and undoubtedly there was one – to pick out the preparations going on on the *Doris'* deck and in the big ships. The sun had gone. Above where it had sunk a small sliver of cloud shone brilliantly gold and then turned to pink as he looked. Twilight was closing in on them.

'Send the hands to the braces, if you please, Mr Bush. Fill the maintops'l and lay her on the starboard tack.'

'Starboard tack. Aye aye, sir.'

Hotspur crept northward through the growing night, following after *Doris*, heading towards the big ships and Point Matthew.

'There goes the semaphore again, sir.'

'Thank you.'

There was just light enough in the darkening sky to see the telegraphic arms silhouetted against it, as they spun round, signalling the latest move on the part of the British, this concentration towards the north – this relaxing of the hold of the British navy on the passages of the south.

'Only just keep her going,' said Hornblower to the quartermasters at the helm. 'Don't let the Frogs see what we're up to.'

'Aye aye, sir.'

Hornblower was feeling nervous; he did not want to leave the Toulinguet Passage too far behind him. He turned his glass towards the Inshore Squadron. Now there was a strip of red sky along the horizon behind it – the last light of day – and against it the sails of the ships of the line stood out in startling black. The red was fading rapidly, and above it Venus could be seen; Pellew over there was holding on to the last possible moment. Pellew was not only a man of iron nerve; he was a man who never underestimated his enemy. At last; the rectangles of the silhouetted topsails shortened, hesitated, and lengthened again.

'Inshore Squadron's hauled its wind, sir.'

'Thank you.'

Already the topsails were out of sight with the complete fading of the sky. Pellew had timed the move perfectly. A Frenchman on Petit Minou could not help but think that Pellew, looking towards the night-covered east, had thought that his ships were now invisible, and had come to the wind without realising that the move could still be seen by an observer looking towards the west. Hornblower stared round him. His eyes were aching, so that with his hands on the hammock netting he closed his eyes to rest them. Never had a minute seemed so long as that one. Then he opened them again. The light was all gone. Venus was shining where once the sun had shone. The figures about him were almost invisible. Now one or two of the brighter stars could be seen, and *Hotspur* must be lost to sight, to that unknown observer on Petit Minou. He gulped, braced himself, and plunged into action.

'Take in the tops'ls and topgallants!'

Hands rushed aloft. In the gentle night the vibration of the shrouds as fifty men ran up the ratlines could be distinctly heard.

'Now, Mr Bush, wear the ship, if you please. Course sou' by west.'

'Sou' by west, sir.'

Soon it was time for the next order.

'Send the topgallant masts down!'

This was the time when drill and practice revealed their value. In the dark night what had once been a mere toilsome exercise was performed without a hitch.

'Set the fore- and maintopmast-stays'ls. Get the fores'l in.'

Hornblower walked over to the binnacle.

'How does she handle under this sail?'

There was a pause while the almost invisible figure at the wheel spun it tentatively this way and that. 'Well enough, sir.'

'Very well.'

Hornblower had altered the silhouette of the *Hotspur* as entirely as he could. With only her fore and aft sails and her main course set, and her topgallant masts sent down, even an experienced seaman on this dark night would have to look twice or thrice to recognize what he saw. Hornblower peered at the chart in the faint light of the binnacle. He concentrated on it, to find the effort unnecessary. For two days now he had been studying it and memorising this particular section; it was fixed in his mind and it seemed as if he would be able to visualize it to his dying day – which might be today. He looked up, to find, as he expected, that exposure to that faint light had temporarily made his eyes quite blind in the darkness. He would not do it again.

'Mr Prowse! You can keep your eye on the chart from now on when you think it necessary. Mr Bush! Choose the best two hands you know with the lead and send them aft to me.' When the two dark figures reported Hornblower gave them curt orders. 'Get into the main chains on each side. I don't want you to make a sound more than you can help. Don't make a cast unless I order it. Haul your lines in and then let 'em out to four fathoms. We're making three knots through the water, and when the flood starts we'll be making next to nothing over the ground. Keep your fingers on your lines and pass the word quietly about what you feel. I'll station hands to pass the word. Understand?'

'Aye aye, sir.'

Four bells struck to mark the end of the second dog watch.

'Mr Bush, that's the last time I want the bell to strike. Now you may clear for action. No, wait a moment, if you please. I want the guns loaded with two rounds of shot each and run out. Have the coigns in and the guns at extreme depression. And as soon as the men are at their quarters I don't want to hear another sound. Not a word, not a whisper. The man who drops a hand-spike on the deck will get two dozen. Not the slightest sound.'

'Aye aye, sir.'

'Very well, Mr Bush. Carry on.'

There was a roar and a rattle as the hands went to their quarters, as the gun ports opened and the guns were run out. Then silence closed in upon the ship. Everything was ready, from the gunner down in the magazine to the look-out in the foretop, as the *Hotspur* reached silently down to the southward with the wind one point abaft the beam.

'One bell in the first watch, sir,' whispered Prowse, turning the sand-glass by the binnacle. An hour ago the flood tide had started to make. In another half-hour the clustered coasters to the southward, huddled under the shelter of the batteries at Camaret, would be casting off; no, they would be doing that at this moment, for there should be just enough water for them. They would be sweeping and kedging out, to run with the flood up the dangerous Toulinguet Passage, round the point and up the Goulet. They would hope to reach the Little Girls and safety, as the tide carried them into Brest Roads where the provisions and the cordage and the canvas with which they were laden were so eagerly awaited by the French fleet. To the north, back at the Petit Minou, Hornblower could imagine the bustle and the excitement. The movements of the Inshore Squadron must have been noted. Sharp eyes on the French shore had told anxious minds of the insufficiently concealed preparations for a concentration of force and a heavy blow. Four ships of the line and two big frigates could muster a landing force – even without drawing on the main fleet – of a thousand men or more. There were probably twice as many French infantry and artillerymen along the coast there, but, spread out along five miles, they were vulnerable to a sharp attack launched at an unexpected point on a dark night. There was a large accumulation of coasting vessels there as well, sheltering under the batteries on the far side of Cape Matthew. They had crept from battery to battery for hundreds of miles – spending weeks in doing so – and now were huddled in the little creeks and bays waiting for a chance to complete the last and most dangerous run into Brest. The menacing approach of the Inshore Squadron would make them nervous in case the British meditated some new attack, a cutting-out expedition, or fire-ships, or bomb-vessels, or even these new-fangled rockets. But at least this concentration of the British strength to the north left the south unwatched, as the signal station of Petit Minou would report. The coasters round Camaret – chasse-marees, tide-chasers – would be able to take advantage of the tide run through the horribly dangerous Toulinguet Passage up into the Goulet. Hornblower was hoping, in fact he was confident, that *Hotspur* had not been seen to turn back to stop this bolt hole. She drew six feet of water less than any frigate, hardly more than the big chasse-marees, and were she boldly handled her arrival among the rocks and shoals of Toulinguet would be totally unexpected.

'Two bells, sir,' whispered Prowse. This was the moment when the tide would be running at its fastest, a four knot tide, rising a full thirty feet, racing up through Toulinguet Passage and round the Council Rocks into the Goulet. The hands were behaving well; only twice had restless individuals started skylarking in the darkness, to be instantly suppressed by stern mutterings from the petty officers.

'Touching bottom to starboard, sir,' came a whisper from the gangway, and instantly afterwards, 'Touching bottom to port.'

The hands at the leads had twenty-four feet of line out between the leads and the surface of the water, but with the ship moving gently in this fashion even the heavy leads trailed behind to some extent. There must be some sixteen feet only – five feet to spare.

'Pass the word. What bottom do you feel?'

In ten seconds the answer came back. 'Sandy bottom, sir.'

'That must be well off Council Rocks, sir,' whispered Prowse.

'Yes. Quartermaster, one point to starboard.'

Hornblower stared through the night-glass. There was the shadowy shore-line just visible. Yes, and there was a gleam of white, the gentlest of surfs breaking on Council Rocks. A whisper from the gangway.

'Rocky bottom now, sir, shoaling a little.'

'Very well.'

On the starboard bow he could see faint whiteness too. That was the surf on all the wild tangle of rocks and shoals outside the Passage – Corbin, Trepieds, and so on. The tiny night breeze was still holding steady.

'Pass the word. What bottom?'

The question awaited an answer for some time, as the chain of communication broke down and the answer had to be repeated. At last it came.

'Rocky bottom, sir. But we're hardly moving over the ground.'

So *Hotspur* was now stemming the rising tide, hanging suspended in the darkness, less than a yard of water under her keel, the tide rushing past her, the wind thrusting her into it. Hornblower worked out problems in his head.

'Quartermaster, two points to port.'

It called for nice calculation, for now *Hotspur* was braced sharp up – twice the staysails had flapped in warning – and there was leeway to be allowed for as *Hotspur* crept crabwise across the tide.

'Mr Bush, go for'rard to the port side main chains and come back to report.'

What a lovely night it was, with this balmy air sighing

through the rigging, the stars shining and the gentle sound of the surf.

'We're moving over the ground, sir,' whispered Bush. 'Rocky bottom, and the port-side lead's under the ship.'

Hotspur's crabwise motion would produce that effect.

'Three bells, sir,' reported Prowse.

There would be water enough now for the coasters to negotiate the shoals off Rougaste and to have entered into the channel. It could not be long now, for the tide flowed for no more than four and a half hours and the coasters could not afford to waste time – or so he had calculated when he had made his suggestion to Pellew, for this moonless night with the tide making at this particular moment. But it might of course all end in a ridiculous fiasco, even if *Hotspur* did not touch on one of the menacing rocks that beset her course.

'Look, sir! Look!' whispered Bush urgently. 'One point before the beam!'

Yes. A shadowy shape, a darker nucleus on the dark surface. More than that; the splash of a sweep at work. More than that; other dark shapes beyond. There had been fifty coasters, by the last intelligence, at Camaret, and the chances were they would try the run all together.

'Get down to the starboard battery, Mr Bush. Warn the guns' crews. Wait for my order, and then make every shot tell.'

'Aye aye, sir.'

Despite the precautions he had taken, *Hotspur* would be far more visible than the coasters; she should have been observed from them by now; except that the Frenchmen would be preoccupied with their problems of navigation. Ah! There was a yell from the nearest coaster, a whole series of hails and shouts and warnings.

'Open fire, Mr Bush!'

A red glare in the darkness, an ear-splitting bang, the smell of powder smoke. Another glare, another bang. Hornblower fumbled for the speaking-trumpet, ready to make himself heard through the firing. But Bush was behaving admirably, and the gunners were keeping their heads, with the guns going off singly as the captains made sure of their targets. With the guns depressed the two round-shot hurtling from each would sweep the smooth surface of the sea. Hornblower thought he could hear shrieks from the stricken coasters, but the guns were firing at only the briefest intervals. The gentle wind swept the smoke along the ship, clouds of it billowing in dark waves round Hornblower. He leaned out to keep clear of it. The din was continuous now, as guns fired, as the carriage-trucks rumbled over the deck, as gun-captains bellowed orders. The flash of a gun illuminated something close overside – a sinking coaster, deck level with the water. Her frail side must have been beaten in by half a dozen round-shot. A yell from the main chains cut through the din.

'Here's one of 'em coming aboard!'

Some desperate swimmer had reached the *Hotspur*; Hornblower could leave Bush to deal with prisoners of that sort. There were more dark shapes to starboard, more targets presenting themselves. The mass of the coasters was being hurried along by the three-knot tide which *Hotspur* was stemming by the aid of the wind. Tug at their sweeps as they might, the French crews could not possibly counter the tide. They could not turn back; to turn aside was possible – but on one side were the Council Rocks, on the other were Corbin and Trepids and the whole tangle of reefs roundabout them. *Hotspur* was having experiences like those of Gulliver; she was a giant compared with these Lilliputian coasters after having been a dwarf in her encounter with the Brobdingnagian *Loire*.

Fine on the port bow Hornblower caught sight of half a dozen pinpoints of fire. That would be the battery on Toulinguet, two thousand yards away. At that range they were welcome to try their luck, firing at *Hotspur's* gun flashes. *Hotspur*, still travelling slowly over the ground, was a moving target, and the French would be disturbed in their aim through fear of hitting the coasters. Night-firing in those conditions was a waste of powder and shot. Foreman was yelling, wild with excitement, to the crew of the quarterdeck carronade.

'She's aground! Drop it – dead 'un!'

Hornblower swung round to look; the coaster there was undoubtedly on the rocks and consequently not worth firing at. He mentally gave a mark of approval to Foreman, who despite his youth and his excitement was keeping his head, even though he made use of the vocabulary of the rat-killing pit.

'Four bells, sir,' reported Prowse amid the wild din. That was an abrupt reminder to Hornblower that he must keep his head, too. It was hard to think and to calculate, harder still to recall his visualization of the chart, and yet he had to do so. He realized that *Hotspur* could have nothing to spare over on the landward side.

'Wear the ship – Mr Prowse,' he said; he remembered

just too late to use the formal address completely naturally. 'Get her over on the port tack.'

'Aye aye, sir.'

Prowse seized the speaking-trumpet and somewhere in the darkness disciplined men hurried to sheets and braces. As *Hotspur* swung about another dark shape came down at her from the channel.

'*Je me rends! Je me rends!*' a voice was shouting from it.

Someone in that coaster was trying to surrender before *Hotspur*'s broadside could blow her out of the water. She actually bumped against the side as the current took her round, and then she was free – her surrender had been premature, for now she was past *Hotspur* and vanishing in the farther darkness.

'Main chains, there,' yelled Hornblower. 'Take a cast of the lead.'

'Two fathoms!' came the answering cry. There was only six inches under *Hotspur*'s keel, but now she was drawing away from the perils on one side and approaching those on the other.

'Man the port-side guns! Keep the lead going on the starboard!'

Hotspur was steady on her new course as another unhappy coaster loomed up. In the momentary stillness Hornblower could hear Bush's voice as he called the port-side guns' crews to attention, and then came the crash of the firing. The smoke billowed round, and through the clouds came the cry of the leadsman.

'By the mark three!'

The smoke and the lead told conflicting stories.

'And a half three!'

'Wind must be backing, Mr Prowse. Keep your eye on the binnacle.'

'Aye aye, sir. And it's five bells, sir.'

The tide was almost at its height; another factor to be remembered. At the port-side quarterdeck carronade the crew were slewing their weapon round to the limit of its arc, and Hornblower, looking over the quarter, could see a coaster escaping past *Hotspur*'s stern. Two flashes from the dark shape, and a simultaneous crash under Hornblower's feet. That coaster had guns mounted, and was firing her pop-gun broadside, and at least one shot had told. A pop-gun broadside perhaps, but even a four-pounder could smash a hole in *Hotspur*'s frail side. The carronade roared out in reply.

'Luff a little,' said Hornblower to the quartermasters; his mind was simultaneously recording the cries of the men at the leads. 'Mr Bush! Stand by with the port-side guns as we luff.'

Hotspur came to the wind; on the maindeck there were creakings and groanings as the guns' crews laboured with hand-spike and crowbar to train their weapons round.

'Take your aim!' shouted Bush, and after some pregnant seconds, 'Fire!'

The guns went off almost together, and Hornblower thought – although he was sure he was wrong – that he could hear instantly afterwards the crash of the shot upon the coasters' hulls. Certainly after that he heard shouts and cries from that direction while the smoke blinded him, but he had no time to spare for that. There was only half an hour of floodtide left. No more coasters could be coming along the channel, for if they did they would not be able to round the Council Rocks before the ebb set in. And it was full time to extricate *Hotspur* from the reefs and shoals that surrounded her. She needed what was left of the flood to carry her out, and even at half-tide she was likely to touch bottom and be left ignominiously stranded, helpless in daylight under the fire of the Toulinguet battery.

'Time to say goodbye,' he said to Prowse. He realized with a shock that he was on the edge of being light-headed with strain and excitement, for otherwise he would not have said such a ridiculous thing. He must keep himself under control for a long while to come. It would be far more dangerous to touch bottom on a falling tide than on a rising one. He gulped and steadied himself, regaining his self-command at the cost of one more fierce effort.

'I'll handle the ship, Mr Prowse.' He raised the trumpet.

'Hands to the braces! Hands wear ship.'

A further order to the wheel brought the ship round on the other tack, with Prowse at the binnacle calling her heading. Now he had to thread his way out through the perils that encompassed her. The hands, completely carefree, were inclined to show their elation by noisy skylarking, but one single savage reproof from Bush silenced them, and *Hotspur* fell as quiet as a church as she crept out.

'Wind's backed three points since sunset, sir,' reported Prowse.

'Thank you.'

With the wind just abaft the beam *Hotspur* handled easily, but by this time instinct had to take the place of calculation. Hornblower had come in to the very limit of safety at high water over shallows hardly covered at high tide. He had to feel his way out, by the aid of the lead, by what could be seen of the shore and the shoals. The wheel spun over and back again as the ship nosed her way out. For a few perilous seconds she was sailing by the lee, but Hornblower was able to order the helm over again in the nick of time.

'Slack water now, sir,' reported Prowse.

'Thank you.'

Slack water, if any of the incalculable factors had not intervened. The wind had been slight but steady for several days from the south-eastward. He had to bear that in mind along with all the other factors.

'By the mark five!' called the leadsman.

'Thank God!' muttered Prowse.

For the first time *Hotspur* had nearly twenty feet of water under her keel, but there were still some outlying pinnacles of rock to menace her.

'Starboard a point,' ordered Hornblower.

'Deep six!'

'Mr Bush!' Hornblower must stay steady and calm. He must betray no relief, no human feelings, although within him the desire to laugh like an idiot welled up in combat with the frightful exhaustion he felt. 'Kindly secure the guns. Then you may dismiss the hands from general quarters.'

'Aye aye, sir.'

'I must thank you, Mr Prowse, for your very able assistance.'

'Me, sir?' Prowse went on in incoherent self-depreciation. Hornblower could imagine the lantern-jaws working in surprise, and he ignored the mumblings.

'You may heave the ship to, Mr Prowse. We don't want dawn to find us under the guns of Petit Minou.'

'No, sir, of course not, sir.'

All was well. *Hotspur* had gone in and come out again. The coasters from the south had received a lesson they would not forget for a long time. And now it was apparent that the night was not so dark; it was not a question of eyes becoming habituated to the darkness, but something more definite than that. Faces were now a blur of white, visible across the deck. Looking aft Hornblower could see the low hills of Quelern standing out in dark relief against a lighter sky, and while he watched a grain of silver became visible over their summits. He had actually forgotten until this moment that the moon was due to rise now; that had been one of the factors he had pointed out in his letter to Pellew. The gibbous moon rose above the hilltops and shone serenely down upon the Gulf. The topgallant masts were being sent up, topsails were being set, staysails got in.

'What's that noise?' asked Hornblower, referring to a dull thumping somewhere forward.

'Carpenter plugging a shot hole, sir,' explained Bush. 'That last coaster holed us just above the waterline on the starboard side right for'ard.'

'Anyone hurt?'

'No, sir.'

'Very well.'

His questions and his formal termination of the conversation were the result of one more effort of will.

'I can trust you not to lose your way now, Mr Bush,'

he said. He could not help being jocular, although he knew it sounded a false note. The hands at the braces were backing the maintopsail, and *Hotspur* could lie hove-to in peace and quiet. 'You may set the ordinary watches, Mr Bush. And see that I am called at eight bells in the middle watch.'

'Aye aye, sir.'

There were four and a half hours of peace and quiet ahead of him. He yearned with all his weary mind and body for rest – for oblivion, rather than rest. An hour after dawn, at the latest, Pellew could expect him to send in his report on the events of the evening, and it would take an hour to compose it. And he must take the opportunity to write to Maria so that the letter could be sent to *Tonnant* along with the report and so have a chance to reach the outside world. It would take him longer to write to Maria than to Pellew. That reminded him of something else. He had to make one more effort.

'Oh, Mr Bush!'

'Sir?'

'I'll be sending a boat to *Tonnant* during the morning watch. If any officer – or if any of the men – wish to send letters that will be their opportunity.'

'Aye aye, sir. Thank you, sir.'

In his cabin he faced one further effort to pull off his shoes, but the arrival of Grimes saved him the trouble. Grimes took off his shoes, eased him out of his coat, unfastened his neckcloth. Hornblower allowed him to do it; he was too weary even to be self-conscious. For one moment he luxuriated in allowing his weary feet free play in his stockings, but then he fell spreadeagled on to his cot, half prone, half on his side, his head on his arms, and Grimes covered him up and left him.

That was not the most sensible attitude to adopt, as he discovered when Grimes shook him awake. He ached in every joint, it seemed, while to dash cold seawater on his face did little enough to clear his head. He had to struggle out of the after-effects of a long period of strain as other men had to struggle out of the after effects of a drinking bout. But he had recovered sufficiently to move his left-handed pen when he sat down and began his report.

> *Sir,*
>   *In obedience to your instructions, dated the 16th instant, I proceeded on the afternoon of the 18th . . .*

He had to leave the last paragraph until the coming of daylight should reveal what he should write in it, and he laid the letter aside and took another sheet. He had to bite the end of his pen before he could even write the salutation in this second letter, and when he had written 'My dear Wife' he had to bite it again before he could continue. It was something of a relief to have Grimes enter at last.

'Mr Bush's compliments, sir, and it's not far off daylight.'

That made it possible to conclude the letter.

> *And now, my dearest –*' Hornblower glanced at Maria's letter to select an endearment – '*Angel, my duty calls me once more on deck, so that I must end this letter with –*'

another reference – *'fondest love to my dear Wife, the loved Mother of the Child to be.*

Your affectionate Husband,
Horatio.

Daylight was coming up fast when he arrived on deck.

'Brace the maintops'l round, if you please, Mr Young. We'll stand to the s'uth'ard a little. Good morning, Mr Bush.'

'Good morning, sir.'

Bush was already trying to see to the southward through his telescope. Increasing light and diminishing distance brought rapid results.

'There they are, sir! God, sir – one, two, three – and there are two others over on the Council Rocks. And that looks like a wreck right in the fairway – that's one we sunk, I'll wager, sir.'

In the glittering dawn the half-tide revealed wrecks littering the shoals and the shore, black against the crystal light, the coasters which had paid the penalty of trying to run the blockade.

'They're all holed and waterlogged, sir,' said Bush. 'Not a hope of salvage.'

Hornblower was already composing in his mind the final paragraph of his report.

'I have reason to believe that not less than ten sail of coasters were sunk or forced to run aground during this encounter. This happy result . . .'

'That's a fortune lost, sir,' grumbled Bush. 'That's a tidy sum in prize money over on those rocks.'

No doubt, but in those decisive moments last night there could have been no question of capture. *Hotspur's* duty had been to destroy everything possible, and not to fill her captain's empty purse by sending boats to take possession, at the cost of allowing half the quarry to escape. Hornblower's reply was cut off short, as the smooth water on the starboard beam suddenly erupted in three successive jets of water. A cannon ball had come skipping towards them over the surface, to make its final plunge a cable's length away. The sound of gunfire reached their ears at the same moment, and their instantly elevated telescopes revealed a cloud of smoke engulfing the Toulinguet battery.

'Fire away, Monseer le Frog,' said Bush. 'The damage is done.'

'We may as well make sure we're out of range,' said Hornblower. 'Put the ship about, if you please.'

He was trying as best he could to reproduce Bush's complete indifference under fire. He told himself that he was only being sensible, and not cowardly, in making certain that there was no chance of *Hotspur*'s being hit by a salvo of twenty-four-pounders, but he was inclined to sneer at himself, all the same.

Yet there was one source of self-congratulation. He had held his tongue when the subject of prize money had come up in the conversation. He had been about to burst out condemning the whole system as pernicious, but he had managed to refrain. Bush thought him a queer character in any case, and if he had divulged his opinion of prize money – of the system by which it was earned and paid – Bush would have thought him more than merely eccentric. Bush would think him actually insane, and liberal-minded, revolutionary, subversive and dangerous as well.

9

Hornblower stood ready to go down the side into the waiting boat. He made the formal, legal speech.

'Mr Bush, you will take command.'

'Aye aye, sir.'

Hornblower remembered to look about him as he prepared to make the descent. He glowered round at the sideboys in the white gloves that Bush had had made for this ceremonial purpose out of white twine by some seaman adept with a hook – 'crochet' was the French name for this process. He ran his eyes up and down the bos'n's mates as they piped his departing salute. Then he went over the side. The piping stopped at the same moment as his foot reached for the thwart – that was a measure of the height of *Hotspur*'s freeboard, for by the rules of ceremonial the honours ceased the moment the departing officer's head was at the level of the deck. Hornblower scrambled into the stern sheets, embarrassed by hat and gloves and sword and boat cloak, and he barked an order to Hewitt. The boathook released its hold and there was a moment of apparent disorder as the boat left the ship's side and four brawny arms at the halliards sent the balance-lug up the mast. There was a decided strangeness at sitting here on a level with the water, with the green waves close at hand; it was over eight weeks since Hornblower had last set foot outside the ship.

The boat settled on her course, running free because the wind had backed southerly several points, and Hornblower looked back at *Hotspur* lying hove-to. He ran a professional eye over her lines, noting, as an observer from the outside again, the relative heights of her masts, the distances at which they were stepped, the rake of the bowspit. He knew a great deal now about the behaviour of the ship under sail, but there was always more to learn. Not at this moment, though, for a stronger puff of wind laid the boat over and Hornblower felt suddenly uncertain both of his surroundings and himself. The little waves of which *Hotspur* took no notice were monstrous when encountered in a small boat, which, besides lying over, was now rising and swooping in a most unpleasant fashion. After the reassuring solidity of *Hotspur*'s deck – after painfully accustoming himself to her motion – these new surroundings and these new antics were most unsettling, especially as Hornblower was excited and tense at the prospect before him. He swallowed hard, battling against the seasickness which had leaped out of ambush for him; to divert his mind he concentrated his attention upon the *Tonnant*, growing slowly nearer – much too slowly.

At her maintopgallant-masthead she sported the coveted broad pendant in place of the narrow one worn by other ships in commission. It was the sign of a captain with executive powers over other ships besides his own. Pellew was not only high up in the captains' list but clearly destined for important command as soon as he reached flag rank; there must be rear admirals in the Channel Fleet bitterly jealous of Pellew's tenure of the Inshore Command. A boat came along her starboard side, painted white picked out with red, and of a design unlike that of the workaday boats supplied by the Navy Office. Hornblower could see the matching red and white uniforms of the boat's crew; this must be some very dandy captain at last, paying a call – or more likely a flag officer. Hornblower saw a ribboned and epauletted figure go up the side, and across the water came the sound of the squealing of the pipes and the boomp-bump noise that to his ears indicated a band playing. Next moment the White Ensign broke out at the fore-topmasthead. A vice-admiral of the White! That could be no other than Cornwallis himself.

Hornblower realized that this meeting to which he had been summoned by the curt signal 'All captains' was something more than a sociable gathering. He looked down in distress at his shabby clothing, reminded as he did so to open his boat cloak and reveal the epaulette on his left shoulder – a shabby brassy thing, dating back to the time of his earlier, disallowed appointment as commander, two years ago. Hornblower distinctly saw the officer of the watch, in attendance at the gangway, turn from his telescope and give an order which sent four of the eight white-gloved sideboys there scurrying out of sight, so that a mere commander should not share the honours given a vice-admiral. The admiral's barge had sheered off and the *Hotspur*'s boat took its place, with Hornblower not too seasick and nervous to worry about the way it was handled, in case it did not reflect credit on his ship. The worry, however, was instantly overlaid by the necessity for concentration on the process of going up the side. This was a lofty two-decker, and although the considerable 'tumble-home' was of help it was a tricky business for the gangling Hornblower to mount with dignity encumbered as he was. Somehow he reached the deck, and somehow, despite his shyness and embarrassment, he remembered to touch his hat in salute to the guard that presented arms to him.

'Captain Hornblower?' enquired the officer of the watch. He knew him by the single epaulette on his left shoulder, the only commander in the Inshore Squadron, perhaps the only one in the Channel Fleet. 'This young gentleman will act as your guide.'

The deck of the *Tonnant* seemed incredibly spacious after the cramped deck of the *Hotspur*, for the *Tonnant* was no mere seventy-four. She was an eighty-four, with dimensions and scantlings worthy of a three-decker. She was a reminder of the era when the French built big ships in the hope of overpowering the British seventy-fours by brute force instead of by skill and discipline. How the venture had turned out was proved by the fact that *Tonnant* now flew the flag of England.

The great poop-cabins had been thrown into a single suite for Pellew, in the absence of a flag-officer permanently on board. It was incredibly luxurious. Once past the sentry the decks were actually carpeted – Wilton carpets in which the foot sank noiselessly. There was an anteroom with a steward in dazzling white ducks to take Hornblower's hat and gloves and cloak.

'Captain Hornblower, sir,' announced the young gentleman, throwing open the door.

The deck-beams above were six feet clear, over the carpet, and Pellew had grown so used to this that he advanced to shake hands with no stoop at all, in contrast with Hornblower, who instinctively crouched with his five-foot-eleven.

'Delighted to see you, Hornblower,' said Pellew. 'Genuinely delighted. There is much to say to you, for letters are always inadequate. But I must make the introductions. The Admiral has already made your acquaintance, I think?'

Hornblower shook hands with Cornwallis, mumbling the same politenesses as he had already addressed to Pellew. Other introductions followed, names known to everyone who had read in the *Gazette* the accounts of naval victories; Grindall of the *Prince*, Marsfield of the *Minotaur*, Lord Henry Paulet of the *Terrible*, and half a dozen others. Hornblower felt dazzled, although he had just come in from the bright outer world. In all this array there was one other officer with a single epaulette, but he wore it on his right shoulder, proof that he, too, had attained the glorious rank of post captain, and had only to go on living to mount a second epaulette on attaining three years' seniority, and – if long life was granted him – eventually to attain the unspeakable heights of flag rank. He was far higher above a commander than a commander was above a lowly lieutenant.

Hornblower sat in the chair offered him, instinctively edging it backward so as to make himself, the most junior, the infinitely junior officer, as inconspicuous as possible. The cabin was finished in some rich material – damask, Hornblower guessed – with a colour scheme of nutmeg and blue unobtrusive and yet incredibly satisfying to the eye. Daylight poured in through a vast stern window, to glint upon the swaying silver lamps. There was a shelf of books, some in good leather bindings, but Hornblower's sharp eye detected tattered copies of the *Mariners' Guide* and the Admiralty publications for the coasts of France. On the far side were two large masses so draped as to be shapely and in keeping so that no uninitiated person could guess that inside were two eighteen-pounder carronades.

'This must take you a full five minutes to clear for action, Sir Edward,' said Cornwallis.

'Four minutes and ten seconds by stopwatch, sir,' answered Pellew, 'to strike everything below, including the bulkheads.'

Another steward, also in dazzling white ducks, entered at this moment and spoke a few words in a low tone to Pellew, like a well-trained butler in a ducal house, and Pellew rose to his feet.

'Dinner, gentlemen,' he announced. 'Permit me to lead the way.'

A door, thrown open in the midships bulkhead, revealed a dining room, an oblong table with white damask, glittering silver, sparkling glasses, while more stewards in white ducks were ranged against the bulkhead. There could be little doubt about precedence, when every captain in the Royal Navy had, naturally, studied his place in the captains' list ever since his promotion; Hornblower and the single-epauletted captain were headed for the foot of the table when Pellew halted the general sorting-out.

'At the Admiral's suggestion,' he announced, 'we are dispensing with precedence today. You will find your names on cards at your places.'

So now every one began a feverish hunt for their names; Hornblower found himself seated between Lord

Henry Paulet and Hosier of the *Fame*, and opposite him was Cornwallis himself.

'I made the suggestion to Sir Edward,' Cornwallis was saying as he leisurely took his seat, 'because otherwise we always find ourselves sitting next to our neighbours in the captains' list. In blockade service especially, variety is much to be sought after.'

He lowered himself into his chair, and when he had done so his juniors followed his example. Hornblower, cautiously on guard about his manners, still could not restrain his mischievous inner self from mentally adding a passage to the rules of naval ceremonial, to the lines of the rule about the officer's head reaching the level of the maindeck – 'when the Admiral's backside shall touch the seat of his chair –'

'Pellew provides good dinners,' said Lord Henry, eagerly, scanning the dishes with which the stewards were now crowding the table. The largest dish was placed in front of him, and when the immense silver dish cover was whipped away a magnificent pie was revealed. The pastry top was built up into a castle, from the turret of which flew a paper Union Jack.

'Prodigious!' exclaimed Cornwallis. 'Sir Edward, what lies below the dungeons here?'

Pellew shook his head sadly. 'Only beef and kidneys, sir. Beef stewed to rags. Our ship's bullock this time, as ever, was too tough for ordinary mortals, and only stewing would reduce his steaks to digestibility. So I called in the aid of his kidneys for a beefsteak and kidney pie.'

'But what about the flour?'

'The Victualling Officer sent me a sack, sir. Unfortunately it had rested in bilge water, as could only be expected, but there was just enough at the top unspoiled for the pie-crust.'

Pellew's gesture, indicating the silver bread barges filled with ship's biscuit, hinted that in more fortunate circumstances they might have been filled with fresh rolls.

'I'm sure it's delicious,' said Cornwallis. 'Lord Henry, might I trouble you to serve me, if you can find it in your heart to destroy those magnificent battlements?'

Paulet set to work with carving knife and fork on the pie, while Hornblower pondered the phenomenon of the son of a Marquis helping the son of an Earl to a steak and kidney pie made from a ration bullock and spoiled flour.

'That's a ragout of pork beside you, Captain Hosier,' said Pellew. 'Or so my chef would call it. You may find it even saltier than usual, because of the bitter tears he shed into it. Captain Durham has the only live pig left in the Channel Fleet, and no gold of mine would coax it from him, so that my poor fellow had to make do with the contents of the brine tub.'

'He has succeeded perfectly with the pie, at least,' commented Cornwallis. 'He must be an artist.'

'I engaged him during the Peace,' said Pellew, 'and brought him with me on the outbreak of war. At quarters he points a gun on the starboard-side lower deck.'

'If his aim is as good as his cooking,' said Cornwallis, reaching for his glass which a steward had filled, 'then – confusion to the French!'

The toast was drunk with murmured acclaim.

'Fresh vegetables!' said Lord Henry ecstatically. 'Cauliflower!'

'Your quota is on the way to your ship at this moment, Hornblower,' said Cornwallis. 'We try not to forget you.'

'*Hotspur*'s like Uriah the Hittite,' said a saturnine captain at the end of the table whose name appeared to be Collins. 'In the forefront of the battle.'

Hornblower was grateful to Collins for that speech, because it brought home to him a truth, like a bright light, that he had not realized before; he would rather be on short commons in the forefront of the battle than back in the main body with plenty of vegetables.

'Young carrots!' went on Lord Henry, peering into each vegetable dish in turn. 'And what's this? I can't believe it!'

'Spring greens, Lord Henry,' said Pellew. 'We still have to wait for peas and beans.'

'Wonderful!'

'How do you get these chickens so fat, Sir Edward?' asked Grindall.

'A matter of feeding, merely. Another secret of my chef.'

'In the public interest you should disclose it,' said Cornwallis. 'The life of a seasick chicken rarely conduces to putting on flesh.'

'Well, sir, since you ask. This ship has a complement of six hundred and fifty men. Every day thirteen fifty-pound bread bags are emptied. The secret lies in the treatment of those bags.'

'But how?' asked several voices.

'Tap them, shake them, before emptying. Not enough to make wasteful crumbs, but sharply enough. Then take out the biscuits quickly, and behold! At the bottom of each bag is a mass of weevils and maggots, scared out of their natural habitat and with no time allowed to seek shelter again. Believe me, gentlemen, there is nothing that fattens a chicken so well as a diet of rich biscuit-fed weevils. Hornblower, your plate's still empty. Help yourself, man.'

Hornblower had thought of helping himself to chicken, but somehow – and he grinned at himself internally – this last speech diverted him from doing so. The beefsteak pie was in great demand and had almost disappeared, and as a junior officer he knew better than to anticipate his seniors' second helpings. The ragout of pork, rich in onions, was at the far end of the table.

'I'll make a start on this, sir,' he said, indicating an untouched dish before him.

'Hornblower has a judgement that puts us all to shame,' said Pellew. 'That's a kickshaw in which my chef takes particular pride. To go with it you'll need these purée potatoes, Hornblower.'

It was a dish of brawn, from which Hornblower cut himself moderately generous slices, and it had dark flakes in it. There was no doubt that it was utterly delicious; Hornblower diving down into his general knowledge, came up with the conclusion that the black flakes must be truffle, of which he had heard but which he had never tasted. The purée potatoes, which he would have called mashed, were like no mashed potatoes he had ever sampled either on shipboard or in a sixpenny ordinary in England. They were seasoned subtly and yet to perfection – if angels ever ate mashed potatoes they would call on Pellew's chef to prepare them. With spring greens and carrots – for both of which he hungered inexpressibly – they made a plateful, along with the brawn, of sheer delight. He found himself eating like a wolf and pulled himself up short, but the glance that he stole round the table reassured him, for the others were eating like wolves too, to the detriment of conversation, with only a few murmured words to mingle with the clash of cutlery.

'Wine with you, sir.' 'Your health, Admiral.' 'Would you give the onions a fair wind, Grindall?' and so on.

'Won't you try the galantine, Lord Henry?' asked Pellew. 'Steward, a fresh plate for Lord Henry.'

That was how Hornblower learned the real name of the brawn he was eating. The ragout of pork drifted his way and he helped himself generously; the steward behind him changed his plate in the nick of time. He savoured the exquisite boiled onions that wallowed in the beatific sauce. Then like magic the table was cleared and fresh dishes made their appearance, a pudding rich with raisins and currants, jellies of two colours; much labour must have gone into boiling down the bullock's feet and into subsequent straining to make that brilliant gelatine.

'No flour for that duff,' said Pellew apologetically. 'The galley staff has done its best with biscuit crumbs.'

That best was as near perfection as mind could conceive; there was a sweet sauce with it, hinting of ginger, that made the most of the richness of the fruit. Hornblower found himself thinking that if ever he became a post captain, wealthy with prize money, he would have to devote endless thought to the organization of his cabin stores. And Maria would not be of much help, he thought ruefully. He was still drifting along with thoughts of Maria when the table was swept clear again.

'Caerphilly, sir?' murmured a steward in his ear. 'Wensleydale? Red Cheshire?'

These were cheeses that were being offered him. He helped himself at random – one name meant no more to him than another – and went on to make an epoch-making discovery, that Wensleydale cheese and vintage port were a pair of heavenly twins, Castor and Pollux riding triumphantly as the climax of a glorious procession. Full of food and with two glasses of wine inside him – all he allowed himself – he felt vastly pleased with the discovery, rivalling those of Columbus and Cook. Almost simultaneously he made another discovery which amused him. The chased silver fingerbowls which were put on the table were very elegant; the last time he had seen anything like them was as a midshipman at a dinner at Government House in Gibraltar. In each floated a fragment of lemon peel, but the water in which the peel floated – as Hornblower discovered by a furtive taste as he dabbed his lips – was plain seawater. There was something comforting in that fact.

Cornwallis' blue eyes were fixed on him.

'Mr Vice, the King,' said Cornwallis.

Hornblower came back from pink hazes of beatitude. He had to take a grip of himself, as when he had tacked *Hotspur* with the *Loire* in pursuit; he had to await the right moment for the attention of the company. Then he rose to his feet and lifted his glass, carrying out the ages old ritual of the junior officer present.

'Gentlemen, the King,' he said.

'The King!' echoed everyone present, and some added phrases like 'God Bless him' and 'Long may he reign' before they sat down again.

'His Royal Highness the Duke of Clarence,' said Lord Henry in conversational tone, 'told me that during his time at sea he had knocked his head – he's a tall man, as you know – so often on so many deck beams while drinking his father's health that he seriously was considering requesting His Majesty's permission, as a special privilege, for the Royal Navy to drink the royal health while sitting down.'

At the other corner of the table Andrews, captain of the *Flora*, was going on with an interrupted conversation.

'Fifteen pounds a man,' he was saying. 'That's what my Jacks were paid on account of prize money, and we were in Cawsand Bay ready to sail. The women had left the ship, not a bumboat within call, and so my men – the ordinary seamen, mind you – still have fifteen pounds apiece in their pockets.'

'All the better when they get a chance to spend it,' said Marsfield.

Hornblower was making a rapid calculation. The *Flora* would have a crew of some three hundred men, who divided a quarter of the prize money between them. The captain had one quarter to himself, so that Andrews would have been paid – on account, not necessarily in full – some four thousand five hundred pounds as a result of some lucky cruise, probably without risk, probably without a life being lost, money for seizing French merchant ships intercepted at sea. Hornblower thought ruefully about Maria's latest letter, and about the uses to which he could put four thousand five hundred pounds.

'There'll be lively times in Plymouth when the Channel Fleet comes in,' said Andrews.

'That is something which I wish to explain to you gentlemen,' said Cornwallis, breaking in on the conversation. There was something flat and expressionless about his voice, and there was a kind of mask-like expression on his good-tempered face, so that all eyes turned on him.

'The Channel Fleet will not be coming in to Plymouth,' said Cornwallis. 'This is the time to make that plain.'

A silence ensued, during which Cornwallis was clearly waiting for a cue. The saturnine Collins supplied it.

'What about water, sir? Provisions?'

'They are going to be sent out to us.'

'Water, sir?'

'Yes. I have had four water-hoys constructed. They will bring us water. Victualling ships will bring us our food. Each new ship which joins us will bring us fresh food, vegetables and live cattle, all they can carry on deck. That will help against scurvy. I'm sending no ship back to replenish.'

'So we'll have to wait for the winter gales before we see Plymouth again, sir?'

'Not even then,' said Cornwallis. 'No ship, no captain, is to enter Plymouth without my express orders. Do I have to explain why, to experienced officers like you?'

The reasons were as obvious to Hornblower as to the others. The Channel Fleet might well have to run for shelter when south-westerly gales blew, and with a gale at southwest the French fleet could not escape from Brest. But Plymouth Sound was difficult; a wind from the eastward would delay the British fleet's exit, prolong it over several days, perhaps, during which time the wind would be fair for the French fleet to escape. There were plenty of other reasons, too. There was disease; every captain knew that ships grew healthier the longer they were at sea. There was desertion. There was the fact that discipline could be badly shaken by debauches on shore.

'But in a gale, sir?' asked someone. 'We could get blown right up-Channel.'

'No,' answered Cornwallis decisively. 'If we're blown off this station our rendezvous is Tor Bay. There we anchor.'

Confused murmurings showed how this information was being digested. Tor Bay was an exposed uncomfortable anchorage, barely sheltered from the west, but it had the obvious advantage that at the first shift of wind the fleet could put to sea, could be off Ushant again before the unwieldy French fleet could file out down the Goulet.

'So none of us will set foot on English soil again until the end of the war, sir?' said Collins.

Cornwallis' face was transfigured by a smile. 'We need never say that. All of you, any one of you, can go ashore . . .' the smile broadened as he paused, 'the moment I set foot ashore myself.'

That caused a laugh, perhaps a grudging laugh, but with an admiring echo. Hornblower, watching the scene keenly, suddenly came to a fresh realization. Collins' questions and remarks had been very apt, very much to the point. Hornblower suspected that he had been listening to a prepared piece of dialogue, and his suspicions were strengthened by the recollection that Collins was First Captain under Cornwallis, somebody whom the French would call a Chief of Staff. Hornblower looked about him again. He could not help feeling admiration for Cornwallis, whose guileless behaviour concealed such unsuspected depths of subtlety. And it was a matter for self-congratulation that he had guessed the secret, he, the junior officer present, surrounded by all these captains of vast seniority, of distinguished records and of noble descent. He felt positively smug, a most unusual and gratifying feeling.

Smugness and vintage port combined to dull his awareness of all the implications at first, and then suddenly everything changed. The new thought sent him sliding down an Avernus of depression. It brought about an actual physical sensation in the pit of his stomach, like the one he felt when *Hotspur*, close-hauled, topped a wave and went slithering and rolling down the farther side. Maria! He had written so cheerfully saying he would be seeing her soon. There were only fifty days' provisions and water left in *Hotspur*; fresh food would eke out the provisions, but little enough could be done (he had thought) regarding water. He had been confident that *Hotspur* would be making periodic calls at Plymouth for food and water and firewood. Now Maria would never have the comfort of his presence during her pregnancy. Nor would he himself (and the violence of this reaction surprised him) have the pleasure of seeing her during her pregnancy. And one more thing; he would have to write to her and tell her that he would not be keeping his promises, that there was no chance of their meeting. He would be causing her terrible pain, not only because her idol would be revealed to her as a man who could not, or perhaps even would not, keep his word.

He was recalled suddenly from these thoughts, from these mental pictures of Maria, by hearing his name spoken during the conversation round the table. Nearly everyone present was looking at him, and he had to ferret hurriedly through his unconscious memory to recapture what had been said. Someone – it must have been Cornwallis himself – had said that the information he had gathered from the French coast had been satisfactory and illuminating. But for the life of him Hornblower could not recall what had next been said, and now here he was, with every eye on him, gazing round the table with a bewilderment that he tried to conceal behind an impassive countenance.

'We are all interested in your sources of information, Hornblower,' prompted Cornwallis, apparently repeating something already said.

Hornblower shook his head in decisive negation; that was his instant reaction, before he could analyse the situation, and before he could wrap up a blunt refusal in pretty words.

'No,' he said, to back up the shaking of his head.

There were all these people present; nothing would remain a secret if known to so large a group. The pilchard fishermen and lobster-pot men with whom he had been having furtive dealings and on whom he had been lavishing British gold – French gold, to be exact – would meet with short shrift if their activities became known to the French authorities. Not only would they die, but they would never be able to supply him with any further news. He was passionately anxious for his secrets to remain secrets, yet he was surrounded by all these senior officers any one of whom might have an influence on his career. Luckily he was already committed by the curt negative that had been surprised out of him – nothing could commit him more deeply than that, and that was thanks to Maria. He must not think about Maria, yet he must find some way of softening his abrupt refusal.

'It's more important than a formula for fattening chickens, sir,' he said, and then, with a bright further inspiration he shifted the responsibility. 'I would not like to disclose my operations without a direct order.'

His sensibilities, keyed to the highest pitch, detected sympathy in Cornwallis' reaction.

'I'm sure there's no need, Hornblower,' said Cornwallis, turning back to the others. Now, before he turned, was it true that the eyelid of his left eye, nearest to Hornblower, flickered a trifle? Was it? Hornblower could not be sure.

As the conversation reverted to a discussion of future operations Hornblower's sense, almost telepathic, became aware of something else in the past atmosphere which called up hot resentment in his mind. These fighting officers, these captains of ships of the line, were content to leave the dirty details of the gathering of intelligence to a junior, to someone hardly worthy of their lofty notice. They would not sully their aristocratic white hands; if the insignificant Commander of an insignificant sloop chose to do the work they would leave it to him in tolerant contempt.

Now the contempt was in no way one-sided. Fighting captains had their place in the scheme of things, but only an insignificant place, and anyone could be a fighting captain, even if he had to learn to swallow down the heart from his mouth and master the tensions that set his limbs a-tremble. Hornblower was experiencing symptoms not unlike these at this moment, when he was in no danger at all. Vintage port and a good dinner, thoughts of Maria and resentment against the captains, combined within him in a witches' brew that threatened to boil over. Luckily the bubbling mixture happened to distil off a succession of ideas, first one and then another. They linked themselves in a logical chain. Hornblower, along with his agitation, could feel the flush of blood under his skin that foretold the development of a plan, in the same way that the witch in Macbeth could tell the approach of something wicked by the pricking in her thumbs. Soon the plan was mature, complete, and Hornblower was left calm and clear-headed after his spiritual convulsion; it was like the clearness of head that follows the crisis of an attack of fever – possibly that was exactly what it was.

The plan called for a dark night, and for half-flood an hour before dawn; nature would supply those sooner or later, following her immutable laws. It called for some good fortune, and it would call for resolution and promptitude of action, but those were accessory ingredients in every plan. It included possibilities of disaster, but was there ever a plan that did not? It also called for the services of a man who spoke perfect French, and Hornblower, measuring his abilities with a cold eye, knew that he was not that man. The penniless noble French refugee who in Hornblower's boyhood had instructed him, with fair success, in French and

Deportment (and, totally unsuccessfully, in Music and Dancing), had never managed to confer a good accent upon his tone-deaf pupil. His grammar and his construction were excellent, but no one would ever mistake him for a Frenchman.

Hornblower had reached every necessary decision by the time the party began to break up, and he made it his business to take his stand, casually, beside Collins at the moment the Admiral's barge was called.

'Is there anyone in the Channel Fleet who speaks perfect French, sir?' he asked.

'You speak French yourself,' replied Collins.

'Not well enough for what I have in mind, sir,' said Hornblower, more struck by the extent of Collins' knowledge than flattered. 'I might find a use for a man who speaks French exactly like a Frenchman.'

'There's Côtard,' said Collins, meditatively rubbing his chin. 'Lieutenant in the *Marlborough*. He's a Guernseyman. Speaks French like a native – always spoke it as a child, I believe. What do you want him to do?'

'Admiral's barge coming alongside, sir,' reported a breathless messenger to Pellew.

'Hardly time to tell you now, sir,' said Hornblower. 'I can submit a plan to Sir Edward. But it'll be no use without someone speaking perfect French.'

The assembled company was now filing to the gangway; Collins, in accordance with naval etiquette, would have to go down the side into the barge ahead of Cornwallis.

'I'll detail Côtard from his ship on special service,' said Andrews hastily. 'I'll send him over to you and you can look him over.'

'Thank you, sir.'

Cornwallis was now thanking his host and saying goodbye to the other captains; Collins unobtrusively yet with remarkable rapidity contrived to do the same, and disappeared over the side. Cornwallis followed, with all the time honoured ceremonial of guard of honour and band and sideboys, while his flag was hauled down from the fortopmast head. After his departure barge after barge came alongside, each gaudy with new paint, with every crew tricked out in neat clothing paid for out of their captains' pockets, and captain after captain went down into them, in order of seniority, and shoved off to their respective ships.

Lastly came *Hotspur*'s drab little quarter-boat, its crew dressed in the clothes issued to them in the slop-ship the day they were sent on board.

'Goodbye, sir,' said Hornblower, holding out his hand to Pellew.

Pellew had shaken so many hands, and had said so many goodbyes, that Hornblower was anxious to cut this farewell as short as possible.

'Goodbye, Hornblower,' said Pellew, and Hornblower quickly stepped back, touching his hat. The pipes squealed until his head was below the level of the main-deck, and then he dropped perilously into the boat, hat, gloves, sword and all, all of them shabby.

IO

'I'll take this opportunity, Mr Bush,' said Hornblower, 'of repeating what I said before. I'm sorry you're not being given your chance.'

'It can't be helped, sir. It's the way of the Service,' replied the shadowy figure confronting Hornblower on the dark quarterdeck. The words were philosophical, but the tone was bitter. It was all part of the general logical madness of war, that Bush should feel bitter at not being allowed to risk his life, and that Hornblower, about to be doing so, should commiserate with Bush, speaking in flat formal tones as if he were not in the least excited – as if he were feeling no apprehension at all.

Hornblower knew himself well enough to be sure that if some miracle were to happen, if orders were to arrive forbidding him to take personal part in the coming raid, he would feel a wave of relief; delight as well as relief. But it was quite impossible, for the orders had definitely stated that 'the landing party will be under the command of Captain Horatio Hornblower of the *Hotspur.*' That sentence had been explained in advance in the preceding one . . . 'because Lieut Côtard is senior to Lieut Bush.' Côtard could not possibly have been transferred from one ship and given command of a landing party largely provided by another; nor could he be expected to serve under an officer junior to him, and the only way round the difficulty had been that

Hornblower should command. Pellew, writing out those orders in the quiet of his magnificent cabin, had been like a Valkyrie in the Norse legends now attaining a strange popularity in England – he had been a Chooser of the Slain. Those scratches of his pen could well mean that Bush would live and Hornblower would die.

But there was another side to the picture. Hornblower had grudgingly to admit to himself that he would have been no more happy if Bush had been in command. The operation planned could only be successful if carried through with a certain verve and with an exactness of timing that Bush possibly could not provide. Absurdly, Hornblower was glad he was to command, and that was one demonstration in his mind of the defects of his temperament.

'You are sure about your orders until I return, Mr Bush?' he said. 'And in case I don't return?'

'Yes, sir.'

Hornblower had felt a cold wave up his spine while he spoke so casually about the possibility of his death. An hour from now he might be a disfigured stiffening corpse.

'Then I'll get myself ready,' he said, turning away with every appearance of nonchalance.

He had hardly reached his cabin when Grimes entered.

'Sir!' said Grimes, and Hornblower swung round and looked at him. Grimes was in his early twenties, skinny, highly strung, and excitable. Now his face was white – his duties as steward meant that he spent little time on deck in the sun – and his lips were working horribly.

'What's the matter?' demanded Hornblower curtly.

'Don't make me come with you, sir!' spluttered Grimes. 'You don't want me with you, sir, do you, sir?'

It was an astonishing moment. In all his years of service Hornblower had never met with any experience in the least similar, and he was taken aback. This was cowardice; it might even be construed as mutiny. Grimes had in the last five seconds made himself liable not merely to the cat but to the noose. Hornblower could only stand and stare, wordless.

'I'll be no use, sir,' said Grimes. 'I – I might scream!'

Now that was a very definite point. Hornblower, giving his orders for the raid, had nominated Grimes as his messenger and aide-de-camp. He had given no thought to the selection; he had been a very casual Chooser of the Slain. Now he was learning a lesson. A frightened man at his elbow, a man made clumsy by fear, could imperil the whole expedition. Yet the first words he could say echoed his earlier thoughts.

'I could hang you, by God!' he exclaimed.

'No, sir! No, sir! Please, sir –' Grimes was on the point of collapse; in another moment he would be down on his knees.

'Oh, for God's sake –' said Hornblower. He was conscious of contempt, not for the coward, but for the man who allowed his cowardice to show. And then he asked himself by what right he felt this contempt. And then he thought about the good of the Service, and then – He had no time to waste in these trivial analyses.

'Very well,' he snapped. 'You can stay on board. Shut your mouth, you fool!'

Grimes was about to show gratitude, but Hornblower's words cut it off short.

'I'll take Hewitt out of the second boat. He can come with me. Pass the word for him.'

The minutes were fleeting by, as they always did with the final touches to put on to a planned scheme. Hornblower passed his belt through the loop on a cutlass sheath, and buckled it round him. A sword hanging on slings could be a hindrance, would strike against obstructions, and the cutlass was a handier weapon for what he contemplated. He gave a final thought to taking a pistol, and again rejected the idea. A pistol might be useful in certain circumstances, but it was a bulky encumbrance. Here was something more silent – a long sausage of stout canvas filled with sand, with a loop for the wrist. Hornblower settled it conveniently in his right hand pocket.

Hewitt reported, and had to be briefly told what was expected of him. The sidelong glance he gave to Grimes revealed much of what Hewitt thought, but there was no time for discussion; that matter would have to be sorted out later. Hewitt was shown the contents of the bundle originally allotted to Grimes – the flint and steel for use if the dark lantern were extinguished, the oily rags, the slow match, the quick match, the blue lights for instant intense combustion. Hewitt took solemn note of each item and weighed his sandbag in his hand.

'Very well. Come along,' said Hornblower.

'Sir!' said Grimes at that moment in a pleading tone, but Hornblower would not – indeed could not – spare time to hear any more.

On deck it was pitch dark, and Hornblower's eyes took long to adjust themselves.

Officer after officer reported all ready.

'You're sure of what you have to say, Mr Côtard?'

'Yes, sir.'

There was no hint of the excitable Frenchman about Côtard. He was as phlegmatic as any commanding officer could desire.

'Fifty-one rank and file present, sir,' reported the captain of marines.

Those marines, brought on board the night before, had lain huddled below decks all day, concealed from the telescopes on Petit Minou.

'Thank you, Captain Jones. You've made sure no musket is loaded?'

'Yes, sir.'

Until the alarm was given not a shot was to be fired. The work was to be done with the bayonet and the butt, and the sandbag – but the only way to be certain of that was to keep the muskets unloaded.

'First landing party all down in the fishing-boat, sir,' reported Bush.

'Thank you, Mr Bush. Very well, Mr Côtard, we may as well start.'

The lobster-boat, seized earlier in the night to the surprise of its crew, lay alongside. The crew were prisoners down below; their surprise was due to the breach of the traditional neutrality enjoyed during the long wars by fishing-boats. These men were all acquainted with Hornblower, had often sold him part of their catch in exchange for gold, yet they had hardly been reassured when they were told that their boat would be returned to them later. Now it lay alongside, and Côtard followed Hewitt, and Hornblower followed Côtard, down into it.

Eight men were squatting in the bottom where the lobster-pots used to lie.

'Sanderson, Hewitt, Black, Downes take the oars. The rest of you get down below the gunnels. Mr Côtard, sit here against my knees, if you please.'

Hornblower waited until they had settled themselves. The black silhouette of the boat must appear no different in the dark night. Now came the moment.

'Shove off,' said Hornblower.

The oars dragged through the water, bit more effectively at the next stroke, pulled smoothly at the third, and they were leaving *Hotspur* behind them. They were setting off on an adventure, and Hornblower was only too conscious that it was his own fault. If he had not been bitten with this idea they might all be peacefully asleep on board; tomorrow men would be dead who but for him would still be alive.

He put the morbid thought to one side, and then immediately he had to do the same with thoughts about Grimes. Grimes could wait perfectly well until his return, and Hornblower would not trouble his mind about him until then. Yet even so, as Hornblower concentrated on steering the lobster-boat, there was a continual undercurrent of thought – like ship's noises during a discussion of plans – regarding how the crew on board would be treating Grimes, for Hewitt, before leaving the ship, would have certainly told the story to his cronies.

Hornblower, with his hand on the tiller, steered a steady course northward towards Petit Minou. A mile and a quarter to go, and it would never do if he missed the little jetty so that the expedition would end in a miserable fiasco. He had the faint outline of the steep hills on the northern shore of the Goulet to guide him; he knew them well enough now, after all these weeks of gazing at them, and the abrupt shoulder, where a little stream came down to the sea a quarter of a mile west of the semaphore, was his principal guide. He had to keep that notch open as the boat advanced, but after a few minutes he could actually make out the towering height of the semaphore itself, just visible against the dark sky, and then it was easy.

The oars groaned in the rowlocks, the blades splashing occasionally in the water; the gentle waves which raised them and lowered them seemed to be made of black glass. There was no need for a silent or invisible approach; on the contrary, the lobster-boat had to appear as if she were approaching on her lawful occasions. At the foot of the abrupt shore was a tiny half-tide jetty, and it was the habit of the lobster-boats to land there and put ashore a couple of men with the pick of the catch. Then, each with a basket on his head containing a dozen live lobsters, they would run along the track over the hills into Brest so as to be ready for the opening of the market, regardless of whether the boat was delayed by wind and tide or not. Hornblower, scouting at a safe distance in the jolly boat, had ascertained during a succession of nights such of the routine as he had not been able to pick up in conversation with the fishermen.

There it was. There was the jetty. Hornblower found his grip tightening on the tiller. Now came the loud voice of the sentry at the end of the jetty.

'Qui va là?'

Hornblower nudged Côtard with his knee, unnecessarily, for Côtard was ready with the answer.

'Camille,' he hailed, and continued in French, 'Lobster-boat. Captain Quillien.'

They were already alongside; the crucial moment on which everything depended. Black, the burly Captain of the Forecastle, knew what he had to do the moment opportunity offered. Côtard spoke from the depths of the boat.

'I have the lobster for your officer.'

Hornblower, standing up and reaching for the jetty, could just see the dark of the sentry looking down, but Black had already leaped up from the bows like a panther, Downes and Sanderson following him. Hornblower saw a swift movement of shadows, but there was not a sound – not a sound.

'All right, sir,' said Black.

Hornblower, with a line in his hand, managed to propel himself up the slippery side, arriving on the top on his hands and knees. Black was standing holding the inanimate body of the sentry in his arms. Sandbags were silent; a vicious blow from behind at the exposed back of the neck, a quick grab, and it was finished. The sentry had not even dropped his musket; he and it were safe in Black's monstrous arms.

Black lowered the body – senseless or dead, it did not matter which – on to the slimy stone flags of the jetty.

'If he makes a sound cut his throat,' said Hornblower.

This was all orderly and yet unreal, like a nightmare. Hornblower, turning to drop a clove-hitch with his line over a bollard, found his upper lip was still drawn up in a snarl like a wild beast's. Côtard was already beside him; Sanderson had already made the boat fast forward.

'Come on.'

The jetty was only a few yards long; at the far end, where the paths diverged up to the batteries, they would find the second sentry. From the boat they passed up a couple of empty baskets, and Black and Côtard held them on their heads and set off, Côtard in the middle, Hornblower on the left, and Black on the right where his right arm would be free to swing his sandbag. There was the sentry. He made no formal challenge, greeting them in jocular fashion while Côtard spoke again about the lobster which was the recognized though unofficial toll paid to the officer commanding the guard for the use of the jetty. It was a perfectly ordinary encounter until Black dropped his basket and swung with his sandbag and they all three leaped on the sentry, Côtard with his hands on the sentry's throat, Hornblower striking madly with his sandbag as well, desperately anxious to make sure. It was over in an instant, and Hornblower looked round at the dark and silent night with the sentry's body lying at his feet. He and Black and Côtard were the thin point of the wedge that had pierced the ring of the French defences. It was time for the wedge to be driven home. Behind them were the half-dozen others who had crouched in the lobster-boat, and following them up were the seventy marines and seamen in the boats of the *Hotspur*.

They dragged the second sentry back to the jetty and left him with the two boat-keepers. Now Hornblower had eight men at his back as he set his face to the steep climb up the path, the path he had only seen through a telescope from *Hotspur's* deck. Hewitt was behind him; the smell of hot metal and fat in the still night air told him that the dark lantern was still alight. The path was stony and slippery, and Hornblower had to exert his self-control as he struggled up it. There was no need for desperate haste, and although they were inside the ring of sentries, in an area where civilians apparently passed fairly freely, there was no need to scramble noisily and attract too much attention.

Now the path became less steep. Now it was level, and here it intersected another path at right angles.

'Halt!' grunted Hornblower to Hewitt, but he took another two paces forward while Hewitt passed the word back; a sudden stop would mean that the people behind would be cannoning into each other.

This was indeed the summit. Owing to the levelling-off of the top this was an area unsearched by telescopes from the *Hotspur*; even from the maintopgallant-masthead, with the ship far out in the Iroise, they had not been able to view the ground here. The towering telegraph had been plainly in view, and at its foot just a hint of a roof, but they had not been able to see what was at ground level here, nor had Hornblower been able to obtain any hint in his conversations with fishermen.

'Wait!' he whispered back, and stepped cautiously forward, his hands extended in front of him. Instantly they came into contact with a wooden paling, quite an ordinary fence and by no means a military obstacle. And this was a gate, an ordinary gate with a wooden latch. Obviously the semaphore station was not closely guarded – fence and gate were only polite warnings to unauthorized intruders – and of course there was no reason why they should be, here among the French coastal batteries.

'Hewitt! Côtard!'

They came up to him and all three strained their eyes in the darkness.

'Do you see anything?'

'Looks like a house,' whispered Côtard.

Something in two storeys. Windows in the lower one, and above that a sort of platform. The crew who worked the telegraph must live here. Hornblower cautiously fumbled with the latch of the gate, and it opened without resistance. Then a sudden noise almost in his ear tensed him rigid, to relax again. It was a cock crowing, and he could hear a fluttering of wings. The semaphore crew must keep chickens in coops here, and the cock was giving premature warning of day. No reason for further delay; Hornblower whispered his orders to his band whom he called up to the gate. Now was the time; and this was the moment when the parties of marines must be halfway up the climb to the battery. He was on the point of giving the final word when he saw something else which stopped him dead, and Côtard grabbed his shoulder at the same moment. Two of the windows before him were showing a light, a tiny glimmer, which nevertheless to their dilated pupils made the whole cottage plain to their view.

'Come on!'

They dashed forward, Hornblower, Côtard, Hewitt, and the two men with axes in one group, the other four musket men scattering to surround the place. The path led straight to a door, again with a wooden latch, which Hornblower feverishly tried to work. But the door resisted; it was bolted on the inside, and at the rattling of the latch a startled cry made itself heard inside. A woman's voice! It was harsh and loud, but a woman's voice, undoubtedly. The axeman at Hornblower's shoulder heaved up his axe to beat in the door, but at the same moment the other axeman shattered a window and went leaping through followed by Côtard. The woman's voice rose to a scream; the bolt was drawn and the door swung open and Hornblower burst in.

A tallow dip lit the odd scene, and Hewitt opened the shutter of the dark lantern to illuminate it further, sweeping its beam in a semicircle. There were large baulks of timber, each set at an angle of forty-five degrees, to act as struts for the mast. Where floor space remained stood cottage furniture, a table and chairs, a rush mat on the floor, a stove. Côtard stood in the centre with sword and pistol, and at the far side stood a screaming woman. She was hugely fat, with a tangle of black hair, and all she wore was a nightshirt that hardly came to her knees. There was an inner door from which emerged a bearded man with hairy legs showing below his shirt-tails. The woman still screamed, but Côtard spoke loudly in French, waving his pistol – empty presumably – and the noise ceased, not, perhaps, because of Côtard's threats but because of the woman's sheer curiosity regarding these dawn intruders. She stood goggling at them, making only the most perfunctory gestures to conceal her nakedness.

But decisions had to be made; those screams might have given the alarm and probably had done so. Against the thick bulk of the semaphore mast a ladder led up to a trap door. Overhead must be the apparatus for working the semaphore-arms. The bearded man in his shirt must be the telegraphist, a civilian perhaps, and he and his wife presumably lived beside their work. It must have been convenient for them that the construction of the working platform overhead made it easy to build these cottage rooms underneath.

Hornblower had come to burn the semaphore, and burn it he would, even if a civilian dwelling were involved. The rest of his party were crowding into the living room, two of the musket men appearing from the bedroom into which they must have made their way by another window. Hornblower had to stop and think for a perceptible space. He had expected that at this moment he would be fighting French soldiers, but here he was already in complete possession and with a woman on his hands. But his wits returned to him and he was able to put his thoughts in order.

'Get out, you musket men,' he said. 'Get out to the fence and keep watch. Côtard, up that ladder. Bring down all the signal books you can find. Any papers there are. Quick – I'll give you two minutes. Here's the lantern. Black, get something for this woman. The clothes from the bed'll do, and then take these two out and guard 'em. Are you ready to burn this place, Hewitt?'

It flashed through his mind that the *Moniteur* in Paris could make a great deal of noise about ill-treatment of a woman by the licentious British sailors, but it would do that however careful he might be. Black hung a ragged quilt over the woman's shoulders and then hustled his charge out of the front door. Hewitt had to stop and think. He had never set about burning a house before, and clearly he did not adapt himself readily to new situations.

'That's the place,' snapped Hornblower, pointing to the foot of the telegraph mast. There were the great baulks of timber round the mast; Hornblower joined with Hewitt in pushing the furniture under them, and then hurried into the bedroom to do the same.

'Bring some rags here!' he called.

Côtard came scrambling down the ladder with one arm full of books.

'Now. Let's start the fire,' said Hornblower.

It was a strange thing to do, in cold blood.

'Try the stove,' suggested Côtard.

Hewitt unlatched the door of the stove, but it was too hot to touch after that. He set his back to the wall and braced his feet against the stove and shoved; the stove fell and rolled, scattering a few embers over the floor. But Hornblower had snatched up a handful of blue lights from Hewitt's bundle; the tallow dip was still burning and available to light the fuses. The first fuse spluttered and then the firework spouted flames. Sulphur and saltpetre with a sprinkling of gunpowder; blue lights were ideal for this purpose. He tossed the blazing thing on to the oily rags, lit another and threw it, lit another still.

This was like some scene in Hell. The uncanny blue gleam lit the room, but soon the haze of smoke made everything dim, and the fumes of the burning sulphur offended their nostrils as the fireworks hissed and roared, while Hornblower went on lighting fuses and thrusting the blue lights where they would be most effective in living room and bedroom. Hewitt in an inspired moment tore the rush mat up from the floor and flung it over the rising flames of the rags. Already the timber was crackling and throwing out showers of yellow sparks to compete with the blue glare and the thickening smoke.

'That'll burn!' said Côtard.

The flames from the blazing mat were playing on one of the sloping timbers, and engendering new flames which licked up the rough wooden surface. They stood and watched fascinated. On this rocky summit there could be no well, no spring, and it would be impossible to extinguish this fire once it was thoroughly started. The laths of the partition wall were alight in two places where Hornblower had thrust blue lights into the crannies; he saw the flames at one point suddenly leap two feet up the partition with a volley of loud reports and fresh showers of sparks.

'Come on!' he said.

Outside the air was keen and clear and they blinked their dazzled eyes and stumbled over inequalities at their feet, but there was a faint tiny light suffusing the air, the first glimmer of daylight. Hornblower saw the vague shape of the fat woman standing huddled in her quilt; she was sobbing in a strange way, making a loud gulping noise regularly at intervals of a couple of seconds or so. Somebody must have kicked over the chicken coop, because there seemed to be clucking chickens everywhere in the half-light. The interior of the cottage was all ablaze, and now there was light enough in the sky for Hornblower to see the immense mast of the telegraph against it, oddly shaped with its semaphore arms dangling. Eight stout cables radiated out from it, attached to pillars sunk in the rock. The cables braced the unwieldy mast against the rude winds of the Atlantic, and the pillars served also to support the tottering picket fence that surrounded the place. There was a pathetic attempt at a garden on small patches of soil that might well have been carried up by hand from the valley below; a few pansies, a patch of lavender, and two unhappy geraniums trodden down by some blunderer.

Yet the light was still only just apparent; the flames that were devouring the cottage were brighter. He saw illuminated smoke pouring from the side of the upper storey, and directly after that flames shot out from between the warping timbers.

'The devil of a collection of ropes and blocks and levers up there,' said Côtard. 'Not much of it left by this time.'

'No one'll put that out now. And we've heard nothing from the marines,' said Hornblower. 'Come along, you men.'

He had been prepared to fight a delaying action with his musket men if the enemy had appeared before the place was well alight. Now it was unnecessary, so well had everything gone. So well, indeed, that it called for a moment or two's delay to collect the men. These leisurely minutes had made all haste appear unnecessary as they filed out through the gate. There was a slight haze lying over the surface of the summer sea; the topsails of the *Hotspur* – maintopsail aback – were far more visible than her hull, a grey pearl in the pearly mist. The fat woman stood at the gate, all modesty gone with the quilt that had fallen from her shoulders, waving her arms and shrieking curses at them.

From the misty valley on their right as they faced the descent came the notes of a musical instrument, some trumpet or bugle.

'That's their reveille,' commented Côtard, sliding down the path on Hornblower's heels.

He had hardly spoken when the call was taken up by other bugles. A second or two later came the sound of a musket shot, and then more musket shots, and along with them the echoing roll of a drum, and then more drums beating the alarm.

'That's the marines,' said Côtard.

'Yes,' snapped Hornblower. 'Come on!'

Musketry meant a bad mark against the landing party that had gone up against the battery. Very likely there was a sentry there, and he should have been disposed of silently. But somehow the alarm had been given. The guard had turned out – say twenty men armed and equipped – and now the main body was being roused. That would be the artillery unit in their hutments below the ridge; not too effective, perhaps, fighting with musket and bayonet, but over the other side there was a battalion of infantry at this very moment being roused from sleep. Hornblower had given his order and broken into a run along the right-hand path towards the battery before these thoughts had formulated themselves quite so clearly. He was ready with his new plan before they topped the ridge.

'Halt!'

They assembled behind him.

'Load!'

Cartridges were bitten open; pans were primed, and charges poured down the barrels of muskets and pistols.

The wadded cartridge papers were thrust into the muzzles, the bullets were spat in on top, and then the ramrods were plied to drive all home.

'Côtard, take the musket men out to the flank. You others, come with me.'

There was the great battery with its four thirty-two-pounders looking through the embrasures of its curving parapet. Beyond it a skirmish line of marines, their uniforms showing scarlet in the growing light, were holding at bay a French force only outlined by musket flashes and puffs of smoke. The sudden arrival of Côtard and his men, an unknown force on their flank caused the momentary withdrawal of this French force.

In the centre of the inner face of the parapet Captain Jones in his red coat with four other men were struggling with a door; beside him was laid out a bundle similar to the one Hewitt carried, blue lights, reels of slow match and quick match. Beyond him lay two dead marines, one of them shot hideously in the face. Jones looked up as Hornblower arrived, but Hornblower wasted no time in discussion.

'Stand aside! Axemen!'

The door was of solid wood and reinforced with iron, but it was only intended to keep out thieving civilians; a sentry was supposed to guard it, and under the thundering of the axes, it gave way rapidly.

'The guns are all spiked,' said Jones.

That was only the smallest part of the business. An iron spike driven into the touch-hole of a gun would render it useless in the heat of the moment, but an armourer working with a drill would clear it in an hour's work. Hornblower was on the step of the parapet looking over the top; the French were rallying for a new attack. But an axe-handle was working as a lever through a gap driven in the door. Black had hold of the edge of a panel and with a wild effort tore it free. A dozen more blows, another wrench, and there was a way open through the door. A crouching man could make his way into the blackness inside.

'I'll go,' said Hornblower. He could not trust Jones or the marines. He could trust no one but himself. He seized the reel of quick match and squeezed through the shattered door. There were timbered steps under his feet, but he expected that and so did not fall down them. He crouched under the roof and felt his way down. There was a landing and a turn, and then more steps, much darker, and then his outstretched hands touched a hanging curtain of serge. He thrust this aside and stepped cautiously beyond it. Here it was utterly black. He was in the magazine. He was in the area where the ammunition party would wear list slippers, because nailed shoes might cause a spark to ignite the gun-powder. He felt cautiously about him; one hand touched the harsh outline of a cask. Those were the powder-barrels – his hand involuntarily withdrew itself, as though it had touched a snake. No time for that sort of idiocy, he was surrounded by violent death.

He drew his cutlass, snarling in the darkness with the intensity of his emotion. Twice he stabbed into the wall of cartridges, and his ears were rewarded by the whispering sound of a cascade of powder-grains pouring out through the gashes he had made. He must have a firm anchorage for the fuse; and he stooped and sank the blade of the cutlass into another cartridge. He unravelled a length of quick match and wound a bight firmly round the hilt, and he buried the end in the pile of powder-grains on the floor; an unnecessarily careful measure, perhaps, when a single spark would set off the explosion. Unreeling the quick match behind him, carefully, very carefully, lest he jerk the cutlass loose, he made his way out past the curtain again, and up the steps, up into the growing light, round the corner. The light through the broken door was dazzling, and he blinked as he came out crouching through it, still unreeling the quick match.

'Cut this!' he snapped, and Black whipped out his knife and sawed through the quick match at the point indicated by Hornblower's hand.

Quick match burned faster than the eye could follow; the fifty feet or so that extended down to the magazine would burn in less than a second.

'Cut me a yard off that!' said Hornblower pointing to the slow match.

Slow match was carefully tested. It burned in still air at exactly thirty inches in one hour, one inch in two minutes. Hornblower had no intention whatever of allowing an hour or more for the combustion of this yard, however. He could hear the muskets banging; he could hear drums echoing in the hills. He must keep calm.

'Cut off another foot and light it!'

While Black was executing this order Hornblower was tying quick match to slow match, making sure they were closely joined. Yet he still had to think of the general situation in addition to these vital details.

'Hewitt!' he snapped, looking up from his work.

'Listen carefully. Run to the lieutenant's party of marines over the ridge there. Tell him we're going to fall back now, and he is to cover our retreat at the last slope above the boats. Understand?'

'Aye aye, sir.'

'Then run.'

Just as well that it was not Grimes who had to be entrusted with the mission. The fuses were knotted together now, and Hornblower looked around him.

'Bring that dead man over here!'

Black asked no questions, but dragged the corpse to the foot of the door. Hornblower had looked first for a stone, but a corpse would be better in every way. It was not yet stiff, and the arm lay limply across the quick match just above the knot, after Hornblower had passed all excess slack back through the shattered door. The dead man served to conceal the existence of the fuse. If the French arrived too early he would gain valuable seconds for the plan; the moment the fire reached the quick match it would flash under the dead man's arm and shoot on down to the powder. If to investigate the magazine they dragged the corpse out of the way, the weight of a fuse inside the door would whisk the knot inside and so gain seconds too – perhaps the burning end would tumble down the steps, perhaps right into the magazine.

'Captain Jones! Warn everybody to be ready to retreat. At once, please. Give me that burning fuse, Black.'

'Let me do that, sir.'

'Shut your mouth.'

Hornblower took the smouldering slow match and

blew on it to quicken its life. Then he looked down at the length of slow match knotted to the quick match. He took special note of a point an inch and a half from the knot; there was a black spot there which served to mark the place. An inch and a half. Three minutes.

'Get up on the parapet, Black. Now. Yell for them to run. Yell!'

As Black began to bellow Hornblower pressed the smouldering end down upon the black spot. After two seconds he withdrew it; the slow match was alight and burning in two directions – in one, harmlessly towards the inoperative excess, and in the other towards the knot, the quick match an inch and a half away. Hornblower made sure it was burning, and then he scrambled to his feet and leaped up on the parapet.

The marines were trooping past him, with Côtard and his seamen bringing up the rear. A minute and a half – a minute, now, and the French were following them up, just out of musket range.

'Better hurry, Côtard. Come on!'

They broke into a dogtrot.

'Steady, there!' yelled Jones. He was concerned about panic among his men if they ran from the enemy instead of retreating steadily, but there was a time for everything. The marines began to run, with Jones yelling ineffectually and waving his sword.

'Come on, Jones,' said Hornblower as he passed him, but Jones was filled with fighting madness, and went on shouting defiance at the French, standing alone with his face to the enemy.

Then it happened. The earth moved back and forth under their feet so that they tripped and staggered, while a smashing, overwhelming explosion burst on their ears, and the sky went dark. Hornblower looked back. A column of smoke was still shooting upwards, higher and higher, and dark fragments were visible in it. Then the column spread out, mushrooming at the top. Something fell with a crash ten yards away, throwing up chips of stone which rattled round Hornblower's feet. Something came whistling through the air, something huge, curving down as it twirled. Selectively, inevitably, it fell, half a ton of rock, blown from where it roofed the magazine right on to Jones in his red coat, sliding along as if bestially determined to wipe out completely the pitiful thing it dragged beneath it. Hornblower and Côtard gazed at it in mesmerized horror as it came to rest six feet from their left hands.

It was the most difficult moment of all for Hornblower to keep his senses, or to regain them. He had to shake himself out of a daze.

'Come on.'

He still had to think clearly. They were at the final slope above the boats. The lieutenant's party of marines, sent out as a flank guard, had fallen back to this point and were drawn up here firing at a threatening crowd of Frenchmen. The French wore white facings on their blue uniforms – infantry men, not the artillery men who had opposed them round the battery. And beyond them was a long column of infantry, hurrying along, with a score of drums beating an exhilarating rhythm – the *pas de charge*.

'You men get down into the boats,' said Hornblower, addressing the rallying group of seamen and marines from the battery, and then he turned to the lieutenant.

'Captain Jones is dead. Make ready to run for it the moment those others reach the jetty.'

'Yes, sir.'

Behind Hornblower's back, turned as it was to the enemy, they heard a sharp sudden noise, like the impact of a carpenter's axe against wood. Hornblower swung round again. Côtard was staggering, his sword and the books and papers he had carried all this time fallen to the ground at his feet. Then Hornblower noticed his left arm, which was swaying in the air as if hanging by a thread. Then came the blood. A musket bullet had crashed into Côtard's upper armbone, shattering it. One of the axemen who had not yet left caught him as he was about to fall.

'Ah – ah – ah!' gasped Côtard, with the jarring of his shattered arm. He stared at Hornblower with bewildered eyes.

'Sorry you've been hit,' said Hornblower, and to the axeman, 'Get him down to the boat.'

Côtard was gesticulating towards the ground with his right hand, and Hornblower spoke to the other axeman.

'Pick those papers up and go down to the boat too.'

But Côtard was not satisfied.

'My sword! My sword!'

'I'll look after your sword,' said Hornblower. These absurd notions of honour were so deeply engrained that even in these conditions Côtard could not bear the thought of leaving his sword on the field of battle. Hornblower realized he had no cutlass as he picked up Côtard's sword. The axeman had gathered up the books and papers.

'Help Mr Côtard down,' said Hornblower, and added,

as another thought struck him. 'Put a scarf round his arm above the wound and strain it tight. Understand?'

Côtard, supported by the other axeman was already tottering down the path. Movement meant agony. That heartrending 'ah – ah – ah!' came back to Hornblower's ears at every step Côtard took.

'Here they come!' said the marine lieutenant.

The skirmishing Frenchmen, emboldened by the near approach of their main body, were charging forward. A hurried glance told Hornblower that the others were all down on the jetty; the lobster-boat was actually pushing off, full of men.

'Tell your men to run for it,' he said, and the moment after they started he followed them.

It was a wild dash, slipping and sliding, down the path to the jetty, with the French yelling in pursuit. But here was the covering party, as Hornblower had ordered so carefully the day before; *Hotspur*'s own thirteen marines, under their own sergeant. They had built a breastwork across the jetty, again as Hornblower had ordered when he had visualized this hurried retreat. It was lower than waist-high, hurriedly put together with rocks and fish-barrels full of stones. The hurrying mob poured over it, Hornblower, last of all, gathering himself together and leaping over it, arms and legs flying, to stumble on the far side and regain his footing by a miracle.

'*Hotspur*'s marines! Line the barricade. Get into the boats, you others!'

Twelve marines knelt at the barricade; twelve muskets levelled themselves over it. At the sight of them the pursuing French hesitated, tried to halt.

'Aim low!' shouted the marine lieutenant hoarsely.

'Go back and get the men into the boats, Mr What's-your-name,' snapped Hornblower. 'Have the launch ready to cast off, while you shove off in the yawl and get away.'

The French were coming forward again; Hornblower looked back and saw the lieutenant drop off the jetty on the heels of the last marine.

'Now sergeant. Let 'em have it.'

'Fire!' said the sergeant.

That was a good volley, but there was not a moment to admire it.

'Come on!' yelled Hornblower. 'Over to the launch!'

With the weight of *Hotspur*'s marines leaping into it the launch was drifting away by the time he was at the edge; there was a yard of black water for Hornblower to leap over, but his feet reached the gunnel and he pitched forward among the men clustered there; he luckily remembered to drop Côtard's sword so that he fell harmlessly into the bottom of the boat without wounding anyone. Oars and boathook thrust against the jetty and the launch surged away while Hornblower scrambled into the stern sheets. He almost stepped on Côtard's face; Côtard was lying apparently unconscious on the bottom boards.

Now the oars were grinding in the rowlocks. They were twenty yards away, thirty yards away, before the first Frenchmen came yelling along the jetty, to stand dancing with rage and excitement on the very edge of the masonry. For an invaluable second or two they even forgot the muskets in their hands. In the launch the huddled men raised their voices in a yell of derision that excited Hornblower's cold rage.

'Silence! Silence, all of you!'

The stillness that fell on the launch was more unpleasant than the noise. One or two muskets banged off on the jetty, and Hornblower, looking over his shoulder, saw a French soldier drop on one knee and take deliberate aim, saw him choose a target, saw the musket barrel foreshorten until the muzzle was pointed directly at him. He was wildly contemplating throwing himself down into the bottom of the boat when the musket went off. He felt a violent jar through his body, and realized with relief that the bullet had buried itself in the solid oak transom of the launch against which he was sitting. He recovered his wits; looking forward he saw Hewitt trying to force his way aft to his side and he spoke to him as calmly as his excitement permitted.

'Hewitt! Get for'ard to the gun. It's loaded with grape. Fire when it bears.' Then he spoke to the oarsmen and to Cargill at the tiller. 'Hard-a-port. Starboard-side oars, back water.'

The launch turned her clumsy length.

'Port side, back water.'

The launch ceased to turn; she was pointed straight at the jetty, and Hewitt, having shoved the other men aside, was cold-bloodedly looking along the sights of the four-pounder carronade mounted in the bows, fiddling with the elevating coign. Then he leaned over to one side and pulled the lanyard. The whole boat jerked sternwards abruptly with the recoil, as though when under way she had struck a rock, and the smoke came back round them in a sullen pall.

'Give way, starboard side! Pull! Hard-a-starboard!' The boat turned ponderously. 'Give way, port side!'

Nine quarter-pound grape-shot balls had swept through the group on the jetty; there were struggling figures, quiescent figures, lying there. Bonaparte had a quarter of a million soldiers under arms, but he had now lost some of them. It could not be called a drop out of the bucketful, but perhaps a molecule. Now they were out of musket shot, and Hornblower turned to Cargill in the stern sheets beside him.

'You managed your part of the business well enough, Mr Cargill.'

'Thank you, sir.'

Cargill had been appointed by Hornblower to land with the marines and to take charge of the boats and prepare them for the evacuation.

'But it might have been better if you'd sent the launch away first and kept the yawl back until the last. Then the launch could have lain off and covered the others with her gun.'

'I thought of that, sir. But I couldn't be sure until the last moment how many men would be coming down in the last group. I had to keep the launch for that.'

'Maybe you're right,' said Hornblower, grudgingly, and then, his sense of justice prevailing, 'In fact I'm sure you're right.'

'Thank you, sir,' said Cargill again, and, after a pause, 'I wish you had let me come with you, sir.'

Some people had queer tastes, thought Hornblower bitterly to himself, having regard to Côtard lying unconscious with a shattered arm at their feet, but he had to smooth down ruffled feelings in these touchy young men thirsting for honour and for the promotion that honour might bring.

'Use your wits, man,' he said, bracing himself once more to think logically. 'Someone had to be in charge on the jetty, and you were the best man for the job.'

'Thank you, sir,' said Cargill all over again, but still wistfully, and therefore still idiotically.

A sudden thought struck Hornblower, and he turned and stared back over his shoulder. He actually had to look twice, although he knew what he was looking for. The silhouette of the hills had changed. Then he saw a wisp of black smoke still rising from the summit. The semaphore was gone. The towering thing that had spied on their movements and had reported every disposition of the Inshore Squadron was no more. Trained British seamen and riggers and carpenters could not replace it – if they had such a job to do – in less than a week's work. Probably the French would take two weeks at least; his own estimate would be three.

And there was *Hotspur* waiting for them, maintopsail aback, as he had seen her half an hour ago; half an hour that seemed like a week. The lobster-boat and the yawl were already going round to her port side, and Cargill steered for her starboard side; in these calm waters and with such a gentle wind there was no need for the boats to be offered a lee.

'Oars!' said Cargill, and the launch ran alongside, and there was Bush looking down on them from close overhead. Hornblower seized the entering-ropes and swung himself up. It was his right as captain to go first, and it was also his duty. He cut Bush's congratulations short.

'Get the wounded out as quick as you can, Mr Bush. Send a stretcher down for Mr Côtard.'

'Is he wounded, sir?'

'Yes.' Hornblower had no desire to enter into unnecessary explanations. 'You'll have to lash him to it and then sway the stretcher up with a whip from the yardarm. His arm's in splinters.'

'Aye aye, sir.' Bush by now had realized that Hornblower was in no conversational mood.

'The surgeon's ready?'

'He's started work, sir.'

A wave of Bush's hand indicated a couple of wounded men who had come on board from the yawl and were being supported below.

'Very well.'

Hornblower headed for his cabin; no need to explain that he had his report to write; no need to make excuses. But as always after action he yearned for the solitude of his cabin even more than he yearned to sink down and forget his weariness. But at the second step he pulled up short. This was not a neat clean end to the venture. No peace for him at the moment, and he swore to himself under this final strain, using filthy black blasphemies such as he rarely employed.

He would have to deal with Grimes, and instantly. He must make up his mind about what he should do. Punish him? Punish a man for being a coward? That would be like punishing a man for having red hair. Hornblower stood first on one foot and then on the other, unable to pace, yet striving to goad his weary mind to further action. Punish Grimes for showing cowardice? That was more to the point. Not that it would do Grimes any good, but it would deter other men from showing cowardice. There were officers who would punish, not in the interests of discipline, but because they thought punishment should be inflicted in payment for crime, as sinners had to go to Hell. Hornblower would not credit himself with the divine authority some officers thought natural.

But he would have to act. He thought of the court martial. He would be the sole witness, but the court would know he was speaking the truth. His word would decide Grimes' fate, and then – the hangman's noose, or at the very least five hundred lashes, with Grimes screaming in pain until he should fall unconscious, to be nursed round for another day of torture, and another after that, until he was a gibbering idiot with neither mind nor strength left.

Hornblower hated the thought. But he remembered that the crew must have already guessed. Grimes must have already started his punishment, and yet the discipline of the *Hotspur* must be preserved. Hornblower would have to do his duty; he must pay one of the penalties for being a naval officer, just as he suffered seasickness – just as he risked his life. He would have Grimes put under arrest at once, and while Grimes was spending twenty-four hours in irons he could make up his mind to the final decision. He strode aft to his cabin, with all relief gone from the thought of relaxation.

Then he opened the door, and there was no problem left; only horror, further horror. Grimes hung there, from a rope threaded through the hook that supported the lamp. He was swaying with the gentle motion of the ship, his feet dragging on the deck so that even his knees were almost on the deck too. There was a blackened face and protruding tongue – actually there was no likeness to Grimes at all in the horrible thing hanging there. Grimes had not the courage to face the landing operation, but when the realization had come to him, when the crew had displayed their feelings, he had yet had the determination to do this thing, to submit himself to this slow strangulation, falling with a small preliminary jerk from a cramped position crouching on the cot.

In all the crew of the *Hotspur* Grimes had been the one man who as captain's steward could find the necessary privacy to do this thing. He had foreseen the flogging or the hanging, he had suffered the scorn of his shipmates; there was bitter irony in the thought that the semaphore station which he had feared to attack had turned out to be defended by a helpless civilian and his wife.

Hotspur rolled gently on the swell, and as she rolled the lolling head and the dangling arms swayed in unison, and the feet scraped over the deck. Hornblower shook off the horror that had seized him, drove himself to be clear-headed once more despite his fatigue and his disgust. He went to the door of the cabin; it was excusable that no sentry had yet been reposted there, seeing that the *Hotspur*'s marines had only just come on board.

'Pass the word for Mr Bush,' he said.

Within a minute Bush hurried in, to pull up short as soon as he saw the thing.

'I'll have that removed at once, if you please, Mr Bush. Put it over the side. Give it a burial, Christian burial, if you like.'

'Aye aye, sir.'

Bush shut his mouth after his formal statement of compliance. He could see that Hornblower was in even less a conversational mood in this cabin than he had been when on deck. Hornblower passed into the chart room and squeezed himself into the chair, and sat still, his hands motionless on the table. Almost immediately he heard the arrival of the working party Bush had sent. He heard loud amazed voices, and something like a laugh, all instantly repressed when they realized that he was next door. The voices died to hoarse whispers. There was a clump or two, and then a dragging noise and he knew the thing was gone.

Then he got to his feet to carry out the resolution formed during his recent clarity of mind. He walked firmly into the cabin, a little like someone unwillingly going into a duel. He did not want to; he hated this place, but in a tiny ship like *Hotspur* he had nowhere else to go. He would have to grow used to it. He put aside the weak thought that he could move himself into one of the screened-off cabins in the 'tween decks, and send, for instance, the warrant officers up here. That would occasion endless inconvenience, and – even more important – endless comment as well. He had to use this place and the longer he contemplated the prospect the less inviting it would be. And he was so tired he could hardly stand. He approached the cot; a mental picture developed in his mind's eye of Grimes kneeling on it, rope round his neck, to pitch himself off. He forced himself coldly to accept that picture, as something in the past. This was the present, and he dropped on to the cot, shoes on his feet, cutlass-sheath at his side, sandbag in his pocket. Grimes was not present to help him with those.

Hornblower had written the address, the date, and the word 'Sir' before he realized that the report would not be so easy to write. He was quite sure that this letter would appear in the *Gazette*, but he had been sure of that from the moment he had faced the writing of it. It would be a '*Gazette* Letter', one of the few, out of the many hundreds of reports coming into the Admiralty, selected for publication, and it would be his first appearance in print. He had told himself that he would simply write a standard straightforward report along the time-honoured lines, yet now he had to stop and think, although stage fright had nothing to do with it. The publication of this letter meant that it would be read by the whole world. It would be read by the whole Navy, which meant that his subordinates would read it, and he knew, only too well, how every careless word would be scanned and weighed by touchy individuals.

Much more important still; it would be read by all England, and that meant that Maria would read it. It would open a peephole into his life that so far she had never been able to look through. From the point of view of his standing with the Navy it might be desirable to let the dangers he had undergone be apparent, in a modest sort of way, but that would be in direct contradiction of the breezy light-hearted letter he intended to write to Maria. Maria was a shrewd little person, and he could not deceive her; to read the *Gazette* letter after his letter would excite her mistrust and apprehension at a moment when she was carrying what might well be the heir to the Hornblower name, with possibly the worst effects both on Maria and on the child.

He faced the choice, and it had to be in favour of Maria. He would make light of his difficulties and dangers, and even then he could still hope that the Navy would read between the lines that which Maria in her ignorance would not guess at. He redipped his pen, and bit the end in a momentary mental debate as to whether all the *Gazette* Letters he had read had been written in the face of similar difficulties, and decided that was probably true of the majority. Well, it had to be written. There was no avoiding it – for that matter there was no postponing it. The necessary preliminary words, 'In accordance with your orders' set him off, started the flow. He had to remember all that he had to put in. 'Mr William Bush, my first lieutenant, very handsomely volunteered his services, but I directed him to remain in command of the ship.' Later on it was no effort to write 'Lieut Charles Côtard, of HMS *Marlborough*, who had volunteered for the expedition, gave invaluable assistance as a result of his knowledge of the French language. I regret very much to have to inform you that he received a wound which necessitated amputation, and his life is still in danger.' Then there was something else he had to put in. 'Mr' – what was his first name? – 'Mr Alexander Cargill, Master's Mate, was allotted by me the duty of superintending the re-embarkation, which he carried out very much to my satisfaction.' The next passage would satisfy Maria. 'The Telegraph

Station was seized by the party under my personal command without the slightest opposition, and was set on fire and completely destroyed after the confidential papers had been secured.' Intelligent naval officers would have a higher opinion of an operation carried through without loss of life than of one which cost a monstrous butcher's bill.

Now for the battery; he had to be careful about this. 'Captain Jones of the Royal Marines, having gallantly secured the battery, was unfortunately involved in the explosion of the magazine, and I much regret to have to report his death, while several other Royal Marines of his party are dead or missing.' One of them had been as useful dead as alive. Hornblower checked himself. He still could not bear to remember those minutes by the magazine door. He went on with his letter. 'Lieutenant Reid of the Royal Marines guarded the flank and covered the retreat with small loss. His conduct calls for my unreserved approbation.'

That was very true, and pleasant to write. So was the next passage. 'It is with much gratification that I can inform you that the battery is completely wrecked. The parapet is thrown down along with the guns, and the gun-carriages destroyed, as will be understood because not less than one ton of gunpowder was exploded in the battery.' There were four thirty-two-pounders in that battery. A single charge for one of these guns was ten pounds of powder, and the magazine, sunk deep below the parapets, must have contained charges for fifty rounds per gun as a minimum. A crater had been left where once the parapet stood.

Not much more to write now. 'The retreat was

effected in good order. I append the list of killed, wounded, and missing.' The rough list lay in front of him, and he proceeded to copy it out carefully; there were widows and bereaved parents who might derive consolation from the sight of those names in the *Gazette*. One seaman had been killed and several slightly wounded. He recorded their names and began a fresh paragraph. 'Royal Marines. Killed. Captain Henry Jones. Privates –' A thought struck him at this moment and he paused with his pen in the air. There was not only consolation in seeing a name in the *Gazette*; parents and widows could receive the back pay of the deceased and some small gratuity. He was still thinking when Bush came hurrying in the door.

'Cap'n, sir. I'd like to show you something from the deck.'

'Very well. I'll come.'

He paused for only a short while. There was a single name in the paragraph headed 'Seamen killed' – James Johnson, Ordinary Seaman. He added another name. 'John Grimes, Captain's Steward' and then he put down the pen and came out on deck.

'Look over there, sir,' said Bush, pointing eagerly ashore and proffering his telescope.

The landscape was still unfamiliar, with the semaphore gone and the battery – easily visible previously – replaced now by a mound of earth. But that was not what Bush was referring to. There was a considerable body of men on horseback riding along the slopes; through the telescope Hornblower could fancy he could detect plumes and gold lace.

'Those must be generals, sir,' said Bush excitedly,

'come out to see the damage. The commandant, and the governor, an' the chief engineer, an' all the rest of 'em. We're nearly in range now, sir. We could drop down without their noticing, run out the guns smartly, full elevation, and – we ought to hit a target that size with one shot in a broadside at least, sir.'

'I think we could,' agreed Hornblower. He looked up at the windvane and over at the shore. 'We could wear ship and –'

Bush waited for Hornblower to complete his speech, but the end never came.

'Shall I give the order, sir?'

There was another pause.

'No,' said Hornblower at last. 'Better not.'

Bush was too good a subordinate to protest, but his disappointment showed plainly enough, and it was necessary to soften the refusal with an explanation. They might kill a general, although the odds were that it would merely be an orderly dragoon. On the other hand they would be drawing most forcible attention to the present weakness of this portion of coast.

'Then they'll be bringing field batteries,' went on Hornblower. 'Only nine-pounders, but –'

'Yes, sir. They might be a nuisance,' said Bush in reluctant agreement. 'Do you have anything in mind, sir?'

'Not me. Him,' said Hornblower. All operations of the Inshore Squadron were Pellew's responsibility and should be to Pellew's credit. He pointed towards the Inshore Squadron where Pellew's broad pendant flew.

But the broad pendant was to fly there no longer. The boat that took Hornblower's report to the *Tonnant* returned not only with stores but with official despatches.

'Sir,' said Orrock, after handing them over, 'the Commodore sent a man with me from the *Tonnant* who carries a letter for you.'

'Where is he?'

He seemed a very ordinary sort of seaman, dressed in the standard clothes of the slop chest. His thick blond pigtail, as he stood hat in hand, indicated that he had long been a seaman. Hornblower took the letter and broke the seal.

My dear Hornblower,

It is with infinite pain to myself that I have to confirm the news, conveyed to you in the official despatches, that your latest report will also be the last that I shall have the pleasure of reading. My flag has come, and I shall hoist it as Rear-Admiral commanding the squadron assembling for the blockade of Rochefort. Rear-Admiral Wm Parker will take over the command of the Inshore Squadron and I have recommended you to him in the strongest terms although your actions speak even more strongly for you. But commanding officers are likely to have their favourites, men with whom they are personally acquainted. We can hardly quarrel on this score, seeing that I have indulged myself in a favourite whose initials are HRH! Now let us leave this subject for another even more personal.

I noted in your report that you have had the misfortune to lose your steward, and I take the liberty to send you James Doughty as a substitute. He was steward of the late Captain Stevens of the Magnificent, and he has been persuaded to volunteer for the Hotspur. I understand that he has had much practical experience in attending to gentlemen's needs, and I hope you will find him suitable

and that he will look after you for many years. If during
that time you are reminded of me by his presence I shall
be well satisfied.

    Your sincere friend,
    Ed. Pellew

Even with all his quickness of mind it took Hornblower a little while to digest the manifold contents of his letter after reading it. It was all bad news; bad news about the change of command, and just as bad, although in a different way, that he was being saddled with a gentleman's gentleman who would sneer at his domestic arrangements. Yet if there was anything that a naval career taught anybody, it was to be philosophic about drastic changes.

'Doughty?' said Hornblower.

'Sir.'

Doughty looked respectful, but there might be something quizzical in his glance.

'You're going to be my servant. Do your duty and you have nothing to fear.'

'Yes, sir. No, sir.'

'You've brought your dunnage?'

'Aye aye, sir.'

'The First Lieutenant will detail someone to show you where to sling your hammock. You'll share a berth with my clerk.'

The captain's steward was the only ordinary seaman in the ship who did not have to sleep in the tiers.

'Aye aye, sir.'

'Then you can take up your duties.'

'Aye aye, sir.'

It was only a few minutes later that Hornblower, in his cabin, looked up to find a silent figure slipping in through the door; Doughty knew that as a personal servant he did not knock if the sentry told him the captain was alone.

'Have you had your dinner, sir?'

It took a moment to answer that question, at the end of a broken day following an entirely sleepless night. During that moment Doughty looked respectfully over Hornblower's left shoulder. His eyes were a startling blue.

'No, I haven't. You'd better see about something for me,' replied Hornblower.

'Yes, sir.'

The blue eyes looked round the cabin and found nothing.

'No. There are no cabin stores. You'll have to go to the galley. Mr Simmonds will find something for me.' The ship's cook, as a warrant officer, rated the 'Mr' in front of his name. 'No. Wait. There are two lobsters somewhere in this ship. You'll find 'em in a barrel of seawater somewhere on the booms. And that reminds me. Your predecessor has been dead for nearly twenty-four hours and that water hasn't been changed. You must do that. Go to the officer of the watch with my compliments and ask him to put the wash-deck pump to work on it. That'll keep one lobster alive while I have the other.'

'Yes, sir. Or you could have this one hot tonight and the other one cold tomorrow if I boil them both now, sir.'

'I could,' agreed Hornblower without committing himself.

'Mayonnaise,' said Doughty. 'Are there any eggs in this ship, sir? Any salad oil?'

'No there are not!' rasped Hornblower. 'There are no cabin stores whatever in this ship except those two damned lobsters.'

'Yes, sir. Then I'll serve this one with drawn butter and I'll see what I can do tomorrow, sir.'

'Do whatever you damned well like and don't trouble me,' said Hornblower.

He was working into a worse and worse temper. He not only had to storm batteries but he also had to remember about keeping lobsters alive. And Pellew was leaving the Brest fleet; the official orders he had just read gave details about salutes to the new flags tomorrow. And tomorrow this damned Doughty and his damned mayonnaise, whatever that was, would be pawing over his patched shirts.

'Yes, sir,' said Doughty, and disappeared as quietly as he had entered.

Hornblower went out on deck to pace off his bad temper. The first breath of the delightful evening air helped to soothe him; so too, did the hurried movement of everyone on the quarterdeck over to the lee side so as to leave the weather side to him. For him there was as much space as heart could desire – five long strides forward and aft – but all the other officers had now to take the air under crowded conditions. Let 'em. He had to write out his report to Pellew three times, the original draft, the fair copy, and the copy in his confidential letter book. Some captains gave that work to their clerks, but Hornblower would not do so. Captain's clerks made a practice of exploiting their confidential position; there were officers in the ship who would be glad to hear what their captain said about them, and what the future plans might be. Martin would never have the chance. He could confine himself to muster-rolls and returns of stores and the other nuisances that plagued a captain's life.

Now Pellew was leaving them, and that was a disaster. Earlier today Hornblower had actually allowed his mind to dally with the notion that some day he might know the inexpressible joy of being 'made Post', of being promoted to Captain. That called for the strongest influence, in the Fleet and in the Admiralty. With Pellew's transfer he had lost a friend in the Fleet. With Parry's retirement he had lost a friend in the Admiralty – he did not know a single soul there. His promotion to Commander had been a fantastic stroke of luck. When *Hotspur* should be paid off there were three hundred ambitious young Commanders all with uncles and cousins and all anxious to take his place. He could find himself rotting on the beach on half-pay. With Maria. With Maria and the child. The reverse side of the penny was no more attractive than the front.

This was not the way to work off the gloom that threatened to engulf him. He had written Maria a letter to be proud of, reassuring, cheerful, and as loving as he had found it possible to make it. Over there was Venus, shining out in the evening sky. This sea air was stimulating, refreshing, delightful. Surely this was a better world than his drained nervous condition allowed him to believe. It took a full hour of pacing to convince him fully of this. At the end of that time the comfortably monotonous exercise had slowed down his overactive mind. He was healthily tired now, and the moment he thought about it he knew he was ravenously hungry. He had seen Doughty flitting about the deck more than once, for however lost in distraction Hornblower might be he nevertheless took instant note, consciously or subconsciously, of everything that went on in the ship. He was growing desperately impatient, and night had entirely closed in, when his pacing was intercepted.

'Your dinner's ready, sir.'

Doughty stood respectfully in front of him.

'Very well. I'll come.'

Hornblower sat himself down at the chart room table, Doughty standing at his chair in the cramped space.

'One moment, sir, while I bring your dinner from the galley. May I pour you some cider, sir?'

'Pour me some . . . ?'

But Doughty was already pouring from jug to cup, and then he vanished. Hornblower tasted gingerly. There was no doubt about it, it was excellent cider, rough and yet refined, fruity and yet in no way sweet. After water months in cask it was heavenly. He only took two preliminary sips before his head went back and the whole cupful shot delightfully down his throat. He had not begun to debate this curious phenomenon when Doughty slipped into the chart room again.

'The plate is hot, sir,' he said.

'What the devil's this?' asked Hornblower.

'Lobster cutlets, sir,' said Doughty, pouring more cider, and then, with a gesture not quite imperceptible, he indicated the wooden saucer he had laid on the table at the same time. 'Butter sauce, sir.'

Extraordinary. There were neat brown cutlets on his plate that bore no outward resemblance to lobster, but when Hornblower cautiously added sauce and tasted, the result was excellent. Minced lobster. And when Doughty took the cover off the cracked vegetable dish there was a dream of delight revealed. New potatoes, golden and lovely. He helped himself hurriedly and very nearly burned his mouth on them. Nothing could be quite as nice as the first new potatoes of the year.

'These came with the ship's vegetables, sir,' explained Doughty. 'I was in time to save them.'

Hornblower did not need to ask from what those new potatoes had been saved. He knew a good deal about Huffnell the purser, and he could guess at the appetite of the wardroom mess. Lobster cutlets and new potatoes and this pleasant butter sauce; he was enjoying his dinner, resolutely putting aside the knowledge that the ship's biscuit in the bread barge was weevily. He was used to weevils, which always showed up after the first month at sea, or earlier if the biscuit had been long in store. He told himself as he took another mouthful of lobster cutlet that he would not allow a weevil in his biscuit to be a fly in his ointment.

He took another pull at the cider before he remembered to ask where it came from.

'I pledged your credit for it, sir,' said Doughty. 'I took the liberty of doing so, to the extent of a quarter of a pound of tobacco.'

'Who had it?'

'Sir,' said Doughty, 'I promised not to say.'

'Oh, very well,' said Hornblower.

There was only one source for cider – the *Camilla,*

the lobster-boat he had seized last night. Of course the Breton fishermen who manned it would have a keg on board, and somebody had looted it; Martin, his clerk, most likely.

'I hope you bought the whole keg,' said Hornblower.

'Only some of it, I am afraid, sir. All that remained.'

Out of a two-gallon keg of cider – Hornblower hoped it might be more – Martin could hardly have downed more than a gallon in twenty-four hours. And Doughty must have noted the presence of a keg in the berth he shared with Martin; Hornblower was quite sure that more pressure than the offer of a mere quarter of a pound of tobacco had been applied to make Martin part with the keg, but he did not care.

'Cheese, sir,' said Doughty; Hornblower had eaten everything else in sight.

And the cheese – the ration cheese supplied for the ship's company – was reasonably good, and the butter was fresh; a new firkin must have come in the boat and Doughty must somehow have got at it although the rancid previous assignment had not been used up. The cider jug was empty and Hornblower felt more comfortable than he had felt for days.

'I'll go to bed now,' he announced.

'Yes, sir.'

Doughty opened the chart room door and Hornblower passed into his cabin. The lamp swayed from the deck beam. The patched nightshirt was laid out on the cot. Perhaps it was because he was full of cider that Hornblower did not resent Doughty's presence as he brushed his teeth and made ready for bed. Doughty was at hand to take his coat as he pulled it off; Doughty retrieved his trousers when he let them fall; Doughty hovered by as he dropped into bed and pulled the blankets over him.

'I'll brush this coat, sir. Here's your bed gown if you're called in the night, sir. Shall I put out the lamp, sir?'

'Yes.'

'Good night, sir.'

It was not until next morning that Hornblower remembered again that Grimes had hanged himself in this cabin. It was not until next morning that he remembered those minutes down in the magazine with the gunpowder. Doughty had already proved his worth.

12

The salutes had been fired. Pellew's flag had been hoisted and then the *Tonnant* had sailed away to initiate the blockade of Rochefort. The *Dreadnought* had hoisted Admiral Parker's flag, and each flag had received thirteen guns from every ship. The French on their hillsides must have seen the smoke and heard the firing, and the naval officers among them must have deduced that one more rear-admiral had joined the Channel Fleet; and must have shaken their heads a little sadly at this further proof that the British Navy was increasing its lead over the French in the race to build up maritime strength.

Hornblower, peering up the Goulet, over the black shapes of the Little Girls, could count the vessels of war swinging to their anchors in Brest Roads. Eighteen ships of the line now, and seven frigates, but with sub-minimum crews and incomplete stores; no match for the fifteen superb ships of the line under Cornwallis who waited for them outside, growing daily in efficiency and in moral ascendancy. Nelson off Toulon and now Pellew off Rochefort similarly challenged inferior French squadrons, and under their protection the merchant fleets of Britain sailed the seas unmolested except by privateers – and the merchant fleet themselves, bunched in vast convoys, received constant close cover from further British squadrons of a total strength even exceeding that of the blockading fleets. Cordage and hemp, timber and iron and copper, turpentine and salt, cotton and nitre, could all flow freely to the British Isles and be as freely distributed round them, maintaining the ship yards in constant activity, whilst the French yards were doomed to idleness, to the gangrene that follows the cutting off of the circulation.

But the situation was nevertheless not without peril. Along the Channel Coast Bonaparte had two hundred thousand soldiers, the most formidable army in the world, and collecting in the Channel Ports, from St Malo to Ostend and beyond was a flotilla of seven thousand flat-bottomed boats. Admiral Keith with his frigates, backed by a few ships of the line, held the Channel secure against Bonaparte's threat; there was no chance of invasion as long as England held naval command of the Channel.

Yet in a sense that command was precarious. If the eighteen ships of the line in Brest Roads could escape, could round Ushant and come up-Channel with Cornwallis distracted in some fashion, Keith might be driven away, might be destroyed. Three days would be sufficient to put Bonaparte's army into the boats and across the Channel, and Bonaparte would be issuing decrees from Windsor Castle as he had already done from Milan and Brussels. Cornwallis and his squadron, *Hotspur* and her mightier colleagues, were what made this impossible; a moment of carelessness, a misjudged movement, and the tricolour might fly over the Tower of London.

Hornblower counted the ships in Brest Roads, and as he did so he was very conscious that this morning routine was the ultimate, most insolent expression of the power of England at sea. England had a heart, a brain, an arm, and he and *Hotspur* were the final sensitive fingertip of that long arm. Nineteen ships of the line at anchor, two of them three-deckers. Seven frigates. They were the ones he had observed yesterday. Nothing had contrived to slip out unnoticed during the night, by the passage of the Four or the Raz.

'Mr Foreman! Signal to the Flag, if you please. "Enemy at anchor. Situation unchanged."'

Foreman had made that signal several times before, but, while Hornblower watched him unobtrusively, he checked the numbers in the signal book. It was Foreman's business to know all the thousand arbitrary signals off by heart, but it was best, when time allowed, that he should corroborate what his memory told him. An error of a digit might send the warning that the enemy was coming out.

'Flag acknowledges, sir,' reported Foreman.

'Very well.'

Poole, as officer of the watch, made note of the incident in the rough log. The hands were washing down the deck, the sun was lifting over the horizon. It was a beautiful day, with every promise of being a day like any other.

'Seven bells, sir,' reported Prowse.

Only half an hour more of the ebb; time to withdraw from this lee shore before the flood set in.

'Mr Poole! Wear the ship, if you please. Course west by north.'

'Good morning, sir.'

'Good morning, Mr Bush.'

Bush knew better than to indulge in further

conversation, besides, he could devote his attention to watching how smartly the hands braced the maintopsail round, and to how Poole handled the ship when the topsails filled. Hornblower swept the northern shore, seeking as ever for any signs of change. His attention was concentrated on the ridge beyond which Captain Jones had met his death, when Poole reported again.

'Wind's come westerly, sir. Can't make west by north.'

'Make it west nor'west,' replied Hornblower, his eye still to the telescope.

'Aye aye, sir. West nor'west, full and bye.' There was a hint of relief in Poole's voice; an officer is likely to be apprehensive when he has to tell his captain that the last order was impossible to execute.

Hornblower was aware that Bush had taken his stand beside him with his telescope trained in the same direction.

'A column of troops, sir,' said Bush.

'Yes.'

Hornblower had detected the head of the column crossing the ridge. He was watching now to see to what length the column would stretch. It continued interminably over the ridge, appearing through his glass like some caterpillar hurrying over the even rougher hillside. Ah! There was the explanation. Beside the caterpillar appeared a string of ants, hurrying even faster along the path. Field artillery – six guns and limbers with a wagon bringing up the rear. The head of the caterpillar was already over the farther ridge before the tail appeared over the nearer one. That was a column of infantry more than a mile long, five thousand men or more – a division of infantry with its attendant battery. It might be merely a portion of the garrison of Brest turning out for exercises and manoeuvres on the hillside, but its movements were somewhat more hurried and purposeful than would be expected in that case.

He swept his glass farther round the coast, and then checked it with a start and a gulp of excitement. There were the unmistakable lugsails of a French coaster coming round the bold headland of Point Matthew. There was another pair – a whole cluster. Could it possibly be that a group of coasters was trying to run the blockade into Brest in broad daylight in the teeth of *Hotspur*? Hardly likely. Now there was a bang – bang – bang of guns, presumably from the field battery, invisible over the farther ridge. Behind the coasters appeared a British frigate, and then another, showing up at the moment when the coasters began to go about; as the coasters tacked they revealed that they had no colours flying.

'Prizes, sir. And that's *Naiad* an' *Doris*,' said Bush.

The two British frigates must have swooped down during the night by the passage of the Four inshore of Ushant and cut out these coasters from the creeks of Le Conquet where they had been huddled for shelter. A neat piece of work, undoubtedly, but bringing them out had only been made possible by the destruction of the battery on the Petit Minou. The frigates tacked in the wake of the coasters, like shepherd dogs following a flock of sheep. They were escorting their prizes in triumph back to the Inshore Squadron, whence, presumably they would be dispatched to England for sale. Bush had taken his telescope from his eye and had turned his gaze full on Hornblower, while Prowse came up to join them.

'Six prizes, sir,' said Bush.

'A thousand pound each, those coasters run, sir,' said Prowse. 'More, if it's naval stores, and I expect it is. Six thousand pound. Seven thousand. An' no trouble selling 'em, sir.'

By the terms of the royal proclamation issued on the declaration of war, prizes taken by the Royal Navy became – as was traditional by now – the absolute property of the captors.

'And we weren't in sight, sir,' said Bush.

The proclamation also laid down the proviso that the value of the prizes, after a deduction for flag officers, should be shared among those ships in sight at the moment the colours came down or possession was secured.

'We couldn't expect to be,' said Hornblower. He was honestly implying that *Hotspur* was too preoccupied with her duty of watching the Goulet, but the others misinterpreted the speech.

'No, sir, not with –' Bush broke off what he was saying before he became guilty of mutiny. He had been about to continue 'not with Admiral Parker in command' but he had more sense than to say it, after Hornblower's meaning had become clear to him.

'One eighth'd be nigh on a thousand pounds,' said Prowse.

An eighth of the prizes was, by the proclamation, to be divided among the lieutenants and masters taking part in the capture of the ships. Hornblower was making a different calculation. The share of the captains was two-eighths; if *Hotspur* had been associated in the venture with *Naiad* and *Doris* he would have been richer by five hundred pounds.

'And it was us that opened the way for 'em, sir,' went on Prowse.

'It was you, sir, who –' Bush broke off his speech for the second time.

'That's the fortune of war,' said Hornblower, lightly. 'Or the misfortune of war.'

Hornblower was quite convinced that the whole system of prize money was vicious, and tended towards making the navy less effective in war. He told himself that this was sour grapes, that he would think differently if he had won great amounts of prize money, but that did not soften his present conviction.

'For'ard, there!' yelled Poole from beside the binnacle. 'Get the lead going in the mainchains.'

The three senior officers beside the hammock nettings came back to the present world with a general start. Hornblower felt a chill wave of horror over his ribs as he realized his inexcusable carelessness. He had forgotten all about the course he had set. *Hotspur* was sailing tranquilly into peril, was in danger of running aground, and it was his fault, the result of his own inattention. He had no time for self-reproach at the present moment, all the same. He lifted his voice, trying to pitch it steadily.

'Thank you, Mr Poole,' he called. 'Belay that order. Put the ship on the other tack, if you please.'

Bush and Prowse were wearing guilty, hangdog looks. It had been their duty, it had been Prowse's particular duty, to warn him when *Hotspur* was running into navigational dangers. They would not meet his eye; they tried to assume a pose of exaggerated interest in Poole's handling of the ship as she went about. The yards creaked as she came round, the sails flapped and then drew again, the wind blew on their faces from a different angle.

'Hard-a-lee!' ordered Poole, completing the manoeuvre. 'Foretack! Haul the bowlines!'

Hotspur settled down on her new course, away from the dangerous shore to which she had approached too close, and all danger was averted.

'You see, gentlemen,' said Hornblower coldly, and he waited until he had the full attention of Bush and Prowse. 'You see, there are many disadvantages about the system of prize money. I am aware now of a new one, and I hope you are too. Thank you, that will do.'

He remained by the hammock netting as they slunk away; he was taking himself to task. It was his first moment of carelessness in a professional career of ten years. He had made mistakes through ignorance, through recklessness, but never carelessness before. If there had been a fool as officer of the watch just now utter ruin would have been possible. If *Hotspur* had gone aground, in clear weather and a gentle breeze, it would have been the end of everything for him. Court martial and dismissal from the service, and then . . . ? In his bitter self-contempt he told himself that he would not be capable even of begging his bread, to say nothing of Maria's. He might perhaps ship before the mast, and with his clumsiness and abstraction he would be the victim of the cat, of the boatswain's rattan. Death would be better. He shuddered with cold.

Now he turned his attention to Poole, standing impassive by the binnacle. What had been the motives that had impelled him to order the lead into use? Had it been mere precaution, or had it been a tactful way of calling his captain's attention to the situation of the ship? His present manner and bearing gave no hint of the answer. Hornblower had studied his officers carefully since *Hotspur* was commissioned; he was not aware of any depths of ingenuity or tact in Poole, but he freely admitted to himself that they might exist, unobserved. In any case, he must allow for them. He sauntered down the quarterdeck.

'Thank you, Mr Poole,' he said, slowly and very distinctly.

Poole touched his hat in reply, but his homely face did not change its expression. Hornblower walked on, nettled – amused – that his questions remained unanswered. It was a momentary relief from the torments of conscience which still plagued him.

The lesson he had learned remained with him during that summer to trouble his conscience. Otherwise during those golden months the blockade of Brest might have been for *Hotspur* and Hornblower a yachting holiday with a certain macabre quality. Just as some lay theologians advanced the theory that in Hell sinners would be punished by being forced to repeat, in unutterable tedium and surfeit, the sins they had committed during life, so Hornblower spent those delightful months doing delightful things until he felt he could not do them any longer. Day after day, and night after night, through the finest summer in human memory, *Hotspur* cruised in the approaches to Brest. She pressed up to the Goulet with the last of the flood, and cannily withdrew in to safety with the last of the ebb. She counted the French fleet, she reported the result of her observations to Admiral Parker. She drifted, hove-to, over calm seas amid gentle breezes. With westerly winds she worked her way out to give the lee shore a wide berth; with easterly winds she beat back again to beard the impotent French in their safe harbour.

They were months of frightful peril for England, with the Grande Armee, two hundred thousand strong, poised within thirty miles of the Kentish beaches, but they were months of tranquillity for *Hotspur*, even with a score of hostile battleships in sight. There were occasional flurries when the coasters tried too boldly to enter or leave; there were occasional busy moments when squalls came down and topsails had to be reefed. There were encounters after dark with fishing vessels, conversations over a glass of rum with the Breton captains, purchases of crabs and lobsters and pilchards – and of the latest decree of the Inscription Maritime, or of a week-old copy of the *Moniteur*.

Hornblower's telescope revealed ant-like hordes of workmen rebuilding the blown-up batteries, and for a couple of weeks he watched the building of scaffolding and the erection of sheers on the Petit Minou, and, for three continuous days, as a result, the slow elevation to the vertical of the new mast of the semaphore station. The subsequent days added horizontal and vertical arms; before the summer was over those arms were whirling about reporting once more the movements of the blockading squadron.

Much good might that do the French, huddled in their anchored ships in the Roads. Inertia and a sense of inferiority would work their will on the unfortunate crews. The ships ready for sea might slowly increase in number; men might slowly be found for them, but every day the balance of fighting quality, of naval power, swung faster and faster over in favour of the British, constantly exercising at sea, and constantly reinforced by the seaborne tribute of the world.

There was a price to be paid; the dominion of the seas was not given free by destiny. The Channel Fleet paid in blood, in lives, as well as in the sacrifice of the freedom and leisure of every officer and man on board. There was a constant petty drain. Ordinary sickness took only small toll; among men in the prime of life isolated from the rest of the world illnesses were few, although it was noticeable that after the arrival of victualling ships from England epidemics of colds would sweep through the fleet, while rheumatism – the sailor's disease – was always present.

The losses were mainly due to other causes. There were men who, in a moment of carelessness or inattention, fell from the yards. There were the men who ruptured themselves, and they were many, for despite the ingenuity of blocks and tackles there were heavy weights to haul about by sheer manpower. There were crushed fingers and crushed feet when ponderous casks of salted provisions were lowered into boats from the storeships and hauled up on to the decks of the fighting ships. And frequently a lacerated limb would end – despite all the care of the surgeons – in gangrene, in amputation, and death. There were the careless men who, during target practice with the cannon, lost their arms by ramming a cartridge into an improperly sponged gun, or who did not remove themselves from the line of the recoil. Three times that year there were men who died in quarrels, when boredom changed to hysteria and knives were drawn; and on each of those occasions another life was lost, a life for a life, a hanging with the other ships clustered round and the crews lining the sides to learn what happened when a man lost his temper. And once the crews manned the sides to see what happened when a wretched young seaman paid the price for a crime worse even than murder – for raising his fist to his superior officer. Incidents of that sort were inevitable as the ships beat back and forth monotonously, over the eternal grey inhospitable sea.

It was as well for the *Hotspur* that she was under the command of a man to whom any form of idleness or monotony was supremely distasteful. The charts of the Iroise were notoriously inaccurate; *Hotspur* set herself to run line after line of soundings, to take series after series of careful triangulations from the headlands and hilltops. When the fleet ran short of silver sand, so necessary to keep the decks spotless white, it was *Hotspur* who supplied the deficiency, finding tiny lost beaches round the coast where a party could land – trespassing upon Bonaparte's vaunted dominion over Europe – to fill sacks with the precious commodity. There were fishing competitions, whereby the lower deck's rooted objection to fish as an item of diet was almost overcome; a prize of a pound of tobacco for the biggest catch by an individual mess set all the messes to work on devising more novel fish-hooks and baits. There were experiments in ship-handling, when obsolescent and novel methods were tested, when by careful and accurate measurement with the log the effect of goose-winging the topsails was ascertained; or, it being assumed that the rudder was lost, the watch-keeping officers tried their hands at manoeuvring the ship by the sails alone.

Hornblower himself found mental exercise in working out observations, and by their aid it was possible to arrive at an accurate determination of longitude – a subject of debate since the days of the Carthaginians – at the cost of endless calculations. Hornblower was determined to perfect himself in this method, and his officers and young gentlemen bewailed the decision, for they, too, had to make lunar observations and work out the resulting sums. The longitude of the Little Girls was calculated on board the *Hotspur* a hundred times that summer, with nearly a hundred different results.

To Hornblower it was a satisfactory occupation, the more satisfactory as it became obvious that he was acquiring the necessary knack. He tried to acquire the same facility in another direction, without the same satisfaction, as he wrote his weekly letters to Maria. There was only a limited number of endearments, only a limited number of ways of saying that he missed her, that he hoped her pregnancy was progressing favourably. There was only the one way of excusing himself for not returning to England as he had promised to do, and Maria was inclined to be a little peevish in her letters regarding the exigencies of the service.

When the water-hoys arrived periodically and the enormous labour had to be undertaken of transferring the already stale liquid into the *Hotspur* Hornblower always found himself thinking that getting those eighteen tons of water on board meant another month of writing letters to Maria.

13

Hotspur's bell struck two double strokes; it was six o'clock in the evening, and the first dogwatch had come to an end in the gathering darkness.

'Sunset, sir,' said Bush.

'Yes,' agreed Hornblower.

'Six o'clock exactly. The equinox, sir.'

'Yes,' agreed Hornblower again; he knew perfectly well what was coming.

'We'll have a westerly gale, sir, or my name's not William Bush.'

'Very likely,' said Hornblower, who had been sniffing the air all day long.

Hornblower was a heretic in this matter. He did not believe that the mere changing from a day a minute longer than twelve hours to one a minute shorter made gales blow from out of the west. Gales happened to blow at this time because winter was setting in, but ninety-nine men out of a hundred firmly believed in a more direct, although more mysterious causation.

'Wind's freshening and sea's getting up a bit, sir,' went on Bush, inexorably.

'Yes.'

Hornblower fought down the temptation to declare that it was not because the sun happened to set at six o'clock, for he knew that if he expressed such an opinion it would be received with the tolerant and concealed disagreement accorded to the opinions of children and eccentrics and captains.

'We've water for twenty-eight days, sir. Twenty-four allowing for spillage and ullage.'

'Thirty-six, on short allowance,' corrected Hornblower.

'Yes, sir,' said Bush, with a world of significance in those two syllables.

'I'll give the order within the week,' said Hornblower.

No gale could be expected to blow for a month continuously, but a second gale might follow the first before the water-hoys could beat down from Plymouth to refill the casks. It was a tribute to the organization set up by Cornwallis that during nearly six continuous months at sea *Hotspur* had not yet had to go on short allowance for water. Should it become necessary, it would be one more irksome worry brought about by the passage of time.

'Thank you, sir,' said Bush, touching his hat and going off about his business along the darkened reeling deck.

There were worries of all sorts. Yesterday morning Doughty had pointed out to Hornblower that there were holes appearing in the elbows of his uniform coat, and he only had two coats apart from full dress. Doughty had done a neat job of patching, but a search through the ship had not revealed any material of exactly the right weatherbeaten shade. Furthermore the seats of nearly all his trousers were paper-thin, and Hornblower did not fancy himself in the baggy slop-chest trousers issued to the lower deck; yet as that store was fast running out he had had to secure a pair for himself before they should all go. He was wearing his thick winter underclothing; three sets had appeared ample last April, but now he faced the prospect, in a gale, of frequent wettings to the skin with small chance of drying anything. He cursed himself and went off to try to make sure of some sleep in anticipation of a disturbed night. At least he had a good dinner inside him; Doughty had braised an oxtail, the most despised and rejected of all the portions of the weekly ration bullock, and had made of it a dish fit for a king. It might be his last good dinner for a long time if the gale lasted – winter affected land as well as sea, so that he could expect no other vegetables than potatoes and boiled cabbage until next spring.

His anticipation of a disturbed night proved correct. He had been awake for some time, feeling the lively motion of the *Hotspur* and trying to make up his mind to rise and dress or to shout for a light and try to read, when they came thundering on his door.

'Signal from the Flag, sir!'

'I'll come.'

Doughty was really the best of servants; he arrived at the same moment, with a storm lantern.

'You'll need your pea-jacket, sir, and oilskins over it. Your sou'wester, sir. Better have your scarf, sir, to keep your pea-jacket dry.'

A scarf round the neck absorbed spray that might otherwise drive in between sou'wester and oilskin coat and soak the pea-jacket. Doughty tucked Hornblower into his clothes like a mother preparing her son for school, while they reeled and staggered on the leaping deck. Then Hornblower went out into the roaring darkness.

'A white rocket and two blue lights from the Flag, sir,' reported Young. 'That means "take offshore stations".'

'Thank you. What sail have we set?' Hornblower could guess the answer by the feel of the ship, but he wanted to be sure. It was too dark for his dazzled eyes to see as yet.

'Double reefed tops'ls and main course, sir.'

'Get that course in and lay her on the port tack.'

'Port tack. Aye aye, sir.'

The signal for offshore stations meant a general withdrawal of the Channel Fleet. The main body took stations seventy miles to seaward off Brest, safe from that frightful lee shore and with a clear run open to them for Tor Bay – avoiding Ushant on the one hand and the Start on the other – should the storm prove so bad as to make it impossible to keep the sea. The Inshore Squadron was to be thirty miles closer in. They were the most weatherly ships and could afford the additional risk in order to be close up to Brest should a sudden shift of wind enable the French to get out.

But there was not merely the question of the French coming out, but of other French ships coming in. Out in the Atlantic there were more than one small French squadron – Bonaparte's own brother was on board one of them, with his American wife – seeking urgently to regain a French port before food and water should be completely exhausted. So *Naiad* and *Doris* and *Hotspur* had to stay close in, to intercept and report. They could best encounter the dangers of the situation. And they could best be spared if they could not. So *Hotspur* had to take her station only twenty miles to the west of

Ushant, where French ships running before the gale could be best expected to make their landfall.

Bush loomed up in the darkness, shouting over the gale.

'The equinox, just as I said, sir.'

'Yes.'

'It'll be worse before it's better, sir.'

'No doubt.'

Hotspur was close-hauled now, soaring, pitching, and rolling over the vast invisible waves that the gale was driving in upon her port bow. Hornblower felt resentfully that Bush was experiencing pleasure at this change of scene. A brisk gale and a struggle to windward was stimulating to Bush after long days of fair weather, while Hornblower struggled to keep his footing and felt a trifle doubtful about the behaviour of his stomach as a result of this sudden change.

The wind howled round them and the spray burst over the deck so that the black night was filled with noise. Hornblower held on to the hammock netting; the circus riders he had seen in his childhood, riding round the ring, standing upright on two horses with one foot on each, had no more difficult task than he had at present. And the circus riders were not smacked periodically in the face with bucketfuls of spray.

There were small variations in the violence of the wind. They could hardly be called gusts; Hornblower took note that they were increases in force without any corresponding decreases. Through the soles of his feet, through the palms of his hands, he was aware of a steady increase in *Hotspur's* heel and a steady stiffening in her reaction. She was showing too much canvas. With his mouth a yard from Young's ear he yelled his order.

'Four reefs in the tops'ls!'

'Aye aye, sir.'

The exaggerated noises of the night were complicated now with the shrilling of the pipes of the bos'n's mates; down in the waist the orders were bellowed at hurrying, staggering men.

'All hands reef tops'ls!'

The hands clawed their way to their stations; this was the moment when a thousand drills bore fruit, when men carried out in darkness and turmoil the duties that had been ingrained into them in easier conditions. Hornblower felt *Hotspur*'s momentary relief as Young set the topsails a-shiver to ease the tension on them. Now the men were going aloft to perform circus feats compared with which his maintenance of his foothold was a trifle. No trapeze artist ever had to do his work in utter darkness on something as unpredictable as a footrope in a gale, or had to exhibit the trained strength of the seaman passing the ear-ring while hanging fifty feet above an implacable sea. Even the lion tamer, keeping a wary eye on his treacherous brutes, did not have to encounter the ferocious enmity of the soulless canvas that tried to tear the topmast men from their precarious footing.

A touch of the helm set the sails drawing again, and *Hotspur* lay over in her fierce struggle with the wind. Surely there was no better example of the triumph of man's ingenuity over the blind forces of nature than this, whereby a ship could wring advantage out of the actual attempt of the gale to push her to destruction.

Hornblower clawed his way to the binnacle and studied the heading of the ship, working out mental problems of drift and leeway against the background of his mental picture of the trend of the land. Prowse was there, apparently doing the same thing.

'I should think we've made our offing, sir.' Prowse had to shout each syllable separately. Hornblower had to do the same when he replied.

'We'll hold on a little longer, while we can.'

Extraordinary how rapidly time went by in these circumstances. It could not be long now until daylight. And this storm was still working up; it was nearly twenty-four hours since Hornblower had detected the premonitory symptoms, and it had not yet reached its full strength. It was likely to blow hard for a considerable time, as much as three days more, possibly even longer than that. Even when it should abate the wind might stay westerly for some considerable further time, delaying the water-hoys and the victuallers in their passage from Plymouth, and when eventually they should come, *Hotspur* might well be up in her station off the Goulet.

'Mr Bush!' Hornblower had to reach out and touch Bush's shoulder to attract his attention in the wind. 'We'll reduce the water allowance from today. Two between three.'

'Aye aye, sir. Just as well, I think, sir.'

Bush gave little thought to hardship, either for the lower deck or for himself. It was no question of giving up a luxury; to reduce the water ration meant an increase in hardship. The standard issue of a gallon a day a head was hardship, even though a usual one; a man could just manage to survive on it. Two-thirds of a gallon a day was a horrible deprivation; after a few days thirst began to colour every thought. As if in mockery the pumps were going at this moment. The elasticity and springiness that kept *Hotspur* from breaking up under these strains meant also that the sea had greater opportunities of penetrating her fabric, working its way in through the straining seams both above and below the waterline. It would accumulate in the bilge, one – two – three feet deep. While the storm blew most of the crew would have six hours' hard physical work a day – an hour each watch – pumping the water out.

Here was the grey dawn coming, and the wind was still increasing, and *Hotspur* could not battle against it any longer.

'Mr Cargill!' Cargill was now officer of the watch. 'We'll heave to. Put her under maintopmast-stays'l.'

Hornblower had to shout the order at the top of his lungs before Cargill nodded that he understood.

'All hands! All hands!'

Some minutes of hard work effected a transformation. Without the immense leverage of the topsails *Hotspur* ceased to lie over quite so steeply; the more gentle influence of the maintopmast-staysail kept her reasonably steady, and now the rudder desisted from its hitherto constant effort to force the little ship to battle into the wind. Now she rose and swooped more freely, more extravagantly yet with less strain. She was leaping wildly enough, and still shipping water over her weather bow, but her behaviour was quite different as she yielded to the wind instead of defying it at the risk of being torn apart.

Bush was offering him a telescope, and pointing to windward, where there was now a grey horizon dimly to be seen – a serrated horizon, jagged with the waves hurrying towards them. Hornblower braced himself to put two hands to the telescope. Sea and then sky raced past the object glass as *Hotspur* tossed over successive waves. It was hard to sweep the area indicated by Bush; that had to be done in fits and starts, but after a moment something flashed across the field, was recaptured – many hours of using a telescope had developed Hornblower's reflex skills – and soon could be submitted to intermittent yet close observation.

'*Naiad*, sir,' shouted Bush into his ear.

The frigate was several miles to windward, hove-to like *Hotspur*. She had one of those new storm-topsails spread, very shallow and without reefs. It might be of considerable advantage when lying-to, for even the reduction in height alone would be considerable, but when Hornblower turned his attention back to the *Hotspur* and observed her behaviour under her main-topmast-staysail he felt no dissatisfaction. Politeness would have led him to comment on it when he handed back the glass, but politeness stood no chance against the labour of making conversation in the wind, and contented himself with a nod. But the sight of *Naiad* out there to windward was confirmation that *Hotspur* was on her station, and beyond her Hornblower had glimpses of the *Doris* reeling and tossing on the horizon. He had done all there was to be done at present. A sensible man would get his breakfast while he might, and a sensible man would resolutely ignore the slight question of stomach occasioned by this new and different motion of the ship. All he had to do now was to endure it.

There was a pleasant moment when he reached his cabin and Huffnell the purser came in to make his morning report, for then it appeared that at the first indication of trouble Bush and Huffnell between them had routed out Simmonds the cook and had set him to work cooking food.

'That's excellent, Mr Huffnell.'

'It was laid down in your standing orders, sir.'

So it was, Hornblower remembered. He had added that paragraph after reading Cornwallis' orders regarding stations to be assumed in westerly gales. Simmonds had boiled three hundred pounds of salt pork in *Hotspur*'s cauldrons, as well as three hundred pounds of dried peas, before the weather had compelled the galley fires to be extinguished.

'Pretty nigh on cooked, anyway, sir,' said Huffnell.

So that for the next three days – four at a pinch – the hands would have something more to eat than dry biscuit. They would have cold parboiled pork and cold pease porridge; the latter was what the Man in the Moon burned his mouth on according to the nursery rhyme.

'Thank you, Mr Huffnell. It's unlikely that this gale will last more than four days.'

That was actually the length of time that gale lasted, the gale that ushered in the worst winter in human memory, following the best summer. For those four days *Hotspur* lay hove-to, pounded by the sea, flogged by the wind, while Hornblower made anxious calculations regarding leeway and drift; as the wind backed northerly his attention was diverted from Ushant to the north to the Isle de Sein to the south of the approaches to Brest. It was not until the fifth day that *Hotspur* was able to set three-reefed topsails and thrash her way back to station while Simmonds managed to start his galley fires again and to provide the crew – and Hornblower – with hot boiled beef as a change from cold boiled pork.

Even then that three-reefed gale maintained the long Atlantic rollers in all their original vastness, so that *Hotspur* soared over them and slithered unhappily down the far side, adding her own corkscrew motion as her weather-bow met the swells, her own special stagger when a rogue wave crashed into her, and the worse lurch when – infrequently – a higher wave than usual blanketed her sails so that she reeled into the sea instead of yielding, with a bursting of green water over her decks. But an hour's work at the pumps every watch kept the bilges clear, and by tacking every two hours *Hotspur* was able to beat painfully out to sea again – not more than half a mile's gain to windward on each tack – and recover the comparative safety of her original station before the next storm.

It was as if in payment for that fair weather summer that these gales blew, and perhaps that was not an altogether fanciful thought; to Hornblower's mind there might be some substance to the theory that prolonged local high pressure during the summer now meant that the pent-up dirty weather to the westward could exert more than its usual force. However that might be, the mere fresh gale that endured for four days after the first storm then worked up again into a tempest, blowing eternally from the westward with almost hurricane force; grey dreary days of lowering cloud, and wild black nights, with the wind howling unceasingly in the rigging until the ear was sated with the noise, until no price seemed too great to pay for five minutes of peace – and yet no price however great could buy even a second of peace. The creaking and the groaning of *Hotspur's* fabric blended with the noise of the wind, and the actual woodwork of the ship vibrated with the vibration of the rigging until it seemed as if body and mind, exhausted with the din and with the fatigues of mere movement, could not endure for another minute, and yet went on to endure for days.

The tempest died down to a fresh gale, to a point when the topsails needed only a single reef, and then, unbelievably, worked up into a tempest again, the third in a month, during which all on board renewed the bruises that covered them as a result of being flung about by the motion of the ship. And it was during that tempest that Hornblower went through a spiritual crisis. It was not a mere question of calculation, it went far deeper than that, even though he did his best to appear quite imperturbable as Bush and Huffnell and Wallis the surgeon made their daily reports. He might have called them into a formal council of war; he might have covered himself by asking for their opinions in writing, to be produced in evidence should there be a court of inquiry, but that was not in his nature. Responsibility was the air he breathed; he could no more bring himself to evade it than he could hold his breath indefinitely.

It was the first day that reefed topsails could be set that he reached his decision.

'Mr Prowse, I'd be obliged if you would set a course to close *Naiad* so that she can read our signals.'

'Aye aye, sir.'

Hornblower, standing on the quarterdeck in the eternal, infernal wind, hated Prowse for darting that inquiring glance at him. Of course the wardroom had discussed his problem. Of course they knew of the shortage of drinking water; of course they knew that Wallis had discovered three cases of sore gums – the earliest symptoms of scurvy in a navy that had overcome scurvy except in special conditions. Of course they had wondered about when their captain would yield to circumstances. Perhaps they had made bets on the date. The problem, the decision, had been his and not theirs.

Hotspur clawed her way over the tossing sea to the point on *Naiad's* lee bow when the signal flags would blow out at right angles to the line of sight.

'Mr Foreman! Signal to *Naiad*, if you please. "Request permission to return to port."'

'Request permission to return to port. Aye aye, sir.'

Naiad was the only ship of the Inshore Squadron – of the Channel Fleet – in sight, and her captain was therefore senior officer on the station. Every captain was senior to the captain of the *Hotspur*.

'*Naiad* acknowledges, sir,' reported Foreman, and then, after ten seconds' wait, '*Naiad* to *Hotspur*, sir, "Interrogative."'

Somehow it might have been more politely put. Chambers of the *Naiad* might have signalled 'Kindly give reasons for request', or something like that. But the single interrogative hoist was convenient and rapid. Hornblower framed his next signal equally tersely.

'*Hotspur* to *Naiad*. "Eight days water."'

Hornblower watched the reply soar up *Naiad's* signal

halliards. It was not the affirmative; if it was permission, it was a qualified permission.

'*Naiad* to *Hotspur*, sir. "Remain four more days."'

'Thank you, Mr Foreman.'

Hornblower tried to keep all expression out of his voice and his face.

'I'll wager he has two months' water on board, sir,' said Bush, angrily.

'I hope he has, Mr Bush.'

They were seventy leagues from Tor Bay; two days' sailing with a fair wind. There was no margin for misfortune. If at the end of four days the wind should shift easterly, as was perfectly possible, they could not reach Tor Bay in a week or even more; the water-hoys might come down-channel, but might easily not find them at once, and then it was not unlikely that the sea would be too rough for boat work. There was an actual possibility that the crew of the *Hotspur* might die of thirst. It had not been easy for Hornblower to make his request; he had no desire to be thought one of those captains whose sole desire was to return to port, and he had waited to the last sensible moment. Chambers saw the problem differently, as a man well might do as regards the possible misfortune of other people. This was an easy way of demonstrating his resolution and firmness. An easy way, a comfortable way, a cheap way.

'Send this signal, if you please, Mr Foreman. "Thank you. Am returning to station. Goodbye." Mr Prowse, we can bear away when that signal is acknowledged. Mr Bush, from today the water ration is reduced. One between two.'

Two quarts of water a day for all purposes – and such

water – to men living on salted food, was far below the minimum for health. It meant sickness as well as discomfort, but the reduction also meant that the last drop of water would not be drunk until sixteen days had passed.

Captain Chambers had not foreseen the future weather, and perhaps he could not be blamed for that, seeing that on the fourth day after the exchange of signals the westerly wind worked up again, unbelievably, into the fourth tempest of that gale-ridden autumn. It was towards the end of the afternoon watch that Hornblower was called on deck again to give his permission for the reefed topsails to be got in and the storm staysail set once more. Significantly it was growing dark already; the days of the equinox when the sun set at six o'clock were long past, and, equally significantly, that roaring westerly gale now had a chilling quality about it. It was cold; not freezing, not icy, but cold, searchingly cold. Hornblower tried to pace the unstable deck in an endeavour to keep his circulation going; he grew warm, not because of his walking, but because the physical labour of keeping his feet was great enough for the purpose. *Hotspur* was leaping like a deer beneath him, and from down below, too, came the dreary sound of the pumps at work.

Six days' water on board now; twelve at half-rations. The gloom of the night was no more gloomy than his thoughts. It was five weeks since he had last been able to send a letter to Maria, and it was six weeks since he had last heard from her, six weeks of westerly gales and westerly tempests. Anything might have happened to her or to the child, and she would be thinking that anything might have happened to the *Hotspur* or to him.

A more irregular wave than usual, roaring out of the darkness, burst upon *Hotspur*'s weather bow. Hornblower felt her sudden sluggishness, her inertia, beneath his feet. That wave must have flooded the waist to a depth of a yard or more, fifty or sixty tons of water piled up on her deck. She lay like something dead for a moment. Then she rolled, slightly at first, and then more freely; the sound of the cataracts of water pouring across could be clearly heard despite the gale. She freed herself as the water cascaded out through the overworked scuppers, and she came sluggishly back to life, to leap once more in her mad career from wave crest to trough. A blow like that could well be her death; some time she might not rise to it; some time her deck might be burst in. Another wave beat on her bow like the hammer of a mad giant, and another after that.

Next day was worse, the worst day that *Hotspur* had experienced in all these wild weeks. Some slight shift in the wind, or the increase in its strength, had worked up the waves to a pitch that was particularly unsuited to *Hotspur*'s idiosyncrasies. The waist was flooded most of the time now, so that she laboured heavily without relief, each wave catching her before she could free herself. That meant that the pumps were at work three hours out of every four, so that even with petty officers and idlers and waisters and marines all doing their share, every hand was engaged on the toilsome labour for twelve hours a day.

Bush's glance was more direct even than usual when he came to make his report.

'We're still sighting *Naiad* now and then, sir, but not a chance of signals being read.'

This was the day when by Captain Chambers' orders they were free to run for harbour.

'Yes. I don't think we can bear away in this wind and sea.'

Bush's expression revealed a mental struggle. *Hotspur*'s powers of resistance to the present battering were not unlimited, but on the other hand to turn tail and run would be an operation of extreme danger.

'Has Huffnell reported to you yet, sir?'

'Yes,' said Hornblower.

There were nine hundred-gallon casks of fresh water left down below, which had been standing in the bottom tier for a hundred days. And now one of them had proved to be contaminated with seawater and was hardly drinkable. The others might perhaps be even less so.

'Thank you, Mr Bush,' said Hornblower, terminating the interview. 'We'll remain hove-to for today at least.'

Surely a wind of this force must moderate soon, even though Hornblower had a premonition that it would not.

Nor did it. The slow dawn of the new day found *Hotspur* still labouring under the dark clouds, the waves still as wild, the wind still as insane. The time had come for the final decision, as Hornblower well knew as he came out on deck in his clammy clothes. He knew the dangers, and he had spent a large part of the night preparing his mind to deal with them.

'Mr Bush, we'll get before the wind.'

'Aye aye, sir.'

Before she could come before the wind she would have to present her vulnerable side to the waves. There would be seconds during which she could be rolled over on to her beam ends, beaten down under the waves, pounded into a wreck.

'Mr Cargill!'

This was going to be a moment far more dangerous than being chased by the *Loire*, and Cargill would have to be trusted to carry out a similar duty as on a tense occasion then. Face close to face, Hornblower shouted his instructions.

'Get for'ard. Make ready to show a bit of the fore-topmast-stays'l. Haul it up when I wave my arm.'

'Aye aye, sir.'

'Get it in the moment I wave a second time.'

'Aye aye, sir.'

'Mr Bush! We shall need the foretops'l.'

'Aye aye, sir.'

'Goose-wing it.'

'Aye aye, sir.'

'Stand by the sheets. Wait for me to wave my arm the second time.'

'The second time. Aye aye, sir.'

Hotspur's stern was nearly as vulnerable as her side. If she presented it to the waves while stationary she would be 'pooped' – a wave would burst over her and sweep her from stern to stem, a blow she would probably not survive. The foretopsail would give her the necessary way, but spreading it before she was before the wind would lay her over on her beam ends. 'Goose-winging it' – pulling down the lower corners while leaving the centre portion still furled – would expose less canvas than the reefed sail; enough in that gale to carry her forward at the necessary speed.

Hornblower took his station beside the wheel, where he could be clearly seen from forward. He ran his eyes aloft to make sure that the preparations for goose-winging the foretopsail were complete, and his gaze lingered for a while longer as he observed the motion of the spars relative to the wild sky. Then he transferred his attention to the sea on the weather side, to the immense rollers hurrying towards the ship. He watched the roll and the pitch; he gauged the strength of the howling wind which was trying to tear him from his footing. That wind was trying to stupefy him, to paralyse him, too. He had to keep the hard central core of himself alert and clear thinking while his outer body was numbed by the wind.

A rogue wave burst against the weather bow in a huge but fleeting pillar of spray, the green mass pounding aft along the waist, and Hornblower swallowed nervously while it seemed as if *Hotspur* would never recover. But she did, slowly and wearily, rolling off the load from her deck. As she cleared herself the moment came, a moment of regularity in the oncoming waves, with her bow just lifting to the nearest one. He waved his arm, and saw the slender head of the fore-topmast-staysail rising up the stay, and the ship lay over wildly to the pressure.

'Hard-a-port,' he yelled to the hands at the wheel.

The enormous leverage of the staysail, applied to the bowsprit, began to swing the *Hotspur* round like a weather vane; as she turned, the wind thrusting more and more from aft gave her steerage way so that the rudder could bite and accelerate the turn. She was down in the trough of the wave but turning, still turning. He waved his arm again. The clews of the fore-topsail showed themselves as the hands hauled on the sheets, and *Hotspur* surged forward with the impact of the wind upon the canvas. The wave was almost upon them, but it disappeared out of the tail of Hornblower's eye as *Hotspur* presented first her quarter and then her stern to it.

'Meet her! Midships!'

The tug of the sail on the foremast would put *Hotspur* right before the wind without the use of the rudder; indeed the rudder would only delay her acquiring all the way she could. Time enough to put the rudder to work again when she was going at her fastest. Hornblower braced himself for the impact of the wave now following them up. The seconds passed and then it came, but the stern had begun to lift and the blow was deprived of its force. Only a minor mass of water burst over the taffrail, to surge aft again as *Hotspur* lifted her bows. Now they were racing along with the waves; now they were travelling through the water ever so little faster. That was the most desirable point of speed; there was no need to increase or decrease even minutely the area of canvas exposed by the goose-winged foretop-sail. The situation was safe and yet unutterably precarious, balanced on a knife edge. The slightest yawing and *Hotspur* was lost.

'Keep her from falling off!' Hornblower yelled to the men at the wheel, and the grizzled senior quartermaster, his wet grey ringlets flapping over his cheeks from out of his sou'wester, nodded without taking his eyes from the foretopsail. Hornblower knew – with his vivid imag-ination he could feel the actual sensation up his arms –

how uncertain and unsatisfactory was the feel of wheel and rudder when running before a following sea, the momentary lack of response to the turning spokes, the hesitation of the ship as a mounting wave astern deprived the foretopsail of some of the wind that filled it, the uncontrolled slithering sensation as the ship went down a slope. A moment's inattention – a moment's bad luck – could bring ruin.

Yet here they were momentarily safe before the wind, and running for the Channel. Prowse was already staring into the binnacle and noting the new course on the traverse board, and at a word from him Orrock and a seaman struggled aft to cast the log and determine the speed. And here came Bush, ascending to the quarterdeck, grinning over the success of the manoeuvre and with the exhilaration of the new state of affairs.

'Course nor'east by east, sir,' reported Prowse. 'Speed better than seven knots.'

Now there was a new set of problems to deal with. They were entering the Channel. There were shoals and headlands ahead of them; there were tides – the tricky tidal streams of the Channel – to be reckoned with. The very nature of the waves would change soon, with the effect upon the Atlantic rollers of the shallowing water and the narrowing Channel and the varying tides. There was the general problem of avoiding being blown all the way up Channel, and the particular one of trying to get into Tor Bay.

All this called for serious calculation and reference to tide tables, especially in face of the fact that running before the wind like this it would be impossible to take soundings.

'We ought to get a sight of Ushant on this course, sir,' yelled Prowse.

That would be a decided help, a solid base for future calculations, a new departure. A shouted word sent Orrock up to the foretopmasthead with a telescope to supplement the look-out there, while Hornblower faced the first stage of the new series of problems – the question of whether he could bring himself to leave the deck – and the second stage – the question of whether he should invite Prowse to share his calculations. The answer to both was necessarily in the affirmative. Bush was a good seaman and could be trusted to keep a vigilant eye on the wheel and on the canvas; Prowse was a fair navigator and was by law co-responsible with Hornblower for the course to be set and so would have just cause for grievance if he was not consulted, however much Hornblower wished to be free of his company.

So it came about that Prowse was with Hornblower in the chart room, struggling with the tide tables, when Foreman opened the door – his knocking not having been heard in the general din – and admitted all the noise of the ship in full volume.

'Message from Mr Bush, sir. Ushant in sight on the starboard beam, seven or eight miles, sir.'

'Thank you, Mr Foreman.'

That was a stroke of good fortune, the first they had had. Now they could plan the next struggle to bend the forces of nature to their will. It was a struggle indeed; for the men at the wheel a prolonged physical ordeal which made it necessary to relieve them every half-hour and for Hornblower a mental ordeal which was to keep him at full strain for the next thirty hours. There was the tentative trying of the wheel, to see if it was possible to bring the wind a couple of points on her port quarter. Three times they made the attempt, to abandon it hastily as wind and wave rendered the ship unmanageable, but at the fourth try it became possible, with the shortening of the waves in their advance up-Channel and the turn of the tide over on the French coast. Now they tore through the water, speed undiminished despite the drag of the rudder as the helmsmen battled with the wheel that kicked and struggled as if it were alive and malignant under their hands, and while the whole strength of the crew handled the braces to trim the yard exactly to make certain there was no danger of sailing by the lee.

At least the danger of running *Hotspur* bodily under water was now eliminated. There was no chance of her putting her bows into the slack back of a dilatory wave and never lifting them again. To balance the leverage of the foretopsail they hauled up the mizzen-staysail, which brought relief to the helmsmen even though it laid *Hotspur* over until her starboard gun ports were level with the water. It lasted for a frantic hour, and it seemed to Hornblower that he was holding his breath during all that time, and until it burst in the centre with a report like a twelve-pounder, splitting into flying pendants of canvas that cracked in the wind like coach-whips as the helmsmen fought against the renewed tendency of *Hotspur* to turn away from the wind. Yet the temporary success justified replacing the sail with the mizzen-topmast-staysail, just a corner of it showing, and the head and the tack still secured by gaskets. It was a brand-new sail, and it managed to endure the strain, to compensate for the labour and difficulty of setting it.

The short dark day drew to an end, and now everything had to be done in roaring night, while lack of sleep intensified the numbness and fatigue and the stupidity induced by the unremitting wind. With his dulled sensitivity Hornblower's reaction was slow to the changed behaviour of *Hotspur* under his feet. The transition was gradual, in any case, but at last it became marked enough for him to notice it, his sense of touch substituting for his sense of sight to tell him that the waves were becoming shorter and steeper; this was the choppiness of the Channel and not the steady sweep of the Atlantic rollers.

Hotspur's motion was more rapid, and in a sense more violent; the waves broke over her bow more frequently though in smaller volume. Although still far below the surface the floor of the Channel was rising, from a hundred fathoms deep to forty fathoms, and there was the turn of the tide to be considered, even though this westerly tempest must have piled up the waters of the Channel far above mean level. And the Channel was narrower now; the rollers that had found ample passage between Ushant and Scilly were feeling the squeeze, and all these factors were evident in their behaviour. *Hotspur* was wet all the time now, and only continuous working of the pumps kept the water down below within bounds – pumps worked by weary men, thirsty men, hungry men, sleepy men, throwing their weight on the long handles each time with the feeling that they could not repeat the effort even once more.

At four in the morning Hornblower was conscious of a shift in the wind, and for a precious hour he was able to order a change of course until a sudden veering of the wind forced them back on the original course again, but he had gained, so his calculations told him, considerably to the northward; there was so much satisfaction in that that he put his forehead down on his forearms on the chart room table and was surprised into sleep for several valuable minutes before a more extravagant leaping of the ship banged his head upon his arms and awakened him to make his way wearily out upon the quarterdeck again.

'Wish we could take a sounding, sir,' shouted Prowse.

'Yes.'

There was no sense in wasting strength in voicing wishes.

Yet now, even in the darkness, Hornblower could feel that the recent gain and the change in the character of the sea made it justifiable to heave to for a space. He could goad his mind to deal with the problem of drift and leeway; he could harden his heart to face the necessity of calling upon the exhausted topmen to make the effort to furl the goose-winged foretopsail while he stood by, alert, to bring the ship to under the mizzenstaysail; bring the helm over at the right moment so that she met the steep waves with her bow. Riding to the wind her motion was wilder and more extravagant than ever, but they managed to cast the deep-sea lead, with the crew lined up round the ship, calling 'Watch! Watch!' as each man let his portion of line loose. Thirtyeight – thirty-seven – thirty-eight fathoms again; the three casts consumed an hour, with everyone wet to the skin and exhausted. It was a fragment more of the data necessary, while heaving-to eased the labour of the worn-out quartermasters and actually imposed so much less strain on the seams that the pumps steadily gained on the water below.

At the first watery light of dawn they set the goose-winged foretopsail again while Hornblower faced the problem of getting *Hotspur* round with the wind over her quarter without laying her over on her beam ends. Then they were thrashing along in the old way, decks continually under water, rolling until every timber groaned, with Orrock freezing at the foretopmasthead with his glass. It was noon before he sighted the land; half an hour later Bush returned to the quarterdeck from the ascent he made to confirm Orrock's findings. Bush was more weary than he would ever admit, his dirty hollow cheeks overgrown with a stubble of beard, but he could still show surprise and pleasure.

'Bolt Head, sir!' he yelled. 'Fine on the port bow. And I could just make out the Start.'

'Thank you.'

Even though it meant shouting, Bush wanted to express his feelings about this feat of navigation, but Hornblower had no time for that, nor the patience, nor, for that matter, the strength. There was the question of not being blown too far to leeward at this eleventh hour, of making preparations to come to an anchor in conditions that would certainly be difficult. There was the tide rip off the Start to be borne in mind, the necessity of rounding to as close under Berry Head as possible. There was the sudden inexpressible change in wind and sea as they came under the lee of the Start; the steep choppiness here seemed nothing compared with what *Hotspur* had been enduring five minutes before, and the land took the edge of the hurricane wind to reduce it to the mere force of a full gale that still kept *Hotspur* flying before it. There was the Newstone and the Blackstones – here as well as in the Iroise – and the final tricky moment of the approach to Berry Head.

'Ships of war at anchor, sir,' reported Bush, sweeping Tor Bay with his glass as they opened it up. 'That's *Dreadnought*. That's *Temeraire*. It's the Channel Fleet. My God! There's one aground in Torquay Roads. Two-decker – she must have dragged her anchors.'

'Yes. We'll back the best bower anchor before we let go, Mr Bush. We'll have to use the launch's carronade. You've time to see about that.'

'Aye aye, sir.'

Even in Tor Bay there was a full gale blowing; where a two-decker had dragged her anchors every precaution must be taken at whatever further cost in effort. The seven hundredweight of the boat carronade, attached to the anchor-cable fifty feet back from the one ton of the best bower, might just save that anchor from lifting and dragging. And so *Hotspur* came in under goose-winged foretopsail and storm mizzen-staysail, round Berry Head, under the eyes of the Channel Fleet, to claw her way in towards Brixham pier and to round-to with her weary men furling the foretopsail and to drop her anchors while with a last effort they sent down the topmasts and Prowse and Hornblower took careful bearings to make sure she was not dragging. It was only then that there was leisure to spare to make her number to the flagship.

'Flag acknowledges, sir,' croaked Foreman.

'Very well.'

It was still possible to do something more without collapsing. 'Mr Foreman, kindly make this signal. "Need drinking water."'

14

Tor Bay was a tossing expanse of white horses. The land lessened the effect of the wind to some extent; the Channel waves were hampered in their entry by Berry Head, but all the same the wind blew violently and the waves racing up the Channel managed to wheel leftwards, much weakened, but now running across the wind, and with the tide to confuse the issue Tor Bay boiled like a cauldron. For forty hours after *Hotspur*'s arrival the *Hibernia*, Cornwallis' big three-decker, flew the signal 715 with a negative beside it, and 715 with a negative meant that boats were not to be employed.

Not even the Brixham fishermen, renowned for their small-boat work, could venture out into Tor Bay while it was in that mood, so that until the second morning at anchor the crew of the *Hotspur* supported an unhappy existence on two quarts of tainted water a day. And Hornblower was the unhappiest man on board, from causes both physical and mental. The little ship almost empty of stores was the plaything of wind and wave and tide; she surged about at her anchors like a restive horse. She swung and she snubbed herself steady with a jerk; she plunged and snubbed herself again. With her topmasts sent down she developed a shallow and rapid roll. It was a mixture of motions that would test the strongest stomach, and Hornblower's stomach was by no means the strongest, while there was the depressing association in his memory of his very first day in a ship of war, when he had made himself a laughing stock by being seasick in the old *Justinian* at anchor in Spithead.

He spent those forty hours vomiting his heart out, while to the black depression of seasickness was added the depression resulting from the knowledge that Maria was only thirty miles away in Plymouth, and by a good road. Cornwallis' representations had caused the government to cut that road, over the tail end of Dartmoor, so that the Channel Fleet in its rendezvous could readily be supplied from the great naval base. Half a day on a good horse and Hornblower could be holding Maria in his arms, he could be hearing news first-hand about the progress of the child, on whom (to his surprise) his thoughts were beginning to dwell increasingly. The hands spent their free moments on the forecastle, round the knightheads, gazing at Brixham and Brixham Pier; even in that wind with its deluges of rain there were women to be seen occasionally, women in skirts, at whom the crew stared like so many Tantaluses. After one good night's sleep, and with pumping only necessary now for half an hour in each watch, those men had time and energy so that their imaginations had free play. They could think about women, and they could think about liquor – most of them dreamed dreams of swilling themselves into swinish unconsciousness on Brixham's smuggled brandy, while Hornblower could only vomit and fret.

But he slept during the second half of the second night, when the wind not only moderated but backed two points northerly, altering the conditions in Tor Bay like magic, so that after he had assured himself at midnight that the anchors were still holding his fatigue took charge and he could sleep without moving for seven hours. He was still only half awake when Doughty came bursting in on him.

'Signal from the Flag, sir.'

There were strings of bunting flying from the halliards of the *Hibernia*; with the shift of wind they could be read easily enough from the quarterdeck of the *Hotspur*.

'There's our number there, sir,' said Foreman, glass at eye. 'It comes first.'

Cornwallis was giving orders for the victualling and rewatering of the fleet, establishing the order in which the ships were to be replenished, and that signal gave *Hotspur* priority over all the rest.

'We're lucky, sir,' commented Bush.

'Possibly,' agreed Hornblower. No doubt Cornwallis had been informed about *Hotspur*'s appeal for drinking water, but he might have further plans, too.

'Look at that, sir,' said Bush. 'They waste no time.'

Two lighters, each propelled by eight sweeps, and with a six-oared yawl standing by, were creeping out round the end of Brixham Pier.

'I'll see about the fend-offs, sir,' said Bush, departing hastily.

These were the water-lighters, marvels of construction, each of them containing a series of vast cast-iron tanks. Hornblower had heard about them; they were of fifty tons' burthen each of them, and each of them carried ten thousand gallons of drinking water, while *Hotspur*, with every cask and hogshead brim full, could not quite store fifteen thousand.

So now began an orgy of fresh water, clear spring-water which had not lain in the cast-iron tanks for more than a few days. With the lighters chafing uneasily along-side, a party from *Hotspur* went down to work the beautiful modern pumps which the lighters carried, forcing the water up through four superb canvas hoses passed in through the ports and then down below. The deck scuttle butt, so long empty, was swilled out and filled, to be instantly emptied by the crew and filled again; just possibly at that moment the hands would rather have fresh water than brandy.

It was glorious waste; down below the casks were swilled and scrubbed out with fresh water, and the swill-ings drained into the bilge whence the ship's pumps would later have to force it overboard at some cost of labour. Every man drank his fill and more; Hornblower gulped down glass after glass until he was full, yet half an hour later found him drinking again. He could feel himself expanding like a desert plant after rain.

'Look at this, sir,' said Bush, telescope in hand and gesturing towards Brixham.

The telescope revealed a busy crowd at work there, and there were cattle visible.

'Slaughtering,' said Bush. 'Fresh meat.'

Soon another lighter was creeping out to them; hanging from a frame down the midship line were sides of beef, carcasses of sheep and pigs.

'I won't mind a roast of mutton, sir,' said Bush.

Bullocks and sheep and swine had been driven over the moors to Brixham, and slaughtered and dressed on the waterfront immediately before shipping so that the meat would last fresh as long as possible.

'Four days' rations there, sir,' said Bush making a practised estimate. 'An' there's a live bullock an' four sheep an' four pigs. Excuse me, sir, and I'll post a guard at the side.

Most of the hands had money in their pockets and would spend it freely on liquor if they were given the chance, and the men in the victualling barges would sell to them unless the closest supervision were exercised. The water-lighters had finished their task and were casting off. It had been a brief orgy; from the moment that the hoses were taken in ship's routine would be re-established. One gallon of water per man per day for all purposes from now on.

The place of the watering barges was taken by the dry victualling barge, with bags of biscuit, sacks of dried peas, kegs of butter, cases of cheese, sacks of oatmeal, but conspicuous on top of all this were half a dozen nets full of fresh bread. Two hundred four-pound loaves – Hornblower could taste the crustiness of them in his watering mouth when he merely looked at them. A beneficent government, under the firm guidance of Cornwallis, was sending these luxuries aboard; the hardships of a life at sea were the result of natural circumstances quite as much as of ministerial ineptitude.

There was never a quiet moment all through that day. Here was Bush touching his hat again with a final demand on his attention.

'You've given no order about wives, sir.'

'Wives?'

'Wives, sir.'

There was an interrogative lift in Hornblower's voice as he said the word; there was a flat, complete absence of expression in Bush's. It was usual in His Majesty's Ship when they lay in harbour for women to be allowed on board, and one or two of them might well be wives. It was some small compensation for the system that forbade a man to set foot on shore lest he desert; but the women inevitably smuggled liquor on board, and the scenes of debauchery that ensued on the lower deck were as shameless as in Nero's court. Disease and indiscipline were the natural result; it took days or weeks to shake the crew down again into an efficient team. Hornblower did not want his fine ship ruined but if *Hotspur* were to stay long at anchor in Tor Bay he could not deny what was traditionally a reasonable request. He simply could not deny it.

'I'll give my orders later this morning,' he said.

It was not difficult, some minutes later, to intercept Bush at a moment when a dozen of the hands were within earshot.

'Oh, Mr Bush!' Hornblower hoped his voice did not sound as stilted and theatrical as he feared. 'You've plenty of work to be done about the ship.'

'Yes, sir. There's a good deal of standing rigging I'd like set up again. And there's running rigging to be rerove. And there's the paint work –'

'Very well, Mr Bush. When the ship's complete in all respects we'll allow the wives on board, but not until then. Not until then, Mr Bush. And if we have to sail before then it will be the fortune of war.'

'Aye aye, sir.'

Next came the letters; word must have reached the post office in Plymouth of the arrival of *Hotspur* in Tor Bay, and the letters had been sent across overland. Seven letters from Maria; Hornblower tore open the last first, to find that Maria was well and her pregnancy progressing favourably, and then he skimmed through the others, to find, as he expected, that she had rejoiced to read her Valiant Hero's *Gazette* letter although she was perturbed by the risks run by her Maritime Alexander, and although she was consumed with sorrow because the Needs of the Service had denied from her eyes the light of his Countenance. Hornblower was halfway through writing a reply when a midshipman came escorted to his cabin door with a note . . .

HMS Hibernia
Tor Bay
Dear Captain Hornblower,
    If you can be tempted out of your ship at three o'clock this afternoon to dine in the flagship it would give great pleasure to
    Your ob't servant,
    Wm Cornwallis, Vice-Ad.
    PS – An affirmative signal hung out in the Hotspur is all the acknowledgement necessary.

Hornblower went out on to the quarterdeck.
'Mr Foreman. Signal "*Hotspur* to Flag. Affirmative."'
'Just affirmative, sir?'
'You heard me.'
An invitation from the Commander-in-Chief was as much a royal command as if it had been signed George R – even if the postscript did not dictate the reply.
Then there was the powder to be put on board, with all the care and precautions that operation demanded;

Hotspur had fired away one ton of the five tons of gunpowder that her magazine could hold. The operation was completed when Prowse brought up one of the hands who manned the powder-barge.

'This fellow says he has a message for you, sir.'

This was a swarthy gypsy-faced fellow who met Hornblower's eye boldly with all the assurance to be expected of a man who carried in his pocket a protection against impressment.

'What is it?'

'Message for you from a lady, sir, and I was to have a shilling for delivering it to you.'

Hornblower looked him over keenly. There was only one lady who could be sending a message.

'Nonsense. That lady promised sixpence. Now didn't she?'

Hornblower knew that much about Maria despite his brief married life.

'Well, yes, sir.'

'Here's the shilling. What's the message?'

'The lady said look for her on Brixham Pier, sir.'

'Very well.'

Hornblower took the glass from its becket and walked forward. Busy though the ship was, there were nevertheless a few idlers round the knightheads who shrank away in panic at the remarkable sight of their captain here. He trained the glass; Brixham Pier, as might be expected, was crowded with people, and he searched for a long time without result, training the glass first on one woman and then on another. Was that Maria? She was the only woman wearing a bonnet and not a shawl. Of course it was Maria; momentarily he had forgotten that this was the end of the seventh month. She stood in the front row of the crowd; as Hornblower watched she raised an arm and fluttered a scarf. She could not see him, or at least she certainly could not recognize him at that distance without a telescope. She must have heard, along with the rest of Plymouth, of the arrival of *Hotspur* in Tor Bay; presumably she had made her way here via Totnes in the carrier's cart – a long and tedious journey.

She fluttered her scarf again, in the pathetic hope that he was looking at her. In that part of his mind which never ceased attending to the ship Hornblower became conscious of the pipes of the bos'n's mate – the pipes had been shrilling one call or another all day long.

'Quarter-boat away-ay-ay!'

Hornblower had never been so conscious of the slavery of the King's service. Here he was due to leave the ship to dine with the Commander-in-Chief, and the Navy had a tradition of punctuality that he could not flout. And there was Foreman, breathless from his run forward.

'Message from Mr Bush, sir. The boat's waiting.'

What was he to do? Ask Bush to write Maria a note and send it by a shore boat? No, he would have to risk being late – Maria could not bear to receive second-hand messages at this time of all times. A hurried scribble with the left-handed quill.

My own darling,
    So much pleasure in seeing you, but not a moment to spare yet. I will write to you at length.
    Your devoted husband,
    H.

He used that initial in all his letters to her; he did not like his first name and he could not bring himself to sign 'Horry'. Damn it all, here was the half-finished letter, interrupted earlier that day and never completed. He thrust it aside and struggled to apply a wafer to the finished note. Seven months at sea had destroyed every vestige of gum and the wafer would not adhere. Doughty was hovering over him with sword and hat and cloak – Doughty was just as aware of the necessity for punctuality as he was. Hornblower gave the open note to Bush.

'Seal this, if you please, Mr Bush. And send it by shore boat to Mrs Hornblower on the pier. Yes, she's on the pier. By a shore boat, Mr Bush; no one from the ship's to set foot on land.'

Down the side and into the boat. Hornblower could imagine the explanatory murmur through the crowd on the pier, as Maria would learn from better informed bystanders what was going on.

'That's the captain going down into the boat.' She would feel a surge of excitement and happiness. The boat shoved off, the conditions of wind and current dictating that her bow was pointing right at the pier; that would be Maria's moment of highest hope. Then the boat swung round while the hands hauled at the halliards and the balance-lug rose up the mast. Next moment she was flying towards the flagship, flying away from Maria without a word or a sign, and Hornblower felt a great welling of pity and remorse within his breast.

Hewitt responded to the flagship's hail, turned the boat neatly into the wind, dropped the sail promptly, and with the last vestige of the boat's way ran her close enough to the starboard mainchains for the bowman to hook on. Hornblower judged his moment and went up the ship's side. As his head reached the level of the main-deck the pipes began to shrill in welcome. And through that noise Hornblower heard the three sharp double strokes of the ship's bell. Six bells in the afternoon watch; three o'clock, the time stated in his invitation.

The great stern cabin in the *Hibernia* was furnished in a more subdued fashion than Pellew had affected in the *Tonnant*, more Spartan and less lavish, but comfortable enough. Somewhat to Hornblower's surprise there were no other visitors; present in the cabin were only Cornwallis, and Collins, the sardonic Captain of the Fleet, and the flag lieutenant, whose name Hornblower vaguely heard as one of these newfangled double-barrelled names with a hyphen.

Hornblower was conscious of Cornwallis' blue eyes fixed upon him, examining him closely in a considering, appraising way that might have unsettled him in other conditions. But he was still a little preoccupied with his thoughts about Maria, on the one hand, while on the other seven months at sea, seven weeks of continuous storms, provided all necessary excuse for his shabby coat and his seaman's trousers. He could meet Cornwallis' glance without shyness. Indeed, the effect of Cornwallis' kindly but unsmiling expression was much modified because his wig was slightly awry; Cornwallis still affected a horsehair bobwig of the sort that was now being relegated by fashion to noblemen's coachmen, and today it had a rakish cant that dissipated all appearance of dignity.

Yet, wig or no wig, there was something in the air,

some restraint, some tension, even though Cornwallis was a perfect host who did the honours of his table with an easy grace. The quality of the atmosphere was such that Hornblower hardly noticed the food that covered the table, and he felt acutely that the polite conversation was guarded and cautious. They discussed the recent weather; *Hibernia* had been in Tor Bay for several days, having run for shelter just in time to escape the last hurricane.

'How were your stores when you came in, Captain?' asked Collins.

Now here was another sort of atmosphere, something artificial. There was an odd quality about Collins' tone, accentuated by the formal 'Captain', particularly when addressed to a lowly Commander. Then Hornblower identified it. This was a stilted and prepared speech, exactly of the same nature at his recent speech to Bush regarding the admission of women to the ship. He could identify the tone, but he still could not account for it. But he had a commonplace answer, so commonplace that he made it in a commonplace way.

'I still had plenty, sir. Beef and pork for a month at least.'

There was a pause a shade longer than natural, as if the information was being digested, before Cornwallis asked the next question in a single word.

'Water?'

'That was different, sir. I'd never been able to fill my casks completely from the hoys. We were pretty low when we got in. That was why we ran for it.'

'How much did you have?'

'Two days at half-rations, sir. We'd been on half-rations for a week, and two-thirds rations for four weeks before that.'

'Oh,' said Collins, and in that instant the atmosphere changed.

'You left very little margin for error, Hornblower,' said Cornwallis, and now he was smiling, and now Hornblower in his innocence realized what had been going on. He had been suspected of coming in unnecessarily early, of being one of those captains who wearied of combating tempests. Those were the captains Cornwallis was anxious to weed out from the Channel Fleet, and Hornblower had been under consideration for weeding out.

'You should have come in at least four days earlier,' said Cornwallis.

'Well, sir –' Hornblower could have covered himself by quoting the orders of Chambers of the *Naiad*, but he saw no reason to, and he changed what he was going to say. 'It worked out all right in the end.'

'You'll be sending in your journals, of course, sir?' asked the flag lieutenant.

'Of course,' said Hornblower.

The ship's log would be documentary proof of his assertions, but the question was a tactless, almost an insulting, impugning of his veracity, and Cornwallis instantly displayed a hot-tempered impatience at this awkwardness on the part of his flag lieutenant.

'Captain Hornblower can do that all in his own good time,' he said. 'Now, wine with you, sir?'

It was extraordinary how pleasant the meeting had become; the change in the atmosphere was as noticable as the change in the lighting at this moment when the stewards brought in candles. The four of them were laughing and joking when Newton, captain of the ship, came in to make his report and for Hornblower to be presented to him.

'Wind's steady at west nor'west, sir,' said Newton.

'Thank you, captain.' Cornwallis rolled his blue eyes on Hornblower. 'Are you ready for sea?'

'Yes, sir.' There could be no other reply.

'The wind's bound to come easterly soon,' meditated Cornwallis. 'The Downs, Spithead, Plymouth Sound – all of them jammed with ships outward bound and waiting for a fair wind. But one point's all you need with *Hotspur*.'

'I could fetch Ushant with two tacks now, sir,' said Hornblower. There was Maria huddled in some lodging in Brixham at this moment, but he had to say it.

'M'm,' said Cornwallis, still in debate with himself. 'I'm not comfortable without you watching the Goulet, Hornblower. But I can let you have one more day at anchor.'

'Thank you, sir.'

'That is if the wind doesn't back any further.' Cornwallis reached a decision. 'Here are your orders. You sail at nightfall tomorrow. But if the wind backs one more point you hoist anchor instantly. That is, with the wind at nor'west by west.'

'Aye aye, sir.'

Hornblower knew how he liked his own officers to respond to his orders, and he matched his deportment with that mental model. Cornwallis went on, his eye still considering him.

'We took some reasonable claret out of a prize a

month ago, I wonder if you would honour me by accepting a dozen, Hornblower?'

'With the greatest of pleasure, sir.'

'I'll have it put in your boat.'

Cornwallis turned to give the order to his steward, who apparently had something to say in return in a low voice; Hornblower heard Cornwallis reply, 'Yes, yes, of course,' before he turned back.

'Perhaps your steward would pass the word for my boat at the same time, sir?' said Hornblower, who was in no doubt that his visit had lasted long enough by Cornwallis' standards.

It was quite dark when Hornblower went down the side into the boat, to find at his feet the case that held the wine, and by now the wind was almost moderate. The dark surface of Tor Bay was spangled with the lights of ships, and there were the lights of Torquay and of Paignton and Brixham visible as well. Maria was somewhere there, probably uncomfortable, for these little places were probably full of naval officers' wives.

'Call me the moment the wind comes nor'west by west,' said Hornblower to Bush as soon as he reached the deck.

'Nor'west by west. Aye aye, sir. The hands managed to get liquor on board, sir.'

'Did you expect anything else?'

The British sailor would find liquor somehow at any contact with the shore; if he had no money he would give his clothes, his shoes, even his earrings in exchange.

'I had trouble with some of 'em, sir, especially after the beer issue.'

Beer was issued instead of rum whenever it could be supplied.

'You dealt with 'em?'

'Yes, sir.'

'Very well, Mr Bush.'

A couple of hands were bringing the case of wine in from the boat, under the supervision of Doughty, and when Hornblower entered his cabin he found the case lashed to the bulkhead, occupying practically the whole of the spare deck space, and Doughty bending over it, having prized it open with a hand-spike.

'The only place to put it, sir,' explained Doughty, apologetically.

That was probably true in two senses; with the ship crammed with stores, even with raw meat hung in every place convenient and inconvenient, there could hardly be any space to spare, and in addition wine would hardly be safe from the hands unless it were here where a sentry constantly stood guard. Doughty had a large parcel in his arms, which he had removed from the case.

'What's that?' demanded Hornblower; he had already observed that Doughty was a little disconcerted, so that when his servant hesitated he repeated the question more sharply still.

'It's just a parcel from the Admiral's steward, sir.'

'Show me.'

Hornblower expected to see bottles of brandy or some other smuggled goods.

'It's only cabin stores, sir.'

'Show me.'

'Just cabin stores, sir, as I said.' Doughty examined the contents while exhibiting them in a manner which proved he had not been certain of what he would find. 'This is sweet oil, sir, olive oil. And here are dried herbs. Marjoram, thyme, sage. And here's coffee – only half a pound, by the look of it. And pepper. And vinegar. And . . .'

'How the devil did you get these?'

'I wrote a note, sir, to the Admiral's steward, and sent it by your coxs'n. It isn't right that you shouldn't have these things, sir. Now I can cook for you properly.'

'Does the Admiral know?'

'I'd be surprised if he did, sir.'

There was an assured superior expression on Doughty's face as he said this, which suddenly revealed to Hornblower a world of which he had been ignorant until then. There might be Flag Officers and Captains, but under that glittering surface was an unseen circle of stewards, with its own secret rites and passwords, managing the private lives of their officers without reference to them.

'Sir!' This was Bush, entering the cabin with hurried step. 'Wind's nor'west by west, sir. Looks as if it'll back further still.'

It took a moment for Hornblower to reorient his thoughts, to switch from stewards and dried herbs to ships and sailing orders. Then he was himself again, rapping his commands.

'Call all hands. Sway the topmasts up. Get the yards crossed. I want to be under way in twenty minutes. Fifteen minutes.'

'Aye aye, sir.'

The quiet of the ship was broken by the pipes and the curses of the petty officers, as they drove the hands to work. Heads bemused by beer and brandy cleared themselves with violent exercise and the fresh air of the chilly night breeze. Clumsy fingers clutched hoists and halliards. Men tripped and stumbled in the darkness and were kicked to their feet by petty officers goaded on by the master's mates goaded on in turn by Bush and Prowse. The vast cumbersome sausages that were the sails were dragged out from where they had been laid away on the booms.

'Ready to set sail, sir,' reported Bush.

'Very well. Send the hands to the capstan. Mr Foreman, what's the night signal for "Am getting under way"?'

'One moment, sir.' Foreman had not learned the night signal book as thoroughly as he should have done in seven months. 'One blue light and one Bengal fire shown together, sir.'

'Very well. Make that ready. Mr Prowse, a course from the Start to Ushant, if you please.'

That would let the hands know what fate awaited them, if they did not guess already. Maria would know nothing at all until she looked out at Tor Bay tomorrow to find Hotspur's place empty. And all she had to comfort her was the curt note he had sent before dinner; cold comfort, that. He must not think of Maria, or of the child.

The capstan was clanking as they hove the ship up towards the best bower. They would have to deal with the extra weight of the boat carronade that backed that anchor; the additional labour was the price to be paid for the security of the past days. It was a clumsy, as well as a laborious operation.

'Shall I heave short on the small bower, sir?'

'Yes, if you please, Mr Bush. And you can get under way as soon as is convenient to you.'

'Aye aye, sir.'

'Make that signal, Mr Foreman.'

The quarterdeck was suddenly illuminated, the sinister blue light blending with the equally sinister crimson of the Bengal fire. The last splutterings had hardly died away before the answer came from the flagship, a blue light that winked three times as it was momentarily screened.

'Flagship acknowledges, sir!'

'Very well.'

And this was the end of his stay in harbour, of his visit to England. He had seen the last of Maria for months to come; she would be a mother when he saw her next.

'Sheet home!'

Hotspur was gathering way, turning on her heel with a fair wind to weather Berry Head. Hornblower's mind played with a score of inconsequential thoughts as he struggled to put aside his overwhelming melancholy. He remembered the brief private conversation that he had witnessed between Cornwallis and the steward. He was quite sure that the latter had been telling his Admiral about the parcel prepared for transmission to *Hotspur*. Doughty was not nearly as clever as he thought he was. That conclusion called up a weak smile as *Hotspur* breasted the waters of the Channel, with Berry Head looming up on her starboard beam.

15

Now it was cold, horribly cold; the days were short and the nights were very, very long. Along with the cold weather came easterly winds – the one involved the other – and a reversal of the tactical situation. For although with the wind in the east *Hotspur* was relieved of the anxiety of being on a lee shore her responsibilities were proportionately increased. There was nothing academic now about noting the direction of the wind each hour; it was no mere navigational routine. Should the wind blow from any one of ten points of the compass out of thirty-two it would be possible even for the lubberly French to make their exit down the Goulet and enter the Atlantic. Should they make the attempt it was *Hotspur*'s duty to pass an instant warning for the Channel Fleet to form line of battle if the French were rash enough to challenge action, and to cover every exit – by the Raz, by the Iroise, by the Four – if, as would be more likely, they attempted merely to escape.

Today the last of the flood did not make until two o'clock in the afternoon, a most inconvenient time, for it was not until then that *Hotspur* could venture in to make her daily reconnaissance at closest range. To do so earlier would be to risk that a failure of the wind, leaving her at the mercy of the tide, would sweep her helplessly up, within range of the batteries on Petit Minou and the Capuchins – the Toulinguet battery; and more assuredly fatal than the batteries would be the reefs, Pollux and the Little Girls.

Hornblower came out on deck with the earliest light – not very early on this almost the shortest day of the year – to check the position of the ship while Prowse took the bearings of the Petit Minou and the Grand Gouin.

'Merry Christmas, sir,' said Bush. It was typical of a military service that Bush should have to touch his hat while saying those words.

'Thank you. The same to you, Mr Bush.'

It was typical, also, that Hornblower should have been acutely aware that it was December 25th and yet should have forgotten that it was Christmas Day; tide tables made no reference to the festivals of the church.

'Any news of your good lady, sir?' asked Bush.

'Not yet,' answered Hornblower, with a smile that was only half-forced. 'The letter I had yesterday was dated the eighteenth, but there's nothing as yet.'

It was one more indication of the way the wind had been blowing, that he should have received a letter from Maria in six days; a victualler had brought it out with a fair wind. That also implied that it might be six weeks before his reply reached Maria, and in six weeks – in one week – everything would be changed, and the child would be born. A naval officer writing to his wife had to keep one eye on the windvane just as the Lords of the Admiralty had to do when drafting their orders for the movements of fleets. New Year's Day was the date Maria and the midwife had decided upon; at that time Maria would be reading the letters he wrote a month ago. He wished he had written more sympathetically, but nothing he could do could recall, alter, or supplement those letters.

All he could do would be to spend some of this morning composing a letter that might belatedly compensate for the deficiencies of its predecessors (and Hornblower realized with a stab of conscience that this was not the first time he had reached that decision) while it would be even more difficult than usual because it would have to be composed with an eye to all eventualities. All eventualities; Hornblower felt in that moment the misgivings of every prospective father.

He spent until eleven o'clock on these unsatisfactory literary exercises, and it was with guilty relief that he returned to the quarterdeck to take *Hotspur* up with the last of the tide with the well-remembered coasts closing in upon her on both sides. The weather was reasonably clear; not a sparkling Christmas Day, but with little enough haze at noon, when Hornblower gave the orders that hove *Hotspur* to, as close to Pollux Reef as he dared. The dull thud of a gun from Petit Minou coincided with his orders. The rebuilt battery there was firing its usual range-testing shot in the hope that this time he had come in too far. Did they recognize the ship that had done them so much damage? Presumably.

'Their morning salute, sir,' said Bush.

'Yes.'

Hornblower took the telescope into his gloved, yet frozen, hands and trained it up the Goulet as he always did. Often there was something new to observe. Today there was much.

'Four new ships at anchor, sir,' said Bush.

'I make it five. Isn't that a new one – the frigate in line with the church steeple?'

'Don't think so, sir. She's shifted anchorage. Only four new ones by my count.'

'You're right, Mr Bush.'

'Yards crossed, sir. And – sir, would you look at those tops'l yards?'

Hornblower was already looking.

'I can't be sure.'

'I think those are tops'ls furled over-all, sir.'

'It's possible.'

A sail furled over-all was much thinner and less noticeable, with the loose part gathered into the bunt about the mast, than one furled in the usual fashion.

'I'll go up to the masthead myself, sir. And young Foreman has good eyes. I'll take him with me.'

'Very well. No, wait a moment, Mr Bush. I'll go myself. Take charge of the ship, if you please. But you can send Foreman up.'

Hornblower's decision to go aloft was proof of the importance he attached to observation of the new ships. He was uncomfortably aware of his slowness and awkwardness, and it was only reluctantly that he exhibited them to his lightfooted and light-hearted subordinates. But there was something about those ships . . .

He was breathing heavily by the time he reached the foretopmasthead, and it took several seconds to steady himself sufficiently to fix the ships in the field of the telescope, but he was much warmer. Foreman was there already, and the regular lookout shrank away out of the notice of his betters. Neither Foreman nor the lookout could be sure about those furled topsails.

They thought it likely, yet they would not commit themselves.

'D'you make out anything else about those ships, Mr Foreman?'

'Well, no, sir. I can't say that I do.'

'D'you think they're riding high?'

'Maybe, yes, sir.'

Two of the new arrivals were small two-deckers – sixty-fours, probably – and the lower tier of gun ports in each case might be farther above the waterline than one might expect. It was not a matter of measurement, all the same; it was more a matter of intuition, of good taste. Those hulls were just not quite right, although, Foreman, willing enough to oblige, clearly did not share his feelings.

Hornblower's glass swept the shores round the anchorage, questing for any further data. There were the rows of hutments that housed the troops. French soldiers were notoriously well able to look after themselves, to build themselves adequate shelter; the smoke of their cooking fires was clearly visible – today, of course, they would be cooking their Christmas dinners. It was from here that had come the battalion that had chased him back to the boats the day he blew up the battery. Hornblower's glass checked itself, moved along and returned again. With the breeze that was blowing he could not be certain, but it seemed to him that from two rows of huts there was no smoke to be seen. It was all a little vague; he could not even estimate the number of troops those huts would house; two thousand men, five thousand men; and he was still doubtful about the absence of cooking smoke.

'Captain, sir!' Bush was hailing from the deck. 'The tide's turned.'

'Very well. I'll come down.'

He was abstracted and thoughtful when he reached the deck.

'Mr Bush, I'll be wanting fish for my dinner soon. Keep a special lookout for the *Duke's Freers*.'

He had to pronounce it that way to make sure Bush understood him. Two days later he found himself in his cabin drinking rum – pretending to drink rum – with the captain of the *Deux Frères*. He had bought himself half a dozen unidentifiable fish, which the captain strongly recommended as good eating. 'Carrelets,' the captain called them – Hornblower had a vague idea that they might be flounders. At any rate, he paid for them with a gold piece which the captain slipped without comment into the pockets of his scale-covered serge trousers.

Inevitably the conversation shifted to the sights to be seen up the Goulet, and from the general to the particular, centring on the new arrivals in the anchorage. The captain dismissed them with a gesture as unimportant.

'*Armé's en flûte*,' he said, casually.

En flûte! That told the story. That locked into place the pieces of the puzzle. Hornblower took an unguarded gulp at his glass of rum and water and fought down the consequent cough so as to display no special interest. A ship of war with her guns taken out was like a flute when her ports were opened – she had a row of empty holes down her side.

'Not to fight,' explained the captain. 'Only for stores, or troops, or what you will.'

For troops especially. Stores could best be carried in merchant ships designed for cargo, but ships of war were constructed to carry large numbers of men – their cooking arrangements and water storage facilities had been built in with that in mind. With only as many seamen on board as were necessary to work the ship there was room to spare for soldiers. Then the guns would be unnecessary, and at Brest they could be immediately employed in arming new ships. Removing the guns meant a vast increase in available deck space into which more troops could be crammed; the more there were the more strain on the cooking and watering arrangements, but on a short voyage they would not have long to suffer. A short voyage. Not the West Indies, nor Good Hope, and certainly not India. A forty-gun frigate armed *en flûte* might have as many as a thousand soldiers packed into her. Three thousand men, plus a few hundred more in the armed escorts. The smallness of the number ruled out England – not even Bonaparte, so improvident with human life, would throw away a force that size in an invasion of England where there was at least a small army and a large militia. There was only one possible target; Ireland, where a disaffected population meant a weak militia.

'They are no danger to me, then,' said Hornblower, hoping that the interval during which he had been making these deductions had not been so long as to be obvious.

'Not even to this little ship,' agreed the Breton captain with a smile.

It called for the exertion of all Hornblower's moral strength to continue the interview without allowing his agitation to show. He wanted to get instantly into action, but he dared not appear impatient; the Breton captain wanted another three-finger glass of rum and was unaware of any need for haste. Luckily Hornblower remembered an admonition from Doughty, who had impressed on him the desirability of buying cider as well as fish, and Hornblower introduced the new subject. Yes, agreed the captain, there was a keg of cider on board the *Deux Frères*, but he could not say how much was left, as they had tapped it already during the day. He would sell what was left.

Hornblower forced himself to bargain; he did not want the Breton captain to know that his recent piece of information was worth further gold. He suggested that the cider, of an unknown quantity, should be given him for nothing extra, and the captain, with an avaricious gleam in his peasant's eye, indignantly refused. For some minutes the argument proceeded while the rum sank lower in the captain's glass.

'One franc, then,' offered Hornblower at last. 'Twenty sous.'

'Twenty sous and a glass of rum,' said the captain, and Hornblower had to reconcile himself to that much further delay, but it was worth it to retain the captain's respect and to allay the captain's suspicions.

So that it was with his head swimming with rum – a sensation he detested – that Hornblower sat down at last to write his urgent despatch, having seen his guest down the side. No mere signal could convey all that he wanted to say, and no signal would be secret enough, either. He had to choose his words as carefully as the rum would permit, as he stated his suspicions that the French might be planning an invasion of Ireland, and as he gave his reasons for those suspicions. He was satisfied at last, and wrote 'H. Hornblower, Commander', at the foot of the letter. Then he turned over the sheet and wrote the address: 'Rear Admiral William Parker, Commanding the Inshore Squadron', on the other side, and folded and sealed the letter. Parker was one of the extensive Parker clan; there were and had been admirals and captains innumerable with that name, none of them specially distinguished; perhaps his letter would alter that tradition.

He sent it off – a long and arduous trip for the boat, and waited impatiently for the acknowledgement.

Sir,

Your letter of this date has been received and will be given my full attention.

Your ob'd serv't,

Wm Parker.

Hornblower read the few words in a flash; he had opened the letter on the quarterdeck without waiting to retire with it to his cabin, and he put it in his pocket hoping that his expression betrayed no disappointment.

'Mr Bush,' he said, 'We shall have to maintain a closer watch than ever over the Goulet, particularly at night and in thick weather.'

'Aye aye, sir.'

Probably Parker needed time to digest the information, and would later produce a plan; until that time it was Hornblower's duty to act without orders.

'I shall take the ship up to the Little Girls whenever I can do so unobserved.'

'The Little Girls? Aye aye, sir.'

It was a very sharp glance that Bush directed at him. No one in his senses – at least no one except under the strongest compulsion – would risk his ship near those navigational dangers in conditions of bad visibility. True; but the compulsions existed. Three thousand well-trained French soldiers landing in Ireland would set that distressful country in a flame from end to end, a wilder flame than had burned in 1798.

'We'll try it tonight,' said Hornblower.

'Aye aye, sir.'

The Little Girls lay squarely in the middle of the channel of the Goulet; on either side lay a fairway a scant quarter of a mile wide, and up and down those fairways raced the tide; it would only be during the ebb that the French would be likely to come down. No, that was not strictly true, for the French could stem the flood tide with a fair wind – with this chill easterly wind blowing. The Goulet had to be watched in all conditions of bad visibility and *Hotspur* had to do the watching.

16

'I beg your pardon, sir,' said Bush, lingering after delivering his afternoon report, and hesitating before taking the next step he had clearly decided upon.

'Yes, Mr Bush?'

'You know, sir, you're not looking as well as you should.'

'Indeed?'

'You've been doing too much, sir. Day and night.'

'That's a strange thing for a seaman to say, Mr Bush. And a King's officer.'

'It's true, all the same, sir. You haven't had an hour's sleep at a time for days. You're thinner than I've ever known you, sir.'

'Thank you, Mr Bush. I'm going to turn in now, as a matter of fact.'

'I'm glad of that, sir.'

'See that I'm called the moment the weather shows signs of thickening.'

'Aye aye, sir.'

'Can I trust you, Mr Bush?'

That brought a smile into what was too serious a conversation.

'You can, sir.'

'Thank you, Mr Bush.'

It was interesting after Bush's departure to look into the speckled chipped mirror and observe his thinness, the cheeks and temples fallen in, the sharp nose and the pointed chin. But this was not the real Hornblower. The real one was inside, unaffected – as yet, at least – by privation or strain. The real Hornblower looked out at him from the hollow eyes in the mirror with a twinkle of recognition, a twinkle that brightened, not with malice, but with something akin to that – a kind of cynical amusement – at the sight of Hornblower seeking proof of the weaknesses of the flesh. But time was too precious to waste; the weary body that the real Hornblower had to drag about demanded repose. And, as regards the weaknesses of the flesh, how delightful, how comforting it was to clasp to his stomach the hot-water bottle that Doughty had put into his cot, to feel warm and relaxed despite the clamminess of the bedclothes and the searching cold that pervaded the cabin.

'Sir,' said Doughty, coming into the cabin after what seemed to be one minute's interval but which, his watch told him, was two hours. 'Mr Prowse sent me. It's snowing, sir.'

'Very well. I'll come.'

How often had he said those words? Every time the weather had thickened he had taken *Hotspur* up the Goulet, enduring the strain of advancing blind up into frightful danger, watching wind and tide, making the most elaborate calculations, alert for any change in conditions, ready to dash out again at the first hint of improvement, not only to evade the fire of the batteries, but also to prevent the French from discovering the close watch that was being maintained over them.

'It's only just started to snow, sir,' Doughty was saying. 'But Mr Prowse says it's set in for the night.'

With Doughty's assistance Hornblower had bundled himself automatically into his deck clothing without noticing what he was doing. He went out into a changed world, where his feet trod a thin carpet of snow on the deck, and where Prowse loomed up in the darkness shimmering in the white coating of snow on his oilskins.

'Wind's nor' by east, sir, moderate. An hour of flood still to go.'

'Thank you. Turn the hands up and send them to quarters, if you please. They can sleep at the guns.'

'Aye aye, sir.'

'Five minutes from now I don't want to hear a sound.'

'Aye aye, sir.'

This was only regular routine. The less the distance one could see the readier the ship had to be to open fire should an enemy loom up close alongside. But there was no routine about his own duties; every time he took the ship up conditions were different, the wind blowing from a different compass point and the tide of a different age. This was the first time the wind had been so far round to the north. Tonight he would have to shave the shallows off Petit Minou as close as he dared, and then, close-hauled, with the last of the flood behind him, *Hotspur* could just ascend the northern channel, with the Little Girls to starboard.

There was spirit left in the crew; there were jokes and cries of surprise when they emerged into the snow from the stinking warmth of the 'tween deck, but sharp orders suppressed every sound. *Hotspur* was deadly quiet, like a ghost ship when the yards had been trimmed and the helm orders given and she began to make her way through the impenetrable night, night more impenetrable than ever with the air full of snowflakes silently dropping down upon them.

A shuttered lantern at the taffrail for reading the log, although the log's indications were of minor importance, when speed over the ground could be so different – instinct and experience were more important. Two hands in the port-side mainchains with the lead. Hornblower on the weather side of the quarterdeck could hear quite a quiet call, even though there was a hand stationed to relay it if necessary. Five fathoms. Four fathoms. If his navigation were faulty they would strike before the next cast. Aground under the guns of Petit Minou, ruined and destroyed; Hornblower could not restrain himself from clenching his gloved hands and tightening his muscles. Six and a half fathoms. That was what he had calculated upon, but it was a relief, nevertheless – Hornblower felt a small contempt for himself at feeling relieved, at his lack of faith in his own judgement.

'Full and bye,' he ordered.

They were as close under Petit Minou as possible, a quarter of a mile from those well-known hills, but there was nothing visible at all. There might be a solid back wall a yard from Hornblower's eyes whichever way he turned them. Eleven fathoms; they were on the edge of the fairway now. The last of the flood, two days after the lowest neaps, and wind north by east; the current should be less than a knot and the eddy off Mengam non-existent.

'No bottom!'

More than twenty fathoms; that was right.

'A good night this for the Frogs, sir,' muttered Bush beside him; he had been waiting for this moment.

Certainly it was a good night for the French if they were determined to escape. They knew the times of ebb and flood as well as he did. They would see the snow. Comfortable time for them to up anchor and get under weigh, and make the passage of the Goulet with a fair wind and ebb tide. Impossible for them to escape by the Four with this wind; the Iroise was guarded – he hoped – by the Inshore Squadron, but on a night as black as this they might try it in preference to the difficult Raz du Sein.

Nineteen fathoms; he was above the Little Girls, and he could be confident of weathering Mengam. Nineteen fathoms.

'Should be slack water now, sir,' muttered Prowse, who had just looked at his watch in the light of the shaded binnacle.

They were above Mengam now; the lead should record a fairly steady nineteen fathoms for the next few minutes, and it was time that he should plan out the next move – the next move but one, rather. He conjured up the chart before his mental eye.

'Listen!' Bush's elbow dug into Hornblower's ribs with the urgency of the moment.

'Avast there at the lead!' said Hornblower. He spoke in a normal tone to make sure he was understood; with the wind blowing that way his voice would not carry far in the direction he was peering into.

There was the sound again; there were other noises. A long drawn monosyllable borne by the wind, and Hornblower's straining senses picked it up. It was a Frenchman calling 'seize', sixteen. French pilots still used the old-fashioned *toise* to measure depths, and the *toise* was slightly greater than the English fathom.

'Lights!' muttered Bush, his elbow at Hornblower's ribs again. There was a gleam here and there – the Frenchman had not darkened his ship nearly as effectively as the *Hotspur*. There was enough light to give some sort of indication. A ghost ship sweeping by within biscuit toss. The topsails were suddenly visible – there must be a thin coating of snow on the after surfaces whose gleaming white could reflect any light there was. And then –

'Three red lights in a row on the mizzen-tops'l yard,' whispered Bush.

Visible enough now; shaded in front, presumably, with the light directed aft to guide following ships. Hornblower felt a surge of inspiration, of instant decision, plans for the moment, plans for the next five minutes, plans for the more distant future.

'Run!' he snapped at Bush. 'Get three lights hoisted the same way. Keep 'em shaded, ready to show.'

Bush was off at the last word, but the thoughts had to come more rapidly like lightning. *Hotspur* dared not tack; she must wear.

'Wear ship!' he snapped at Prowse – no time for the politenesses he usually employed.

As *Hotspur* swung round he saw the three separated red lights join together almost into one, and at the same moment he saw a blue glare; the French ship was altering course to proceed down the Goulet and was burning a blue light as an indication to the ships following to up helm in succession. Now he could see the second French ship, a second faint ghost – the blue light helped to reveal it.

Pellew in the old *Indefatigable*, when Hornblower was

a prisoner in Ferrol, had once confused a French squadron escaping from Brest by imitating the French signals, but that had been in the comparatively open waters of the Iroise. It had been in Hornblower's mind to try similar tactics, but here in the narrow Goulet there was a possibility of more decisive action.

'Bring her to the wind on the starboard tack,' he snapped at Prowse, and *Hotspur* swung round further still, the invisible hands hauling at the invisible braces.

There was the second ship in the French line just completing her turn, with *Hotspur*'s bows pointing almost straight at her.

'Starboard a little.' *Hotspur*'s bows swung away. 'Meet her.'

He wanted to be as close alongside as he possibly could be without running foul of her.

'I've sent a good hand up with the lights, sir.' This was Bush reporting. 'Another two minutes and they'll be ready.'

'Get down to the guns,' snapped Hornblower, and then, with the need for silence at an end, he reached for the speaking-trumpet.

'Maindeck! Man the starboard guns! Run 'em out.'

How would the French squadron be composed? It would have an armed escort, not to fight its way through the Channel Fleet, but to protect the transports, after the escape, from stray British cruising frigates. There would be two big frigates, one in the van and one bringing up the rear, while the intermediate ships would be defenceless transports, frigates armed *en flûte*.

'Starboard! Steady!'

Yard arm to yard arm with the second ship in the

line, going down the Goulet alongside her, ghost ships side by side in the falling snow. The rumble of gun-trucks had ceased.

'Fire!'

At ten guns, ten hands jerked at the lanyards, and *Hotspur*'s side burst into flame, illuminating the sails and hull of the Frenchman with a bright glare; in the instantaneous glare of the gunfire snowflakes were visible as if stationary in mid air.

'Fire away, you men!'

There were cries and shouts to be heard from the French ship, and then a French voice speaking almost in his ear – the French captain hailing him from thirty yards away with his speaking-trumpet pointed straight at him. It would be an expostulation, the French captain wondering why a French ship should be firing into him, here where no British ship could possibly be. The words were cut off abruptly by the bang and the flash of the first gun of the second broadside, the others following as the men loaded and fired as fast as they could. Each flash brought a momentary revelation of the French ship, a flickering, intermittent picture. Those nine-pounder balls were crashing into a ship crammed with men. At this very moment, as he stood there rigid on the deck, men were dying in agony by the score just over there, for no more reason than that they had been forced into the service of a continental tyrant. Surely the French would not be able to bear it. Surely they would flinch under this unexpected and unexplainable attack. Ah! She was turning away, although she had nowhere to turn to except the cliffs and shoals of the shore close overside. There were the three red lights on her mizzen-topsail yard. By accident or design she had put her helm down. He must make sure of her.

'Port a little.'

Hotspur swung to starboard, her guns blazing. Enough.

'Starboard a little. Steady as you go.'

Now the speaking-trumpet. 'Cease fire!'

The silence that followed was broken by the crash as the Frenchman struck the shore, the clatter of falling spars, the yells of despair. And in this darkness, after the glare of the guns, he was blinder than ever, and yet he must act as if he could see; he must waste no moment.

'Back the maintops'l! Stay by the braces!'

The rest of the French line must be coming down, willy-nilly; with the wind over their quarter and the ebb under their keels and rocks on either side of them they could do nothing else. He must think quicker than they; he still had the advantage of surprise – the French captain in the following ship would not yet have had time to collect his thoughts.

The Little Girls were under their lee; he must not delay another moment.

'Braces, there!'

Here she came, looming up, close, close, yells of panic from her forecastle.

'Hard-a-starboard!'

Hotspur had just enough way through the water to respond to her rudder; the two bows swung from each other, collision averted by a hair's breadth.

'Fire!'

The Frenchman's sails were all a-shiver; she was not under proper control, and with those nine-pounder balls sweeping her deck she would not recover quickly. *Hotspur* must not pass ahead of her; he still had a little time and a little room to spare.

'Maintops'l aback!'

This was a well-drilled crew; the ship was working like a machine. Even the powder-boys, climbing and descending the ladders in pitch darkness, were carrying out their duties with exactitude, keeping the guns supplied with powder, for the guns never ceased from firing, bellowing in deafening fashion and bathing the Frenchman with orange light while the smoke blew heavily away on the disengaged side.

He could not spare another moment with the maintopsail aback. He must fill and draw ahead even if it meant disengagement.

'Braces, there!'

He had not noticed until now the infernal din of the quarterdeck carronades beside him; they were firing rapidly, sweeping the transport's deck with grape. In their flashes he saw the Frenchman's masts drawing aft as *Hotspur* regained her way. Then in the next flash he saw something else, another momentary picture – a ship's bowsprit crossing the Frenchman's deck from the disengaged side, and he heard a crash and the screams. The next Frenchman astern had run bows on into her colleague. The first rending crash was followed by others; he strode aft to try to see, but already the darkness had closed like a wall round his blinded eyes. He could only listen, but what he heard told him the story. The ship that rammed was swinging with the wind, her bowsprit tearing through shrouds and halliards until it snapped against the mainmast. Then the foretopmast would fall, yards would fall. The two ships were locked together and helpless, with the Little Girls under their lee. Now he saw blue lights burning as they tried to deal with the hopeless situation; with the ships swinging the blue lights and the red lights on the yards were revolving round each other like some planetary system. There was no chance of escape for them; as wind and current carried him away he thought he heard the crash as they struck upon the Little Girls, but he could not be sure, and there was no time – of course there was no time – to think about it. At this stage of the ebb there was an eddy that set in upon Pollux Reef and he must allow for that. Then he would be out in the Iroise, whose waters he used to think so dangerous before he had ventured up the Goulet, and an unknown number of ships was coming down from Brest, forwarned now by all the firing and the tumult that an enemy was in their midst.

He took a hasty glance into the binnacle, gauged the force of the wind on his cheeks. The enemy – what there was left of them – would certainly, with this wind, run for the Raz du Sein, and would certainly give the Trepieds shoal a wide berth. He must post himself to intercept them; the next ship in the line must be close at hand in any case, but in a few seconds she would no longer be confined to the narrow channel of the Goulet. And what would the first frigate be doing, the one he had allowed to pass without attacking her?'

'Mainchains, there! Get the lead going.'

He must keep up to windward as best he could.

'No bottom! No bottom with this line.'

He was clear of Pollux, then.

'Avast, there, with the lead.'

They stood on steadily on the starboard tack; in the impenetrable darkness he could hear Prowse breathing heavily at his side and all else was silence round him. He would have to take another cast of the lead soon enough. What was that? Wind and water had brought a distinctive sound to his ears, a solemn noise, of a solid body falling into the water. It was the sound of a lead being cast – and then followed, at the appropriate interval, the high-pitched cry of the leadsman. There was a ship just up there to windward, and now with the distance lessening and with his hearing concentrated in that direction he could hear other sounds, voices, the working of yards. He leaned over the rail and spoke quietly down into the waist.

'Stand by your guns.'

There she was, looming faintly on the starboard bow.

'Starboard two points. Meet her.'

They saw *Hotspur* at that same moment; from out of the darkness came the hail of a speaking-trumpet, but in the middle of a word Hornblower spoke down into the waist again.

'Fire!'

The guns went off so nearly together that he felt *Hotspur*'s light fabric heel a little with the force of the recoil, and there again was the shape of a ship lit up by the glare of the broadside. He could not hope to force her on the shoals; there was too much sea-room for that. He took the speaking-trumpet.

'Elevate your guns! Aim for her spars!'

He could cripple her. The first gun of the new broadside went off immediately after he said the words – some fool had not paid attention. But the other guns fired after the interval necessary to withdraw the coigns, flash after flash, bang after bang. Again and again and again. Suddenly a flash revealed a change in the shape of the illuminated mizzen-topsail, and at the same moment that mizzen-topsail moved slowly back abaft the beam. The Frenchman had thrown all aback in a desperate attempt to escape this tormentor, risking being raked in the hope of passing under *Hotspur*'s stern to get before the wind. He would wear the *Hotspur* round and bring her under the fire of the port broadside and chase her on to the Trepieds; the speaking-trumpet was at his lips when the darkness ahead erupted into a volcano of fire.

Chaos. Out of the black snow-filled night had come a broadside, raking the *Hotspur* from bow to stern. Along with the sound and the flash came the rending crash of splintered woodwork, the loud ringing noise as a cannon ball hit the breech of a gun, the shriek of the flying splinters, and following on that came the screaming of a wounded man, cutting through the sudden new stillness.

One of the armed frigates of the escort – the leader of the line, most likely – had seen the firing and had been close enough to intervene. She had crossed *Hotspur*'s bows to fire in a raking broadside.

'Hard-a-starboard!'

He could not tack, even if he were prepared to take the chance of missing stays with the rigging as much cut up as it must be, for he was not clear of the transport yet. He must wear, even though it meant being raked once more.

'Wear the ship!'

Hotspur was turning even as her last guns fired into the transport. Then came the second broadside from ahead, flaring out of the darkness, a fraction of a second between each successive shot, crashing into *Hotspur*'s battered bows, while Hornblower stood, trying not to wince, thinking what he must do next. Was that the last shot? Now there was a new and rending crash forward, a succession of snapping noises, another thundering crash, and cries and shrieks from forward. That must be the foremast fallen. That must be the foretopsail yard crashing on the deck.

'Helm doesn't answer, sir,' called the quartermaster at the wheel.

With the foremast down *Hotspur* would tend to fly up in the wind, even if the wreckage were not dragging alongside to act as a sea-anchor. He could feel the wind shifting on his cheek. Now *Hotspur* was helpless. Now she could be battered to destruction by an enemy twice her size, with four times her weight of metal, with scantlings twice as thick to keep out *Hotspur*'s feeble shot. He would have to fight despairingly to the death. Unless . . . The enemy would be putting his helm a-starboard to rake *Hotspur* from astern, or he would be doing so as soon as he could make out in the darkness what had happened. Time would pass very fast and the wind was still blowing, thank God, and there was the transport close on his starboard side still. He spoke loudly into the speaking-trumpet.

'Silence! Silence!'

The bustle and clatter forward, where the hands had been struggling with the fallen spars, died away. Even the groaning wounded fell silent; that was discipline, and not the discipline of the cat o' nine tails. He could just hear the rumble of the French frigate's gun-trucks as they ran out the guns for the next broadside, and he could hear shouted orders. The French frigate was turning to deliver the *coup de grâce* as soon as she made certain of her target. Hornblower pointed the speaking-trumpet straight upwards as if addressing the sky, and he tried to keep his voice steady and quiet. He did not want the French frigate to hear.

'Mizzen-topsail yard! Unmask those lights.'

That was a bad moment; the lights might have gone out, the lad stationed on the yard might be dead. He had to speak again.

'Show those lights!'

Discipline kept the hand up there from hailing back, but there they were – one, two, three red lights along the mizzen-topsail yard. Even against the wind he heard a wild order being shouted from the French frigate, excitement, even panic in the voice. The French captain was ordering his guns not to fire. Perhaps he was thinking that some horrible mistake had already been made; perhaps in the bewildering darkness he was confusing *Hotspur* with her recent victim not so far off. At least he was holding fire; at least he was going off to leeward, and a hundred yards to leeward in that darkness was the equivalent of a mile in ordinary conditions.

'Mask those lights again!'

No need to give the Frenchman a mark for gunfire or an objective to which to beat back when he should clear up the situation. Now a voice spoke out of the darkness close to him.

'Bush reporting, sir. I've left the guns for the moment,

if you give me leave, sir. Foretops'ls all across the starboard battery. Can't fire those guns in any case yet.'

'Very well, Mr Bush. What's the damage?'

'Foremast's gone six feet above the deck, sir. Everything went over the starboard side. Most of the shrouds must have held – it's all trailing alongside.'

'Then we'll get to work – in silence, Mr Bush. I want every stitch of canvas got in first, and then we'll deal with the wreckage.'

'Aye aye, sir.'

Stripping the ship of her canvas would make her far less visible to the enemy's eyes, and would reduce *Hotspur*'s leeway while she rode to her strange sea-anchor. Next moment it was the carpenter, up from below.

'We're making water very fast, sir. Two feet in the hold. My men are plugging one shot hole, aft by the magazine, but there must be another one for'ard in the cable tier. We'll need hands at the pumps, sir, an' I'd like half a dozen more in the cable tier.'

'Very well.'

So much to be done, in a nightmare atmosphere of unreality, and then came an explanation of some of the unreality. Six inches of snow lay on the decks, piled in deeper drifts against the vertical surfaces, silencing as well as impeding every movement. But most of the sense of unreality stemmed from simple exhaustion, nervous and physical, and the exhaustion had to be ignored while the work went on, trying to think clearly in the numbing darkness, with the knowledge that the Trepieds shoal lay close under their lee, on a falling tide. Getting up sail when the wreckage had been cleared away, and discovering by sheer seaman's instinct how to handle *Hotspur* under sail without her foremast, with only the feel of the wind on his cheeks and the wavering compass in the binnacle to guide him, and the shoals waiting for him if he miscalculated.

'I'd like you to set the spritsail, Mr Bush, if you please.'

'Aye aye, sir.'

A dangerous job for the hands that had to spread the spritsail under the bowsprit in the dark, with all the accustomed stays swept away by the loss of the foremast, but it had to be done to supply the necessary leverage forward to keep *Hotspur* from turning into the wind. Setting the ponderous main-course, because the main-topmast could not be trusted to carry sail. Then creeping westward, with the coming of the dawn and the cessation of the snowfall. Then it was light enough to see the disorder of the decks and the trampled snow – snow stained pink here and there, in wide areas. Then at last came the sight of the *Doris*, and help at hand; it might almost be called safety, except that later they would have to beat back against contrary winds and with a jury fore-mast and in a leaky ship, to Plymouth and refitting.

It was when they saw *Doris* hoisting out her boats, despatching additional manpower, that Bush could turn to Hornblower with a conventional remark. Bush was not aware of his own appearance, his powder-blackened face, his hollow cheeks and his sprouting beard, but even without that knowledge the setting was bizarre enough to appeal to Bush's crude sense of humour.

'A Happy New Year to you, sir,' said Bush, with a death's head grin.

It was New Year's Day. Then to the two men the same thought occurred simultaneously, and Bush's grin was replaced by something more serious.

'I hope your good lady . . .'

He was taken unawares, and could not find the formal words.

'Thank you, Mr Bush.'

It was on New Year's Day that the child was expected. Maria might be in labour at this moment while they stood there talking.

17

'Will you be having dinner on board, sir?' asked Doughty.

'No,' replied Hornblower. He hesitated before he launched into the next speech that had occurred to him, but he decided to continue. 'Tonight Horatio Hornblower dines with Horatio Hornblower.'

'Yes, sir.'

No joke ever fell as flat as that one. Perhaps – certainly – it was too much to expect Doughty to catch the classical allusion, but he might at least have smiled, because it was obvious that his captain had condescended so far as to be facetious.

'You'll need your oilskins, sir. It's raining heavily still,' said Doughty of the almost immovable countenance.

'Thank you.'

It seemed to have rained every single day since *Hotspur* had crawled into Plymouth Sound. Hornblower walked out from the dockyard with the rain rattling on his oilskins as if it were hail and not rain, and it continued all the time it took him to make his way to Driver's Alley. The landlady's little daughter opened the door to his knock, and as he walked up the stairs to his lodgings he heard the voice of the other Horatio Hornblower loudly proclaiming his sorrows. He opened the door and entered the small, hot stuffy room where Maria was standing with the baby over her shoulder, its long clothes hanging below her waist. Her face lit with pleasure when she saw him, and she could hardly wait for him to peel off his dripping oilskins before she came to his arms. Hornblower kissed her hot cheek and tried to look round the corner at little Horatio, but the baby only put his face into his mother's shoulder and wailed.

'He's been fractious today, dear,' said Maria, apologetically.

'Poor little fellow! And what about you, my dear?' Hornblower was careful to make Maria the centre of his thoughts whenever he was with her.

'I'm well enough now, dear. I can go up and down the stairs like a bird.'

'Excellent.'

Maria patted the baby's back.

'I wish he would be good. I want him to smile for his father.'

'Perhaps I could try?'

'Oh, no!'

Maria was quite shocked at the notion that a man should hold a crying baby, even his own, but it was a delightful kind of shock, all the same, and she yielded the baby to his proffered arms. Hornblower held his child – it was always a slight surprise to find how light that bundle of clothes was – and looked down at the rather amorphous features and the wet nose.

'There!' said Hornblower. The act of transfer had quieted little Horatio for a moment at least.

Maria stood bathed in happiness at the sight of her husband holding her son. And Hornblower's emotions were strangely mixed; one emotion was astonishment at finding pleasure in holding his child, for he found it hard to believe that he was capable of such sentiment.

Maria held the back of the fireside armchair so that he could sit down in it, and then, greatly daring, kissed his hair.

'And how is the ship?' she asked, leaning over him.

'She's nearly ready for sea,' said Hornblower.

Hotspur had been in and out of dock, her bottom cleaned, her seams recaulked, her shot holes patched. Her new foremast had been put in, and the riggers had set up the standing rigging. She only had to renew her stores.

'Oh dear,' said Maria.

'Wind's steady in the west,' said Hornblower. Not that that would deter him from beating down Channel if he could once work *Hotspur* down the Sound – he could not think why he had held out this shred of hope to Maria.

Little Horatio began to wail again.

'Poor darling!' said Maria. 'Let me take him.'

'I can deal with him.'

'No. It – it isn't right.' It was all wrong, in Maria's mind, that a father should be afflicted by his child's tantrums. She thought of something else. 'You wished to see this, dear. Mother brought it in this afternoon from Lockhart's Library.'

She brought a magazine from the side table, and gave it in exchange for the baby, whom she clasped once more to her breast.

The magazine was the new number of the *Naval Chronicle*, and Maria with her free hand helped Hornblower to turn the pages.

'There!' Maria pointed to the relevant passage, on almost the last page. 'On January 1st last . . .' it began, it was the announcement of little Horatio's birth.

'The Lady of Captain Horatio Hornblower of the Royal Navy, of a son,' read Maria. 'That's me and little Horatio. I'm – I'm more grateful to you, dear, than I can ever tell you.'

'Nonsense,' replied Hornblower. That was just what he thought it was, but he made himself look up with a smile that took out any sting from what he said.

'They call you "Captain",' went on Maria, with an interrogative in the remark.

'Yes,' agreed Hornblower. 'That's because –'

He embarked once more on the explanation of the profound difference between a Commander by rank (and a Captain only by courtesy) and a Post Captain. He had said it all before, more than once.

'I don't think it's right,' decided Maria.

'Very few things are right, my dear,' said Hornblower, a little absently. He was leafing through the other pages of the *Naval Chronicle*, working forward from the back page where he had started. Here was the Plymouth Report, and here was one of the things he was looking for.

'Came in HM Sloop *Hotspur* under jury rig, from the Channel Fleet. She proceeded at once into dock. Captain Horatio Hornblower landed at once with despatches.' Then came the Law Intelligence, and the Naval Courts Martial, and the Monthly Register of Naval Events, and the Naval Debates in the Imperial Parliament, and then, between the Debates and the Poetry, came the *Gazette* Letters. And here it was. First, in italics, came the introduction.

'*Copy of a letter from Vice-Admiral Sir William Cornwallis* to Sir Evan Nepean, Bart., dated on board of HMS Hibernia, the 2nd instant.'

Next came Cornwallis' letter.

Sir,

I herewith transmit for their Lordships' information, copies of letters I have received from Captains Chambers of HMS Naiad and Hornblower of HM Sloop Hotspur, acquainting me of the capture of the French national frigate Clorinde and of the defeat of an attempt by the French to escape from Breast with a large body of Troops. The conduct of both these officers appears to me to be highly commendable. I enclose also a copy of a letter I have received from Captain Smith of HMS Doris.

I have the honour to be, with deepest respect,
Your ob'd't serv't,
Wm Cornwallis.

Chambers' report came next. *Naiad* had caught *Clorinde* near Molene and had fought her to a standstill, capturing her in forty minutes. Apparently the other French frigate which had come out with the transports had escaped by the Raz du Sein and had still not been caught.

Then at last came his own report. Hornblower felt the flush of excitement he had known before on reading his own words in print. He studied them afresh at this interval, and was grudgingly satisfied. They told, without elaboration, the bare facts of how three transports had been run ashore in the Goulet, and of how *Hotspur* while attacking a fourth had been in action with a French frigate and had lost her foremast. Not a word about saving Ireland from invasion; the merest half-sentence about the darkness and the snow and the navigational perils, but men who could understand would understand.

Smith's letter from the *Doris* was brief, too. After meeting *Hotspur* he had pushed in towards Brest and had found a French frigate, armed *en flûte*, aground on the Trepieds with shore boats taking off her troops. Under the fire of the French coastal batteries *Doris* had sent in her boats and had burned her.

'There's something more in the *Chronicle* that might interest you, dear,' said Hornblower. He proffered the magazine with his finger indicating his letter.

'Another letter from you, dear!' said Maria. 'How pleased you must be!'

She read the letter quickly.

'I haven't had time to read this before,' she said, looking up. 'Little Horatio was so fractious. And – and – I never understand all these letters, dear. I hope you are proud of what you did. I'm sure you are, of course.'

Luckily little Horatio set up a wail at that moment to save Hornblower from a specific answer to that speech. Maria pacified the baby and went on.

'The shopkeepers will know about this tomorrow and they'll all speak to me about it.'

The door opened to admit Mrs Mason, her pattens clattering on her feet, raindrops sparkling on her shawl. She and Hornblower exchanged 'good evenings' while she took off her outer clothing.

'Let me take that child,' said Mrs Mason to her daughter.

'Horry has another letter in the *Chronicle*,' countered Maria.

'Indeed?'

Mrs Mason sat down across the fire from Hornblower and studied the page with more care than Maria had done, but perhaps with no more understanding.

'The Admiral says your conduct was "very Commendable",' she said, looking up.

'Yes.'

'Why doesn't he make you a real captain, "post", as you call it?'

'The decision doesn't lie with him,' said Hornblower. 'And I doubt if he would in any case.'

'Can't admirals make captains?'

'Not in home waters.'

The god-like power of promotion freely exercised on distant stations was denied to commanders-in-chief where speedy reference to the Admiralty was possible.

'And what about prize money?'

'There's none for the *Hotspur*.'

'But this – this *Clorinde* was captured?'

'Yes, but we weren't in sight.'

'But you were fighting, weren't you?'

'Yes, Mrs Mason. But only ships in sight share in prize money. Except for the flag officers.'

'And aren't you a flag officer?'

'No. Flag officer means "Admiral", Mrs Mason.'

Mrs Mason sniffed.

'It all seems very strange. So you do not profit at all by this letter?'

'No, Mrs Mason.' At least not in the way Mrs Mason meant.

'It's about time you made some prize money. I hear all the time about the ships that have made thousands.

330

Eight pounds a month for Maria, and her with a child.'
Mrs Mason looked round at her daughter. 'Threepence
a pound for neck of mutton! The cost of things is more
than I can understand.'

'Yes, mother. Horry gives me all he can, I'm sure.'

As captain of a ship below the sixth rate Hornblower's pay was twelve pounds a month, and he still
needed those new uniforms. Prices were rising with
wartime demand, and the Admiralty, despite many
promises, had not yet succeeded in obtaining an increase
in pay for naval officers.

'Some captains make plenty,' said Mrs Mason.

It was prize money, and the possibility of gaining it,
that kept the Navy quiet under the otherwise intolerable conditions. The great mutinies at Spithead and the
Nore were less than ten years old. But Hornblower felt
he would be drawn into a defence of the prize money
system shortly if Mrs Mason persisted in talking as she
did. Luckily the entrance of the landlady to lay the table
for supper changed the subject of conversation. With
another person in the room neither Mrs Mason nor
Maria would discuss such a low subject as money, and
they talked about indifferent matters instead. They sat
down to dinner when the landlady brought in a steaming
tureen.

'The pearl barley's at the bottom, Horatio,' said Mrs
Mason, supervising him as he served the food.

'Yes, Mrs Mason.'

'And you'd better give Maria that other chop – that
one's meant for you.'

'Yes, Mrs Mason.'

Hornblower had learned to keep a still tongue in his

head under the goadings of tyranny when he was a lieutenant in the old *Renown* under Captain Sawyer's command, but he had well-nigh forgotten those lessons by now, and was having painfully to relearn them. He had married of his own free will – he could have said 'no' at the altar, he remembered – and now he had to make the best of a bad business. Quarrelling with his mother-in-law would not help. It was a pity that *Hotspur* had come in for docking at the moment when Mrs Mason had arrived to see her daughter through her confinement, but he need hardly fear a repetition of the coincidence during the days – the endless days – to come.

Stewed mutton and pearl barley and potatoes and cabbage. It might have been a very pleasant dinner, except that the atmosphere was unfavourable; in two senses. The room, with its sea-coal fire, was unbearably hot. Thanks to the rain no washing could be hung out of doors, and Hornblower doubted if in the vicinity of Driver's Alley washing could be hung out of doors unwatched in any case. So that on a clothes-horse on the other side of the room hung little Horatio's clothing, and somehow nature arranged it that every stitch little Horatio wore had to be washed, as often as several times a day. Hanging on the horse were the long embroidered gowns, and the long flannel gowns with their scalloped borders, and the flannel shirts, and the binders, as well as the innumerable napkins that might have been expected to sacrifice themselves, like a rearguard, in the defence of the main body. Hornblower's wet oilskins and Mrs Mason's wet shawl added variant notes to the smells in the room, and Hornblower suspected that little

Horatio, now in the cradle beside Maria's chair, added yet another.

Hornblower thought of the keen clean air of the Atlantic and felt his lungs would burst. He did his best with his dinner, but it was a poor best.

'You're not making a very good dinner, Horatio,' said Mrs Mason, peering suspiciously at his plate.

'I suppose I'm not very hungry.'

'Too much of Doughty's cooking, I expect,' said Mrs Mason.

Hornblower knew already, without a word spoken, that the women were jealous of Doughty and ill at ease in his presence. Doughty had served the rich and the great; Doughty knew of fancy ways of cooking; Doughty wanted money to bring the cabin stores of the *Hotspur* up to his own fastidious standards; Doughty (in the women's minds, at least) was probably supercilious about Driver's Alley and the family his captain had married into.

'I can't abide that Doughty,' said Maria – the word was spoken now.

'He's harmless enough, my dear,' said Hornblower.

'Harmless!' Mrs Mason said only that one word, but Demosthenes could not have put more vituperation into a whole Philippic; and yet, when the landlady came in to clear the table, Mrs Mason contrived to be at her loftiest.

As the landlady left the room Hornblower's instincts guided him into an action of which he was actually unconscious. He threw up the window and drew the icy evening air deep into his lungs.

'You'll give him his death!' said Maria's voice, and Hornblower swung round, surprised.

Maria had snatched up little Horatio from his cradle and stood clasping him to her bosom, a lioness defending her cub from the manifest and well-known perils of the night air.

'I beg your pardon, dear,' said Hornblower. 'I can't imagine what I was thinking of.'

He knew perfectly well that little babies should be kept in stuffy heated rooms, and he was full of genuine contrition regarding little Horatio. But as he turned back and pulled the window shut again his mind was dwelling on the Blackstones and the Little Girls, on bleak harsh days and dangerous nights, on a deck that he could call his own. He was ready to go to sea again.

18

With the coming of spring a new liveliness developed in the blockade of Brest. In every French port during the winter there had been much building of flat-bottomed boats. The French army, two hundred thousand strong, was still poised on the Channel coast, waiting for its chance to invade, and it needed gun-boats by the thousand to ferry it over when that chance should come. But the invasion coast from Boulogne to Ostend could not supply one-tenth, one-hundredth of the vessels needed; these had to be built whenever there were facilities, and then had to be moved along the coast to the assembling area.

To Hornblower's mind Bonaparte – the Emperor Napoleon, as he was beginning to call himself – was displaying a certain confusion of ideas in adopting this course of action. Seamen and shipbuilding materials were scarce enough in France; it was absurd to waste them on invasion craft when invasion was impossible without a covering fleet, and when the French navy was too small to provide such a fleet. Lord St Vincent had raised an appreciative smile throughout the Royal Navy when he had said in the House of Lords regarding the French army, 'I do not say they cannot come. I only say they cannot come by sea.' The jest had called up a ludicrous picture in everyone's mind of Bonaparte trying to transport an invading army by Montgolfier balloons, and the impossibility of such an attempt underlined the impossibility of the French building up a fleet strong enough to command the Channel even long enough for the gun-boats to row across.

It was only by the time summer was far advanced that Hornblower fully understood Bonaparte's quandary. Bonaparte had to persist in this ridiculous venture, wasting the substance of his empire on ships and landing-craft even though a sensible man might well write off the whole project and devote his resources to some more profitable scheme. But to do so would be an admission that England was impregnable, could never be conquered, and such an admission would not only hearten his potential Continental enemies but would have a most unsettling effect on the French people themselves. He was simply compelled to continue along this road, to go on building his ships and his gun-boats to make the world believe there was a likelihood that England would soon be overthrown, leaving him dominant everywhere on earth, lord of the whole human race.

And there was always chance, even if it were not one chance in ten or one chance in a hundred, but one in a million. Some extraordinary, unpredictable combination of good fortune, of British mismanagement, of weather, and of political circumstances might give him the week he needed to get his army across. If the odds were enormous at least the stakes were fantastic. In itself that might appeal to a gambler like Bonaparte even without the force of circumstance to drive him on.

So the flat-bottomed boats were built at every little fishing village along the coast of France, and they crept from their places of origin towards the great military camp of Boulogne, keeping to the shallows, moving by oar more than by sail, sheltering when necessary under the coastal batteries, each boat manned by fifty soldiers and a couple of seamen. And because Bonaparte was moving these craft, the Royal Navy felt bound to interfere with the movement as far as possible.

That was how it came about that *Hotspur* found herself momentarily detached from the Channel Fleet and forming a part of a small squadron under the orders of Chambers of the *Naiad* operating to the northward of Ushant, which was doing its best to prevent the passage of half a dozen gun-boats along the wild and rocky shore of Northern Brittany.

'Signal from the Commodore, sir,' reported Foreman.

Chambers spent a great deal of time signalling to his little squadron.

'Well?' asked Hornblower; Foreman was referring to his signal book.

'Take station within sight bearing east nor'east, sir.'

'Thank you, Mr Foreman. Acknowledge. Mr Bush, we'll square away.'

A pleasant day, with gentle winds from the south east, and occasional white clouds coursing over a blue sky. Overside the sea was green and clear, and two miles off on the beam was the coast with its white breakers; the chart showed strange names, Aber Wrack and Aber Benoit, which told of the relationship between the Breton tongue and Welsh. Hornblower divided his attention between the *Naiad* and the coast as *Hotspur* ran down before the wind, and he experienced something of the miser's feeling at some depletion of his gold. It might be necessary to go off like this to leeward, but every hour so spent might call for a day of beating back to windward. The decisive strategical point was outside Brest where lay the French ships of the line, not here where the little gun-boats were making their perilous passage.

'You may bring-to again, Mr Bush.'

'Aye aye, sir.'

They were now so far from *Naiad* that it would call for a sharp eye and a good glass to read her signals.

'We're the terrier at the rat hole, sir,' said Bush, coming back to Hornblower as soon as *Hotspur* had lain-to with her maintopsail to the mast.

'Exactly,' agreed Hornblower.

'Boats are cleared away ready to launch, sir.'

'Thank you.'

They might have to dash in to attack the gun-boats when they came creeping along just outside the surf.

'Commodore's signalling, sir,' reported Foreman again. 'Oh, it's for the lugger, sir.'

'There she goes!' said Bush.

The small armed lugger was moving in towards the shore.

'That's the ferret going down the hole, Mr Bush,' said Hornblower, unwontedly conversational.

'Yes, sir. There's a gun! There's another!'

They could hear the reports, borne on the wind, and could see the gusts of smoke.

'Is there a battery there, sir?'

'Maybe. Maybe the gun-boats are using their own cannon.'

Each gun-boat mounted one or two heavy guns in

the bows, but they laboured under the disadvantage that half a dozen discharges racked the little vessels to pieces by the recoil. The theory behind those guns was that they were to be used for clearing beaches of defending troops where the invasion should take place and the gunboats should be safely beached.

'Can't make out what's happening,' fumed Bush; a low headland cut off their view.

'Firing's heavy,' said Hornblower. 'Must be a battery there.'

He felt irritated; the Navy was expending lives and material on an objective quite valueless, in his opinion. He beat his gloved hands together in an effort to restore their warmth, for there was an appreciable chilliness in the wind.

'What's that?' exclaimed Bush, excitedly training his telescope. 'Look at that, sir! Dismasted, by God!'

Just visible round the point now was a shape that could not instantly be recognized. It was the lugger, drifting disabled and helpless. Everything about the situation indicated that she had run into a well-planned ambush.

'They're still firing at her, sir,' remarked Prowse. The telescope just revealed the splashes round her as cannon balls plunged into the sea.

'We'll have to save her,' said Hornblower, trying to keep the annoyance out of his voice. 'Square away, if you please, Mr Prowse, and we'll run down.'

It was extremely irritating to have to go into danger like this, to redeem someone else's mismanagement of an expedition unjustified from the start.

'Mr Bush, get a cable out aft ready to tow.'

'Aye aye, sir.'

'Commodore's signalling, sir.' This was Foreman speaking. 'Our number. "Assist damaged vessel."'

'Acknowledge.'

Chambers had ordered that signal before he could see that *Hotspur* was already on the move.

Hornblower scanned the shore on this side of the headland. There was no gun-smoke on this side, no sign of any battery. With luck all he would have to do was to haul the lugger round the corner. Down in the waist the voices of Bush and Wise were urging a working party to their utmost efforts as they took the ponderous cable aft. Things were happening fast, as they always did at crises. A shot screamed overhead as Hornblower reached for the speaking-trumpet.

'*Grasshopper*! Stand by to take a line!'

Somebody in the disabled lugger waved a handkerchief in acknowledgement.

'Back the maintops'l, Mr Prowse, and we'll go down to her.'

That was when the *Grasshopper* disintegrated, blew apart, in two loud explosions and a cloud of smoke. It happened right under Hornblower's eyes, as he leaned over with his speaking-trumpet; one second there was the intact hull of the lugger, with living men working on the wreckage, and the next the smoking explosions, the flying fragments, the billowing smoke. It must have been a shell from the shore; there were howitzers or mortars mounted there. Most likely a field howitzer battery, light and easily moved across country, which had been brought up to protect the gun-boats. A shell must have dropped into the lugger and burst in the magazine.

Hornblower had seen it all, and when the cloud of smoke dispersed the bow and stern did not disappear from sight. They were floating waterlogged on the surface, and Hornblower could see a few living figures as well, clinging to the wreckage among the fragments.

'Lower the quarter-boat! Mr Young, go and pick up those men.'

This was worse than ever. Shell fire was a horrible menace to a wooden ship that could so easily be set into an inextinguishable blaze. It was utterly infuriating to be exposed to these perils for no profit. The quarter-boat was on its way back when the next shell screamed overhead. Hornblower recognized the difference in the sound from that of a round-shot; he should have done so earlier. A shell from a howitzer had a belt about it, a thickening in the centre which gave its flight, as it arched across the sky, the peculiarly malevolent note he had already heard.

It was the French army that was firing at them. To fight the French navy was the essence of *Hotspur*'s duty, and of his own, but to expose precious ships and seamen to the attack of soldiers who cost almost nothing to a government that enforced conscription was bad business, and to expose them without a chance of firing back was sheer folly. Hornblower drummed on the hammock cloths over the netting in front of him with his gloved hands in a fury of bad temper, while Young rowed about the wreckage picking up the survivors. A glance ashore coincided with the appearance of a puff of white smoke. That was one of the howitzers at least – before the wind dispersed it he could clearly see the initial upward direction of the puff; howitzers found their best range at an angle of fifty degrees, and at the end of their trajectory the shells dropped at sixty degrees. This one was behind a low bank, or in some sort of ditch; his glass revealed an officer standing above it directing the operation of the gun at his feet.

Now came the shriek of the shell, not so far overhead; even the fountain of water that it threw up when it plunged into the sea was different in shape and duration from those flung up by round-shot from a cannon. Young brought the quarter-boat under the falls and hooked on; Bush had his men ready to tail away at the tackles, while Hornblower watched the operation and fumed at every second of delay. Most of the survivors picked up were wounded, some of them dreadfully. He would have to go and see they were properly attended to – he would have to pay a visit of courtesy – but not until *Hotspur* were safely out of this unnecessary peril.

'Very well, Mr Prowse. Bring her before the wind.'

The yards creaked round; the quartermaster spun the wheel round into firm resistance, and *Hotspur* slowly gathered way, to leave this hateful coast behind her. Next came a sudden succession of noises, all loud, all different, distinguishable even though not two seconds elapsed between the first and the last – the shriek of a shell, a crash of timber aloft, a deep note as the main-topmast backstay parted, a thud against the hammock nettings beside Hornblower, and then a thump three yards from his feet, and there on the deck death, sizzling death, was rolling towards him and as the ship heaved death changed its course with the canting of the deck in a blundering curve as the belt round the shell deflected its roll. Hornblower saw the tiny thread of

smoke, the burning fuse one-eighth of an inch long. No
time to think. He sprang at it as it wobbled on its belt,
and with his gloved hand he extinguished the fuse,
rubbing at it to make sure the spark was out, rubbing
at it again unnecessarily before he straightened up. A
marine was standing by and Hornblower gestured to
him.

'Throw the damned thing overboard!' he ordered; the
fact that he swore indicated his bad temper.

Then he looked round. Every soul on that crowded
little quarterdeck was rigid, posed in unnatural attitudes,
as if some Gorgon's head had turned them all into stone,
and then with his voice and his gesture they all came
back to life again, to move and relax – it was as if time
had momentarily stood still for everyone except himself.
His bad temper was fanned by the delay, and he lashed
out with his tongue indiscriminately.

'What are you all thinking about? Quartermaster, put
your helm over! Mr Bush! Just look at that mizzen-tops'l
yard! Send the hands aloft this minute! Splice that backstay! You, there! Haven't you coiled those falls yet? Move,
damn you!'

'Aye aye, sir! Aye aye, sir!'

The automatic chorus of acknowledgements had a
strange note, and in the midst of the bustle Hornblower
saw first Bush from one angle and then Prowse from
another, both looking at him with strange expressions
on their faces.

'What's the matter with you?' he blazed out, and with
the last word understanding came to him.

That extinguishing of the fuse appeared to them in
monstrous disproportion, as something heroic, even

perhaps as something magnificent. They did not see it in its true light as the obvious thing to do, indeed the only thing to do; nor did they know of the instinctive flash of action that had followed his observation of that remaining one-eighth of an inch of fuse. All there was to his credit was that he had seen and acted quicker than they. He had not been brave, and most certainly not heroic.

He returned the glance of his subordinates, and with all his senses still keyed up to the highest pitch he realized that this was the moment of the conception of a legend, that the wildest tales would be told later about this incident, and he was suddenly hideously embarrassed. He laughed, and before the laugh was finished he knew it was a self-conscious laugh, the motiveless laugh of an idiot, and he was angrier than ever with himself and with Chambers of the *Naiad* and with the whole world. He wanted to be away from all this, back in the approaches to Brest, doing his proper work and not engaged in these hare-brained actions that did not forward the defeat of Bonaparte an iota.

Then another thought struck him, occasioned by the discovery that the fuse had burned a hole in his right-hand glove. Those were the gloves Maria had given him on that dark morning when he had walked with her from the George to take *Hotspur* to sea.

19

In the Iroise, comfortably sheltered with the wind to the east of south, *Hotspur* was completing her stores again. This was the second time since her refitting in Plymouth that she had gone through this laborious process, refilling her casks from the water-hoys, replacing the empty beef and pork barrels from the victuallers, and coaxing all the small stores she could from the itinerant slop-ship that Cornwallis had put into commission. She had been six months continuously at sea, and was now ready for three more.

Hornblower watched with something of relief the slop-ship bearing away; that six months at sea had barely been sufficient to get his ship clear of all the plagues that had come on board at Plymouth; disease, bed bugs, fleas and lice. The bed bugs had been the worst; they had been hunted from one hiding place in the woodwork to another, scorched with smouldering oakum, walled in with the paint, time after time, and each time that he had thought he had extirpated the pests some unfortunate seaman would approach his division officer and with a knuckling of his forehead would report, 'Please, sir, I think I've got 'em this time.'

He had seven letters from Maria to read – he had opened the last one already to make sure that she and little Horatio were well – and he had already completed this task when Bush came knocking at his door. Sitting at the chart-table Hornblower listened to what Bush had to report; trifles, only, and Hornblower wondered at Bush disturbing his captain about them. Then Bush produced something from his side pocket, and Hornblower, with a sigh, knew what had been the real object of this visit. It was the latest number of the *Naval Chronicle*, come on board with the mail; the wardroom mess subscribed to it jointly. Bush thumbed through the pages, and then laid the open magazine before him, a gnarled finger indicating the passage he had found. It only took Hornblower a couple of minutes to read it; Chambers' report to Cornwallis on the affray off Aber Wrack, which apparently had been published in the *Gazette* to inform the public regarding the circumstances in which *Grasshopper* had been lost. Bush's finger pointed again to the last four lines. 'Captain Hornblower informs me that *Hotspur* suffered no casualties although she was struck by a five-inch shell which did considerable damage aloft but which fortunately failed to explode.'

'Well, Mr Bush?' Hornblower put a stern lack of sympathy in his voice to warn Bush as much as he could.

'It isn't right, sir.'

This routine of serving so close to home had serious disadvantages. It meant that in only two or three months the fleet would be reading what had appeared in the *Gazette* and the newspapers, and it was extraordinary how touchy men were about what was written about them. It could well be subversive of discipline, and Hornblower meant to deal with that possibility from the start.

'Would you kindly explain, Mr Bush?'

Bush was not to be deterred. He blunderingly repeated himself. 'It isn't right, sir.'

'Not right? Do you mean that it wasn't a five-inch shell?'

'No, sir. It . . .'

'Do you imply that it didn't do considerable damage aloft?'

'Of course it did, sir, but . . .'

'Perhaps you're implying that the shell really did explode?'

'Oh no, sir. I . . .'

'Then I fail to see what you are taking exception to, Mr Bush.'

It was highly unpleasant to be cutting and sarcastic with Mr Bush, but it had to be done. Yet Bush was being unusually obstinate.

''Tisn't right, sir. 'Tisn't fair. 'Tisn't fair to you, sir, or the ship.'

'Nonsense, Mr Bush. What d'you think we are? Actresses? Politicians? We're King's officers, Mr Bush, with a duty to do, and no thought to spare for anything else. Never speak to me again like this, if you please, Mr Bush.'

And there was Bush looking at him with bewildered eyes and still stubborn.

''T'isn't fair, sir,' he repeated.

'Didn't you hear my order, Mr Bush? I want to hear no more about this. Please leave this cabin at once.'

It was horrible to see Bush shamble out of the cabin, hurt and depressed. The trouble with Bush was that he had no imagination; he could not envisage the other side. Hornblower could – he could see before his eyes at that moment the words he would have written if Bush had had his way. 'The shell fell on the deck and with my own hands I extinguished the fuse when it was about to explode.' He could never have written such a sentence. He could never have sought for public esteem by writing it. Moreover, and more important, he would scorn the esteem of a public who could tolerate a man who would write such words. If by some chance his deeds did not speak for themselves he would never speak for them. The very possibility revolted him, and he told himself that this was not a matter of personal taste, but a well-weighed decision based on the good of the service; and in that respect he was displaying no more imagination than Bush.

Then he caught himself up short. This was all lies, all self-deception, refusal to face the truth. He had just flattered himself that he had more imagination than Bush; more imagination, perhaps, but far less courage. Bush knew nothing of the sick horror, the terrible moment of fear which Hornblower had experienced when the shell dropped. Bush did not know how his admired captain had had a moment's vivid mental picture of being blown into bloody rags by the explosion, how his heart had almost ceased to beat – the heart of a coward. Bush did not know the meaning of fear, and he could not credit his captain with that knowledge either. And so Bush would never know why Hornblower had made so light of the incident of the shell, and why he had been so irascible when it was discussed. But Hornblower knew, and would know, whenever he could bring himself to face facts.

There were orders being bellowed on the quarterdeck, a rush of bare feet over the planking, a clatter of ropes against woodwork, and *Hotspur* was beginning to lean over on a new course. Hornblower was at the cabin door bent on finding out what was the meaning of this activity which he had not ordered, when he found himself face to face with Young.

'Signal from the Flag, sir. "*Hotspur* report to Commander-in-Chief."'

'Thank you.'

On the quarterdeck Bush touched his hat.

'I put the ship about as soon as we read the signal, sir,' he explained.

'Very good, Mr Bush.'

When a commander-in-chief demanded the presence of a ship no time was to be wasted even to inform the captain.

'I acknowledged the signal, sir.'

'Very good, Mr Bush.'

Hotspur was turning her stern to Brest; with the wind comfortably over her quarter she was running out to sea, away from France. For the commander-in-chief to demand the attendance of his farthest outpost must be of significance. He had summoned the ship, not merely the captain. There must be something more in the wind than this gentle breeze.

Bush called the crew to attention to render passing honours to Parker's flagship, the flagship of the Inshore Squadron.

'Hope he has as good a ship as us to replace us, sir,' said Bush, who evidently had the same feeling as Hornblower, to the effect that the departure was only the beginning of a long absence from the Iroise.

'No doubt,' said Hornblower. He was glad that Bush was bearing no malice for his recent dressing-down. Of course this sudden break in routine was a stimulant in itself, but Hornblower in a moment of insight realized that Bush, after a lifetime of being subject to the vagaries of wind and weather, could manage to be fatalistic about the unpredictable vagaries of his captain.

This was the open sea; this was the wide Atlantic, and there on the horizon was a long line of topsails in rigid order – the Channel Fleet, whose men and whose guns prevented Bonaparte from hoisting the Tricolour over Windsor Castle.

'Our number from the Commander-in-Chief, sir. "Pass within hail."'

'Acknowledge. Mr Prowse, take a bearing, if you please.'

A pleasant little problem, to set a course wasting as little time as possible, with *Hibernia* close-hauled under easy sail and *Hotspur* running free under all plain sail. It was a small sop to Prowse's pride to consult him, for Hornblower had every intention of carrying out the manoeuvre by eye alone. His orders to the wheel laid *Hotspur* on a steadily converging course.

'Mr Bush, stand by to bring the ship to the wind.'

'Aye aye, sir.'

A big frigate was foaming along in *Hibernia*'s wake. Hornblower looked and looked again. That was the *Indefatigable*, once Pellew's famous frigate – the ship in which he had served during those exciting years as midshipman. He had no idea she had joined the Channel Fleet. The three frigates astern of *Indefatigable* he knew at once; *Medusa*, *Lively*, *Amphion*, all veterans of the Channel Fleet. Bunting soared up *Hibernia*'s halliards.

'"All captains," sir!'

'Clear away the quarter-boat, Mr Bush!'

It was another example of how good a servant Doughty was, that he appeared on the quarterdeck with sword and boat cloak within seconds of that signal being read. It was highly desirable to shove off in the boat at least as quickly as the boats from the frigates, even though it meant that Hornblower had to spend longer pitching and tossing in the boat while his betters went up *Hibernia*'s side before him, but the thought that all this presaged some new and urgent action sustained Hornblower in the ordeal.

In the cabin of the *Hibernia* there was only one introduction to be made, of Hornblower to Captain Graham Moore of the *Indefatigable*. Moore was a strikingly handsome burly Scotsman; Hornblower had heard somewhere that he was the brother of Sir John Moore, the most promising general in the army. The others he knew, Gore of the *Medusa*, Hammond of the *Lively*, Sutton of the *Amphion*. Cornwallis sat with his back to the great stern window, with Collins on his left, and the five captains seated facing him.

'No need to waste time, gentlemen,' said Cornwallis abruptly. 'Captain Moore has brought me despatches from London and we must act on them promptly.'

Even though he began with these words he spent a second or two rolling his kindly blue eyes along the row of captains, before he plunged into his explanations.

'Our Ambassador at Madrid –' he went on, and that name made them all stir in their seats; ever since the outbreak of war the Navy had been expecting Spain to resume her old rôle of ally to France.

Cornwallis spoke lucidly although rapidly. British agents in Madrid had discovered the content of the secret clauses of the treaty of San Ildefonso between France and Spain; the discovery had confirmed long cherished suspicions. By those clauses Spain was bound to declare war on England whenever requested by France, and until that request was made she was bound to pay a million francs a month into the French treasury.

'A million francs a month in gold and silver, gentlemen,' said Cornwallis.

Bonaparte was in constant need of cash for his war expenses; Spain could supply it thanks to her mines in Mexico and Peru. Every month waggon-loads of bullion climbed the Pyrenean passes to enter France. Every year a Spanish squadron bore the products of the mines from America to Cadiz.

'The next *flota* is expected this autumn, gentlemen,' said Cornwallis. 'Usually it brings about four millions of dollars for the Crown, and about the same amount on private account.'

Eight millions of dollars, and the Spanish silver dollar was worth, in an England cursed by a paper currency, a full seven shillings. Nearly three million pounds.

'The treasure that is not sent to Bonaparte,' said Cornwallis, 'will largely go towards re-equipping the Spanish navy, which can be employed against England whenever Bonaparte chooses. So you can understand why it is desirable that the *flota* shall not reach Cadiz this year.'

'So it's war, sir?' asked Moore, but Cornwallis shook his head.

'No. I am sending a squadron to intercept the *flota*, and I expect you've already guessed that it is your ships that I'm sending, gentlemen. But it is not war. Captain Moore, the senior officer, will be instructed to request the Spaniards to alter course and enter an English port. There the treasure will be removed and the ships set free. The treasure will not be seized. It will be retained by His Majesty's Government as a pledge, to be returned to His Most Catholic Majesty on the conclusion of a general peace.'

'What ships are they, sir?'

'Frigates. Ships of war. Three frigates, sometimes four.'

'Commanded by Spanish naval officers, sir?'

'Yes.'

'They'll never agree, sir. They'll never violate their orders just because we tell 'em to.'

Cornwallis rolled his eyes up to the deck-beams above and then down again.

'You will have written orders to compel them.'

'Then we'll have to fight them, sir?'

'If they are so foolish as to resist.'

'And that will be war, sir.'

'Yes. His Majesty's Government is of the opinion that Spain without eight million dollars is less dangerous as an open enemy than she would be as a secret enemy with that money available. Is the situation perfectly clear now, gentlemen?'

It was instantly obvious. It could be grasped even more quickly than the problem in simple mental arithmetic could be solved. Prize money; one-quarter of three million pounds for the captains – something approaching eight hundred thousand pounds. Five captains. Say a hundred and fifty thousand pounds each. An enormous fortune; with that sum a captain could buy a landed estate and still have sufficient left over to provide an income on which to live in dignity when invested in the Funds. Hornblower could see that every one of the four other captains was working out that problem too.

'I see you all understand, gentlemen. Captain Moore will issue his orders to you to take effect in case of separation, and he will make his own plans to effect the interception. Captain Hornblower –' every eye came round '– will proceed immediately in *Hotspur* to Cadiz to obtain the latest information from His Britannic Majesty's Consul there, before joining you at the position selected by Captain Moore. Captain Hornblower, will you be kind enough to stay behind after these gentlemen have left?'

It was an extremely polite dismissal of the other four, whom Collins led away to receive their orders, leaving Hornblower face to face with Cornwallis. Cornwallis' blue eyes, as far as Hornblower knew, were always kindly, but apart from that they were generally remarkably expressionless. As an exception, this time they had an amused twinkle.

'You've never made a penny of prize money in your life, have you, Hornblower?' asked Cornwallis.

'No, sir.'

'It seems likely enough that you will make several pennies now.'

'You expect the Dons to fight, sir?'

'Don't you?'

'Yes, sir.'

'Only a fool would think otherwise, and you're no fool, Hornblower.'

An ingratiating man would say 'Thank you, sir', to that speech, but Hornblower would do nothing to ingratiate himself.

'Can we fight Spain as well as France, sir?'

'I think we can. Are you more interested in the war than in prize money, Hornblower?'

'Of course, sir.'

Collins was back in the cabin again, listening to the conversation.

'You've done well in the war so far, Hornblower,' said Cornwallis. 'You're on the way towards making a name for yourself.'

'Thank you, sir.' He could say that this time, because a name was nothing.

'You have no interest at Court, I understand? No friends in the Cabinet? Or in the Admiralty?'

'No, sir.'

'It's a long, long step from Commander to Captain, Hornblower.'

'Yes, sir.'

'You've no young gentlemen with you in *Hotspur*, either.'

'No, sir.'

Practically every captain in the Navy had several boys of good family on board, rated as volunteers or as servants, learning to be sea officers. Most families had a younger son to be disposed of, and this was as good a way as any. Accepting such a charge was profitable to the captain in many ways, but particularly because by conferring such a favour he could expect some reciprocal favour from the family. A captain could even make a monetary profit, and frequently did, by appropriating the volunteer's meagre pay and doling out pocket money instead.

'Why not?' asked Cornwallis.

'When we were commissioned I was sent four volunteers from the Naval Academy, sir. And since then I have not had time.'

The main reason why young gentlemen from the Naval Academy – King's Letter Boys – were detested by captains was because of this very matter; their presence cut down on the number of volunteers by whom the captain could benefit.

'You were unfortunate,' said Cornwallis.

'Yes, sir.'

'Excuse me, sir,' said Collins, breaking in on the conversation. 'Here are your orders, captain, regarding your conduct in Cadiz. You will of course receive additional orders from Captain Moore.'

'Thank you, sir.'

Cornwallis still had time for a moment more of gossip.

'You were fortunate the day *Grasshopper* was lost that that shell did not explode, were you not, Hornblower?'

'Yes, sir.'

'It is quite unbelievable,' said Collins, adding his contribution to the conversation, 'what a hotbed of gossip a fleet can be. The wildest tales are circulating regarding that shell.'

He was looking narrowly at Hornblower, and Hornblower looked straight back at him in defiance.

'You can't hold me responsible for that, sir,' he said.

'Of course not,' interposed Cornwallis, soothingly. 'Well, may good fortune always go with you, Hornblower.'

20

Hornblower came back on board *Hotspur* in a positively cheerful state of mind. There was the imminent prospect of a hundred and fifty thousand pounds in prize money. That ought to satisfy Mrs Mason, and Hornblower found it possible not to dwell too long on the picture of Maria as chatelaine of a country estate. He could avoid that subject by thinking about the immediate future, a visit to Cadiz, a diplomatic contact, and then the adventure of intercepting a Spanish treasure fleet in the broad Atlantic. And if that were not sufficiently ample food for pleasant day dreams, he could recall his conversation with Cornwallis. A Commander-in-Chief in home waters had small power of promotion, but surely his recommendations might have weight. Perhaps –?

Bush, with his hand to his hat, welcoming him aboard again, was not smiling. He was wearing a worried, anxious look.

'What is it, Mr Bush?' asked Hornblower.

'Something you won't like, sir.'

Were his dreams to prove baseless? Had *Hotspur* sprung some incurable leak?

'What is it?' Hornblower bit back at the 'damn you' that he nearly said.

'Your servant's under arrest for mutiny, sir.' Hornblower could only stare as Bush went on. 'He struck his superior officer.'

Hornblower could not show his astonishment or his distress. He kept his face set like stone.

'Signal from the Commodore, sir!' This was Foreman breaking in. 'Our number. "Send boat."'

'Acknowledge. Mr Orrock! Take the boat over at once.'

Moore in the *Indefatigable* had already hoisted the broad pendant that marked him as officer commanding a squadron. The frigates were still hove-to, clustered together. There were enough captains there to constitute a general court martial, with power to hang Doughty that very afternoon.

'Now, Mr Bush, come and tell me what you know about this.'

The starboard side of the quarterdeck was instantly vacated as Hornblower and Bush walked towards it. Private conversation was as possible there as anywhere in the little ship.

'As far as I can tell, sir,' said Bush, 'it was like this –'

Taking stores on board at sea was a job for all hands, and even when they were on board there was still work for all hands, distributing the stores through the ship. Doughty, in the working-party in the waist, had demurred on being given an order by a bos'n's mate, Mayne by name. Mayne had swung his 'starter', his length of knotted line that petty officers used on every necessary occasion – too frequently, in Hornblower's judgement. And then Doughty had struck him. There were twenty witnesses, and if that were not enough, Mayne's lip was cut against his teeth and blood poured down.

'Mayne's always been something of a bully, sir,' said Bush. 'But this –'

'Yes,' said Hornblower.

He knew the Twenty-Second Article of War by heart. The first half dealt with striking a superior officer; the second half with quarrelling and disobedience. And the first half ended with the words 'shall suffer death'; there were no mitigating words like 'or such less punishment'. Blood had been drawn and witnesses had seen it. Even so, some petty officers in the give and take of heavy labour on board ship might have dealt with the situation unofficially, but not Mayne.

'Where's Doughty now?' he asked.

'In irons, sir.' That was the only possible answer.

'Orders from the Commodore, sir!' Orrock was hastening along the deck towards them, waving a sealed letter which Hornblower accepted.

Doughty could wait; orders could not. Hornblower thought of returning to his cabin to read them at leisure, but a captain had no leisure. As he broke the seal Bush and Orrock withdrew to give him what little privacy was possible when every idle eye in the ship was turned on him. The opening sentence was plain enough and definite enough.

Sir,

You are requested and required to proceed immediately in HM Sloop Hotspur *under your command to the port of Cadiz.*

The second paragraph required him to execute at Cadiz the orders he had received from the Commander-in-Chief. The third and last paragraph named a rendezvous, a latitude and longitude as well as a distance and bearing from Cape St Vincent, and required him to proceed there 'with the utmost expedition' as soon as he had carried out his orders for Cadiz.

He reread, unnecessarily, the opening paragraph. There was the word 'immediately'.

'Mr Bush! Set all plain sail. Mr Prowse! A course to weather Finisterre as quickly as possible, if you please. Mr Foreman, signal to the Commodore. "Hotspur to Indefatigable. Request permission to proceed."'

Only time for one pacing of the quarterdeck, up and down, and then, '"Commodore to Hotspur. Affirmative."'

'Thank you, Mr Foreman. Up helm, Mr Bush. Course sou'west by south.'

'Sou'west by south. Aye aye, sir.'

Hotspur came round, and as every sail began to fill she gathered way rapidly.

'Course sou'west by south, sir,' said Prowse, breathlessly returning.

'Thank you, Mr Prowse.'

The wind was just abaft the beam, and Hotspur foamed along as sweating hands at the braces trimmed the yards to an angle that exactly satisfied Bush's careful eye.

'Set the royals, Mr Bush. And we'll have the stuns'l booms rigged out, if you please.'

'Aye aye, sir.'

Hotspur lay over to the wind, not in any spineless fashion, but in the way in which a good sword-blade bends under pressure. A squadron of ships of the line lay just down to leeward, and Hotspur tore past them, rendering passing honours as she did so. Hornblower could imagine the feelings of envy in the breasts of the hands over there at the sight of this dashing little sloop racing off towards adventure. But in that case they did not allow for a year and a half spent among the rocks and shoals of the Iroise.

'Set the stuns'ls, sir?' asked Bush.

'Yes, if you please, Mr Bush. Mr Young, what d'you get from the log?'

'Nine, sir. A little more, perhaps – nine an' a quarter.'

Nine knots, and the studding sails not yet set. This was exhilarating, marvellous, after months of confinement.

'The old lady hasn't forgotten how to run, sir,' said Bush, grinning all over his face with the same emotions; and Bush did not know yet that they were going to seek eight million dollars. Nor – and at that moment all Hornblower's pleasure suddenly evaporated.

He fell from the heights to the depths like a man falling from the main royal yard. He had forgotten until then all about Doughty. That word 'immediately' in Moore's orders had prolonged Doughty's life. With all those captains available, and the Commander-in-Chief at hand to confirm the sentence, Doughty could have been court-martialled and condemned within the hour. He could be dead by now; certainly he would have died tomorrow morning. The captains in the Channel Fleet would be unmerciful to a mutineer.

Now he had to handle the matter himself. There was no desperate emergency; there was no question of a conspiracy to be quelled. He did not have to use his emergency powers to hang Doughty. But he could foresee a dreary future of Doughty in irons and all the ship's company aware they had a man in their midst destined for the rope. That would unsettle everyone. And Hornblower would be more unsettled than anyone else – except perhaps Doughty. Hornblower sickened at the thought of hanging Doughty. He knew at once that he had grown fond of him. He felt an actual respect for Doughty's devotion and attention to duty; along with his tireless attention Doughty had developed skills in making his captain comfortable comparable with those of a tarry-fingered salt making long splices.

Hornblower battled with his misery. For the thousandth time in his life he decided that the King's service was like a vampire, as hateful as it was seductive. He could not think what to do. But first he had to know more about the business.

'Mr Bush, would you be kind enough to order the master-at-arms to bring Doughty to me in my cabin?'

'Aye aye, sir.'

The clank of iron; that was what heralded Doughty's arrival at the cabin door, with gyves upon his wrists.

'Very well, master-at-arms. You can wait outside.'

Doughty's hard blue eyes looked straight into his.

'Well?'

'I'm sorry, sir. I'm sorry to put you out like this.'

'What the hell did you do it for?'

There had always been a current of feeling – as Hornblower had guessed – between Mayne and Doughty. Mayne had ordered Doughty to do some specially dirty work, at this moment when Doughty wished to preserve his hands clean to serve his captain's dinner. Doughty's protest had been the instant occasion for Mayne to wield his starter.

'I – I couldn't take a blow, sir. I suppose I've been too long with gentlemen.'

Among gentlemen a blow could only be wiped out in blood; among the lower orders a blow was something to be received without even a word. Hornblower was captain of his ship, with powers almost unlimited. He could tell Mayne to shut his mouth; he could order Doughty's irons to be struck off, and the whole incident forgotten. Forgotten? Allow the crew to think that petty officers could be struck back with impunity? Allow the crew to think that their captain had favourites?

'Damn it all!' raved Hornblower, pounding on the chart room table.

'I could train someone to take my place, sir,' said Doughty, 'before – before . . .'

Even Doughty could not say those words.

'No! No! No!' It was utterly impossible to have Doughty circulating about the ship with every morbid eye upon him.

'You might try Bailey, sir, the gunroom steward. He's the best of a bad lot.'

'Yes.'

It made matters no easier to find Doughty still so cooperative. And then there was a glimmer of light, the faintest hint of a possibility of a solution less unsatisfactory than the others. They were three hundred leagues and more from Cadiz, but they had a fair wind.

'You'll have to await your trial. Master-at-arms! Take this man away. You needn't keep him in irons, and I'll give orders about his exercise.'

'Goodbye, sir.'

It was horrible to see Doughty retaining the unmoved

364

countenance so carefully cultivated as a servant, and yet to know that it concealed a dreadful anxiety. Hornblower had to forget about it, somehow. He had to come on deck with *Hotspur* flying along with every inch of canvas spread racing over the sea like a thoroughbred horse at last given his head after long restraint. The dark shadow might not be forgotten, but at least it could be lightened under this blue sky with the flying white clouds, and by the rainbows of spray thrown up by the bows, as they tore across the Bay of Biscay on a mission all the more exciting to the ship's company in that they could not guess what it might be.

There was the distraction – the counter irritation – of submitting to the clumsy ministrations of Bailey, brought up from the gunroom mess. There was the satisfaction of making a neat landfall off Cape Ortegal, and flying along the Biscay coast just within sight of the harbour of Ferrol, where Hornblower had spent weary months in captivity – he tried vainly to make out the Dientes del Diablo where he had earned his freedom – and then rounding the far corner of Europe and setting a fresh course, with the wind miraculously still serving, as they plunged along, close-hauled now, to weather Cape Roca.

There was a night when the wind backed round and blew foul but gently, with Hornblower out of bed a dozen times, fuming with impatience when *Hotspur* had to go on the port tack and head directly out from the land, but then came the wonderful dawn with the wind coming from the south west in gentle puffs, and then from the westward in a strong breeze that just allowed studding sails to be spread as *Hotspur* reached southward to make a noon position with Cape Roca just out of sight to leeward.

That meant another broken night for Hornblower to make the vital change of course off Cape St Vincent so as to head, with the wind comfortably over *Hotspur*'s port quarter and every stitch of canvas still spread, direct for Cadiz. In the afternoon, with *Hotspur* still flying along at a speed often reaching eleven knots, the lookout reported a blur of land, low-lying, fine on the port bow, as the coastwise shipping – hastily raising neutral Portuguese and Spanish colours at sight of this British ship of war – grew thicker. Then minutes later another hail from the masthead told that the landfall was perfect, and ten minutes after that Hornblower's telescope, trained fine on the starboard bow, could pick up the gleaming white of the city of Cadiz.

Hornblower should have been pleased at his achievement, but as ever there was no time for self-congratulation. There were the preparations to be made to ask permission of the Spanish authorities to enter the port; there was the excitement of the prospect of getting into touch with the British representative; and – now or never – there was the decision to be reached regarding his plan for Doughty. The thought of Doughty had nagged at him during these glorious days of spread canvas, coming to distract him from his daydreams of wealth and promotion, to divert him from his plans regarding his behaviour in Cadiz. It was like the bye-plots in Shakespeare's plays, rising continually from the depths to assume momentarily equal importance with the development of the main plot.

Yet, as Hornblower had already admitted to himself,

it was now or never. He had to decide and to act at this very minute; earlier would have been premature, and later would be too late. He had risked death often enough in the King's service; perhaps the service owed him a life in return – a threadbare justification, and he forced himself to admit to mere self-indulgence as he finally made up his mind. He shut up his telescope with the same fierce decision that he had closed with the enemy in the Goulet.

'Pass the word for my steward,' he said. No one could guess that the man who spoke such empty words was contemplating a grave dereliction from duty.

Bailey, all knees and elbows, with the figure of a youth despite his years, put his hand to his forehead in salute to his captain within sight, and (more important) within earshot of a dozen individuals on the quarterdeck.

'I expect His Majesty's Consul to sup with me tonight,' said Hornblower. 'I want something special to offer him.'

'Well, sir –' said Bailey, which was exactly what, and all, Hornblower had expected him to say.

'Speak up, now,' rasped Hornblower.

'I don't exactly know, sir,' said Bailey. He had suffered already from Hornblower's irascibility – unplanned, during these last days, but lucky now.

'Damn it, man. Let's have some ideas.'

'There's a cut of cold beef, sir –'

'Cold beef? For His Majesty's Consul? Nonsense.'

Hornblower took a turn up the deck in deep thought, and then wheeled back again.

'Mr Bush! I'll have to have Doughty released from confinement this evening. This ninny's no use to me.

See that he reports to me in my cabin the moment I have time to spare.'

'Aye aye, sir.'

'Very well, Bailey. Get below. Now, Mr Bush, kindly clear away No. 1 carronade starboard side for the salutes. And isn't that the *guarda costa* lugger lying-to for us there?'

The sun declining towards the west bathed the white buildings of Cadiz to a romantic pink as *Hotspur* headed in, and as health officers and naval officers and military officers came on board to see that Cadiz was guarded against infection and violations of her neutrality. Hornblower put his Spanish to use – rusty now, as he had not spoken Spanish since the last war, and more awkward still because of his recent use of French – but despite its rustiness very helpful during the formalities, while *Hotspur* under topsails glided in towards the entrance to the bay, so well remembered despite the years that had passed since his last visit in the *Indefatigable*.

The evening breeze carried the sound of the salutes round the bay, as *Hotspur*'s carronade spoke out and Santa Catalina replied, and while the Spanish pilot guided *Hotspur* between the Pigs and the Sows – Hornblower had a suspicion that the Pigs were Sea Pigs, Porpoises, in Spanish – and the hands stood by to take in sail and drop anchor. There were ships of war lying at anchor already in the bay, and not the Spanish navy, whose masts and yards Hornblower could just make out in the inner harbours.

'Estados Unidos,' said the Spanish naval officer, with a gesture towards the nearer frigate. Hornblower saw the Stars and Stripes, and the broad pendant at the main-topmast-head.

'Mr Bush! Stand by to render passing honours.'

'*Constitution*. Commodore Preble,' added a Spanish officer.

The Americans were fighting a war of their own, at Tripoli far up the Mediterranean; and presumably this Preble – Hornblower could not be sure of the exact name as he heard it – was the latest of a series of American commanders-in-chief. Drums beat and men lined the side and hats were lifted in salute as *Hotspur* crept by.

'French frigate *Félicité*,' went on the Spanish officer, indicating the other ship of war.

Twenty-two ports on a side – one of the big French frigates, but there was no need to pay her further attention. As enemies in a neutral harbour they would ignore each other, cut each other dead, as gentlemen would do if by unlucky chance they met in the interval between the challenge and the duel. Lucky that he did not have to give her further thought, too, seeing that the sight of the *Constitution* was causing modification in his other plans – the bye-plot was intruding on the main plot again.

'You can anchor here, Captain,' said the Spanish officer.

'Helm-a-lee! Mr Bush!'

Hotspur rounded-to, her topsails were taken in with commendable rapidity, and the anchor cable roared out through the hawse. It was as well that the operation went through faultlessly, seeing that it was carried out under the eyes of the navies of three other nations. A flat report echoed round the bay.

'Sunset gun! Take in the colours, Mr Bush.'

The Spanish officers were standing formally in line, hats in hand, as they bowed their farewells. Hornblower put on his politest manner and took off his hat with his politest bow as he thanked them and escorted them to the side.

'Here comes your consul already,' said the naval officer just before he went down.

In the gathering darkness a rowing skiff was heading out to them from the town, and Hornblower almost cut his final farewells short as he tried to recall what honours should be paid to a consul coming on board after sunset. The western sky was blood red, and the breeze dropped, and here in a bay it seemed breathless and stifling after the airy delights of the Atlantic. And now he had to deal with secrets of state and with Doughty.

Recapitulating his worries to himself revived another one. There would now be a break in his letters to Maria; it might be months before she heard from him again, and she would fear the worst. But there was no time to waste in thinking. He had to act instantly.

21

With the wind dropping *Hotspur* had swung to her anchors, and now from the stern window of the chart room USS *Constitution* was visible, revealed by her lights as she rode idly in slack water.

'If you please, sir,' asked Doughty, as respectful as ever, 'what is this place?'

'Cadiz,' replied Hornblower; his surprise was only momentary at the ignorance of a prisoner immured below – it was possible that some even of the crew still did not know. He pointed through the cabin window. 'And that's an American frigate, the *Constitution*.'

'Yes, sir.'

Until Hornblower had seen the *Constitution* at anchor he had been visualising a drab future for Doughty, as a penniless refugee on the waterfront at Cadiz, not daring to ship as a hand before the mast in some merchant ship for fear of being pressed and recognized, starving at worst as a beggar, at best as a soldier enlisted in the ragged Spanish army. A better future than the rope, all the same. Now there was a better one still. Ships of war never had enough men, even if Preble did not need a good steward.

Bailey came in from the cabin with the last bottle of claret.

'Doughty will decant that,' said Hornblower. 'And Doughty, see that those glasses are properly clean. I want them to sparkle.'

'Yes, sir.'

'Bailey, get for'ard to the galley. See that there's a clear fire ready for the marrow bones.'

'Aye aye, sir.'

It was as simple as that as long as each move was well-timed. Doughty applied himself to decanting the claret while Bailey bustled out.

'By the way, Doughty, can you swim?'

Doughty did not raise his head.

'Yes, sir,' his voice was hardly more than a whisper. 'Thank you, sir.'

Now the expected knock on the door.

'Boat's coming alongside, sir!'

'Very well, I'll come.'

Hornblower hurried out on to the quarterdeck and down the gangway to greet the visitor. Darkness had fallen and Cadiz Bay was quite placid, like a dark mirror.

Mr Carron wasted no time; he hurried aft ahead of Hornblower with strides that equalled Hornblower's at his hastiest. When he sat in a chair in the chart room he seemed to fill the little place completely, for he was a big heavily built man. He mopped his forehead with his handkerchief and then readjusted his wig.

'A glass of claret, sir?'

'Thank you.' Mr Carron still wasted no time, plunging into business while Hornblower filled the glasses.

'You're from the Channel Fleet?'

'Yes, sir, under orders from Admiral Cornwallis.'

'You know about the situation then. You know about the *flota*?' Carron dropped his voice at the last words.

'Yes, sir. I'm here to take back the latest news to the frigate squadron.'

'They'll have to act. Madrid shows no sign of yielding.'

'Very well, sir.'

'Godoy's terrified of Boney. The country doesn't want to fight England but Godoy would rather fight than offend him.'

'Yes, sir.'

'I'm sure they're only waiting for the *flota* to arrive and then Spain will declare war. Boney wants to use the Spanish navy to help out his scheme for invading England.'

'Yes, sir.'

'Not that the Dons will be much help to him. There isn't a ship here ready for sea. But there's the *Félicité* here. Forty-four guns. You saw her, of course?'

'Yes, sir.'

'She'll warn the *flota* if she gets an inkling of what's in the wind.'

'Of course, sir.'

'My last news is less than three days old. The courier had a good journey from Madrid. Godoy doesn't know yet that we've found out about the secret clauses in the treaty of San Ildefonso, but he'll guess soon enough by the stiffening of our attitude.'

'Yes, sir.'

'So the sooner you get away the better. Here's the despatch for the officer commanding the intercepting squadron. I prepared it as soon as I saw you coming into the Bay.'

'Thank you, sir. He's Captain Graham Moore in the *Indefatigable*.'

Hornblower put the despatch into his pocket. He had

been aware for some time of sounds and subdued voices from the cabin next door, and he guessed the reason. Now there was a knock and Bush's face appeared round the door.

'One moment, please, Mr Bush. You ought to know I'm busy. Yes, Mr Carron?'

Bush was the only man in the ship who would dare to intrude at that moment, and he only if he thought the matter urgent.

'You had better leave within the hour.'

'Yes, sir. I was hoping you might sup with me this evening.'

'Duty before pleasure, although I thank you. I'll cross the bay now and make the arrangements with the Spanish authorities. The land breeze will start to make before long, and that will take you out.'

'Yes, sir.'

'Make every preparation for weighing anchor. You know of the twenty-four hour rule?'

'Yes, sir.'

Under the rules of neutrality a ship of one contending nation could not leave a neutral harbour until one whole day after the exit of a ship of another contending nation.

'The Dons may not enforce it on the *Félicité*, but they'll certainly enforce it on you if you give them the opportunity. Two-thirds of *Félicité*'s crew are in the taverns of Cadiz at this moment, so you must take your chance now. I'll be here to remind the Dons about the twenty-four hour rule if she tries to follow you. I might delay her at least. The Dons don't want to offend us while the *flota*'s still at sea.'

'Yes, sir. I understand. Thank you, sir.'

Carron was already rising to his feet, with Hornblower following his example.

'Call the Consul's boat,' said Hornblower as they emerged on to the quarterdeck. Bush still had something to say, but Hornblower still ignored him.

And even when Carron had left there was still an order for Bush with which to distract him.

'I want the small bower hove in, Mr Bush, and heave short on the best bower.'

'Aye aye, sir. If you please, sir –'

'I want this done in silence, Mr Bush. No pipes, no orders that *Félicité* can hear. Station two safe men at the capstan with old canvas to muffle the capstan pawls. I don't want a sound.'

'Aye aye, sir. But –'

'Go and attend to that yourself personally, if you please, Mr Bush.'

No one else dare intrude on the captain as he strode the quarterdeck in the warm night. Nor was it long before the pilot came on board; Carron had certainly succeeded in hastening the slow process of the Spanish official mind. Topsails sheeted home, anchor broken out, *Hotspur* glided slowly down the bay again before the first gentle puffs of the nightly land breeze, with Hornblower narrowly watching the pilot. It might be a solution of the Spaniard's problem if *Hotspur* were to take the ground as she went to sea, and Hornblower determined that should not happen. It was only after the pilot had left them and *Hotspur* was standing out to the south westward that he had a moment to spare for Bush.

'Sir! Doughty's gone.'

'Gone?'

It was too dark on the quarterdeck for Hornblower's face to be seen, and he tried his best to make his voice sound natural.

'Yes, sir. He must have nipped out of the stern window of your cabin, sir. Then he could have lowered himself into the water by the rudder-pintles, right under the counter where no one could see him, and then he must have swum for it, sir.'

'I'm extremely angry about this, Mr Bush. Somebody will smart for it.'

'Well, sir –'

'Well, Mr Bush?'

'It seems you left him alone in the cabin when the Consul came on board, sir. That's when he took his chance.'

'You mean it's my fault, Mr Bush?'

'Well, yes, sir, if you want to put it that way.'

'M'm. Maybe you're right, even if I do say it.' Hornblower paused, still trying to be natural. 'God, that's an infuriating thing to happen. I'm angry with myself. I can't think how I came to be so foolish.'

'I expect you had a lot on your mind, sir.'

It was distasteful to hear Bush standing up for his captain in the face of his captain's self-condemnation.

'There's just no excuse for me. I'll never forgive myself.'

'I'll mark him as "R" on the ship's muster, sir.'

'Yes. You'd better do that.'

Cryptic initials in the ship's muster rolls told various stories – 'D' for 'discharged', 'D D' for 'dead', and 'R' for 'run' – deserted.

'But there's some good news, too, Mr Bush. In accordance with my orders I must tell you, Mr Bush, in case of something happening to me, but none of what I'm going to say is to leak out to the ship's company.'

'Of course, sir.'

Treasure; prize money, doubloons and dollars. A Spanish treasure fleet. If there were anything that could take Bush's mind off the subject of Doughty's escape from justice it was this.

'It'll be millions, sir!' said Bush.

'Yes. Millions.'

The seamen in the five ships would share one quarter of the prize money – the same sum as would be divided between five captains – and that would mean six hundred pounds a man. Lieutenants and masters and captains of marines would divide one-eighth. Fifteen thousand pounds for Bush, at a rough estimate.

'A fortune, sir!'

Hornblower's share would be ten of those fortunes.

'Do you remember, sir, the last time we captured a *flota*? Back in '99, I think it was, sir. Some of our Jacks when they got their prize money bought gold watches an' *fried* 'em on Gosport Hard, just to show how rich they were.'

'Well, you can sleep on it, Mr Bush, as I'm going to try to do. But remember, not a word to a soul.'

'No, sir. Of course not, sir.'

The project might still fail. The *flota* might evade capture and escape into Cadiz; it might have turned back; it might never have sailed. Then it would be best if the Spanish government – and the world at large

– did not know that such an attempt had ever been contemplated.

These thoughts, and these figures, should have been stimulating, exciting, pleasant, but tonight, to Hornblower, they were nothing of the sort. They were Dead Sea fruit, turning to ashes in the mouth. Hornblower snapped at Bailey and dismissed him; then he sat on his cot, too low-spirited even to be cheered by the swaying of the cot under his seat to tell him that *Hotspur* was at sea again, bound on a mission of excitement and profit. He sat with drooping head, deep in depression. He had lost his integrity, and that meant he had lost his self-respect. In his life he had made mistakes, whose memory could still make him writhe, but this time he had done far more. He had committed a breach of duty. He had connived at – he had actually contrived – the escape of a deserter, of a criminal. He had violated his sworn oath, and he had done so from mere personal reasons, out of sheer self-indulgence. Not for the good of the service, not for his country's cause, but because he was a soft-hearted sentimentalist. He was ashamed of himself, and the shame was all the more acute when his pitiless self-analysis brought up the conviction that, if he could relive those past hours, he would do the same again.

There were no excuses. The one he had used, that the Service owed him a life after all the perils he had run, was nonsense. The mitigating circumstance that discipline would not suffer, thanks to the new exciting mission, was of no weight. He was a self-condemned traitor; worse still, he was a plausible one, who had carried through his scheme with deft neatness that marked the born conspirator. That first word he had thought of was the correct one; integrity, and he had lost it. Hornblower mourned over his lost integrity like Niobe over her dead children.

22

Captain Graham Moore's orders for the disposition of the frigate squadron so as to intercept the *flota* were so apt that they received even Hornblower's grudging approval. The five ships were strung out on a line north and south to the limit of visibility. With fifteen miles between ships and with the northernmost and southernmost ships looking out to their respective horizons a stretch of sea ninety miles wide could be covered. During daylight they beat or ran towards America; during the night they retraced their course towards Europe, so that if by misfortune the *flota* should reach the line in darkness the interval during which it could be detected would be by that much prolonged. The dawn position was to be in the longitude of Cape St Vincent – 9° west – and the sunset position was to be as far to the west of that as circumstances should indicate as desirable.

For this business of detecting the needle of the *flota* in the haystack of the Atlantic was a little more simple than might appear at first sight. The first point was that by the cumbrous law of Spain the *flota* had to discharge its cargo at Cadiz, and nowhere else. The second point was that the direction of the wind was a strong indication of the point of the compass from which the *flota* might appear. The third point was that the *flota*, after a long sea passage, was likely to be uncertain of its longitude; by sextant it could be reasonably sure of its latitude, and could be counted on to run the final stages of its course along the latitude of Cadiz – 36° 30' north – so as to make sure of avoiding the Portuguese coast on the one hand and the African coast on the other.

So that in the centre of the British line, squarely on latitude 36° 30' north, lay the Commodore in the *Indefatigable*, with the other ships lying due north and due south of him. A flag signal by day or a rocket by night would warn every ship in the line of the approach of the *flota*, and it should not be difficult for the squadron to concentrate rapidly upon the signalling ship, a hundred and fifty miles out from Cadiz with plenty of time and space available to enforce their demands.

An hour before dawn Hornblower came out on deck, as he had done every two hours during the night – and every two hours during all the preceding nights as well. It had been a clear night and it was still clear now.

'Wind nor'east by north, sir,' reported Prowse. 'St Vincent bearing due north about five leagues.'

A moderate breeze; all sail to the royals could be carried, although the *Hotspur* was under topsails, stealing along close-hauled on the port tack. Hornblower trained his telescope over the starboard beam, due south, in the direction where *Medusa* should be, next in line; *Hotspur*, as befitted her small importance, was the northernmost ship, at the point where it was least likely for the *flota* to appear. It was not quite light enough yet for *Medusa* to be visible.

'Mr Foreman, get aloft, if you please, with your signal book.'

Of course every officer and man in *Hotspur* must be puzzled about this daily routine, this constant surveillance of a single stretch of water. Ingenious minds might even guess the true objective of the squadron. That could not be helped.

'There she is, sir!' said Prowse. 'Beating sou' by west. We're a little ahead of station.'

'Back the mizzen-tops'l, if you please.'

They might be as much as a couple of miles ahead of station – not too unsatisfactory after a long night. It was easy enough to drop back to regain the exact bearing, due north from *Medusa*.

'Deck, there!' Foreman was hailing from the main-topmasthead. '*Medusa*'s signalling. "Commodore to all ships."'

Medusa was relaying the signal from *Indefatigable* out of sight to the southward.

'Wear ship,' went on Foreman. 'Course west. Topsails.'

'Mr Cheeseman, kindly acknowledge.'

Cheeseman was the second signal officer, learning his trade as Foreman's deputy. 'Send the hands to the braces, Mr Prowse.'

It must be a gratifying experience for Moore to manoeuvre a line of ships sixty miles long by sending up and hauling down flags.

'Deck!' There was a different tone in Foreman's voice, not the tone of matter of fact routine. 'Sail in sight on the port bow, nearly to windward, sir. Coming down before the wind, fast.'

Hotspur was still waiting for *Medusa*'s signal to come down to indicate the exact moment to wear.

'What do you make of her, Mr Foreman?'

'She's a ship of war, sir. She's a frigate. She looks French to me, sir. She might be the *Félicité*, sir.'

She might well be the *Félicité*, coming out from Cadiz. By now word could easily have reached Cadiz regarding the British cordon out at sea. *Félicité* would come out; she could warn, and divert, the *flota*, if she could get past the British line. Or she could hang about on the horizon until the *flota* should appear, and then interfere with the negotiations. Bonaparte could make great play in the *Moniteur* regarding the heroic French navy coming to the aid of an oppressed neutral fleet. And *Félicité*'s presence might have great weight in the scale should it come to a fight; a large French frigate and four large Spanish ones against one large British frigate, three small ones, and a sloop.

'I'll get aloft and have a look at her myself, sir.' This was Bush, in the right place at the right time as usual. He ran up the ratlines with the agility of any seaman.

'Signal's down, sir!' yelled Foreman.

Hotspur should put up her helm at this moment, for all five ships to wear together.

'No, Mr Prowse. We'll wait.'

On the horizon *Medusa* wore round. Now she was before the wind, increasing her distance rapidly from *Hotspur* on the opposite course.

'That's *Félicité* for certain, sir!' called Bush.

'Thank you, Mr Bush. Kindly come down at once. Drummer! Beat to quarters. Clear for action. Mr Cheeseman, send this signal. "Have sighted French frigate to windward."'

'Aye aye, sir. *Medusa*'s going out of sight fast.'

383

'Hoist it, anyway.'

Bush had descended like lightning, to exchange glances for one moment with Hornblower before hurrying off to supervise clearing for action. For that moment there was an enquiring look in his eye. He alone in this ship beside Hornblower knew the objective of the British squadron. If *Hotspur* was parted from the other ships when the *flota* should be sighted she would lose her share of the prize money. But prize money was only one factor; the *flota* was a primary objective. *Hotspur* would disregard *Medusa*'s signals and turn aside from the objective, at her peril – at Hornblower's peril. And Bush knew, too, the disparity of force between *Hotspur* and *Félicité*. A battle broadside to broadside could only end with half *Hotspur*'s crew dead and the other half prisoners of war.

'*Medusa*'s out of sight, sir. She hasn't acknowledged.' This was Foreman, still aloft.

'Very well, Mr Foreman. You can come down.'

'You can see her from the deck, sir,' said Prowse.

'Yes.' Right on the horizon the Frenchman's topsails and topgallants were plainly in view. Hornblower found it a little difficult to keep them steady in the field of the telescope. He was pulsing with excitement; he could only hope that his face did not reveal him to be as anxious and worried as he felt.

'Cleared for action, sir,' reported Bush.

The guns were run out, the excited guns' crews at their stations.

'She's hauled her wind!' exclaimed Prowse.

'Ah!'

Félicité had come round on the starboard tack,

heading to allow *Hotspur* to pass far astern of her. She was declining battle.

'Isn't she going to fight?' exclaimed Bush.

Hornblower's tensions were easing a little with this proof of the accuracy of his judgement. He had headed for *Félicité* with the intention of engaging in a scrambling long range duel. He had hoped to shoot away enough of the *Félicité*'s spars to cripple her so that she would be delayed in her mission of warning the *flota*. And the Frenchman had paralleled his thoughts. He did not want to risk injury with his mission not accomplished.

'Put the ship about, if you please, Mr Prowse.'

Hotspur tacked like a machine.

'Full and bye!'

Now she headed to cross *Félicité*'s bows on a sharply converging course. The Frenchman, in declining battle, had it in mind to slip round the flank of the British line so as to escape in the open sea and join the Spaniards ahead of the British, and Hornblower was heading him off. Hornblower watched the topsails on the horizon, and saw them swing.

'He's turning away!'

Much good that would do him. Far, far beyond the topsails was a faint blue line on the horizon, the bold coast of Southern Portugal.

'He won't weather St Vincent on that course,' said Prowse.

Lagos, St Vincent, Sagres; all great names in the history of the sea, and that jutting headland would just baulk *Félicité* in her attempt to evade action. She would have to fight soon, and Hornblower was visualising the kind of battle it would be.

'Mr Bush!'

'Sir!'

'I want two guns to bear directly astern. You'll have to cut away the transoms aft. Get to work at once.'

'Aye aye, sir.'

'Thank you, Mr Bush.'

Sailing ships were always hampered in the matter of firing directly ahead or astern; no satisfactory solution of the difficulty had ever been found. Guns were generally so useful on the broadside that they were wasted on the ends of the ship, and ship construction had acknowledged the fact. Now the cry for the carpenter's crew presaged abandoning all the advantages that had been wrung from these circumstances by shipbuilders through the centuries. *Hotspur* was weakening herself in exchange for a momentary advantage in a rare situation. Under his feet Hornblower felt the crack of timber and the vibration of saws at work.

'Send the gunner aft. He'll have to rig tackles and breechings before the guns are moved.'

The blue line of the coast was now much more sharply defined; the towering headland of St Vincent was in plain view. And *Félicité* was hull-up now, the long, long, line of guns along her side clearly visible, run out and ready for action. Her maintopsail was a-shiver, and she was rounding-to. Now she was challenging action, offering battle.

'Up helm, Mr Prowse. Back the maintops'l.'

Every minute gained was of value. *Hotspur* rounded-to as well. Hornblower had no intention of fighting a hopeless battle; if the Frenchman could wait he could wait as well. With this gentle breeze and moderate sea

Hotspur held an advantage over the bigger French ship which was not lightly to be thrown away. *Hotspur* and *Félicité* eyed each other like two pugilists just stepping into the ring. It was such a beautiful day of blue sky and blue sea; it was a lovely world which he might be leaving soon. The rumble of gun-trucks told him that one gun-carriage at least was being moved into position, and yet at this minute somehow he thought of Maria and of little Horatio – madness; he put that thought instantly out of his mind.

The seconds crept by; perhaps the French captain was holding a council of war on his quarterdeck; perhaps he was merely hesitating, unable to reach a decision at this moment when the fate of nations hung in the balance.

'Message from Mr Bush, sir. One gun run out ready for action, sir. The other one in five minutes.'

'Thank you, Mr Orrock. Tell Mr Bush to station the two best gun-layers there.'

Félicité's maintopsail was filling again.

'Hands to the braces!'

Hotspur stood in towards her enemy. Hornblower would not yield an inch of sea room unnecessarily.

'Helm a-weather!'

That was very long cannon shot as *Hotspur* wore round. *Félicité*'s bow was pointing straight at her; *Hotspur*'s stern was turned squarely to her enemy, the ships exactly in line.

'Tell Mr Bush to open fire!'

Even before the message could have reached him Bush down below had acted. There was the bang-bang of the guns, the smoke bursting out under the counter, eddying up over the quarterdeck with the following wind. Nothing visible to Hornblower's straining eye at the telescope; only the beautiful lines of *Félicité*'s bows, her sharply steeved bowsprit, her gleaming canvas. The rumble of the gun-trucks underfoot as the guns were run out again. Bang! Hornblower saw it. Standing right above the gun, looking straight along the line of flight, he saw the projectile, a lazy pencil mark against the white and blue, up and then down, before the smoke blew forward. Surely that was a hit. The smoke prevented his seeing the second shot.

The long British nine-pounder was the best gun in the service as far as precision went. The bore was notoriously true, and the shot could be more accurately cast than the larger projectiles. And even a nine-pounder shot, flying at a thousand feet a second, could deal lusty blows. Bang! The Frenchman would be unhappy at receiving this sort of punishment without hitting back.

'Look at that!' said Prowse.

Félicité's forestaysail was out of shape, flapping in the wind; it was hard to see at first glance what had happened.

'His forestay's parted, sir,' decided Prowse.

That Prowse was correct was shown a moment later when *Félicité* took in the forestaysail. The loss of the sail itself made little difference, but the forestay was a most important item in the elaborate system of checks and balances (like a French constitution before Bonaparte seized power) which kept a ship's masts in position under the pressure of the sails.

'Mr Orrock, run below and say "Well done" to Mr Bush.'

Bang! As the smoke eddied Hornblower saw *Félicité* round-to and as her broadside presented itself to his sight it vanished in a great bank of leaping smoke. There was the horrid howl of a passing cannon ball somewhere near; there were two jets of water from the surface of the sea, one on each quarter, and that was all Hornblower saw or heard of the broadside. An excited crew, firing from a wheeling ship, could not be expected to do better than that, even with twenty-two guns.

A ragged cheer went up from the *Hotspur*'s crew, and Hornblower, turning, saw that every idle hand was craning out of the gun ports, peering aft at the Frenchman. He could hardly object to that, but when he turned back to look at *Félicité* again he saw enough to set the men hurriedly at work. The Frenchman had not yawed merely to fire her broadside; she was hove-to, mizzen-topsail to the mast, in order to splice the forestay. Lying like that, her guns would not bear. But not a second was to be lost, with *Hotspur* before the wind and the range increasing almost irretrievably.

'Stand by your guns to port! Hands to the braces! Hard-a-starboard!'

Hotspur wore sweetly round on to the port tack. She was on *Félicité*'s port quarter where not a French gun would bear. Bush came running from aft to keep his eye on the port-side guns; he strode along from gun to gun, making sure by eye that elevation and training were correct as *Hotspur* fired her broadside into her helpless enemy. Very long range, but some of those shots must have caused damage. Hornblower watched the bearing of *Félicité* altering as *Hotspur* drew astern of her.

'Stand-by to go about after the next broadside!'

The nine guns roared out, and the smoke was still eddying in the waist as *Hotspur* tacked.

'Starboard side guns!'

Excited men raced across the deck to aim and train; another broadside, but *Félicité*'s mizzen-topsail was wheeling round.

'Helm a-weather!'

By the time the harassed Frenchman had come before the wind again *Hotspur* had anticipated her; both ships were again in line and Bush was racing aft to supervise the fire of the stern chasers once more. This was revenge for the action with the *Loire* so long ago. In this moderate breeze and smooth sea the handy sloop held every advantage over the big frigate; what had gone on up to now was only a sample of what was to continue all through that hungry weary day of golden sun and blue sea and billowing powder smoke.

The leeward position that *Hotspur* held was a most decided advantage. To leeward over the horizon lay the British squadron; the Frenchman dared not chase her for long in that direction, lest he find himself trapped between the wind and overwhelming hostile strength. Moreover the Frenchman had a mission to perform; he was anxious to find and warn the Spanish Squadron, yet when he had won for himself enough sea-room to weather St Vincent and to turn away his teasing little enemy hung on to him, firing into his battered stern, shooting holes in his sails, cutting away his running rigging.

During that long day *Félicité* fired many broadsides, all at long range, and generally badly aimed as *Hotspur* wheeled away out of the line of fire. And during all that long day Hornblower stood on his quarterdeck, watching the shifts of the wind, rapping out his orders, handling his little ship with unremitting care and inexhaustible ingenuity. Occasionally a shot from *Félicité* struck home; under Hornblower's very eyes an eighteen-pounder ball came in through a gun-port and struck down five men into a bloody heaving mass. Yet until long after noon *Hotspur* evaded major damage, while the wind backed round southerly and the sun crept slowly round to the west. With the shifting of the wind his position was growing more precarious, and with the passage of time fatigue was numbing his mind.

At a long three-quarters of a mile *Félicité* at last scored an important hit, one hit out of the broadside she fired as she yawed widely off her course. There was a crash aloft, and Hornblower looked up to see the mainyard sagging in two halves, shot clean through close to the centre, each half hanging in the slings at its own drunken angle, threatening, each of them, to come falling like an arrow down through the deck. It was a novel and cogent problem to deal with, to study the dangling menaces and to give the correct helm order that set the sails a-shiver and relieve the strain.

'Mr Wise! Take all the men you need and secure that wreckage!'

Then he could put his glass again to his aching eye to see what *Félicité* intended to do. She could force a close action if she took instant advantage of the opportunity. He would have to fight now to the last gasp. But the glass revealed something different, something he had to look at a second time before he could trust his swimming brain and his weary eye. *Félicité* had filled away. With every sail drawing she was reaching towards the sunset. She had turned tail and was flying for the horizon away from the pest which had plagued all the spirit out of her in nine continuous hours of battle.

The hands saw it, they saw her go, and someone raised a cheer which ran raggedly along the deck. There were grins and smiles which revealed teeth strangely white against the powder blackened faces. Bush came up from the waist, powder blackened like the others.

'Sir!' he said. 'I don't know how to congratulate you.'

'Thank you, Mr Bush. You can keep your eye on Wise. There's the two spare stuns'l booms – fish the mainyard with those.'

'Aye aye, sir.'

Despite the blackening of his features, despite the fatigue that even Bush could not conceal, there was that curious expression in Bush's face again, inquiring, admiring, surprised. He was bursting with things that he wanted to say. It called for an obvious effort of will on Bush's part to turn away without saying them; Hornblower fired a parting shot at Bush's receding back.

'I want the ship ready for action again before sunset, Mr Bush.'

Gurney the Gunner was reporting.

'We've fired away all the top tier of powder, sir, an' we're well into the second tier. That's a ton an' a half of powder. Five tons of shot, sir. We used every cartridge; my mates are sewing new ones now.'

The carpenter next, and then Huffnell the purser and Wallis the surgeon; arrangements to feed the living, and arrangements to bury the dead.

The dead whom he had known so well; there was a bitter regret and a deep sense of personal loss as Wallis read the names. Good seamen and bad seamen, alive this morning and now gone from this world, because he had done his duty. He must not think along those lines at all. It was a hard service to which he belonged, hard and pitiless like steel, like flying cannon shot.

At nine o'clock at night Hornblower sat down to the first food he head eaten since the night before, and as he submitted to Bailey's clumsy ministrations, he thought once more about Doúghty, and from Doughty he went on – the step was perfectly natural – to think about eight million Spanish dollars in prize money. His weary mind was purged of the thought of sin. He did not have to class himself with the cheating captains he had heard about, with the peculating officers he had known. He could grant himself absolution; grudging absolution.

23

With her battered sides and her fished mainyard, *Hotspur*
beat her way back towards the rendezvous appointed
in case of separation. Even in this pleasant latitude of
Southern Europe winter was asserting itself. The nights
were cold and the wind blew chill, and *Hotspur* had to
ride out a gale for twenty-four hours as she tossed about;
St Vincent, bearing north fifteen leagues, was the place
of rendezvous, but there was no sign of the frigate
squadron. Hornblower paced the deck as he tried to
reach a decision, as he calculated how far off to leeward
the recent gale might have blown *Indefatigable* and her
colleagues, and as he debated what his duty demanded
he should do next. Push eyed him from a distance as he
paced; even though he was in the secret regarding the
flota he knew better than to intrude. Then at last came
the hail from the masthead.

'Sail ho! Sail to windward! Deck, there! There's
another. Looks like a fleet, sir.'

Now Bush could join Hornblower.

'I expect that's the frigates, sir.'

'Maybe.' Hornblower hailed the maintopmasthead.
'How many sail now?'

'Eight, sir. Sir, they look like ships of the line, some
of them, sir. Yes, sir, a three-decker an' some two-
deckers.'

A squadron of ships of the line, heading for Cadiz.

They might possibly be French – fragments of Bonaparte's navy sometimes evaded blockade. In that case it was his duty to identify them, risking capture. Most likely they were British, and Hornblower had a momentary misgiving as to what their presence would imply in that case.

'We'll stand towards them, Mr Bush. Mr Foreman! Hoist the private signal.'

There were the topsails showing now, six ships of the line ploughing along in line ahead, a frigate out on either flank.

'Leading ship answers 264, sir. That's the private signal for this week.'

'Very well. Make our number.'

Today's grey sea and grey sky seemed to reflect the depression that was settling over Hornblower's spirits.

'*Dreadnought*, sir. Admiral Parker. His flag's flying.'

So Parker had been detached from the fleet off Ushant; Hornblower's unpleasant conviction was growing.

'Flag to *Hotspur*, sir. "Captain come on board."'

'Thank you, Mr Foreman. Mr Bush, call away the quarter-boat.'

Parker gave an impression of greyness like the weather when Hornblower was led aft to *Dreadnought*'s quarterdeck. His eyes and his hair and even his face (in contrast with the swarthy faces round him) were of a neutral grey. But he was smartly dressed, so that Hornblower felt something of a ragamuffin in his presence, wishing, too, that his morning's shave had been more effective.

'What are you doing here, Captain Hornblower?'

'I am on the rendezvous appointed for Captain Moore's squadron, sir.'

'Captain Moore's in England by this time.'

The news left Hornblower unmoved, for it was what he was expecting to hear, but he had to make an answer.

'Indeed, sir?'

'You haven't heard the news?'

'I've heard nothing for a week, sir.'

'Moore captured the Spanish treasure fleet. Where were you?'

'I had an encounter with a French frigate, sir.'

A glance at *Hotspur* lying hove-to on the *Dreadnought*'s beam could take in the fished mainyard and the raw patches on her sides.

'You missed a fortune in prize money.'

'So I should think, sir.'

'Six million dollars. The Dons fought, and one of their frigates blew up with all hands before others surrendered.'

In a ship in action drill and discipline had to be perfect; a moment's carelessness on the part of a powder-boy or a gun-loader could lead to disaster. Hornblower's thoughts on this subject prevented him this time from making even a conversational reply, and Parker went on without waiting for one.

'So it's war with Spain. The Dons will declare war as soon as they hear the news – they probably have done so already. This squadron is detached from the Channel Fleet to begin the blockade of Cadiz.'

'Yes, sir.'

'You had better return north after Moore. Report to the Channel Fleet off Ushant for further orders.'

'Aye aye, sir.'

The cold grey eyes betrayed not the least flicker of humanity. A farmer would look at a cow with far more interest than this Admiral looked at a Commander.

'A good journey to you, Captain.'

'Thank you, sir.'

The wind was well to the north of west; *Hotspur* would have to stand far out to weather St Vincent, and farther out still to make sure of weathering Cape Roca. Parker and his ships had a fair wind for Cadiz and although Hornblower gave his orders the moment he reached the deck they were over the horizon almost as soon as *Hotspur* had hoisted in her boat and had settled down on the starboard tack, close-hauled, to begin the voyage back to Ushant. And as she plunged to the seas that met her starboard bow there was something additional to be heard and felt about her motion. As each wave crest reached her, and she began to put her bows down, there was a sudden dull noise and momentary little shock through the fabric of the ship, to be repeated when she had completed her descent and began to rise again. Twice for every wave this happened, so that ear and mind came to expect it at each rise and fall. It was the fished mainyard, splinted between the two spare studding sail booms. However tightly the frapping was strained that held the joint together, a little play remained, and the ponderous yardarms settled backward and forward with a thump, twice with every wave, until mind and ear grew weary of its ceaseless monotony.

It was on the second day that Bailey provided a moment's distraction for Hornblower while *Hotspur* still reached out into the Atlantic to gain her offing.

'This was in the pocket of your nightshirt, sir. I found it when I was going to wash it.'

It was a folded piece of paper with a note written on it, and that note must have been written the evening that *Hotspur* lay in Cadiz Bay – Bailey clearly did not believe in too frequent washing of nightshirts.

Sir –

> The Cabin Stores are short of Capers and Cayenne.
> Thank you, Sir. Thank you, Sir.
> Your Humble obedient Servant
> J. Doughty.

Hornblower crumpled the paper in his hand. It was painful to be reminded of the Doughty incident. This must be the very last of it.

'Did you read this, Bailey?'

'No, sir. I'm no scholar, sir.'

That was the standard reply of an illiterate in the Royal Navy, but Hornblower was not satisfied until he had taken a glance at the ship's muster rolls and seen the 'X' against Bailey's name. Most Scotsmen could read and write – it was fortunate that Bailey was an exception.

So *Hotspur* continued close-hauled, first on the starboard tack and then on the port, carrying sail very tenderly on her wounded mainyard, while she made her way northward over the grey Atlantic until at last she weathered Finisterre and could run two points free straight for Ushant along the hypotenuse of the Bay of Biscay. It snowed on New Year's Eve just as it had snowed last New Year's Eve when *Hotspur* had baulked

Bonaparte's attempted invasion of Ireland. It was raining and bleak, and thick weather closely limited the horizon when *Hotspur* attained the latitude of Ushant and groped her way slowly forward in search of the Channel Fleet. The *Thunderer* loomed up in the mist and passed her on to the *Majestic*, and the *Majestic* passed her on until the welcome word 'Hibernia' came back in reply to Bush's hail. There was only a small delay while the news of *Hotspur*'s arrival was conveyed below to the Admiral before the next hail came; Collins' voice, clearly recognisable despite the speaking-trumpet.

'Captain Hornblower?'

'Yes, sir.'

'Would you kindly come aboard?'

Hornblower was ready this time, so closely shaved that his cheeks were raw, his best coat on, two copies of his report in his pocket.

Cornwallis was shivering, huddled in a chair in his cabin, a thick shawl over his shoulders and another over his knees, and presumably with a hot bottle under his feet. With his shawls and his wig he looked like some old woman until he looked up with his china-blue eyes.

'Now what in the world have you been up to this time, Hornblower?'

'I have my report here, sir.'

'Give it to Collins. Now tell me.'

Hornblower gave the facts as briefly as he could.

'Moore was furious at your parting company, but I think he'll excuse you when he hears about this. *Medusa* never acknowledged your signal?'

'No, sir.'

'You did quite right in hanging on to *Félicité*. I'll

endorse your report to that effect. Moore ought to be glad that there was one ship fewer to share his prize money.'

'I'm sure he didn't give that a thought, sir.'

'I expect you're right. But you, Hornblower. You could have turned a blind eye to the *Félicité* – there's a precedent in the Navy for turning a blind eye. Then you could have stayed with Moore and shared the prize money.'

'If *Félicité* had escaped round Cape St Vincent there might not have been any prize money, sir.'

'I see. I quite understand.' The blue eyes had a twinkle. 'I put you in the way of wealth and you disdain it.'

'Hardly that, sir.'

It was a sudden revelation to Hornblower that Cornwallis had deliberately selected him and *Hotspur* to accompany Moore and share the prize money. Every ship must have been eager to go; conceivably this was a reward for months of vigilance in the Goulet.

Now Collins entered the conversation.

'How are your stores?'

'I've plenty, sir. Food and water for sixty more days on full rations.'

'What about your powder and shot?' Collins tapped his finger on Hornblower's report, which he had been reading.

'I've enough for another engagement, sir.'

'And your ship?'

'We've plugged the shot holes, sir. We can carry sail on the mainyard as long as it doesn't blow too strong.'

Cornwallis spoke again.

'Would it break your heart if you went back to Plymouth?'

'Of course not, sir.'

'That's as well, for I'm sending you in to refit.'

'Aye aye, sir. When shall I sail?'

'You're too restless even to stay to dinner?'

'No, sir.'

Cornwallis laughed outright. 'I wouldn't like to put you to the test.'

He glanced up at the telltale windvane in the deck-beams above. Men who had spent their whole lives combating the vagaries of the wind all felt alike in that respect; when a fair wind blew it was sheer folly to waste even an hour on a frivolous pretext.

'You'd better sail now,' went on Cornwallis. 'You know I've a new second in command?'

'No, sir.'

'Lord Gardner. Now that I have to fight the Dons as well as Boney I need a vice-admiral.'

'I'm not surprised, sir.'

'If you sail in this thick weather you won't have to salute him. That will save the King some of his powder that you're so anxious to burn. Collins, give Captain Hornblower his orders.'

So he would be returning once more to Plymouth. Once more to Maria.

24

'It really was a magnificent spectacle,' said Maria.

The *Naval Chronicle*, at which Hornblower was glancing while conversing with her, used those identical words 'magnificent spectacle'.

'I'm sure it must have been, dear.'

Under his eyes was a description of the landing of the Spanish treasure at Plymouth from the frigates captured by Moore's squadron. Military precautions had of course been necessary when millions of pounds in gold and silver had to be piled into wagons and dragged through the streets up to the Citadel, but the fanfare had exceeded military necessity. The Second Dragoon Guards had provided a mounted escort, the Seventy-First Foot had marched with the waggons, the local militia had lined the streets, and every military band for miles round had played patriotic airs. And when the treasure was moved on to London troops had marched with it and their bands had marched with them, so that every town through which the convoy passed had been treated to the same magnificent spectacle. Hornblower suspected that the government was not averse to calling the attention of as many people as possible to this increase in the wealth of the country, at a moment when Spain had been added to the list of England's enemies.

'They say the captains will receive hundreds of thousands of pounds each,' said Maria. 'I suppose it will never be our good fortune to win anything like that, dear?'

'It is always possible,' said Hornblower.

It was astonishing, but most convenient, that Maria was quite unaware of any connection between *Hotspur's* recent action with *Félicité* and Moore's capture of the *flota*. Maria was shrewd and sharp, but she was content to leave naval details to her husband, and it never occurred to her to inquire how it had come about that *Hotspur*, although attached to the Channel Fleet off Ushant, had found herself off Cape St Vincent. Mrs Mason might have been more inquisitive, but she, thank God, had returned to Southsea.

'What happened to that Doughty?' asked Maria.

'He deserted,' answered Hornblower; luckily, again. Maria was not interested in the mechanics of desertion and did not inquire into the process.

'I'm not sorry, dear,' she said. 'I never liked him. But I'm afraid you miss him.'

'I can manage well enough without him,' said Hornblower. It was useless to buy capers and cayenne during this stay in Plymouth; Bailey would not know what to do with them.

'Perhaps one of these days I'll be able to look after you instead of these servants,' said Maria.

There was the tender note in her voice again, and she was drawing nearer.

'No one could do that better than you, my darling,' answered Hornblower. He had to say it. He could not hurt her. He had entered into this marriage voluntarily, and he had to go on playing the part. He put his arm round the waist that had come within reach.

'You are the kindest husband, darling,' said Maria. 'I've been so happy with you.'

'Not as happy as I am when you say that,' said Hornblower. That was the base intriguer speaking again, the subtle villain – the man who had plotted Doughty's escape from justice. No; he must remember that his conscience was clear now in that respect. That self-indulgence had been washed away by the blood that had poured over the decks of *Félicité*.

'I often wonder why it should be,' went on Maria, with a new note in her voice. 'I wonder why you should be so kind to me, when I think about – you, darling – and me.'

'Nonsense,' said Hornblower, as bluffly as he could manage. 'You must always be sure of my feelings for you, dear. Never doubt me.'

'My very dearest,' said Maria, her voice changing again, the note of inquiry dying out and the tenderness returning. She melted into his arms. 'I'm fortunate that you have been able to stay so long in Plymouth this time.'

'That was my good fortune, dear.'

Replacing the transoms which Bush had so blithely cut away in *Hotspur*'s stern for the fight with *Félicité* had proved to be a laborious piece of work – *Hotspur*'s stern had had to be almost rebuilt.

'And the Little One has been sleeping like a lamb all the evening,' went on Maria; Hornblower could only hope that this did not involve his crying all night.

A knock at the door made Maria tear herself away from Hornblower's embracing arm.

'Gentleman to see you,' said the landlady's voice.

It was Bush, in pea-jacket and scarf, standing hesitating on the threshold.

'Good evening, sir. Your servant, ma'am. I hope I don't intrude.'

'Of course not,' said Hornblower, wondering what shift of wind or politics could possibly have brought Bush here, and very conscious that Bush's manner was a little odd.

'Come in, man. Come in. Let me take your coat – unless your news is urgent?'

'Hardly urgent, sir,' said Bush rather ponderously, allowing himself, with embarrassment, to be relieved of his coat. 'But I felt you would like to hear it.'

He stood looking at them both, his eyes not quite in focus, yet sensitive to the possibility that Maria's silence might be a sign that to her he was unwelcome; but Maria made amends.

'Won't you take this chair, Mr Bush?'

'Thank you, ma'am.'

Seated, he looked from one to the other again; it was quite apparent to Hornblower by now that Bush was a little drunk.

'Well, what is it?' he asked.

Bush's face split into an ecstatic grin.

'Droits of Admiralty, sir,' he said.

'What do you mean?'

'Moore and the frigates – I mean Captain Moore, of course, begging your pardon, sir.'

'What about them?'

'I was in the coffee room of the Lord Hawke, sir – I often go there of an evening – and last Wednesday's newspapers came down from London. And there it was, sir. Droits of Admiralty.'

Wrecks; stranded whales; flotsam and jetsam; Droits

of Admiralty dealt with things of this sort, appropriating them for the Crown, and, despite the name, they were of no concern to Their Lordships. Bush's grin expanded into a laugh.

'Serves 'em right, doesn't it, sir?' he said.

'You'll have to explain a little further.'

'All that treasure they captured in the *flota*, sir. It's not prize money at all. It goes to the Government as Droits of Admiralty. The frigates don't get a penny. You see, sir, it was time of peace.'

Now Hornblower understood. In the event of war breaking out with another country, the ships of that country which happened to be in British ports were seized by the Government as Droits of Admiralty; prize money came under a different category, for prizes taken at sea in time of war were Droits of the Crown, and were specifically granted to the captors by an order in Council which waived the rights of the Crown.

The government was perfectly justified legally in its action. And however much that action would infuriate the ships' companies of the frigates, it would make the rest of the navy laugh outright, just as it had made Bush laugh.

'So we didn't lose anything, sir, on account of your noble action. Noble – I've always wanted to tell you it was noble, sir.'

'But how could you lose anything?' asked Maria.

'Don't you know about that, ma'am?' asked Bush, turning his wavering gaze upon her. Wavering or not, and whether he was drunk or not, Bush could still see that Maria had been left in ignorance of the opportunity that *Hotspur* had declined, and he still was sober enough to make the deduction that it would be inadvisable to enter into explanations.

'What was it that Captain Hornblower did that was so noble?' asked Maria.

'Least said soonest mended, ma'am,' said Bush. He thrust his hand into his side pocket and laboriously fished out a small bottle. 'I took the liberty of bringing this with me, ma'am, so that we could drink to the health of Captain Moore an' the *Indefatigable* an' the Droits of Admiralty. It's rum, ma'am. With hot water an' lemon an' sugar, ma'am, it makes a suitable drink for this time o' day.'

Hornblower caught Maria's glance.

'It's too late tonight, Mr Bush,' he said. 'We'll drink that health tomorrow. I'll help you with your coat.'

After Bush had left (being helped on with his coat by his captain flustered him sufficiently to make him almost wordless) Hornblower turned back to Maria.

'He'll find his way back to the ship all right,' he said.

'So you did something noble, darling,' said Maria.

'Bush was drunk,' replied Hornblower. 'He was talking nonsense.'

'I wonder,' said Maria. Her eyes were shining. 'I always think of you as noble, my darling.'

'Nonsense,' said Hornblower.

Maria came forward to him, putting her hands up to his shoulders, coming close so that he could resume the interrupted embrace.

'Of course you must have secrets from me,' she said. 'I understand. You're a King's officer, as well as my darling husband.'

Now that she was in his arms she had to put her head far back to look up at him.

'It's no secret,' she went on, 'that I love you, my dear, noble love. More than life itself.'

Hornblower knew it was true. He felt his tenderness towards her surging up within him. But she was still speaking.

'And something else that isn't a secret,' went on Maria. 'Perhaps you've guessed. I think you have.'

'I thought so,' said Hornblower. 'You make me very happy, my dear wife.'

Maria smiled, her face quite transfigured. 'Perhaps this time it will be a little daughter. A sweet little girl.'

Hornblower had suspected it, as he said. He did not know if he was happy with his knowledge, although he said he was. It would only be a day or two before he took *Hotspur* to sea again, back to the blockade of Brest, back to the monotonous perils of the Goulet.

25

Hotspur lay in the Iroise, and the victualler was heaving-to close alongside, to begin again the toilsome labour of transferring stores. After sixty days of blockade duty there would be much to do, even though the pleasant sunshine of early summer would ease matters a little. The fend-offs were over the side and the first boat was on its way from the victualler bringing the officer charged with initiating the arrangements.

'Here's the post, sir,' said the officer, handing Hornblower the small package of letters destined for the ship's company. 'But here's a letter from the Commander-in-Chief, sir. They sent it across to me from the *Hibernia* as I passed through the Outer Squadron.'

'Thank you,' said Hornblower.

He passed the packet to Bush to sort out. There would be letters from Maria in it, but a letter from the Commander-in-Chief took precedence. There was the formal address:

Horatio Hornblower, Esq.
Master and Commander
HM Sloop Hotspur

The letter was sealed with an informal wafer, instantly broken.

My dear Captain Hornblower,

    I hope you can find it convenient to visit me in Hibernia, as I have news for you that would best be communicated personally. To save withdrawing Hotspur *from her station, and to save you a long journey by boat, you might find it convenient to come in the victualler that brings this letter. You are therefore authorized to leave your First Lieutenant in command, and I will find means for returning you to your ship when our business is completed. I look forward with pleasure to seeing you.*

    Your ob'd't servant,

    Wm Cornwallis.

Two seconds of bewilderment, and then a moment of horrid doubt which made Hornblower snatch the other letters back from Bush and hurriedly search through them for those from Maria.

'Best communicated personally' – Hornblower had a sudden secret fear that something might have happened to Maria and that Cornwallis had assumed the responsibility of breaking the news to him. But here was a letter from Maria only eight days old, and all was well with her and with little Horatio and the child to be. Cornwallis could hardly have later news than that.

Hornblower was reduced to rereading the letter and weighing every word like a lover receiving his first love letter. The whole letter appeared cordial in tone, until Hornblower forced himself to admit that if it was summons to a reprimand it might be worded in exactly the same way. Except for the opening word 'My'; that was a departure from official practice – yet it might be a mere slip. And the letter concerned itself with 'news' – but Cornwallis would call official information 'news' too. Hornblower took a turn up the deck and forced himself to laugh at himself. He really was behaving like a love-lorn youth. If after all these years of service he had not learned to wait patiently through a dull hour for an inevitable crisis the Navy had not taught him even his first lesson.

The stores came slowly on board; there were the receipts to sign, and of course there were the final hurried questions hurled at him by people afraid of accepting responsibility.

'Make up your own mind about that,' snapped Hornblower, and, 'Mr Bush'll tell you want to do, and I hope he'll put a flea in your ear.'

Then at last he was on a strange deck, watching with vast curiosity the handling of a different ship as the victualler filled away and headed out of the Iroise. The victualler's captain offered him the comfort of his cabin and suggested sampling the new consignment of rum, but Hornblower could not make himself accept either offer. He could only just manage to make himself stand still, aft by the taffrail, as they gradually left the coast behind, and picked their way through the Inshore Squadron and set a course for the distant topsails of the main body of the Channel Fleet.

The huge bulk of the *Hibernia* loomed up before them, and Hornblower found himself going up the side and saluting the guard. Newton, the captain of the ship, and Collins, the Captain of the Fleet, both happened to be on deck and received him cordially enough; Hornblower hoped they did not notice his gulp of excitement as he returned their 'good afternoon'. Collins prepared to show him to the Admiral's quarters.

'Please don't trouble, sir. I can find my own way,' protested Hornblower.

'I'd better see you past all the Cerberuses that guard these nether regions,' said Collins.

Cornwallis was seated at one desk, and his flag lieutenant at another, but they both rose at his entrance, and the flag lieutenant slipped unobtrusively through a curtained door in the bulkhead while Cornwallis shook Hornblower's hand – it could hardly be a reprimand that was coming, yet Hornblower found it difficult to sit on more than the edge of the chair that Cornwallis offered him. Cornwallis sat with more ease, yet bolt upright with his back quite flat as was his habit.

'Well?' said Cornwallis.

Hornblower realized that Cornwallis was trying to conceal his mood, yet there was – or was there not? – a twinkle in the china-blue eyes; all these years as Commander-in-Chief still had not forged the Admiral into the complete diplomat. Or perhaps they had. Hornblower could only wait; he could think of nothing to say in reply to that monosyllable.

'I've had a communication about you from the Navy Board,' said Cornwallis at length, severely.

'Yes, sir?' Hornblower could find a reply to this speech; the Navy Board dealt with victualling and supplies and such like matters. It could be nothing vital.

'They've called my attention to the consumption of stores by the *Hotspur*. You appear to have been expensive, Hornblower. Gunpowder, shot, sails, cordage – you've been using up these things as if *Hotspur* were a ship of the line. Have you anything to say?'

'No, sir.' He need not offer the obvious defence, not to Cornwallis.

'Neither have I.' Cornwallis smiled suddenly as he said that, his whole expression changing. 'And that is what I shall tell the Navy Board. It's a naval officer's duty to shoot and be shot at.'

'Thank you, sir.'

'I've done all I need to do in transmitting this information.'

The smile died away from Cornwallis' face, and was replaced by something bleak, something a little sad. He looked suddenly much older. Hornblower was making ready to rise from his chair; he could see that Cornwallis had sent for him so that this censure from the Navy Board should be deprived of all its sting. In the Service anticipated crises sometimes resolved themselves into anti-climaxes. But Cornwallis went on speaking; the sadness of his expression was echoed in the sadness of the tone of his voice.

'Now we can leave official business,' he said, 'and proceed to more personal matters. I'm hauling down my flag, Hornblower.'

'I'm sorry to hear that, sir.' Those might be trite, mechanical words, but they were not. Hornblower was genuinely, sincerely sorry, and Cornwallis could hardly think otherwise.

'It comes to us all in time,' he went on. 'Fifty-one years in the Navy.'

'Hard years, too, sir.'

'Yes. For two years and three months I haven't set foot on shore.'

'But no one else could have done what you have done, sir.'

No one else could have maintained the Channel Fleet as a fighting body during those first years of hostilities, thwarting every attempt by Bonaparte to evade its crushing power.

'You flatter me,' replied Cornwallis. 'Very kind of you, Hornblower. Gardner's taking my place, and he'll do just as well as me.'

Even in the sadness of the moment Hornblower's ever observant mind took notice of the use of that name without the formal 'Lord' or 'Admiral'; he was being admitted into unofficial intimacy with a Commander-in-Chief, albeit one on the point of retirement.

'I can't tell you how much I regret it, all the same, sir,' he said.

'Let's try to be more cheerful,' said Cornwallis. The blue eyes were looking straight through Hornblower, extraordinarily penetrating. Apparently what they observed was specially gratifying. Cornwallis' expression softened. Something appeared there which might almost be affection.

'Doesn't all this mean anything to you, Hornblower?' he asked.

'No, sir,' replied Hornblower, puzzled. 'Only what I've said. It's a great pity that you have to retire, sir.'

'Nothing else?'

'No, sir.'

'I didn't know such disinterestedness was possible. Don't you remember what is the last privilege granted a retiring Commander-in-Chief?'

'No, sir.' That was true when Hornblower spoke;

realization came a second later. 'Oh, of course –'

'Now it's beginning to dawn on you. I'm allowed three promotions. Midshipman to Lieutenant. Lieutenant to Commander. Commander to Captain.'

'Yes, sir.' Hornblower could hardly speak those words; he had to swallow hard.

'It's a good system,' went on Cornwallis. 'At the end of his career a Commander-in-Chief can make those promotions without fear or favour. He has nothing more to expect in this world, and so he can lay up store for the next, by making his selections solely for the good of the service.'

'Yes, sir.'

'Do I have to go on? I'm going to promote you to Captain.'

'Thank you, sir. I can't –' Very true. He could not speak.

'As I said, I have the good of the service in mind. You're the best choice I can make, Hornblower.'

'Thank you, sir.'

'Mark you, this is the last service I can do for you. A fortnight from now I'll be nobody. You've told me you have no friends in high places?'

'Yes, sir. No, sir.'

'And commands still go by favour. I hope you find it, Hornblower. And I hope you have better luck in the matter of prize money. I did my best for you.'

'I'd rather be a captain and poor than anyone else and rich, sir.'

'Except perhaps an Admiral,' said Cornwallis; he was positively grinning.

'Yes, sir.'

Cornwallis rose from his chair. Now he was a Commander-in-Chief again, and Hornblower knew himself dismissed. Cornwallis raised his voice in the high-pitched carrying hail of the Navy.

'Pass the word for Captain Collins!'

'I must thank you, sir, most sincerely.'

'Don't thank me any more. You've thanked me enough already. If ever you become an admiral with favours to give you'll understand why.'

Collins had entered and was waiting at the door.

'Goodbye, Hornblower.'

'Goodbye, sir.'

Only a shake of the hand; no further word, and Hornblower followed Collins to the quarterdeck.

'I've a water-hoy standing by for you,' said Collins. 'In a couple of tacks she'll fetch *Hotspur*.'

'Thank you, sir.'

'You'll be in the *Gazette* in three weeks' time. Plenty of time to make your arrangements.'

'Yes, sir.'

Salutes, the squealing of pipes, and Hornblower went down the side and was rowed across to the hoy. It was an effort to be polite to the captain. The tiny crew had hauled up the big lugsails before Hornblower realized that this was an interesting process which he would have done well to watch closely. With the lugsails trimmed flat and sharp the little hoy laid herself close to the wind and foamed forward towards France.

Those last words of Collins' were still running through Hornblower's mind. He would have to leave the *Hotspur*; he would have to say goodbye to Bush and all the others, and the prospect brought a sadness that quite took the edge off the elation that he felt. Of course he would have to leave her; *Hotspur* was too small to constitute a command for a Post Captain. He would have to wait for another command; as the junior captain on the list he would probably receive the smallest and least important sixth rate in the navy. But for all that he was a Captain. Maria would be delighted.

Also by
C.S. FORESTER...

Mr Midshipman

Lieutenant Hornblower

Hornblower and the Hotspur

Hornblower and the Atropos

The Happy Return

A Ship of the Line

Flying Colours

The Commodore

Lord Hornblower

Hornblower in the West Indies

Hornblower and the Crisis

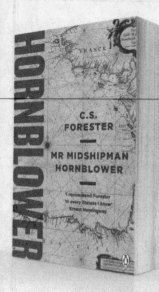

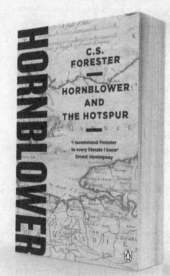

Available July 2017

He just wanted a decent book to read ...

Not too much to ask, is it? It was in 1935 when Allen Lane, Managing Director of Bodley Head Publishers, stood on a platform at Exeter railway station looking for something good to read on his journey back to London. His choice was limited to popular magazines and poor-quality paperbacks – the same choice faced every day by the vast majority of readers, few of whom could afford hardbacks. Lane's disappointment and subsequent anger at the range of books generally available led him to found a company – and change the world.

'We believed in the existence in this country of a vast reading public for intelligent books at a low price, and staked everything on it'
Sir Allen Lane, 1902–1970, founder of Penguin Books

The quality paperback had arrived – and not just in bookshops. Lane was adamant that his Penguins should appear in chain stores and tobacconists, and should cost no more than a packet of cigarettes.

Reading habits (and cigarette prices) have changed since 1935, but Penguin still believes in publishing the best books for everybody to enjoy. We still believe that good design costs no more than bad design, and we still believe that quality books published passionately and responsibly make the world a better place.

So wherever you see the little bird – whether it's on a piece of prize-winning literary fiction or a celebrity autobiography, political tour de force or historical masterpiece, a serial-killer thriller, reference book, world classic or a piece of pure escapism – you can bet that it represents the very best that the genre has to offer.

Whatever you like to read – trust Penguin.